# THE AVON ROMANCE

### Four years old and better than ever!

We're celebrating our fourth anniversary...and thanks to you, our loyal readers, "The Avon Romance" is stronger and more exciting than ever! You've been telling us what you're looking for in top-quality historical romance—and we've been delivering it, month after wonderful month.

Since 1982, Avon has been launching new writers of exceptional promise—writers to follow in the matchless tradition of such Avon superstars as Kathleen E. Woodiwiss, Johanna Lindsey, Shirlee Busbee and Laurie McBain. Distinguished by a ribbon motif on the front cover, these books were quickly discovered by romance readers everywhere and dubbed "the ribbon books."

Every month "The Avon Romance" has continued to deliver the best in historical romance. Sensual, fast-paced stories by new writers (and some favorite repeats like Linda Ladd!) guarantee reading *without* the predictable characters and plots of formula romances.

"The Avon Romance"—our promise of superior, unforgettable historical romance. Thanks for making us such a dazzling success!

Avon Books are available at special quantity discounts for bulk purchases for sales promotions, premiums, fund raising or educational use. Special books, or book excerpts, can also be created to fit specific needs.

For details write or telephone the office of the Director of Special Markets, Avon Books, Dept. FP, 1790 Broadway, New York, New York 10019, 212-399-1357.

# PASSION'S HONOR

## DIANE WICKER DAVIS

**AVON**
PUBLISHERS OF BARD, CAMELOT, DISCUS AND FLARE BOOKS

AVON BOOKS
A division of
The Hearst Corporation
1790 Broadway
New York, New York 10019

Copyright © 1987 by Diane Wicker Davis
Published by arrangement with the author
Library of Congress Catalog Card Number: 86-90999
ISBN: 0-380-75097-X

First Avon Printing: April 1987

AVON TRADEMARK REG. U.S. PAT. OFF. AND IN OTHER COUNTRIES, MARCA REGISTRADA, HECHO EN U.S.A.

Printed in the U.S.A.

K–R 10 9 8 7 6 5 4 3 2 1

With love
to my parents,
Ben and Katrina Wicker

# Chapter 1

Muted laughter rippled across the cloister to where Amicia of Bellay sat on a stone bench beneath the yellowing leaves of an apple tree. With her small feet neatly aligned, leather-clad toes peeping from the hem of her mulberry cotte, and her fragile hands reposing in her lap, she was the image of composure. An image that was disturbed by a single sobbing breath.

A frown marred the symmetry of her satin-smooth chestnut eyebrows, which were framed by the soft mulberry-colored folds of her linen wimple. The tender bow of her lips flattened as she struggled to recapture the shredding fabric of her peace.

It was impossible. Her nerves were stretched as taut as the string of a crossbow. Her hands moved restlessly, fingers entwining one another and palms gripping. The silken brush of her lashes fluttered as her glistening sapphire eyes lifted above the refectory's thatched roof to the soaring tumult of snow-capped mountain peaks. Through the lavender haze cloaking the boulder-strewn tors her gaze rested on the knifelike cleft—the single dangerous defile through the rampart of mountains that protected the peace of the valley, just as the high stone wall protected the sanctity of the convent. She could visualize the gorge's rocky path that could even now be striking sparks from the shod hooves of her father's destrier.

Her lower lip quivered. She sucked it between her teeth,

1

biting it to control the trembling. Tomorrow he would
come as he did every year. Never a day early. Never a day
late. Always on Michaelmas—the day she was born and
brought to Holmby Priory, a swaddled babe. For twenty-
one years. Never a day early. Never a day late.

Tomorrow the gate bell would peal an impatient triplet
of notes. Plump Sister Edwenna would guide him to the
guest chamber and she would be summoned. Every year
was the same. Eustace, Lord of Bellay, would sit sprawled
in a high-backed chair, garbed as if for imminent battle.
Not a word would he say while she entered; she would be
so atremble her teeth would chatter would they not be
clenched so tightly her jaws ached. His vengeful stare
would force her to her knees, as though he had set a hand
to her shoulder. He would shift, his mail scratching dully
across the polished oak as he leaned forward . . .

Amicia's lashes fanned down to her ashen cheeks. Tomorrow she would hear again the only words he had ever
spoken to her: "This is the day you murdered your mother."

A shudder, encompassing body, heart, and soul, shook
her like a devil-brewed cat with a hapless mouse. Betimes
she thought her father barely restrained himself from sheath-
ing his sword into her heart. More often, she wondered
why he did not. It would be kinder than this yearly visita-
tion to remind her of her guilt.

"This, too, shall pass, my child."

The mellow serenity of Mother Margaret's familiar voice
flowed across Amicia, soothing the ravages of dread and
fear. Her eyes opened, tears spangling the curve of her
lashes and blurring her view of the loving, ethereally
unlined face of the Prioress of Holmby.

"I know," she said softly. "It's just . . ."

"Difficult?" Sorrow plumbed the violet depths of Mother
Margaret's eyes. " 'Tis His way of teaching us acceptance. Betimes the lesson can be hard." As her mournful
gaze lifted toward the direction of the autumn music singing through the apple tree's leaves, her frail, blue-veined
hand dropped to the short length of split cane, which
dangled from the plain rope girdle binding her waist.

Amicia watched the gentle tips of her fingers lovingly
trace the smooth spans and knobby joints, then pause to

lightly thumb the worn and dirtied roll of parchment barely jutting from the end. The cane was dried and cracking, its length polished by touch, though it was as new to Mother Margaret as the heavy weight of sadness that had gripped her in the last months.

That sadness had been the source of unending speculation by Amicia and the girls fostering at the convent. A break in the changeless routine of their lives that had leaped out at them as swine to beech mast. Why the sadness, no one knew. They only knew it had begun during the visit of the bovinely placid, yet occasionally sharp-tongued Lady Sybilla of Carrickmuir, widow of the old Lord of Eden. The length of cane had appeared at Mother Margaret's waist after that visit, as irresistible an attraction for her hand as the heavy gold cross at her breast had once been.

"Bitterly difficult," the nun breathed softly to herself.

Her sigh held the blight of mourning, of unconquerable pain endlessly suffered. Amicia's gaze lifted to Mother Margaret's angular face with its translucent skin and sad violet eyes. The face that had leaned over her cradle as a babe and sweetly smiled upon her first perfect rendition of the Pater Noster. Always pale, her skin was now marked by an unhealthy pallor, and a tinge of blue ringed her lips. A quiver of alarm raced through Amicia.

"Mother Margaret," she whispered, her voice soft with compassion, "are you not well?"

The nun's chin dipped, her eyes focusing upon Amicia with an obvious effort. "I am as God wills. And you, my child? Why do you sit here alone?"

"My . . ." Her hands clenched into knotted fists in her lap. "My father comes on the morrow." She should not add to the Prioress's burdens. She should not, but . . . "If only you would speak to him, he would listen to you!"

"No, child. I go into retreat as always at Michaelmas."

"Please, I beg of you." Amicia slipped from the bench and dropped to her knees, clasping the prioress's cool hand and drawing the heavy seal ring to her lips. "I want to become a novice, to dedicate myself to God and his works. I want . . ."

"You want." The sorrowful voice halted Amicia's fervor. Cool fingers trailed along her cheek and cupped her chin, tilting her head up. "You want, Amicia? Have you not learned it is not what we want for ourselves, but what God wills for us?"

"Naught has this to do with God's will!" she burst out. " 'Tis my father's!"

Mother Margaret offered a smile so infinitely sad it brought the ache of tears to Amicia's throat. "How, my child, do you know it is not God working through your father? His ways are . . ." There was the slightest break in her voice before she continued. "His ways are not for us to question."

Amicia searched the steady violet gaze. "Do you never question, Mother?"

"I am human and a sinner, child. There are times when I cry the words of our Savior, 'God! God! Why hast thou forsaken me?' Acceptance is never easy. It is our burden to bear."

"But, Mother Margaret, 'tis my father. If he would . . ."

"Shh, child." A cool finger dammed the words spilling from Amicia's lips. "We cannot accept you without a dower, and your father has refused it these six years past. When he brought you here as an infant he ordered us straightly to train you to take your place as the lady of a great castle."

"But I don't want . . ."

"Child"—her head shook slowly —"how do you know what you want? Naught have you seen beyond this vale. Naught have you seen of men, but your father and the serfs here. Do you choose the cloister for the love of God or your fear of the unknown?"

"I have known no other place. I would not leave those I love. I beg of you—"

"I cannot."

Few words to give birth to such despair. It seemed such a small thing to ask. Amicia's throat convulsed. "He . . . he hates me, Mother." She blinked away tears. "I fear should he take me from this place."

A hissing breath as sharply defined as the honed edge of a dagger snapped Amicia's head up. She stared transfixed by the struggle carving the prioress's face into deep grooves of torment. A tiny blue vein throbbed beneath the pale translucence of her temple while her wide eyes stared at the heavens as though seeking an answer or peace, or perhaps both. Her gaze dropped, stabbing into Amicia's with a hard, hating look that sent gelid fingers of shock across her nape.

"The Lord of Bellay despises beauty even as he desires it." The harsh unrecognizable voice rasped across Amicia's nerves. "He is an evil—"

The words choked off, leaving a silence filled by the gusting wind rustling through the leaves above and the heavy thudding of Amicia's heart in her ears. Mother Margaret knew her father! Knew him and . . . hated him! She reeled before the shock of that revelation. Why had she never once said so in all of these years? Why had she acted as though he were as much a stranger to her as the fathers of all the girls fostering at Holmby?

Mother Margaret's hands, clenched into shaking fists beneath her chin, dropped slowly to the heavy gold cross suspended on a linked chain around her neck. She unfurled her thin fingers, pausing over the cross as though she would grasp it. Her face twisted with pain, and the feathery sweep of chestnut lashes lowered to shield her eyes. Her hands moved to the length of split cane at her waist, and she pulled it up to the quivering blue of her lips and kissed it, as if driven by penance rather than love.

"Mother Margaret"—Amicia found her voice—"you know him? You know my father?"

"Nay!" She recoiled, her eyes revealing a stark and bitter horror. The cane fell from her hands, swinging erratically on the wool thread anchoring it to the girdle. Her hands flew to her mouth as though to dam a threatening flood of speech. She moaned and whirled, the black of her habit flaring like a dark and haunting night settling over the light of day. Her slippered feet crushing scudding autumn leaves, she rushed to the arcade fronting the dorter.

Amicia, stricken mute, followed the nun's flight with a disbelieving stare. Mother Margaret stumbled and caught herself on a thick column with hands as lifelessly pale as the dull gray stone. Her normally erect body was bent as though carrying an oppressive weight. Pushing herself away, she wove an unsteady path through the dappled light of the arcade.

Amicia's senseless turmoil parted for a single coherent thought. *She is ill!* her mind screamed with the terror of a child recognizing the mortality of a parent. Mother Margaret had been the only "parent" she had known. The only person who had given her the security and comfort of an unselfish love.

A cold hand of wind lifted a fold of Amicia's wimple and slapped it across her face. She caught it with one shaking hand, staring toward the dark tunnel at the end of the arcade where the prioress had vanished. As the wind gusted, dead leaves rained with faint crackling sounds. A twig bounced off of Amicia's shoulder and she jerked as from a blow.

A surge of energy propelled her to her feet. Hands lifting her hem, she began to race after Mother Margaret. The air was cooler in the shade of the arcade, where she sped by doors opening into the dorter. Intent on pursuit, she scarcely heard the impatient triplet of notes pealing from the gate bell.

Rounding the door into the prioress's private hall, she paused to catch her breath. The hall, streaked with ribbons of light pouring through the window slits, was empty. Amicia hurried to the wooden staircase hugging the back wall, the smell of sweet flag rising from the rushes rustling beneath her feet.

The solar above was a stark chamber with a writing table, a stool, a straw pallet, and a heavy chest. Above the chest was a painting on parchment depicting in gory detail the martyrdom of St. Edmund, the Anglo-Saxon king slain by the warring Danes.

A muffled sob pulled Amicia into the chamber. Her gaze moved to the huddled figure kneeling at the prie dieu beneath a tall wooden cross. Struck by the despair emanating from the prioress in palpable waves of grief, she faltered, knowing that even now Mother Margaret was silently crying the words she had so lately said: "God! God! Why hast thou forsaken me?" The bent form shifted, her head raising to stare at the rood of the Savior above.

Amicia waited for that cry from the heart to spill out in spoken travail of the soul.

"Robert! Robert! Why? Dear God! Why?"

Amicia started, chilled to the bone by the agony in the wrenching words. Backing away . . . one step . . . two . . . she turned to flee. One hand reached for the safety of the stairs. A guttural groan halted her. Fearfully, her gaze moved to the prie-dieu. Mother Margaret, her hands clenched upon the railing, leaned back, bowing over like a longbow bending its notch to the string. Her hands slipped from the rail. She tumbled from the kneeling bench and fell into the rush-strewn floor, clutching at her chest.

Amicia flew to her side. "Mother! Mother Margaret!"

"The letter! A-Amicia!" she groaned, flinging out one hand to scrabble for the length of split cane resting against the base of the prie-dieu. "The letter!"

Amicia leaned over her, grasping the cane and pressing it into her hands. "Mother, I will get Sister . . ."

"Nay! Nay!" The prioress's fingers curled around her arm like the claws of a falcon. "Stay with me!"

Amicia stared down at her bluish lips and alarming pallor, shaken by a terrible fear. She bent low, her hand trembling against the icy sweat-dewed brow. "You need—"

"It . . . it will pass. It . . . it has ere this."

The hush of the solar was broken by the gasping of Mother Margaret's breath and the muted whispers of the rushes shifting with her restless movements. As Amicia waited, fear twisted her heart and questions trembled on her lips. Her muscles locked to prevent her from flying for the aid she desperately needed to ease Mother Margaret's pain and her own sense of helplessness.

"Help . . . help me to my pallet."

Her head jerked up, the frantic prayers stilling on her lips. Half dragging the frightfully wasted body, she moved the prioress to her straw-stuffed pallet and raced to the chest to withdraw a woven wool coverlet. "Here"—she tucked it in place—"this will warm you."

"Naught will warm me." Mother Margaret's desolate gaze added the dankness of hopelessness to Amicia's sinking spirits. "Child, read this. Read this for me."

"Mother, you should have Sister . . ."

"Nay, child. I need this more. Read it."

Cautiously, Amicia reached for the length of cane, withdrawing the tightly rolled parchment with its crumbling evidence of a long-broken seal. It crackled and curled in upon itself, as though resisting the sight of human eyes. Amicia moved the rushes aside and laid it flat on the cool oak floor, one slender hand spread at the top, one at the bottom. Her questioning gaze moved to Mother Margaret, who nodded and closed her eyes as if bracing for a blow.

" 'Be it known to all that I, Robert, Lord of Eden' " —Amicia read the ink-splattered script written as though by an unsteady hand—" 'do forswear my oaths to my lord, Ranulf, Earl of Chester, and my lord, John, King of England.

" 'I do give my pledge by the rood that from this day I will be faithful to Prince Louis of France, soon to be my lord Louis, King of England, and will maintain my homage against my man, in good faith and without . . .' " Sputtered ink obscured the word. Amicia bent low to decipher the wavering scrawl.

" 'Deception,' " Mother Margaret whispered. " 'Without deception.' "

Amicia's curious sapphire eyes met the sorrowing violet gaze. "Mother, what could his oath mean when he was forsworn?"

"Ay, what?" A bitter smile curled along her mouth, welling tears lending a spurious sparkle to the eyes staring at the smoke-blackened rafters above. "Read."

" 'Written by the hand of Robert, Lord of Eden, on this Hocktide in the seventeenth year of the reign of John, King of England.' "

"At the bottom," Mother Margaret prompted.

Amicia spread the curling corners of the parchment and stared at the words written in a bold hand so unlike those above they might have been written by a different man. " 'Death before dishonor,' " she whispered, her eyes lifting to the grimace of pain that twisted across the prioress's bluish lips.

"To the left. There is . . . something else," Mother Margaret murmured and raised her clenched knuckles to press her eyes.

"A . . . a drawing," Amicia said softly. "The two-faced god Janus. Before the face looking forward is written, 'Honor.' Before the one looking back is written, 'Dishonor.' " She looked up, her forehead puckering in a frown. "What does it mean?"

"It means, child, that he chose his honor above his love."

Amicia sat on her heels, studying Mother Margaret's white hands as they ceaselessly rubbed her eyes. She had never thought about the life the nun who had been mother and mentor had had before she donned the black habit of her calling. "Were . . . were you his love?" she asked, her voice threaded with curiosity and compassion.

The clenched fingers ceased their massaging as if startled into immobility. They moved slowly to lie atop the gold cross. The nun's head turned, tears sliding into the draping black of her wimple. "Ay," she whispered, "I was."

"Do you . . . do you blame him?"

"Nay," she sighed on a tremulous forlorn note. "I loved him for the man he was. Being that man, he had no choice. That he went so far as to write this letter is proof of the struggle he suffered before his decision was made."

Amicia touched the hands feverishly stroking the cross. "Mother . . ."

The prioress's sad sorrowing gaze turned to her. She cradled Amicia's hand between the corpselike cold of her palms. "Child, you think to follow my path and dedicate yourself to God and his works. You are wrong to believe that I have ever done so. I came here broken in body and spirit. Holmby was a haven from despair where I could hide from myself and . . . another. I came with no calling and no desire to serve God. I stayed because I had nowhere else to go."

"But, Mother, you are a shining light for us all . . ."

"Amicia, my love of God came after a torment I hope you will never know." She struggled up, her eyes burning with intensity. "Child, your place is not here. Naught should you fear of life. Nay, rather you should rush toward it with outstretched arms. Fold it to your breast and glory in its sweetness. And if you find love, Amicia, fight for it with every breath in your body. Let no one and nothing come between you and the one you love. For, if you do, your years will be a bitter long season of regret.''

''Mother Margaret! Mother Margaret!'' Sister Edwenna's breathy voice called with its usual harried and harassed air. ''We can't find . . . oh! Here you are! Demoiselle Amicia, the Lord of Bellay awaits you in the guest chamber.'' Her plump fingers fanned the air as if batting away the problems, much of her own making, that continually beset her. ''Do hurry. He shouts so when he must wait.''

Mother Margaret's hand clenched Amicia's in a painful grip that wrenched an involuntary sound from her throat. ''He . . . he is come early!'' the prioress exclaimed.

Tortured violet eyes locked with Amicia's of purest midnight blue, and a thrill of alarm scampered the length of her spine. ''What could it mean?''

''I know not. Merciful heavens! I know not.'' She yearned toward Amicia like a reed bending in the wind.

''Do hurry!'' Sister Edwenna urged breathlessly.

Amicia shook her head to clear the cobwebs of confusion. Her fearful gaze latched onto the nun's round face with its flaring spots of color high on plump cheeks. ''Did . . . did he say why he is come this day?''

''Naught of his will did he speak. Only that you should come with all haste.''

''Mother Margaret is ill,'' Amicia whispered.

''Ill? Mother Margaret?'' Sister Edwenna echoed, wheeling around in an agitated circle with one step toward the stairs, then another toward the pallet. ''I must get Sister . . . nay, that will not do. I must stay here, but then there will be no one . . .''

''Sister Edwenna''—Amicia, despite the impatience that abraded her mood, gently attempted to calm the nun's flutterings—''if you but stay here, I will summon Sister Catherine on my way to the guest chamber.''

''Ay, just the thing to do,'' the nun said with a sweetly abstracted smile. ''Now, why did I not think of that?''

''Mother Margaret,'' Amicia said, cradling the cold hands in hers and chafing warmth into them, ''I must go.''

''He . . . he has never before come early,'' the Prioress

said, her eyes wide with an apprehension that mirrored Amicia's own.

"Nay, never." She swallowed a lump of fear.

"Promise me, wherever you go and whatever happens, you will remember what I have said."

"Never will I forget aught you have taught me."

"Go, child. Always look ahead, never back."

"Toward honor, Mother Margaret?" she asked softly.

"Honor is for men. We look ahead to life."

*Naught should you fear of life. Nay, rather you should rush toward it with outstretched arms.* Mother Margaret's words were still running through Amicia's mind when she paused before the guest chamber's oaken door, gathering her strength for the ordeal ahead. Her fears now seemed paltry, insignificant things. Surely she could face them with but a tithe of Mother Margaret's courage. So easy to think, so hard to do. The trembling began deep within her. In a rush of rejection against her cowardice, she pushed the door open.

Eustace, Lord of Bellay, sprawled across the intricately carved high-backed chair before a blazing hearth fire. He turned slowly, the mail coif shoved back to hang at his nape catching the light with a metallic sparkle. His eyes, the dark midnight hue of her own, narrowed and glittered with a virulent loathing.

The inner trembling spread, a subsurface vibration quivering through her legs. Amicia moved forward, an inching step at a time. Slowly, those glittering eyes staring out of that time- and temper-ravaged face pressed her to her knees. Her chin sank to her chest, her eyes resting on her clenched hands.

The silence stretched. Her trembling grew worse. The pressure of those vicious blue eyes raked across her face and a silent scream clawed at the back of her throat. The fire crackled and spit. The scream of a hunting hawk pierced the window slit. She waited . . . and waited . . .

He would say it soon. Let him hurry. Let him say it and free her for another year.

Instead of the words she expected to hear, a laugh spilled into the chamber. Low, rough, and utterly lacking in humor, it struck her with the odorous mucky feel of the bog in the thick wood at the end of the vale. Never, never once had she heard him laugh. Foreboding raised the fine hair on the back of her neck.

"You are to be wed, demoiselle."

The hard harsh voice, tinged with malice, brought her head up with a snap. "Wed?" she choked out.

"Ay." He relaxed into the chair, a malevolent smile drawing wolfishly over yellowing teeth. "You are to wed my bitterest and most dread enemy. A man who would see the end of me and mine could he but find the way."

Color fled Amicia's cheeks, leaving them as icy cold as her heart. His bitterest and most dread enemy. Had he at last found the way to be rid of her?

"Come, demoiselle. Are you not curious to know who he is?"

Her tongue slicked across her dry lips. "Who?"

His smile widened. His eyes sparkling with unholy glee, he leaned forward. "Tristan, Lord of Eden."

# Chapter 2

Only hours from the priory and Amicia was frozen to the bone by the raw bite of unseasonable winter, which fell across the land as quickly as her life had changed. Icy wind whined through the high mountain pass. Frozen gusts of air snatched at her mantle, whipping it around her. Her palfrey danced restively, its shod hooves ringing against the gray stone outcroppings dusted with snow. Amicia tried to control the dainty mare, but her gloved hands were so cold she could not judge the force she need apply to the reins.

"Odo!" Her father's voice boomed like a crack of thunder—angry thunder that echoed back from his place at the head of his motley troop of men-at-arms. "Lead her palfrey, lest we be the day at this task! Did they teach you naught but your prayers and your needle, demoiselle?"

The sneering question reverberated down the defile. Odo, the master-at-arms, wheeled his sway-backed mount, crowding the palfrey on the narrow path wedged between the steep slopes. "Lady," he growled, his voice as scratchy as a hair shirt. He leaned to gather the reins in one chilblained hand.

"Odo?" Amicia released the reins and reached out to lay her hand gently atop his. "I would look back on all I leave behind."

His one good eye, staring out of a battle-savaged and scarred face, met hers with a look of surprise, then settled on her hand. "The lord be a man without patience, my lady."

"I beg of you a moment only to say my farewell."

That single eye, as darkly cast as the gray shadows falling across the rocky slopes, searched her face with the wary look of a hare running before a pack of belling hounds. His gaze dropped to her hand for a moment, a frown pulling at the puckered scar that split his brow into uneven halves.

"The lady would look back!" He climbed in his stirrups to shout at the line of men. "Dismount that she may see!"

A low rumble of groaning and grumbling accompanied the creaking of saddle leather while Odo backed his horse and turned Amicia's across the path.

The serene vale, framed in the knifelike cleft, lay far below. The tiny beck, babbling across stones worn smooth with the ages, coiled over the sweep of autumn-gold turf like a silvery serpent. It was this beck where she had so often shed her hose and lifted her skirts to delight in its cool gurgling water.

At the near end, cottages—filled with faces as familiar as her own—clustered around the village church like chicks around a hen. Midway, cone-shaped hayricks dotted the landscape, and sheep, cropping stubbled fields, looked no larger than the snowflakes aswirl on the wind. Beyond, the convent was sheltered behind its high curtain wall.

Amicia studied the oak-shingled roof of the church where she had spent so many hours, the golden thatch of the refectory where silent meals were accompanied by readings from the lives of the saints, and the autumn-straggled limbs of the apple tree. Never again would she sit in its cool shade, her mind drifting beyond the jagged peaks to the lives lived beyond the vale.

The heavy hand of impending loss wrapped fingers of sadness around her heart. She had been happy there and safe among those she loved. Now she was being spirited away with no farewell to any, not even Mother Margaret, whose wise counsel she desperately needed.

Her gaze moved to the sloping thatch of the Prioress's Hall. She pictured Mother Margaret lying there, her face as white as parchment, her memories eroding her will to live; the aged woman's heart had been torn like a strip of worn linen because a man had chosen honor over love. Now, cruel fate was sending her, the hated daughter of the Lord of Bellay, to wed that man's son—her father's bitterest and most dread enemy.

A shudder of revulsion and terror began in Amicia's heart, working its way to fingertips and toes that had long since lost all sensation in the biting cold.

"My lady," Odo began.

"God's eyes! What do you here? I gave no order to halt!"

Amicia's head snapped around. Her father bore down upon her, his eyes as cold and steady as his destrier's were wild and rolling. His mailed fist leaped from the folds of his mantle like a bolt of lightning and struck Odo's jaw with a sickening thud that quivered along Amicia's raw nerves.

The blow lifted Odo from the saddle and sent him sliding into a drift of snow beneath his mount's milling hooves. He grunted and tumbled away to safety, his long ungainly arms pulling up his squat torso and short legs to brace against the rough stone.

Amicia stared at the blood pouring from the ragged cut angling along his jaw, then shifted an incredulous gaze to her father. "I but wished to look once more upon all I leave behind," she cried. "He was—"

The destrier surged closer, his steaming breath fanning her shoulder. Shrinking back, her horrified gaze riveted to the threat of that great tossing head, she did not see the slap that whipped her head around in a grind of fragile bones and blinding flash of pain. Blood spurting warm across her lip, she hung low in the saddle, her hand climbing to the stinging welts raised on her tender skin by the linked mail glove.

"The man is mine! Mine, demoiselle! It is I who bid him go or stay! It is I he obeys like the lymers I take to hunt! He is mine until I release him and it is my will he follows!"

The tirade hammered at Amicia like a battering ram thudding against a castle gate. She straightened, searching his twisted and ruddied face. His nostrils flared away from the thin blade of his nose. His lips writhed over yellowing, lupine teeth. His eyes glowed with an invidious ire.

Her gaze skimmed slack lines of self-indulgence, seeking some sign of the love he must have once felt. The love he had given her mother, long dead now in her bearing. Why else had he taken her to Holmby, a swaddled babe scarce from the womb? Why else had he returned yearly to remind her of her guilt?

His face, raddled with a spider-webbing of veins, gave no sign that love had ever softened the heat of his eyes or crimped the corners of his mouth in a smile. It showed nothing but discontent and malice—which matched his voice's bitter tone as he revealed his frenzied obsession with mastering his possessions.

The dream she hugged so close to her heart quivered uncertainly. The dream of loving parents and the life she might have known, if only her mother had lived.

"Like my man, you need lessoning in obedience."

His sharp voice penetrated the bubbling stew of Amicia's thoughts. He bent over the saddle bow, resting one mail-clad arm atop it, and skewered her with a cruel stare.

"Eden will bring you to heel." His lips curled back over his teeth. "Neither man nor beast dares say him nay within his own demesne, for all that he follows his mother's will in the least matter. You, demoiselle, will be naught but an unwanted wife foisted upon him by a crotchet of his overlord and mine."

Amicia's chest fluttered like the pennant whipping at the head of its column. "He weds me against his will?"

"Ay." His smile widened in a travesty of humor. "He does so at the bidding of the Earl of Leicester, who hopes to end the warring between us. He will not accept that between Eden and Bellay there can be no end till one of us is dead. He does not know that you, his instrument of peace, will be my excuse to carry this quarrel to its only end."

Satisfaction glittered in his eyes. Amicia's mouth dried at the sight, lending a pungent reality to the taste of the blood oozing from her lip. "How . . ." Her voice failed her. "How will this come to pass, my lord?"

"Why, demoiselle, the Lord of Eden will see you dead.

Then I, your grieving father," he said with an insincere droop to his mouth, "may seek his end without let or hindrance from any man."

The frigid lash of shock repelled her from his mildly inquiring gaze, and he tilted his face to the scudding clouds and laughed. The blithe tenor pealed on waves of mirth as he pulled at the reins. The destrier neighed and reared to paw the air, before speeding up the path under a vicious raking of spurs.

Amicia's heart flung itself against the cage of her ribs in erratic bursts of turmoil. He wanted her dead. He would mourn no more over her murder at the hands of his enemy than over a flea crushed between his nails. Indeed, he would be glad of it.

Her gaze moved slowly, settling upon Odo. His one gray eye stared steadily, then dropped in submission. He moved, gathering her reins and mounting his sway-backed horse. Amicia lurched in the saddle as the slow, clopping pace began.

She must escape, but how? Plans reeled through her head like ribands led around a Maypole. Wildly impossible plans for flight were studied and discarded as the crest was mounted and the steep descent begun. If she escaped, where could she go? It would be impossible to return to Holmby Vale. Her father would expect it and seek her there. Yet, she knew nowhere else. There was no one to give her succor . . .

Her head strained upward, her eyes eagerly scanning the barren mountains. Surely they would pass through a village. And that village would have a church. If only she could get to it, she could claim the right of sanctuary!

By the third day, hard pressed by her father's angry urgency, Amicia felt her life had been spent swaying in the saddle. The peace of the mountain vale had receded, becoming more dreamlike than real. It seemed she had never been warm, never felt safe, never known a moment of love.

At mid-morning a gusting south wind swept her into the last high pass, a deep bowl scoured out of the red sandstone by wind and rain. Land met sky at the horizon in a haze of sapphire blue. The mountain fell away to low undulating foothills, which spread and split for the vale and river below.

Amicia roused herself to look about. "What is this place?"

"The Vale of Eden, my lady," Odo answered.

His rough scratchy voice jerked her attention from the far distance. "Do . . . do you know him?"

"Nay, my lady."

"Do you know *of* him?" she pleaded, leaning across the pommel as though she could drag the words from him.

"Ay, it is said that he guarded the Earl of Leicester's back in Gascony. It is said that he loses himself in battle like a warrior of old. His sword can cleave a man's head from his neck with a tap, or split a man from crown to crack with a single blow. Men say he is fierce to behold with the bloodlust upon him."

Amicia quelled a surge of nausea. "But the man, Odo. What of the man? Is he as cruel as—" She stopped abruptly, her eyes darting guiltily toward her father.

"I know naught but what I have heard, my lady. It is said that he is merciless to those who do him a despite. Others say he is a man whose pride is in his honor. His sworn word is as certain as death."

Death. Amicia's eyes squeezed shut. The remembered smell of sweet flag filled her gently flaring nostrils. She heard again the crackle of parchment and saw the bold firm script, *Death before dishonor*.

It seemed he might be a man such as his father, and Robert, the Lord of Eden, had chosen his honor over his love. Mayhap this Tristan would choose his honor over vengeance wreaked on her for her father's misdeeds. It was a frail reed of hope to grasp.

The sun hung low on the round peaks to the west when the shadows of a thick wood swallowed the head of the file, beckoning Amicia to the destiny she longed to escape. Overhead, hazelnuts ripened. Nearby, a wild service tree blazed in its autumn garment of crimson and scarlet.

The wind whistled through the thickening canopy, but the forest floor was eerily still with a penetrating chill. A thorn snatched at Amicia's hems and she bent to release it. Her nose twitched and sniffed, separating a whif of smoke from the rich pungency of damp earth. The smell strengthened. Oblique columns of sunlight reaching into the shadows foretold a clearing ahead.

The wail of a child stopped abruptly, as though a hand had been clapped over its mouth. Silence fell, broken by the dull clopping of hooves upon loamy soil. The file of armed men passed through the clearing, where busy charcoal-burners froze at their tasks to raise soot-blackened faces and round wary eyes. Smoke spiraled gently from a series of smoldering piles. A woman with a babe on her hip and a wooden bowl at her lips stared over the rim like a startled doe ready to bolt. A girl stood at the entry to a wattle-and-daub hut, her hand frozen in the act of lifting a strand of hair from her face.

At the far side, Amicia turned in the saddle to stare back, wondering at the fear permeating the air like the acrid smoke.

The pace quickened until a halt was called at a small stream chuckling across a series of miniature rocky falls. Odo lifted Amicia from her palfrey. Grateful for the rest, she sank against the trunk of an alder and huddled in the folds of her mantle. Her father gave low-voiced orders to a quartet of men-at-arms, who rode away with their formerly sullen faces split by broad smiles that left her uneasy and agitated.

Odo passed nearby with the heavy weight of her woolen tent.

"Where do they go?" Amicia asked.

He frowned and shifted from foot to foot, his gaze sliding away from hers. "You will know soon enough, my lady."

She watched his rapid, almost angry, erection of the tent, her thoughts drifting to the mountain vale. She had never seen fear there such as she had seen in the faces of the charcoal-burners. Indeed, in Holmby Vale the serfs had been eager to leave their plows or flails or sickles to greet wanderers. They gladly offered horns of cold water in hopes of hearing tales of golden-haired King Henry, third of that name.

A yearning grew in her for the peace of that greening valley guarded by its rampart of mountains. There was no fear there, but trust. The men met her eyes with honesty and care, not with the surreptitious, sliding glances of her father's men—glances that left her feeling unclean and unclothed.

She braced her chin on her knuckles, favoring the swollen bruising left by her father's hand. Staring into the clear water foaming around a smooth ice-glazed rock, she wondered if nature's forces grieved with her, so unseasonably cold was it.

"My lady, the tent is ready."

Her gaze shifted upward, pausing at the fire beginning to crackle beneath the prodding of a thick-set man-at-arms. "I would warm myself first, Odo."

His scarred face tightened, livid seams gliding across the surface of his weathered skin. But while his face twisted in a grotesque scowl, that single darkly gray eye softened to plead. "Your tent, my lady."

"But, Odo, I am chilled nigh unto—"

"Your tent, demoiselle," her father barked from his perch on a low folding stool. He leaned toward her, one fist braced on the knee of his chausses. A smile colder than the ice-flecked breeze curled across his lips. "Your tent . . . lest you wish to bed your new-wed husband without that which he will expect to take."

His meaning escaped Amicia, even as the knowledge of a threat bloomed with a rank floweret of fear. She was vaguely aware that Odo had made an involuntary movement toward her—one as quickly checked as begun—but her fullest care was given to the sneer in those blue eyes so like her own.

"My men, as you can see"—he scanned the group caught in various poses of avid interest—"would gladly rid you of that prize if you find it so burdensome."

"Lady, get you to your tent." Odo's voice was the merest breath of a wail that traveled no farther than her ear.

Her heart hammered painfully, though comprehension eluded her. She ought to rise and run to that shelter, but her muscles would not obey her frantic urgings.

" 'Twill be rape he sees done, my lady," Odo whispered harshly, his gnarled hands curling into fists.

Her fear burst with the scald of lye dripping from wet ashes. Amicia's eyes widened even as she surged to her feet and raced to the meager protection offered by her tent. The flaps fluttering behind her, she threw herself to her pallet and snatched up a coverlet to shield herself. A chime of laughter pierced the air and vibrated along her nerves like music plucked from a psaltery.

"Ay, Odo," her father snarled, "it would be a merry jest upon the cub of Eden. No maid would he get, but a whore swelling with a villein's brat."

"Ay, my lord. A merry jest indeed," Odo answered with a low grating laugh that stilled Amicia's heart in her breast.

Dread marked in every drooping line, her face climbed from the cradle of her hands to stare at the slit of light glowing through the tent flaps. Odo? Was she wrong to think there was some softness in him that did not exist in these others?

The flap jerked open. Odo's head jutted into the dimness. Amicia gasped and shrank back.

"Do not show your face beyond your tent this night," he hissed. "No matter what you hear! Do not if you would save your honor for the Lord of Eden!"

Her shoulders sank with relief, her lashes sagging over her eyes. This was the Odo she thought she knew. The nearest thing to a friend she had in this foreign, frightful world. How strange this odd feeling of kinship with him was.

"Do you heed me, my lady? No matter what you hear," he warned again and was gone.

Amicia sank to the pallet and curled into a ball of misery. She was hungry and thirsty, but hunger and thirst were of little moment compared to—

A woman's shrill, mindless scream propelled Amicia to her knees. Another scream scrabbled above the last, and she dove for the tent flap, the woolen coverlet flying. Her shaking hand fumbled for the edge. She whipped it open and froze. A woman lay naked and writhing upon the ground. Men-at-arms pinned her spread-eagled arms and legs. Another rose from between her thighs with his chausses around his knees, the jutting rod of his member swollen and red and glistening.

A blow to Amicia's shoulder sent her tumbling backward. She screamed, recoiling from the fury that blazed in Odo's eyes and lividly engorged the patchwork of scars seaming his face.

"Do you seek to join their play, my lady?" he grated.

"Odo"—she swallowed the bitter acid of nausea—"I beg of you, help her!"

"I cannot! 'Tis the way of men to take what they want!"

The flap fell. Amicia watched it float to and fro, revealing the ragged folds of Odo's mantle where he guarded the entrance. His last words rang in her ears like the deep-toned bell at Holmby calling all to their prayers: *'Tis the way of men to take what they want!*

A scream clawed through the air and Amicia started, her hand climbing to her throat. It was not hers. Her screams shrilled in her mind with senseless, savage despair. Odo had saved her for but a moment. She would soon be given to a man who would have all rights over her. None would say him nay if he took her like a ravening beast. None would halt his hand if he beat her unto death. Her life would rest in the hollow of his palm.

*Why, demoiselle, the Lord of Eden will see you dead*, her father's cruel voice slithered from the hidden passages of memory. *Dead . . .*

Amicia bowed low and wept until there were no tears left to shed. Hollow-eyed and aching, she climbed to her knees and folded her hands at her breast. Her wide eyes, swimming with fear and disillusionment, were slowly shielded by the heavy weight of spiky wet lashes. Her prayers came in slow, halting phrases. Pleas for aid for the women screaming in the night. Pleas for aid for herself. Rash promises and thanks given for the serenity she had known at Holmby. A serenity that had deserted her as had the peace she always achieved at prayer.

At some time during the night the screaming died. Low moans accompanied the crackling of the fire and the rustling of leaves—and the frenzied whirl of Amicia's thoughts. Thoughts that whipped in endless plans for escape.

Morning rushed upon her with the sounds of the stirring camp. Odo called softly and parted the flaps. "It is time, my lady. We reach Castle Eden this day."

"The woman, Odo?"

"She lives," he said gruffly, thrusting a horn of heated wine into her hands.

It was sour and of the poorest quality, but she drank it to the dregs. She would need what little strength it offered. Though it seemed to take forever, the tents were down and the ride begun before she could finish the prayers she sent winging heavenward.

Frost crackled with every plodding step. Weak rays of sunlight penetrated the forest canopy, moving at ever more acute angles until they stood like straight columns. The deep wood thinned overhead, while the bracken and brambles thickened. The wind rose, seeming to carry the brightening rays of the sun.

They left the wood behind. Before her lay the bare expanse of a village commons sinking gently to the frozen ruts of a cart track. Amicia's heart thudded and began to race. Her gaze climbed to the twin row of cruck cottages lining the track and pointing to the tall red sandstone walls of a church, whose open doors beckoned her to shelter and safety.

A swiftly whispered prayer of thanksgiving steamed from her icy lips. She tried to move her toes, but could not feel them. She flexed her fingers, but had to look to see if they moved. The head of her party reached the cart track . . . and crossed it, moving toward the bleating sheep spread across a low hill.

Amicia's gaze shifted from the fluttering pennant to the sandstone church and back again, her heart sinking. They would not pass it! Her only hope! Energy born of desperation surged through her. She tilted precariously across the palfrey's mane and yanked the reins from Odo's loose grip. Her heels dug into the dun-colored flanks. The mare shied and lurched up the track, nearly unseating her. Behind her, a shout rose from the column. The wild thunder of her heart blended with the thunder of hooves giving chase. She bounced and bobbled and lost the reins, and the wild-eyed mare sprinted into an all-out race.

''*No!*'' The despairing scream poured from Amicia as she hooked her hands around the tall pommel and fought for balance. The first cruck cottage rushed past and the sound of pounding hooves diminished behind her. The welcoming doors of the church grew large, but the palfrey veered to follow the curve of the track and she was too terrified to chance a tumbling roll from the saddle.

Looming ahead was a small body of mounted men. A ragged row of four astonished faces blurred and vanished behind the thick dappled gray chest of a destrier rearing to paw the air. The palfrey whinnied and reared, dancing a quarter turn before lunging into the stubbled field lining the rutted track—and flinging Amicia from the saddle . . . straight at the flashing hooves of the destrier.

In the split second before she slammed into the frozen ruts with a force that sliced off the trailing ribbon of her scream, it seemed that she saw every movement as separate and distinct: the rusted iron shoe arcing around the massive hoof that flailed the air; the deep muscular chest rippling beneath a splotch of blue-gray; the polished gleam of the leather trappings; a star of light winking from the gold spur fastened to a huge leather shoe set in a heavy stirrup.

The hoof thudded scant inches from her head. She flinched but could not move away. She lay still and gasped for breath, while every muscle screamed a protest at this new, bone-jarring punishment after days in the saddle. Her head, propped against the rising ridge of a rut, crooked her neck at an angle that pulled painfully at her nape. She moaned, a soft sound that became one with the jumbled shouts of men and the neighs of their frightened steeds.

Her eyes fluttered open on the glaring brilliance of the sun. A brilliance that was eclipsed by the shadow of a giant. She heard a voice whose words made no sense, but whose sound was a deeply soothing melody that strummed the tension from her. The giant knelt in one graceful motion. One hand, huge and firm and gentle, so very gentle, cradled her cheek in its palm.

''Demoiselle?'' The disembodied voice wafted on a current of compassion and concern. "Demoiselle, are you hurt?"

Her hand climbed to cup his against her cheek. Slowly, the glare subsided as she focused on eyes as warmly blue as a midsummer sky. "Help me," she whispered breathlessly. "Must get to the church."

"Shh, do not try to speak. Can you sit up?"

Cautiously, he eased his hand beneath her and raised her to sit leaning against the brace of his forearm. Her head rested against the wine-red mantle folded across his shoulder and her eyes climbed to the bold square of his jaw.

Her voice came threaded with exhaustion. "I . . . I must stand."

"Rest a moment, then you may rise," he soothed.

Her lashes fanned closed, twin tears squeezing out to trickle across her cheeks. "The church. Must . . ."

Pounding hooves vibrated the earth beneath her. Her father bore down upon her, his face terrible to behold. Rolling against the hard chest at her back, Amicia tangled her hands in the man's fine woolen surcoat and raised her wild pleading gaze to his.

"Help me! I beg of you! I must gain sanctuary!"

A frown snapped thick red-gold brows into a solid line over the sky-blue eyes that questioned her, then shifted up to the approaching men. He looked back down, the frown centered in the darkening hue of his eyes. "You flee Eustace of Bellay?"

"I beseech you, my lord. Help me!"

"Fear not, demoiselle." He scooped her into his arms and stood. "I would give aid to the most heinous criminal if he wished to escape that spawn of Satan."

"I will keep you in my prayers for this kindness, my lord," she said, resting her head upon his shoulder and giving herself up to a weakening flood of relief. She was safe at last.

There was no time to wonder how easily she had given herself to this man's keeping with absolute faith that he would protect her. Her father's breakneck pace slowed to a canter and he was upon them. The hard chest pressing against her side ridged and rippled and grew taut while the steady heartbeat quickened.

Sly amusement gleamed in her father's eyes and a wolfish smile pulled his lips back from his teeth. A horse snorted, pawing the ground, and the *kraak-kraaak* of a raven sounded. But in the widening circle of full-armed men there was only a tense silence.

"Bellay," her savior said, his voice guttural with loathing

"Eden"—her father's eyes locked with those of the man in whose arms she lay—"I would make you known to my daughter, Amicia of Bellay."

# Chapter 3

Eden!

Amicia's head whipped around and up. The muscular arms beneath her knees and at her back jerked into taut rods as hard and unyielding as iron.

Tristan, Lord of Eden. The man she was to wed! She sifted the paltry seeds of knowledge gleaned from Odo, but it was her father's utter assurance Eden would see her dead that fell across the surface of her mind like chaff from wheat. Yet the huge palm that cupped her cheek had been gentle. So very gentle, she dared greatly to . . . hope.

Rapidly searching the rich honey-gold arrogance of his face, framed in a wind-tossed tumult of cropped red-gold curls, she found no sign of gentleness—so recently there, so quickly gone—to feed the faint stirring of that hope.

Her wide gaze met summer-sky eyes—met and saw them become as cold as the crystalline brilliance of sunlight stabbing through a crust of ice. Her morbid fascination with his ice-rimmed stare was interrupted by the movement of nostrils flaring as though repulsed by a noisome odor. And below, another movement. The long beautifully shaped lips that had so recently moved to speak words of compassion and concern now thinned in a grimace, then shifted to a sneer.

Her illusion of safety dissipated like smoke in the wind. Hope died, while an assurance equal to her father's took

27

root in her mind and heart. She would find no kindness in the Lord of Eden. Another might, but not the daughter of Eustace of Bellay.

His heart pounded furiously against her ribs. A racing, throbbing beat moving in unison with hers. She knew what pushed hers to the limits of endurance. Fear of her father, of him, of a new and unknown life she wanted not at all. But what of him? There was no sign that fear would ever find a dwelling place behind those icy eyes. Revulsion, yes. She could feel his inner shrinking as if she were an adder he hugged to his breast.

With slow distaste, his rigid arm eased from beneath her knees. He bent, his wintry gazed locked on hers. Her toes touched the ground. Her heels settled, and the cold of the frozen earth seeped through her thin leather soles, crawling through her trembling limbs to settle like frost around her heart. The support of his arm peeled away as though he could not release her quickly enough. She stumbled, nearly falling.

His hand clamped around her wrist. The numbing grip jerked her upright with a gasp. Her gaze flew upward, her chin tilted back, and her eyes locked on his once more. Anger flickered in the depths of his eyes like light glinting from the heart of a gem. His effort to smooth it away was evident in the pinched corners of his lips, an effort that left his gaze passionless and pure, as if purposefully robbed of the heat and life that throbbed in the vein at his temple.

"I bid you," he began in a flat voice bereft of its former musical timbre, then paused. The thick column of his throat worked as though it refused the impulse of further speech. And while his throat worked, his long fingers clenched her wrist in a painful vise. "I bid you . . . welcome, demoiselle," he said with the warmth of a winter wind howling out of the high mountains to pelt the ground with snow and sleet.

His words were mere whispers in Amicia's ears, like the distant buzzing of a fly. Her future and her life were centered on the huge hand that bound her wrist, grinding fragile bone against fragile bone. Long graceful fingers, nicked and scarred by battle. A silken haze of red-gold hair glittered across the knuckles and spread over the back of his hand. A man's hand, strong, hard, hurting . . . like the hard, hurting hands that had pressed the flailing limbs of the serf-woman into the cold earth. She saw again the man-at-arms rising from between the woman's thighs with the rigid—

Fear sliced through her, peaking on abject panic. She wrenched her arm back. His grip held and she cried out, a high wordless sound of terror. His grip loosened abruptly. Free, she whirled, her eyes darting like a wild hunted doe until she found a break in the circle of stamping horses and armed men. She was through it in a flash, fleet steps carrying her toward the red sandstone walls of the church.

The chorus of shouts trailing after her died on her father's thundering shout of "Hold fast!" A stone bruised her heel. Gusts of wind snagged her wimple and cotte like clutching hands. Aching muscles pulled at ankles and knees and hips, but she ignored them for the lure of sanctuary and the hope of escape.

The hope was curtailed in an instant of time. One moment the sandstone walls filled her vision; the next, her father's destrier with his rippling black hide and rolling eyes was there, his breath flowing hot across her face. She fell back, wavered on the lip of a deep gouged hole, and tumbled. Before she could right herself, her father's hand closed over her shoulder in a pincer's grip that threatened to splinter bone.

"By God's Eyes! You will not thwart me in this!" he snarled. "You will wed Tristan of Eden or I will see you regret it! There is no torture devised that I will not do unto you! There is no man so low I will not give him the use of your body! Even unto the dog boys that live in the kennels with my hounds! If your intent is to missay the vows at the church door, then think on that, demoiselle." His voice lowered deeply and ominously. "Not even the church will halt my vengeance if you dare hinder my plan."

Deaf to the sounds of running feet and the vibration of hoofbeats, Amicia knew the soul-scarring hopelessness of defeat. There was no succor she could seek beyond the reach of his will. Her sapphire gaze, starred with tears, moved to the walls of the church, rising sturdy and strong against the blue sky.

"Do you heed me, demoiselle?" he snarled.

His open-handed slap crushed her lips against her teeth, snapping her head back. Simultaneously came a deep-throated roar of outrage.

Her father leaped to his feet, his hand on his sword's hilt. Amicia fell back on her elbow, one hand cupping her throbbing cheek. Her gaze rapidly traveled up the long chausses-clad length of Eden's legs to the azure surcoat that danced across the heaving width of his chest, and up to the face whose golden hue was bronzed by rage. Her breath trapped in her throat, she stared, transfixed by the white heat firing his eyes.

"She is my daughter!" her father shouted. "It is my right to lesson her to obedience!"

"She is my betrothed!" Eden boomed like a spring storm gathering strength over the high tors. "Only I have the right to lay hand to her!"

Amicia lay on the ground between them, caught like a hare in the noose of a snare. And like a hare, she lay perfectly still as though by the single drop of an eyelash she might spring the trap of enmity that radiated from the towering men.

Steel scraped on steel with a sibilant hiss. Eden's brawny fist uncurled, leaping out to grip his enemy's forearm. Sunlight glinted from the half-sheathed sword her father fruitlessly attempted to draw. Eden's arm, bulging against the white sleeve of his tunic, held him as still as a rock.

"I will kill you for this!" the Lord of Bellay growled.

"I would gladly meet you in armed combat had I not given sword-oath to Leicester. You are a festering pustule on God's good earth."

Amicia's gaze flickered from the sneer curling her father's mouth to the loathing pulling Eden's lips thin and flat. She realized she had been forgotten. She had been merely the immediate cause of an old quarrel that needed little to bring it to eruption. She could take no heart in Eden's leaping to her defense. He was as her father, obsessively concerned with what he possessed. Though he protected her from her father, there would be no one and nothing to protect her from him.

Even as her heart sank, a third voice insinuated itself into the circle of angry silence surrounding the combatants.

"Tristan, Tristan." A hint of masculinity deepened the sweet tones lilting from the region blocked from her view by Eden's flexing arm. "Leicester awaits. Would you profane your much-lauded honor while he sits at leisure within your keep? Cease this useless wrangling, I say. Neither you nor Bellay would dare thwart the Earl's will, and well do you both know it."

The man hove into view. Short and square and swarthy, he knelt on thick legs, his barrel chest drawing his bright gold surcoat tight and smooth. "Demoiselle," he said in the high light voice that so ill matched his burly frame, "you flee as though the lymers snapped at your heels. Tristan's face has had riotous effect on ladies from Gascony to the Borders, but never, to my knowledge, has one fled *from* him. I vow I do wonder why."

Amicia's wide gaze raced over his square face with its thick jaw and small nose, lingered on the tender curve of a smile that threatened to assume a merry tilt, and rose to the dark brown eyes. Here, she paused to a thrill of unease so slight as to be more imagined than felt. In contrast to the mobility of his face, his eyes were utterly still, a watchful presence that neither invited nor rejected—nor participated in the gentle cajolery of his voice.

"Come, come, demoiselle," the soft singsong entreated, "you may speak naught but the truth here. The Earl would not push you to your marriage bed did he but know it was against your wish. And Tristan"—those watchful eyes shifted upward and his smile grew wide and merry—"would gladly cling to his lonely estate."

Amicia's gaze followed his to Eden's bronzed face and hot eyes. Eyes that were riveted upon her father as though he had heard no word spoken. She needed nothing more to convince her that they were the deadliest of foes, but she had it in that hot gaze with its rapt expression. Did he, even now, plot the revenge he would gain on her father through her?

She chanced a glance at her father and found his relentless eyes boring into her. Eyes that spoke of promises made and kept. Her tongue slid across lips gone dry. There would be none to protect her from him. There was no course left her but marriage to Tristan of Eden. Better the cruel heel of one man, than the host her father promised. It was small comfort, but better than none. She must accustom herself to the fate she must now seek. Surely, there would be time. The betrothal papers must be signed and the banns announced on the Sabbaths in the forty days to follow. Weeks. Just weeks . . .

"This marriage—" Her voice broke, and she paused to draw a deep and bracing breath. "This marriage is not against my wish."

A current swept through the darkness of those brown eyes. Regret? Anger? Whatever it was, it came and was gone too quickly for Amicia to grasp its meaning. As if sensing her unease, he lowered his lashes. When they rose once more, tiny points of light filled his eyes with humor, and laugh lines crowded the corners. His merry smile sprang to life and her unease vanished as quickly.

He reached out. The shadow of Eden's arm fell across the thick square hand with spatulate fingers delicately arched in a gesture of confident expectation.

Amicia's hesitation was brief. Her imagination played tricks upon her. None with so merry a smile could be evil. Did she allow it, she would begin to believe every man followed the path of her father and her betrothed. She would truly go mad, ever looking for threat and never for goodness.

She reached out. His hand closed around hers with warmth and strength and tenderness. Eden stepped back, his leather shoe scuffing the frozen earth, his shadow falling away from their entwined hands.

"I am Aimery, soon to be your brother by marriage. Come, demoiselle," he urged, gently helping her to her feet and placing an arm about her waist to draw her against the solidity of his body. A solidity that was as comforting as the rampart of mountains protecting the Priory of Holmby.

Aimery's gaze lifted to his brother's face and Amicia's followed. The passionless blue eyes resting upon her slowly stiffened her spine and brought her chin up with unconscious defiance. Had she been aware of that defiance, caution would have meekly lowered her eyes. Her father

had taught her the price of outright defiance and she had
not the least wisp of a doubt that the Lord of Eden would
leap to brutality as quickly.

The impassive blue of his eyes stirred to life with an
expression so like approval Amicia was left stunned and
shaken by the sprouting kernel of new hope.

"Tristan," Aimery began, "it ill becomes us to keep
Demoiselle Amicia in the chill wind when she could rest
within the keep. She is worn unto death by the labor of her
travel."

Eden stood tall and taut with the wind threading the
fiery silk of his hair and lifting a corner of his wine-red
mantle. His gaze, sharp and impenetrable, lingered at the
swollen corner of her mouth. Amicia felt a welt of sensation, as though he had reached out a gentle finger to touch
it. A quiver raced across her lip and his gaze climbed to
plunge deeply into hers. A frown smoothed the arch from
his brows and flattened the line of his lips. He nodded
once, an abrupt dip of his head, then turned to mount his
dapple-gray destrier—leaving her, his soon-to-be-betrothed,
to the attentions of his brother.

"My lady, here is your mantle," Odo said softly. "It
was lost in your tumble from the palfrey."

Amicia pulled her attention from Eden's departing back.
Obviously she was not to be extended even the small
courtesy due any wayfarer at his door. Ignoring a disquiet-
ing sense of abandonment, she smiled upon Odo while
Aimery set the mantle around her shoulders. Here, at least,
were two she seemed to need not fear.

"You will ride with me, demoiselle," Aimery began,
and paused to look up the cart track. "Mayhap not. Tristan
returns, and in a foul mood, lest my eyes deceive me."

Tristan cantered up, sitting as straight as the quarrel of a
crossbow. A deep tinge of red rode high on his cheekbones
as he stared down at her with a scowl that weakened her
knees and sent her hand flying to the supporting arm of his
brother.

"You will ride with me," he said with the enthusiasm
of a man approaching the executioner's axe.

She swallowed hard and wished his destrier was not so

big and he not so tall and his frown not so fierce. "My palfrey—"

"Has not been found. She flew into the wasteland beyond the fields. Aimery"—his sharp gaze cut toward his brother—"lift Demoiselle Amicia to my saddle."

"I . . ." Terrified at the thought of riding with him, she lurched into speech. "I could ride pillion behind Odo here."

"You will ride with me," he said flatly, shifting over the high cantle to leave the saddle for her.

There was nothing to do but allow herself to be lifted, to settle uneasily, and stiffly hold herself from the thick chest at her back. His arms encircled her and she quelled a shudder, her eyes dropping to the thick seal ring upon his finger. She saw the intaglio of the two-headed Janus set in a medallion of letters and thought of Mother Margaret and the love she had known and lost. A love that she, herself, would never know.

"Ride ahead, Aimery, and take the lady's man with you."

Amicia started with surprise. She would be alone with him. Alone, and she greatly feared his intent. She could not now quell the shudder that began in her heart and trembled across her shoulders. Her eyes darted to Odo, who had paused in mounting his steady mount. His scarred face lifted to her and his eye narrowed.

"My lady?" he questioned.

"I would have private speech with my betrothed," Tristan of Eden said coldly. "Follow the lead of my brother and be off."

Amicia saw the play of emotions racing across Odo's face like clouds scudding before the wind. Hesitancy, fear, and a resolution that jutted his jaw.

"As you said, my lord, I am the lady's man. I go where she wills."

A silence fell. A silence so acute it seemed to Amicia that she could hear his furied heart beating. She wanted to urge Odo to go, but was stricken mute by his daring and his loyalty.

"Demoiselle," Eden said, his voice as dry as dust.

"Odo," she said quickly, wincing at the hoarse scrape of her own voice, "do as he commands."

Odo yet paused in indecision.

"No harm will come to her at my hands," the deep flat voice of her captor affirmed.

Could she have believed it, her heart might have stopped hammering against her ribs. She watched Odo pull his forelock and mount, then trot toward the group vanishing beyond the crest of a far hill. The cold of the wind bit deep, and she shivered. But that cold was as nothing to the chill of forsaken solitude that filled her mind and made her sway. His hard hand caught her arm, pulling her back against his chest.

"Are you ill?"

She was, but it was not an illness of the body. Instead, it was a sickness of the soul. Partly yearning for the peace of Holmby, partly fear of the life ahead, but mostly the realization that she was alone and would ever be. Odo was but a villein, and what aid he could offer was limited by his estate. Aimery was Eden's brother. His loyalty would lie within him. Her father . . .

She blinked the haze of tears from her eyes. It was best not to think of her father.

"Demoiselle?"

"Nay, my lord," she said softly. "I am only weary. The journey has been long."

"I am sorry to keep you longer from your rest," he said, sounding not at all sorry.

Her gaze climbed to a single sparrow skimming across the fabric of the sky. It wheeled and dipped and sang its song with a freedom that filled Amicia with envy. It could come or go as it pleased, while she . . .

The thick fringe of her lashes lowered to shield her eyes from the sight.

The destrier stamped restlessly, tossing his great head and snorting. Eden's chest bunched and rolled at her back as his hands tightened upon the reins. "Hold, Vainqueur!"

*Vainqueur*. Conqueror. It was so apt, Amicia would have smiled had she not been so dulled by the defeat of her hopes.

The stallion pranced to the side and settled. She heard

Eden draw breath for speech. "Do you still wish to reach the church and gain sanctuary, demoiselle?"

The words acted upon Amicia like a goad. Her spine snapped straight and she twisted in the saddle, her eyes rising to Eden's face. She scanned the clenched line of his jaw, the taut lips, and aquiline nose with flaring nostrils before her wide midnight eyes met wintry blue.

"You . . . you would take me there?" she asked breathlessly, disbelief written on every feature of her small face.

"Ay."

"Why?"

"I would not press you to this joining against your will, and I cannot, after the events past, believe it is your will."

"As it is not yours?" she asked.

His gaze shifted from her and the thick arch of his brows crawled down to shadow his eyes. "True."

"Because . . ." Breath failed her. "Because I am the daughter of the Lord of Bellay."

His eyes shifted to hers. "Ay."

"I am not my father, my lord," she murmured softly.

"But I am mine, demoiselle." The stillness of his eyes gave way to flickering shades of torment. "Were he alive he would be sickened by this thing I do."

"Then why have you agreed, my lord?"

The barest hint of a smile lent a cynical quirk to his lips. "For a reason no woman would ever understand."

"Mayhap you do a disservice to us."

"Do I?" His frown yielded to derisive amusement. "I have years on you, demoiselle, and have seen much. I have yet to meet the woman who understands honor in its full meaning to a man."

Honor. Amicia's curious gaze hardened and cooled. She knew about honor and the havoc it wreaked. She knew about his father's honor and what it had done to Mother Margaret. "You are right, my lord." Tension abraded her soft voice. "I do not understand. Is it honor to join yourself to one you despise?"

His eyes narrowed. "It is my duty to my overlord."

"Does nothing come above this honor you claim?"

"Nothing."

"Not even love, my lord?"

"Least of all love."

Her lips thinned. He was his father's son. It mattered naught who suffered, so long as his honor was preserved.

"You disapprove, demoiselle?" His voice sliced at her.

She stared steadily into his glittering eyes and dared that which she would never have dared with her father. "Ay, my lord. I have seen the result of honor carried beyond sense and it is a sad sight to behold."

"You would live your life without honor?" he asked, distaste curling along his lip.

Amicia's heart hammered uncomfortably within her breast. "Nay, my lord. I would but give honor its proper place."

"A woman's place."

"Ay, my lord."

"Then I am proven right, am I not? No woman can understand honor in its full meaning to a man."

Her lashes fanned down to her cheeks. "Ay, my lord."

"So meek, demoiselle. Yet," he continued with an edge in his voice, "I suspect you yield naught which you do not wish to yield."

"I have been called stubborn, my lord."

"No doubt," he said dryly. "I would ask once more, demoiselle. Do you wish to claim sanctuary in the church?"

Her gaze drifted past his shoulder to linger wistfully on the sandstone walls, then moved in a slow circle to the road ahead. She stared at the crest of the hill where her father had vanished from sight. "I am stubborn, my lord, but not a fool. I will wed you despite your distaste and my . . ."

The pause spun long and his knuckle gently nudged at her chin until her eyes met his. "Your what, demoiselle?"

"My fear," she said simply.

He stared for a moment as if surprised by what she had said. A frown pleated his brow and darkened the vivid blue of his eyes. "You have naught to fear so long as you remember that your honor becomes mine when we are wed."

"That I fear above all, my lord," she said whisper-soft, her dark eyes searching his.

And she did. Her very life was nestled upon the callused palm of his honor.

# Chapter 4

Tristan, the Lord of Eden, a knight whose bold courage was renowned from sunny Gascony to the mist-shrouded northern lands of the Scots, stared into Amicia of Bellay's fear-illumined eyes and felt a rill of doubt disturb his hard-won convictions. Impulse urged him to allay her fear. Reason flayed him with the cynical whip of embattled defenses.

She was a woman, he assured himself, and it was better to accept the faith of that blustering weathercock King Henry than of a woman. She was the daughter of Bellay, and it was better to expect truth from Satan himself than from that demon. She was beautiful, but who better than he knew that the face of an angel could cover an inner rot that despoiled all it touched. Yet there was in that clear steady gaze much that spoke of faith and truth, and an inner beauty that reached out to gently stroke the core of loneliness that had been his since his first memory.

A frown darkened his face. "We must be away," he said harshly, and felt the tension seep from her body as she dipped her chin and faced forward.

His spurs touched the flanks of the destrier, who leaped ahead, settling into a smooth trot. Tristan's pale eyes roamed the stubbled fields to the east and lingered on the circling wood, but he saw nothing of the autumn-hued leaves. Instead, his vision was filled by the small face he could not now see. Flawless skin, pale with fear. Cheeks reddened by wind and cold. Huge eyes as darkly blue as night and ringed by violet shadows of exhaustion. Eyes filled with caution and fear, confusion and resolve. Lips, softly sweet with a childlike innocence . . .

Bellay's daughter—and the apple never fell far from the tree, he reminded himself.

The Earl had decided this marriage would end the warring between his two vassals, but Tristan knew better. Bellay was set upon the destruction of the house of Eden. Nothing would stop him. Now he would have a spy planted in the keep.

A spy. Tristan's gaze lingered on the woolen folds of the wimple. A reluctant one? Why had she first tried to claim sanctuary, then denied it? *Peste!* What had Bellay said before he slapped her? And why had he, himself, been catapulted into rage by that blow? The girl was nothing to him. If her father wished to lesson her, it was none of his concern. Who knew but what she was a disobedient wench who would not learn her place.

Tristan reined in Vainqueur on the crest of the far hill. In the distance lay Castle Eden. Ever did new sight of it tear him between love and pride, hate and despair. There was much to give him pleasure: the demesne farm with its healthy serfs who filled his granaries with wheat and oats and his coffers with silver; the sturdy stone curtain wall with evenly spaced square towers, which had repelled numerous invasions by the ravaging Scots; and the people who gave him a trust equal to that they had afforded his father and his brother Robert. Without the keep he was content, but within . . .

"My lord—" Amicia's hesitant voice intruded on his thoughts—"is . . . is that your—"

"Yes," he bit out.

She studied the thick stone keep with crenelated corner turrets silhouetted against the cloudless sky. What would she find there? Death, if her father was right. Death from the very arms that encircled her now. If this Tristan of Eden were her father instead, she would have no doubt. Yet, he was not. Could a man who had betrayed such compassion and concern in those moments before he learned her identity be so cruel for so little reason? Dare she allow herself a hope as thin and easily broken as a strand of spun wool?

He had not struck her as her father would have done when she was driven to speak her mind to him. She quailed inwardly at that folly. Even as she did, though, she felt the seeping ooze of relief. He might have done anything to her, but he had not done so much as raise his voice, despite his evident displeasure. Was it possible he was not the man her father thought he was?

Impelled by a need greater than her dread, she shifted in the saddle and half turned to study him. She saw clean lines and honey tones. A square angularity, softened by silky cropped curls that captured the sunlight in gilded streaks of gold set upon copper. She saw, too, a strength that called to some secret part of herself—a part that cried, I am alone and afraid.

His gaze dropped to hers. While the destrier stamped on his great hooves and the cold wind snatched the steam of unsteady breaths from their lips, two sets of eyes questioned and parried—and withdrew behind walls that shielded the weaknesses that might be found and used against them.

Amicia was the first to break contact, her gaze falling to the rapid pulse in his throat. Had she seen that terrifying solitude? That bitter unhappiness? He was a great lord, the center of all he surveyed. From whence came his unhappiness?

His pulse sprinted against the thick haze of golden hair that stopped at a neat line where his beard was scraped away. He swallowed, a sticky sound that sent her eyes climbing to his once more, but he stared over her head.

"How does Castle Eden compare to Castle Bellay, demoiselle?" he asked as though pushed into undesired speech by some irritant of emotion.

"I know not, my lord. I have never seen Castle Bellay."

His eyes, shifting down to hers, frowned a question.

"I was taken a swaddled babe to Holmby Priory and abided there until my father came for me these few days past. I know naught but the valley and the nuns and the peace of that life."

"You know naught of . . . ." His nostrils flared as though

the air were filled with a vile stench. "'You know naught of Bellay?''

Amicia's gaze fled the intense pressure of his. She wanted to cry that she knew much of her father. She knew he was cruel beyond measure. She knew his heart was black with the venom of hate. She suddenly wanted to warn this giant of a man, whose stark soul had been so briefly revealed, of her father's evil intent. The urgency of that impulse passed quickly. She was her father's daughter, and so suspect in Eden's eyes.

She drew an unsteady breath. "I know little of him."

Long, graceful fingers cupped her chin and tilted her face up. "Do you know that I am enemy to him?"

"Ay, my lord."

"I would know now, before the vows are spoken—" a thread of steel laced word to word—"does this make me enemy to you?"

Amicia gazed steadily into his eyes. "If I said ay, my lord, would you missay your sword-oath to the Earl and deny this marriage?"

"Nay," he said flatly. "I seek only to know if I need guard my back from the thrust of your dainty dagger."

"And I, my lord? What assurance have I that you will not use me hardly to gain your vengeance on my father?"

A flush of anger turned his cheeks to a ruddy hue beneath a lowering scowl. "I do not make war upon women, demoiselle!"

"Then, my lord, your back is safe." Her voice trembled from a rush of relief so acute she felt weakened by it. She did not pause to ask herself why she believed utterly and surely any word he said. She went on to confide, "My . . . my father has given me little reason to make his enemies my own."

His eyes dropped to the bruise swelling upon her lip and cheek, and his scowl grew darker. His gaze plunged deep into hers. She felt the touch of his finger. A touch as gentle as the brush of goose down. "I see that he has not. You need not worry . . ." His voice trailed into silence while the ember of rage flickered and died in the depths of his eyes.

The cool remoteness of the pristine blue warmed, and a

strange, inexplicable emotion feathered down her spine. His expression was so like the surreptitious glances of the men-at-arms, she felt a belling of alarm. Yet there was something different about it. Something clean and honest that purged it of the stain of evil. Something that wakened her restless longings for life and its unexplored mysteries. Something that recalled Mother Margaret's heartfelt cry: *Naught should you fear of life. Nay, rather you should rush toward it with outstretched arms.*

He blinked, the lush thickness of dark coppery-brown lashes falling like a curtain to shield thought and desire. When they rose once more, she saw stunned confusion and wondered at it, as she did at the frown that quickly took its place. Slowly, as if his every effort to resist were useless, his eyes were drawn back to her face. They settled upon her mouth. Her lips swelled and prickled. His thumb wafted across the sensitive fullness of her mouth and her breath caught in her throat.

"Have you ever known a man's lips, demoiselle?" he asked, his voice low and rich and seductively melodic.

"Nay, my lord," she whispered, wondering at the spell he cast upon her, a spell robbing her of breath and will. If he ever bent his finger and beckoned, would she follow without question?

"Not even your father's kiss of peace?" he asked, his eyes never leaving her lips.

"Peace, my lord," she said so softly he bent closer to hear, "is the last thing my father would wish for me."

Their breaths mingled and their eyes sought and meshed. Time slowed as their beating hearts raced.

"Your father is a fool."

"Ay, my lord."

"Have you no loyalty to him, demoiselle?"

"He is my father, my lord."

"And I, demoiselle? What will I be to you?"

"My . . . husband, my lord."

"And will I have your loyalty, demoiselle?"

Amicia searched his questioning gaze. "I will gladly yield to you all that you merit, my lord," she answered softly.

His seeking gaze warmed and twinkled with humor. A

humor that tugged one corner of his mouth into a half smile. "As I said, demoiselle, I believe you yield naught which you do not wish to yield."

She felt her own lips tilting upward in visible proof of the smile that grew in her heart. "Nay, my lord."

His smile faded while his gaze heated, burning into hers. "Then, demoiselle, I will find it all the sweeter when you yield me your all."

With a lighter heart and brimming with hope, Amicia approached the wooden gate tower surmounting the palisaded wall that surrounded the outer ward. The banner of Eden—the black head of Janus on a background of scarlet sendal—proudly flew from a turret. The wardcorne, peering through a crenel in the parapet, blew a shrill note upon his horn to announce the lord's return. The gate guard shouted, and the wooden gate creaked open in welcome.

A squawking hen darted through with a barking hound in pursuit. Behind them was a gnome of a man with a bent back and a shiny bald plate, giving chase with a hitching step. Thumbless fists punching the air, he shouted, "Mange-ridden beastie! You'll not have her for your—"

He skidded to a halt and canted to one side, peering up with a rosy face and a snaggle-toothed smile. "My lord—" He bobbed and grinned. "He's at it again as you can see."

"He is a hunter, Giles. She is but sport for him."

"Ay, my lord." The man's heaving sigh betrayed frustration and amused affection. "She'll not give an egg for a week!"

"Do you fear to suffer an empty belly?"

The smile in Tristan's voice eased Amicia. This was what she had known at Holmby. The affection born of absolute trust between the nuns and the serfs who worked their demesne. It told her much of the Lord of Eden— much that pleased her and dulled her forebodings for the future.

"Nay, my lord," Giles replied fervently. "You have ever seen my belly full and the hard lot of my life eased. Ay, even when others claimed me beyond worth because of these." He held up the thumbless flats of his hands and spat upon the hoof tracks in the frozen ground. His eyes narrowed and he spat once more. "The devil has entered your gate, my lord," he intoned ominously.

"Ay, Giles, that he has," Eden affirmed. "Fear not. We will be rid of him soon."

Giles's narrowed eyes shifted to Amicia, his mouth turning as ugly as the hate that pierced her heart with dread. "Ay, but his seed is planted here to flower and bear the fruit of his evil."

Even as Amicia felt the icy jolt of shock, Eden stiffened at her back. "His *seed* will be your lady," he said harshly. "Do not forget it."

The destrier surged through the gate, galloping up the incline of the track crossing the deep outer ward. A full-armed knight jousted at the quintain set at the far curve of the sloping hill. Geese and ducks and hens strutted in search of delicacies crawling across the earth bared of grass. Hounds lazed in the sun. Men-at-arms patrolling the *alure,* the wall-walk set behind the parapet, stomped and slapped their arms around their bodies and blew steamy breath upon their hands.

All was as she expected. Movements in harmony with the season and the life behind the curtain walls. Yet she viewed it through a pall of renewed foreboding. She drew breath and stared ahead at the rush-lined moat footing the hill that stepped up to the stone wall in rubbled-stone revetments.

"He hates me, my lord," she said, her voice as unsteady as the erratic race of her heart.

"With reason, demoiselle."

The coldness in his voice knifed through her. "I know naught of him, nor have I ever done evil unto him."

"You are bone and blood of your father. Giles does not judge the difference."

The cold crept through her, chilling her mood and heart and hand. Her spine stiffened and held her from contact with the broad chest at her back. "And you, my lord? Think you that I come from evil, therefore I am evil?"

She waited for his answer as they drew near the foot of the drawbridge crossing the moat. The destrier's hooves clopped in dull thuds upon the wood, coinciding with the heavy beat of her heart. Would she be forced to prove not only the woman she was, but the woman she was not?

"Giles was once the best forester in Eden Chase and was held high in my father's esteem." His evasion gave unwelcome answer to her question. "Your father disputed the boundary between Bellay Chase and ours. He took Giles as a poacher, had his thumbs hewn from his hands and his back and legs broken. He was returned in an ox wain as warning to the villeins who work the wood."

Amicia's lips quivered and pinched together. She swallowed the bile spewing acid into the back of her throat. The sickness roiled within her, making her weak with revulsion. No wonder Giles looked upon her with hate and distrust. No wonder Eden had been so repulsed upon their first meeting. No wonder he evaded a true answer to her question. She was her father's . . . *seed*.

"My father gathered his vassals," Eden continued. "We invested Castle Bellay and would have taken it had he not appealed to the Earl who demanded that we come to terms."

He paused, his anger palpable in the very air, and Amicia found her voice, "Surely, yours was the right, my lord."

"Ay, but it was not in the Earl's best interests then, or now, to have a vassal rendered unfit to perform his obligations to him."

The hollow echoes of the drawbridge gave way to the solidity of transverse logs half-buried in the steep bank to give greater purchase for wheel and hoof. Despite her effort to lean forward, Amicia was inexorably cast back into his hard chest. Did his lip curl with disgust at her touch? Could she blame him if it did? How could any man—even her father—be so cruel as to lame a helpless villein?

The high stone gate-tower loomed ahead with the heavy iron portcullis raised, its lower edge jutting like teeth into the arch overhead. Sunlight pulled them through the thick cavern of the gateway into the inner ward. With the brilliance of that light stabbing into Amicia's eyes came a strident clamor of sounds: the ringing of steel from the smithy set against the curtain wall; the sawing of a log in the carter's shop adjacent; the disparate voices of horse, dog, swine, and sheep; the screams of falcons in the mews near the kennels; the low murmurs of men's voices; the higher-pitched chatter of women; and the shrill squeals of children playing a game of ball with the bladder of a swine.

The silence began with the hard-faced men-at-arms clustered before their quarters rimming the wall beside the gate. It spread like ripples in a pool, bringing the smith from his anvil and the carter from his shop. It reached the women drawing water from the well and the falconer with a merlin upon his wrist. It flowed across the prancing children, who stopped their play to stare wide-eyed and open-mouthed. It rippled on to the bakehouse tower and the kitchens beside it, drawing the cooks into the ward, spoons and knives in hand. Soon no sound was heard but the solitary neigh of a horse and the shuffling of oblivious swine.

All eyes were turned to the soon-to-be Lady of Eden, and in every eye there was a hostility that dug claws of despair into Amicia. She wanted to shrink against the comforting expanse of Eden's chest, but no comfort would be found there. She was alone and there was nothing to do but push herself erect and tilt her chin at a proud angle. She lifted her eyes to the whipping banner atop the turret. Like the sable head of Janus she could look forward or back. Like Mother Margaret, beloved of Tristan's father, she knew the futility of yearning for things which could not be changed.

So stiff was her backbone, she was jarred by every step the destrier made. Though she could hold herself proudly erect, she could do nothing about the flaming and paling of her skin or the sickness curling deep in her belly. She had no need to ask were there others who had suffered at her father's hand. They were all around her, judging her on her father's action and repute. Their eyes, hard and hating, curious and condemning, followed her every movement.

She would find no true "Welcome, my lady," from these. From the lowest dog boy to the lord of them all, she was Bellay's get, and neither she nor they would ever forget. Her spirits plummeted and exhaustion claimed her.

The exhaustion of days of travel and days of fear—only to find she had reason to fear.

The gray square keep was, to her sensitive gaze, as hostile as the eyes that followed her progress. It rose in mammoth proportions, dwarfing the tableau of the inner ward.

After running from his perch on the flight of stone steps that led up the shadowed east wall, a page grasped the destrier's halter while Eden dismounted.

"Demoiselle," the lord said, lifting his arms to her.

For the briefest of moments, dread ruled sense and she resisted. It was foolish. She could not wheel the steed about and fly from this place. There was nowhere to go and no one to care. Whether she willed it or not, her future was here.

His hand settled over hers where they clasped the high pommel with desperation's grip. She felt his warmth, his strength and surprisingly, the comfort he offered. "I am the lord of this place and you will be my lady. None shall do you harm, lest they answer to me," he said, his voice unnecessarily loud in the hushed quiet, as if he wished to give warning to all.

Amicia stared sorrowfully into the steady blue of his eyes. Her voice dropped low for no ears but his. "It can be no easy thing to live amidst such hate, my lord."

A savage current of pain swept through the depths of his eyes. Turning her hand in his, she curled her fingers about the heel of his hand as though she would take that pain unto herself.

"It *is* no easy thing, demoiselle," he said roughly. "But needs must is a hard master. In time, if you are not another such as your father, my people will see it. They are kind and good, and respond to kindness and goodness."

"And you, my lord? Can you forget that I am . . ." She paused and felt his hand squeeze hers lightly as if urging her to finish. "That I am bone and blood of my father."

"I begin to think, demoiselle, that you could charm the hare from its burrow and the bird from its nest." The words were lightly spoken as of a courtier to his lady fair, though his somber expression belied that mood. "But if ever I find your charm is but a mask for a woman's false heart—'' his voice hardened—''I will see you regret it to your last breath.''

He meant every word he spoke, and Amicia knew it. He would carry out that threat with the same thorough disregard for life and heart as her father would. But where her father was driven to that end by a rapacious hate, Eden would be driven by . . . what? Would he think to give this warning had he not been played false by a woman's heart? Would he think to give it had his soul not been scarred? It surprised her to realize that his threat held no fear for her. Other things might make her quiver and tremble, but not this.

''I know but one way to be, my lord,'' she said as softly as the whispering swish of samite, ''and that is as I am.''

He said no more. He lifted her from the saddle and settled her on the beaten earth of the ward. For a moment his hands remained at her waist, and her hands clung to his upper arms as if each sought to gain strength from the other.

The silence grew awkward. His hands fell from her waist and balled into fists. Hers dropped to her sides. She looked away and met the gaping stare of the page. Tristan looked at the platform fronting the entrance tower archway.

''There will be much here that is different from what you have known, demoiselle,'' he said, as if impelled to give warning.

Amicia's gaze climbed to his face, tracing his smooth profile and the slight concavity of his cheeks. ''I am well trained in the arts of a lady, my lord. I hope not to shame you or myself with my ignorance.''

''I am no youngling to be impatient of a trifle. You will have time to accustom yourself to our ways and your duties.'' His gaze moved toward hers, but shifted away before making contact.

The awkward silence descended upon them once more.

Time to accustom herself to their ways and her duties. She needed that. Time to recover from the journey. Time to learn more of this man who would become one with her in the eyes of God and man. Time . . . Her gaze moved slowly around the clustering groups of whispering men, women, and children. She needed time to move among these and prove she was not one such as her father. The weeks while the banns were spoken would not be enough, but would be a beginning. A time to season herself to the duties of a wife. Mayhap even time enough to shed her terror of the bedding ceremony. Would that she could have remained at Holmby, safe and . . . untouched.

Her eyes, wide and fearful, climbed to his face, lingering on the bright curl floating on a breath of wind, before moving to the hard line of his lips. Her own lips fulled and tingled as though his thumb wafted across them once more. He had been gentle. Though he knew who she was, though he hated her father, he had still been gentle with her. Her fingers wound about the wrist he had squeezed so mercilessly. Had he been aware of his strength? She could not believe that he had been. She could not believe that he would fall upon her as the men-at-arms had fallen upon the serf woman at the camp. She could not, because she did not dare. She would go mad with terror did she think it so.

Time. She would have time to learn of him. She would have time to learn if he . . .

"Demoiselle—" his voice, distant and hollow, sliced through her thoughts—"we but delay. Come, it is fitting that you greet Earl Simon and my . . . Lady Sybilla, ere you seek your rest."

He extended his forearm and she placed her hand atop his. They climbed the broad stone steps to the platform fronting the entrance tower. Through the shadowed arch and into the sunlight once more, they climbed another series of steps, crossed the wooden drawbridge, and were met by the bobbing head of the porter in the entrance chamber.

"My lord, I bid you welcome." Dark eyes stabbed hate at Amicia. "My lady."

Amicia nodded, her cheeks heating. Would there be none here to give her the hand of peace?

The garrison hall was crowded elbow-to-elbow with servants waiting at table and men-at-arms taking their leisure. An odor of stale sweat, dusty rushes, and cast-off food assailed Amicia's nostrils. Once more the silence dropped like a pebble in a pool, spreading in widening ripples to the far corners of the filth-ridden hall. Men stopped in the act of chewing. Others raised their heads from the swords they sharpened. All eyes narrowed and stared, and only one was well disposed.

Amicia saw the concern on Odo's face and nodded her head to say that all was well. The concern did not leave him but deepened as he scanned the quiet hall. He frowned as she moved slowly by with her hand upon her lord's.

The pressure of those hard, narrowed eyes sent tension crawling up Amicia's shins to tremble in her knees. It spread up her back and across her shoulders. Her fingers curled unconsciously, nails digging into Eden's hand. He stared straight ahead, as though he were unaware of the silence that followed their passage to the archway opening onto the mural stair spiraling up the corner turret.

Suppressing a sigh of relief that they were alone once more, she lifted her skirt and preceded him up the dank, dim stairway lit by the westering sun. She wondered that he did not speak and chanced a glance back, finding his face as rigidly molded as the bronze it resembled when brightened by the sun. His eyes had reassumed the crystal-line brilliance of ice. His movements lacked the easy flow of moments past. It was as if he dreaded this meeting as much as she.

At the door leading onto the lord's hall, she paused and waited until he stepped beside her. Without a look or a word, he raised his forearm once more. "My lord?" she questioned, her heart hammering within her breast.

"Let us be done with this!" he hissed viciously, and led her into the hall.

Threading a path through the gathered throng, he led her toward the dais at the far end. Her father sat upon a stool with an enigmatic curl to his lips. Behind him, Aimery hovered with a touch of anxiety in his merry smile. Beside them, Lady Sybilla, whom Amicia had seen from afar at Holmby, claimed her right of eminence in the canopied chair. Beringed hands lovingly fingered her costly samite cotte, while her large brown eyes measured Amicia as though wondering whether she would be friend or foe. But the one who caught and held Amicia's attention was the strange man in the matching canopied chair. He could be no other than Simon de Montfort, the Earl of Leicester, a man whose power sat lightly upon his capable shoulders and whose magnetically dark eyes seemed to miss nothing at all.

"Earl Simon, I present to you the lady Amicia of Bellay."

Amicia curtsied low, her hand resting gracefully atop Eden's, and prayed that her trembling knees would not send her sprawling ignominiously at her overlord's feet.

"Rise, demoiselle, that I might see you."

Exhaustion, fear, and trembling combined to betray her. She tried to rise, felt herself falling, and clutched at Eden's hand. He moved quickly, one arm sweeping around her waist, the other holding her hand as he pulled her upright and supported her.

Her face flaming, she heard him say, "Her journey has been long, my lord. Might we save these greetings till she is rested?"

"Mayhap 'tis not the journey that does make her fall," Lady Sybilla observed cryptically in a voice that was low and husky and should have been pleasing to her ear but, somehow, was not.

Amicia felt Eden coiling like a skein wound tight for the launch of a catapult. Her eyes moved slowly to his mother—his mother, staring at him with a look that made what Amicia had faced in the ward and hall seem insignificant in comparison. It was a look of hatred that made her father's hatred of her pale to nothing.

Amicia's gaze darted to her father. His smile was losing its enigmatic quality as the corners of his mouth scaled his cheeks in wry self-satisfied amusement.

"Mayhap 'tis marriage to one such as you that does make her fail," came that husky feminine voice, sharpened by malice.

Eden's hand clenched around Amicia's, grinding knuckle against knuckle. Her face flew up to his face. She saw a look of hate that returned his mother's, full measure and more, which gave rise to a shudder that shook her from head to toe.

"Mayhap," Lady Sybilla continued, "she knows what little use you have for a wife. So little that you let your last wife die upon her birthing bed alone, though she called your name as though it were amulet against the approaching feet of death.''

Amicia's eyes met the dark glitter of triumph in her father's eyes, which screamed of putrescent amusement and perverted zeal. His smirk seemed to say, ''I have told you and it is so. Your end is near and I glory in its coming.''

A tremor raced through Eden, communicating itself to Amicia through clasped hands. Her head swung around and her eyes rose to his face. She waited with bated breath, but he made no denial or rebuttal of his mother's accusation. He only stared at the gloating woman as though he longed to set his hands at her throat and squeeze the life from her.

''The past is done and best forgotten.'' Earl Simon placed himself between mother and son, his hand clapping hard upon Eden's shoulder as if to break him from the trance of his hate. ''Take Lady Amicia to the women's solar that she may seek her rest. The ceremony will be early on the morrow.''

Amicia's horrified gaze wrenched from Tristan. ''The ceremony?''

''Ay, demoiselle, it is planned for the morrow.''

''But . . . but the banns, my lord,'' her voice climbed on a keening note of dismay.

''Your father signed the betrothal agreement and the banns were spoken these weeks past.''

Amicia's head swirled with the blackness of defeat. There was no time. No time to prepare herself. No time . . .

She swayed, and was caught up in strong arms and crushed against a hard chest. She vaguely sensed movement and the dimming light of the mural stair.

''Begone! All of you!'' Tristan of Eden boomed, and Amicia felt the softness of a bed and the gentle touch of a knuckle drawing along her cheek.

Her lashes fluttered and climbed. His face was close to hers, his eyes dark with turmoil and torment. He suffered, and that suffering called to the part of her that seemed to have suffered as he had. She pulled her hand up to lie along his cheek. Her liquid gaze, heavy lidded with exhaustion, searched his.

''What does the morrow bring for us, my lord?''

His eyes squeezed shut as if he could not bear to look upon her face. Yet his hand caught hers and pulled it to his lips. A kiss anointed her palm. "Do not look to me for assurances," he warned huskily. "There are none in me."

"Nor in me, my lord," she whispered and closed her eyes and slept with her hand still in his.

# Chapter 5

Tristan stared at her small hand. Lost as it was in the callused darkness of his, it looked too frail and helpless to withstand the currents of hate and deceit flowing within these moisture-seeping walls like the restless tide of Solway Firth lapping at the mouth of the River Eden. He studied the hand's smooth back and delicately tapered fingers, wondering how she could look to him for assurance.

If she but knew he was as helpless to act as she, she would not look to him for aid. His eyes climbed slowly to her face, roaming restlessly from feature to feature as though he might find answers to the descending plague of questions.

It was as dark as his heart there in the privacy of the turret chamber, lit only by the twilight piercing the scraped skins covering the lancet windows to the south and east. It was darker still in the shadow of the canopied bed with its draping of heavy woolen curtains. Yet her face seemed to glow like the illuminated faces of the saints in paintings.

The wimple had pulled away from her temple, revealing the springy thickness of hair the dark red hue of ripened chestnuts. Dark brows with the sheen of silk arched above her bruised-lavender lids. Her lashes, long and thick and curling, lay upon her cheeks like the wings of moths that court death in a candle's flame. Her nose was fine and straight, neither short nor long, but pleasantly in between. Her mouth . . .

His gaze lingered on her mouth and a curl of heat unfurled in his loins. *Have you ever known a man's lips, demoiselle?* He heard the echo of his own voice. *Nay, my lord,* her answer whispered and he experienced anew the surge of gladness that answer had given him. Gladness that fled before onrushing anger.

Dare he forget she was a woman? No matter the sweetness of those lips, they could spill venom to suck a man as dry of his pride as a physic's leeches could suck him dry of his blood. Lips that could smile so very sweetly, even as they betrayed.

As if responding to that thought, Amicia's lips tilted upward. Tristan's heart lurched. Her mouth twisted and she moaned in her sleep, her head rolling restlessly to the side to reveal the mottled bruising on cheek and lip.

The anger surging through his temple with a giddying rush of blood was directed anew to her father, soon to be his father-by-marriage. The thought lay upon his tongue like wine gone sour. Whatever she was—faithful or faithless, truthful or truthless—she was no sport for a man's ill-temper, even her own father's.

"Papa?"

Tristan's head snapped up. Tension crawled across his shoulders, drawing them as rigid as the expression carving his face like ice molded by wind and sun. His nostrils flared. His jaw clenched until his teeth hurt. Cautiously, he began to detach his hand from Amicia's, pausing when she moaned and clenched it tighter. He waited for her breathing to grow even once more, then placed her hand at her side and stood to face his daughter.

His eyes scanned the room, lingering on the empty passageway before dropping to Megotta's small upturned face. "Lady Sybilla?" he asked, his voice flat and controlled and cold.

"*Grand-mère* is in hall below," she whispered, a sparkle leaping bright in the nut-brown of her eyes.

"The women?"

"They cluster at the far end of the solar, trembling and whispering. You gave them a fright, Papa."

"Did I?" His tension seeped away and the suggestion of a smile pulled at the corners of his mouth.

Megotta cast an anxious glance at the shadowed bed, her sparkling gaze dimming. "The lady, Papa?"

"Sleeps," he answered, his smile spreading as wide as the arms that reached for her.

Her smile arcing across wan cheeks, she raced the few steps to him and leaped into his arms with a giggle. Tristan hugged her close, his heart pounding as though it would explode.

Megotta twined her arms around his neck and rubbed her cheek against his. "I have missed you, Papa."

"And I you, heartling." The agony of his helplessness ate at him and his voice trembled beyond control. "You should not have come, but I am glad, so very glad you did."

"When might we ride out again?" she asked wistfully.

"Soon," he whispered against the downy softness of her cheek. "As soon as we may."

"I hate her, Papa!" she whispered fiercely.

"Shh, heartling. Père André says . . ."

"We must love one another," Megotta said as by rote. "But she is mean and full of spite, Papa, and she does keep us apart!"

"I know. I know, heartling," Tristan soothed as he moved to a nearby stool and lowered himself to it. He settled Megotta on his knee and cupped her chin in his fingers. She was too pale and too thin and too innocent to play the pawn in his mother's game, he thought with a shaft of fear. "Naught can be done for now. Lady Sybilla . . ."

"Fear not, Papa." Velvety eyes, too wise for her years, met his. "I will do naught to bring her ire upon us."

"Come, Megotta. Let us not waste these precious moments upon what cannot be changed." Casting off the heaviness of his spirits, he set his thumb to her chin and quirked a brow high. "I could swear that I did espy a hole where a tooth had been."

Dark eyes brightening with pride, Megotta pulled her lower lip down for his inspection. "I almost swallowed it!" she lisped around the hindrance of her forefinger. "Enid said—"

"That it should have been pulled long since."

Enid's practical voice cut through Tristan like a knife.

Megotta squealed and flung herself against his chest, one small hand rising to curl around his neck, while he crushed her to him and frowned over her head. "God's Blood, Enid!" he hissed furiously. "You walk with the feet of a cat!"

"Ay, my lord." Enid propped her hands on her broad hips and frowned. "Nor am I the only one in this place that does so. What chance do you take here? What if I had been another?"

"By all that's Holy," Tristan gritted in frustration, "I weary of this game!"

"Do you, my lord?" Enid queried gruffly. "Do you grow so weary you would end it and bring pain to an innocent heart?"

Tristan met Enid's resolute stare. His rage drained away leaving him hollow and aching with remorse. His hand cupped Megotta's cheek and he studied her nut-brown eyes and feathery black lashes, the tilt of her nose and her rose-hued lips.

"God help me," he breathed and crushed her to him, his hand cupping her head. Another that looked to him for aid and assurance, he thought in consuming despair. Another that needed what he could not give.

"You have been too long alone without voice raised, my lord," Enid intruded, her gruff tones scrubbed smooth by compassion. "Tongues will wag where they should not."

"A moment longer can make no difference," Tristan whispered, his shadowed eyes raising to hers in pleading.

"An ill-timed moment could bring misfortune for us all."

"Ay," he agreed heavily, lifting Megotta from his lap and settling her before him. He brought her hands to his lips. Gently, he kissed first one, then the other. "Go, heartling. We have been foolishly bold this day."

"But, Papa," she protested, tears hanging heavy on the rim of her lashes.

"Go—"

"Slap her, my lord," Enid said flatly.

Tristan's head jerked up with a look of horror and disgust.

"Does she go from here with a light heart, there will be those to carry the tale," the serving woman added.

Tristan reached for Megotta, his fingers curling around her thin arms to draw her away from the threat Enid posed. "You will not, will you, Megotta? You will wail of your cruel Papa."

Tears spilled from her nut-brown eyes. Tears that dripped like acid across Tristan's heart. "You must, Papa. Else *Grand-mère* will plague me with questions that have no end."

"I cannot," he said hoarsely. "I cannot!"

Megotta stepped between his knees, pressed a kiss to his cheek, and set her small hand against it in a strangely adult gesture of consolation. "Do not fear, Papa. Enid will do it for you," she said softly and turned to walk away.

Tristan sank his face into his hands and set every muscle like rock. He could not do it. He could not stop it. He was helpless. As helpless as a fly caught in a spider's web. No matter how he twisted and turned and fought against it, he was only ensnared the harder.

It came. The ringing sound of flesh upon flesh. He flinched and shuddered—and hated with a white heat of rage. Megotta's scream skimmed down his back like an icy drop of sleet, and the sobs that tore from her throat ripped at his own.

"It is done, my lord. She is gone."

Enid's hand settled upon his nape, offering comfort. His head raised, his eyes met hers. Eyes filled with such a lust to see murder done that she gasped. "She is your mother, my lord."

"She is the devil's handmaiden," Tristan snarled.

"Hush, my lord. You will wake the lady."

"If she did not wake when Megotta . . ." Tristan's throat closed over further speech and he leaped to his feet. Pacing to the narrowing passage in the twelve-foot thickness of the walls, he stared at the skin-covered window as though he might see the wooded hills of Eden Chase through it. "I know not how much longer I can hold this course, Enid," he said softly.

"Eight winters you have done it, my lord. All for the

sake of the child. Would you destroy her now in a fit of temper?''

"Nay, but . . .'' He kneaded the tension from his nape. "It grows harder with time, not easier, as I hoped.''

"Needs must is a hard master, my lord.''

Tristan's gaze drifted to the shadows lying deep inside the bedcurtains. Bitterness twisted his mouth. So quickly his own words were flung into his face. "So it is, Enid,'' he whispered and probed the shadows for the pale gleam of Amicia's face.

"She sleeps like the dead.'' Enid's voice came rife with distaste.

"She is weary. Bellay pushed her beyond her strength.'' He looked up and caught Enid's eye. "The lady has brought none to serve her. I would have you taken as her maidservant.''

"And Megotta?'' she countered.

"Will do well with your daughter. This one has more need of you.''

Enid drew herself up, her broad face flattening with a lack of expression that told Tristan much of her misliking for his request. "I beseech you find another, my lord.''

"There is no other that I may trust as you,'' he said firmly.

"Have you forgotten what her father did to my brother Giles?'' Her face crumpled in a mass of grief. "How may you ask me to serve her who shares the guilt of the deed?''

"What guilt, Enid?'' Tristan queried gently. "Do her mother's sins rest upon Megotta's head? Am I to hate her for naught but that she is bone and blood of her . . .'' He stopped, his eyes moving to the pale purity of Amicia's profile. A frown tugged his brows flat while a memory stirred to life: *And you, my lord? Think you that I come from evil, therefore I am evil?*

Mayhap for his own safety and the safety of those in his care, he should think her so, but he could not. His eyes shifted to Enid. "I would wager my life she is not another such as her father,'' he said with a thread of wonder that he said it—and believed it.

"You do,'' she said bitterly. "It would be easy for her to slip poison in your cup or a knife between your ribs.

You must beware, my lord. 'Tis not like you to be bewitched by a woman.''

"When, Enid, have I ever been bewitched by a woman?" His voice came as hard and cold as the stone walls of Castle Eden.

"Never, my lord, but there is a first time for everything under the sun," she warned.

He frowned and restrained himself by the hardest effort from glancing once more into those beckoning shadows. "I would not force you to act as her woman, do you not wish it."

"Nay, my lord. I will serve her though it curdles my belly. Do you act the fool in this, it would be best to have one who watches with clear eyes."

His frown darkened. "You test my patience, woman."

"I am too long in the tooth to change my ways, my lord." Her head bent submissively, but her tone held naught of meekness.

"More like as stubborn as an ass that sets himself against bridle and bit." His gaze flicked toward the bed and away. "She says that she, too, is stubborn."

"As is her father, my lord."

"Nay, Enid. There is a difference, though I could not set my tongue to what it is. She is . . . gentle."

"Would that it were so, my lord," Enid said with muted sorrow. "There has been none of that in your life."

"Nay, but then, I have little need for gentleness."

"Have you not, my lord?" Enid asked softly.

Tristan's eyes met hers and danced away. He straightened and moved to pass her by, but paused to lay hand to her shoulder. "Enid, be mindful that the lady has come to live among those who are strange to her. She has here no single one to call friend and will meet with hate at every turn. It would please me did you ease her lot where you can."

"For you, my lord, I will try."

"I can ask no more."

The Great Hall was full merry when Tristan set foot from the mural stair. A log, burning red in the hearth, stained the faces of a gathered group as though they blushed at an ill-timed jest. A bardy-coat in a madder-yellow tunic held court in the near corner, plucking his harp and singing a ballade of Henry of yore and his fair Rosamonde. A juggler's daring drew gasps of dismay and sharp cries of admiration from a group of laughing ladies. Earl Simon's own minstrel, gaudily bright in a parti-colored tunic, perched upon a stool below the dais and played a lighthearted frolic upon his lute.

The liquid darkness of the Earl's eyes met Tristan's across the length of the room, assuming the keen piercing quality that had brought him as great a renown as his sword arm. He beckoned with a nod of his head, and a sable wave of hair sank across his brow. Tristan moved toward him, pulled to a halt by one then another who pressed upon him their good wishes. At the foot of the dais, he paused, never glancing at Lady Sybilla or puffy-eyed Megotta standing at her side. It was best not to look upon his daughter in open hall. It was best for them both, and so he set his jaw and almost found success.

The Earl relaxed, one muscular leg stretched out, the other bent at the knee. One finger, dark hued and graceful, traced a thoughtful path across his lips, while his dark, magnetic eyes measured Tristan. "Demoiselle Amicia?" he asked, hooded eyes giving a deceptively lazy bent to his expression.

"Sleeps, my lord."

"She has been misused."

"Ay, my lord."

The tracing finger stilled. "You?"

"Nay, my lord."

"Bellay, I would have speech with you," Earl Simon's voice rose with crisp authority. "Stay, Tristan."

He watched the Earl's dark eyes study Bellay's approach. They assumed a polished hardness that betrayed naught of Leicester's thoughts, but Tristan had fought too long at his overlord's back not to know the expression shielded a personal distaste that was all but ungovernable. The knowledge did him little good. He would not use it to gain his way of Leicester, even if he could. Were he in his overlord's place, he, too, would force agreement among his vassals to protect his interests.

Bellay stepped near, and Leicester's eyes narrowed. "Sir Aimery tells me the girl wished to claim sanctuary in the church. Is this true?"

"A womanish fancy, my lord. She is young and just come from Holmby. I fear I left her with the nuns too long. She thought to take the veil, but has decided against it."

Leicester's lean, hard body coiled forward, one forearm propped atop the armrest, the other hand grasping his knee. "Does she or does she not come willingly into this marriage?"

"Willingly, my lord," Bellay said quickly.

Dark eyes knifed a question at Tristan. He hesitated. "She has said she comes willingly, my lord, but . . ." He paused longer. "I believe she agrees only from fear of her father's punishment, does she not?"

"Bellay?" The Earl's frown came like the threat of thunder on the spring horizon.

"Put it to the test, my lord. Ask her, and see what answer she gives."

"Tristan—" the Earl's head swung toward him—"I have leave to enter your women's solar?"

"Ay, my lord."

Something nudged Amicia from the welcomed peace of sleep. She swam up from its deepest layers and paused, hovering in indecision. Vaguely, she remembered being wakened by an ungentle hand, pulled from the bed, and stripped of her garments, then bundled under the coverlet by a silent, broad-faced woman. More strongly, she remembered the pinched lips and the hard eyes and the air of hostility that greeted her at the gate. She would not wake to face that again.

A hand shook her shoulder. A voice as crisp as watercress pierced her slumber. "My lady! The Earl would have speech with you!"

She tried, but her bones had melted like honeycombs rendered down to honey and wax, and her eyelids seemed weighted with lead.

"My lord, she will not wake and no wonder. She is wearied unto death. Can this not wait?"

"Nay, Enid. The Earl must have answer."

The bed sank. Amicia rolled against the hardness of a knee. The leather thong of cross-gartering scraped at her arm. Finely woven woolen chausses caressed her elbow. She struggled to open her eyes and felt an arm slide beneath her and lift her up. The knee slid behind her and she reclined against the chest that had become so familiar in so short a time.

She should have been afraid that he was sharing this bed with her, but somehow she was not. She pondered the thought, turning it this way and that to find the truth of it. And the truth was that she had never felt so safe and protected, in the full score years of her life. Her father was wrong about him, her heart told her—and her mind listened.

"Demoiselle, you must wake."

Her head rolled and her cheek touched the silk of his surcoat. She felt the steady beating of his heart, which seemed to skip once and sprint into a race. Her lashes fluttered and climbed and her blurry gaze focused on the square of his chin. She sighed heavily and licked her dry lips.

"My lord," she whispered on a wisp of sound. The light of the torch set high on a wall bracket was reflected from his eyes like molten pools of silver. But his eyes did not look into hers. It was a moment before she felt the coolness of the air upon her bare shoulders and lower, upon her breasts. It was yet another moment before she realized where that silvered gaze lay.

The realization acted upon her like the gouge of a spur in a destrier's flanks. She snapped up with a gasp. Her hands dived to the covers folded about her hips and dragged them to her chin. She huddled there, the glossy silk of her chestnut hair rippling down her quivering back and falling in wild tangles across the bed. Eyes huge with disbelief, she stared across the room into the midnight dark eyes of her father. Eyes so like, yet so unlike her own. Eyes that gave warning of promises kept and vicious deeds done.

"There is no need for fear, demoiselle."

Amicia's gaze jerked toward the Earl of Leicester.

"I come but to ask of you a question. When I am done you may seek your rest."

His tone was so kind and gentle Amicia felt a new welling of sorrow for all she had left behind at Holmby. Awake now, with her mind ruling her heart, she feared the Earl would take with him the last kindness she would know in this place.

"How may I help you, my lord?" Strain sharpened the soft modulation of her voice.

"With the truth, demoiselle. Do you come to this marriage willingly?"

Those black eyes seemed capable of scouring the hidden corners of her soul. Her tongue peeped out to wet her dry lips. "Why do you wish to know, my lord?" She parried for time while her mind scurried like a hare through the bracken.

Did she say nay, her father would have his revenge upon her. Did she say yea, Eden might have his revenge upon her. She was caught in the cleft of a stick with certain doom on one side and feared doom on the other.

"I would not have you missay the vows at the church door. Do you plan such, I would know it now."

Her fingers whitened as they gripped the thick woven coverlet. "I . . . I have no such plan, my lord."

"I do this to achieve peace between my vassals, demoiselle. I will not have all undone by the crotchet of a woman. I must know if you will take Sir Tristan to husband and be good wife to him in all ways."

She looked away then, her eyes pulling easily from magnetic black to the stronger attraction of sky blue. Tristan was so near she could see the widening of his black pupils as though he, too, labored under the force of some emotion. So near she could see the betraying throb of a vein running blue beneath his honey-gold temple. She studied the firm slant of his mouth and found no cruelty in it. She searched the paleness of his eyes and saw no sign of cruelty there, either. She might find no kindness in him, but neither did she think to find a malicious cruelty to equal her father's. Mayhap if she performed her duties with care . . .

"I will take Sir Tristan to husband, my lord, and seek in all ways to be good wife to him," she pledged softly, her eyes locked with his.

There was no sign of pleasure or displeasure. He simply stared, the light in his eyes as brittle as her mood, his expression wooden as though he dared yield naught of his thoughts.

"Tristan, Bellay," the Earl said abruptly, "I would have a moment's private speech with Lady Amicia."

Eden stood, his eyes still locked with hers. "I bid you good-night, demoiselle."

"My lord," she said, and wondered why her heart pounded like that of a bird caught in a snare and why his eyes, drifting now to the bareness of her shoulder, made her feel as though she had been caressed instead by his hand.

She watched him lead her father from her chamber and saw the look of evil triumph that the man who sired her cast back before he was swallowed by the shadows of the passageway.

"You gave no answer to my question, demoiselle." The Earl sat on the bed beside her. "Men well skilled in the arts of prattling evasion have failed where you have tried. So now, I will have answer, and truth with it."

"The truth, my lord, is that I come"—she paused, gathering strength to give the lie, and found to her horror that the truth slipped out instead—"unwillingly."

"So I thought." Sable lashes narrowed about his vivid eyes. "Yet you gave just now a pledge—"

"That I will keep, my lord," Amicia interrupted. "I do swear that I will."

He frowned and reached out, setting one long brown forefinger beneath her chin to tilt her face to the torchlight. "I am hard pressed to believe that you are your father's daughter, demoiselle. Do you, I wonder, know how beautiful you are?"

"I am as others, my lord, no better and no worse. At Holmby we were taught that the beauty of the body is fleeting and the beauty of the soul everlasting."

"And you, demoiselle? Have you a beautiful soul?"

"Nay, my lord," Amicia responded with the faint twitch of a rueful smile. "I am quite sinfully pleased to be told of this beauty you see."

His smile came quick and bright, a slash of whiteness in the lean darkness of his face. "I think, demoiselle, that I have done better than I knew. I thought only to settle this endless warring between your father and Tristan in a way easiest upon myself. Now I find that I am giving Tristan the one thing he needs to leech the blackness from his heart. I would that I could remain to see the winter's sport.''

''Sport, my lord?''

''Ay, demoiselle. Have you ever seen a destrier broken to the saddle?''

''Nay, my lord.''

''You will, demoiselle.'' He chuckled as at some private jest. ''You will,'' he repeated and stood and laughed once more.

Amicia watched the shaking width of his shoulders until he was swallowed by the shadowed passageway as her father had been, then turned a wondering gaze to the broad-faced woman who waited quietly in the corner. ''What meant he by that?''

''Give it no heed, my lady. It is but a man's foolishness.''

The woman's expression of dislike, caution, and curiosity killed Amicia's wonder about the Earl's amusement. Tomorrow she would pledge her life into Tristan's hands. Thereafter, she would be surrounded by those who viewed her thus. It was a daunting expectation. One that sent her to her prie-dieu seeking the lost solace of prayer.

Tristan waited in the glow of the torches set in brackets on both sides of the arch leading from the mural stair. He listened to the buzz of voices, the laughter and music. His eyes roamed the Great Hall seeking the faces of the women. He told himself Amicia had lied, and he was angry that she was as any woman. His head said many things that made his heart revolt.

She was not as other women. He had given her chance to spill lying promises without measure. Another woman, knowing her future rested with him, would have given full-blown assurance to his question: *And will I have your loyalty, demoiselle?* She would have placed her hand upon his arm and driven a soulful look into his eyes and said, ''Ay, my lord. Always, my lord. All shall be as you wish, my lord.''

This one had not. Instead, her eyes had met his with a steadiness he was not sure he could have matched in like circumstances. Instead, she sat proud and straight and said: "I will gladly yield to you all that you merit, my lord."

*All that you merit.* Now, as then, he was unsure whether to feel gladness or anger at her heedlessness. Were he another such as her father, she would have suffered for it. Bellay would have seen it as insolence; he saw it as courage whose like he had not met ere this.

What strength did she draw upon when the stiff set of her shoulders and the quiver in her lower lip and the tumult in those night-dark eyes all betrayed a terror whose fearsomeness he could only imagine?

"Tristan." The Earl clapped a heavy hand to his shoulder.

"My lord." He turned. "All is well?"

"Well?" A broad smile split the swarthiness of Leicester's face. "It is better than well. Come, let us break bread and split a ewer of wine. Nay, better yet, a full butt. I would make merry with you on this your last night of peace."

The contagiousness of the Earl's gay spirits pulled the corners of Tristan's mouth into a smile. "My last night of peace, my lord?"

"Ay, Tristan." His hearty laugh rolled. "Women, God bless them, can do more to break a man's peace—and mend it—than aught else I know."

Tristan's smile faded, his gaze straying to the dais, where Lady Sybilla held court in the canopied chair. "I know naught of peace mended, my lord."

"Ay." The Earl's gaze followed his to the dais and his nostrils flared much as Tristan's had done at scent of Bellay. "Why do you not set her in her dower castle and be rid of her? It is your right to do so."

All expression smoothed from Tristan's face until naught was left but the bright hot glitter of his eyes. "I cannot."

"What hold has she upon you that you follow her will like a falcon at leash? And do not tell me she has none!" he said harshly when Tristan whirled to him. "I know you too well as boon companion and bold knight not to know that no woman could lead you against your will, least of all, that one!"

"Do not ask me, my lord," Tristan gritted between

clenched teeth. "It is not such as would bring harm to you and yours."

"I do not ask for that!" Leicester burst out in frustration. "Do you think I know you so little that I do not know such would be brought to me forthwith? I ask not as your overlord, but as your friend. What may I do to help you?"

"Naught, my lord," he said bitterly. "Lest you could add a plea to your prayers that God should strike her dead and Satan gather her to his fold."

A sharp breath of shock hissed between Leicester's teeth. "She is your mother," he said softly.

"The sows that rut in the ward know more of mothering than she," Tristan burst out and instantly regretted it. His hand came up to scrub at the ache between his brows. "I beg forgiveness, my lord. Such should not be spoken. If you will make your way to the dais, I will call the buttler and give him order to tend your thirst."

A cascade of laughter from a nearby group filled the silence and scraped Tristan's raw nerves. At length, Leicester reached out to grip his arm. "If you should ever have need of me—"

"You have worries and more of your own, my lord."

"And you have pride enough for ten. Do not let that pride be your undoing, my friend."

"If I have my honor, I need naught else," he said stiffly.

"We all need something else, Tristan," the Earl said softly and turned away.

Tristan did not immediately call a servant to summon the buttler. Instead, he watched Leicester make his way to the dais through the crowded length of the hall. He respected and admired the Earl as a man cast in his own mold. But in this he thought him wrong. Honor was all that made a man a man. It was all that distinguished him from two-legged beasts like Bellay. Honor was love and pride. Without it, he would be nothing.

His gaze moved to the dais where his mother sat. So seldom did he think of her as that—his mother—he could almost forget she was. He stared at her as though at a stranger. Some called her handsome. Big and large-boned, though graceful with it, she had a placidity of expression that begged indulgence. Few could distinguish the gleam of vindictive malice from the lazy glow of those large brown eyes he had heard called beautiful. If there was anything of beauty about her, he could not see it. He knew her too well.

Knowing her, he wondered at the indolent smile she bestowed upon Aimery, sitting on a stool at her feet. Aimery, her youngest son, for whom she had nothing left to give from her obsessive love for Robert, her eldest, and her obsessive hate for himself. He had thought for a while that Robert's death in Gascony would drive her mad with grief. Would that it had.

She had found in her hatred of him a reason to cling to life and sanity as she knew it. Her beloved Robert had died, while he had lived. It was an error in God's plan that she had intent to rectify. But not until she had wrung the last drop of suffering from him.

So now she sat like a spider in the heart of her web. Spinning, spinning, ever spinning her sticky skeins, she wrapped him about like a hapless fly so that he could move neither here nor there to escape his final doom.

He thought of the woman sleeping above. Amicia. So fragile and frightened to be brought here and made new prey for his mother's ambition to see his end. Would she be friend to his mother and foe to him? And if she would be friend to him, dare he allow it?

# Chapter 6

Tristan woke with his mouth tasting like a garderobe pit and his head filled with a score of tiny smiths wielding hammers.

"God's greeting to you." Earl Simon's booming laugh echoed from the ice-sheeted walls of the mural chamber. "Hold not your ears. Take this instead. Enid sends a cure for your head."

"God's Wounds!" He gingerly gripped his tousled crown. "Did we drain the butt to the dregs?"

"Near enough. Here, drink and all will be well."

Tristan eyed the steaming cup askance.

"Ay, a foul odor it has and fouler taste, but I have supped of mine and see how it left me."

"Grinning like a lackwit," he grumbled. "I would rather—"

"Tristan"—Earl Simon's dark eyes sparkled—"I've seen you a sword's thrust from death and facing it with more valor."

"Ay, my lord. So tell me"—he reached for the cup, raising it in toast—"did you drain yours with that grin you wear now?"

"Nay"—the Earl laughed—"though I had little choice but to sup. Enid stood over me as if I were a page to be chastened. I feared she would have my chausses about my knees and a paddle to my rump, did I refuse."

"And you speak to me of valor?"

The Earl cocked a brow as shiny black as a raven's wing. "Am I to find no respect in this keep? Drink, bold knight, and greet your wedding day. I vow it would be easier to deseisen you and Bellay, than to get you and his daughter to pledge one to the other. You drink yourself into a stupor, muttering about gentle maids and tangled webs, while she wakes, so Enid says, as white as the frost afield."

Tristan lurched up, his hand shackling the Earl's thick wrist. "She is ill?"

"Nay"—Earl Simon's curious gaze traveled quickly across his frowning features—"only fearful, it would seem."

His rigid back wilted with relief, then snapped straight once more. Had the girl slipped beneath his skin like the sharp thorn of a rose? She was nothing to him. So why was he haunted by those dreams . . . nay, nightmares of his mother's tongue spewing a silken thread to ensnare her.

"Drink up," the Earl ordered, "and wipe the scowl from your face lest you fright Demoiselle Amicia into missaying her vows."

Tristan's hollow gaze followed the Earl from his chamber. A curl of steam tickled his nose with a noxious odor. Steeling himself to the deed, he tilted the cup high, drained it to the bitter dregs, and blinked his tearing eyes. His belly aquiver with revulsion, he bellowed for his squires.

"A bath I would have to wash the stench away!"

Sliding his arms into his camelin robe, he bent and spat into the chamber pot. *Peste!* Did he trust Enid less he might think she poisoned him. His narrowed gaze shifted to the better-groomed youth. He sniffed mightily, once, twice, and a smile stole across his mouth. "I vow, someone here smells as sweet as a rose. None of that in my bath. Plain soap will do me. I will await without while you see the tub filled."

"Ay, my lord," the squires echoed and grinned.

Striding into the Great Chamber, astir and askew with squires and pages running and knights and lords at leisure, Tristan paused for a word with this one and that. As he spoke his gaze turned again and again to the spine wall

splitting the keep in two, with the women's solar opposite.
At length he made his way to the roaring hearth fire and
stood with feet spread and head thrown back to stare
across the room.

He saw nothing of the aged wainscoting or the whitewashed wall, darkened by soot. Nor of the banners, bright
in the gloom, nor the gleaming weapons arrayed between
dingy wall-hangings. Though his eyes looked, his mind
saw only the fragile features of Amicia of Bellay . . . as
white as the frost afield. What were her thoughts on this
morning she was to wed her father's enemy?

Was madness afoot? Amicia's gaze wandered the solar
at will. Ought not the day when two were joined unto
eternity be a solemn occasion honored by reverence, penitence, and prayer, as all such occasions had been honored
at the priory? Where was the reverence in these women
who cackled like hens caged at the village fair? Where
was the penitence in these who jealously vied for the
costliest display of cloth and jewels? Where were the
prayers for God's grace and sanction on the two to be
wed? Surely naught were sent aloft from here, save hers
alone.

Though her knees ached from the night spent kneeling at
her prie-dieu, she yearned to slip away to quiet contemplation in the chapel below. Mayhap there she could have found
the peace that eluded her, had she been given leave to seek
it. Instead, she had been pulled from her bed and thrust
into her bath, and now sat atop a low stool before the
raging hearth fire with Enid at her back, drying her fresh-
washed hair.

"Unnatural it is for mother and son to hold such hate,
Guinella!" The whisper pulled Amicia's gaze to a pair of
women hovering over a traveling chest. "I fear Demoiselle
Amicia will have no moment's peace in this place."

"That which lies between Lady Sybilla and Tristan will
be the least of her worries, Burnetta. Ay, his enemy's
daughter and unwanted by him. *I* would not wish to be in
her place," dainty Guinella confided with a toss of her
burnished gold hair.

"Sir Tristan is a man of honor," Burnetta proclaimed

with a crank of her scrawny neck. "He would do her no despite—"

"Would he not?" Guinella's sharp question sent cold fingers of foreboding tripping the length of Amicia's spine. "His first wife came with blood ties to Chester and lands aplenty. This one brings naught but paltry hides of land and the blood of a man Tristan despises. Think you he will set her high in his esteem when he set Lady Ruella so low he would not give her comfort, though she lay dying in childbed?"

Amicia's gaze dropped to the fists curling in her lap. Mayhap that first wife sought in no way to please him. Mayhap she set a foot awry in the strange twists and turns of a man's honor. It was a frail reed to grasp and, with it, a frailer hope. Did she take care, mayhap the same fate would not be hers.

"You never saw them together, as I did, Burnetta. Comely she was and sweet-tempered. When Tristan was near, she had eyes for no other. Ay, it was near blasphemy the way she looked upon him. As if she knelt at chapel and gazed upon the rood above the altar. And he? She could have been a trestle table in the filth of the hall below for all the note he took. Nay, less. The table he would see when he sat to feast."

To be looked upon and not seen. To give love where it was not wanted. To die calling a man who would not come. Amicia swallowed the painful lump in her throat. Could any life be more bitter? Had the kindness she glimpsed in him been no more than her own fervent wish for it to be so?

"You stretch the tale, Guinella. He must have taken note at some time, if she carried his child."

"Ay, he is a man with no love of women, though he has a man's need of them. Who knows what passed in the privacy of his chamber? I, myself, saw her bruises soon after his return to Gascony. Lady Sybilla removed to her dower castle of Carrickmuir with Lady Ruella and Aimery. My lord and I passed a while there, and even he, with a heavy hand of his own, said Tristan had far surpassed a man's duty to chastise an erring wife."

"You think he will misuse this one, too?"

"Who can say what such a man will do?"

Amicia's lashes fanned across her burning eyes. Her wrist, bruised from Tristan's grip, panged sharply. A reminder she did not need. Yet he had said himself that he did not make war upon women. Was it a lie, or did he think a wife different somehow?

Her gaze climbed. No sound pierced the massive wooden doors flanking the spine wall or slipped through the shuttered center well shaft. No sound, though the Great Chamber must be astir. *He* must be there, surrounded as was she, with curious eyes shifting to catch his least smile or frown. She stared as if her fearful gaze could pierce plaster and stone, flesh and bone to read his soul as easily as script on parchment. What manner of man . . .

. . . *am I?* Tristan wondered. *Will I forever be chained by her thinnest hair to that fiend who bore me? How much longer must I dance to the tune of her will? What will she do to the child I dare to love? What will she do to this new one who steps unwittingly into her circle of hate? God, has there not been suffering enough!*

"My lord, your bath awaits."

Tristan turned a blind gaze to his squire. What brought his thoughts round to *her* again and again? Comely the maid was, but no more so than others. Her features taken one by one were no more than pleasant, yet looked upon as a whole . . .

Warmth stole through his middle. A soothing warmth like the touch of Enid's hand on his brow when he had had a fever as a boy. He had felt it upon the track and again in the night . . .

"My lord, your bath awaits."

He shook his head and scowled.

"My, l-lord, have I done aught amiss?"

The boy's fear yanked Tristan up like the reins on a destrier. "Nay, Roger, it is I who go astray. Come."

He strode toward his mural chamber with a black look that choked voices all around. He would wed Amicia of Bellay. He would bed her to bind the vows as he must, but he dare not feel these strange feelings. He must have a care to Megotta . . .

A thought knifed through his mind. Tonight he must spend his seed in Amicia's virgin womb—and pray God it found no fertile field. He stumbled to a halt, his breath whistling through his throat. Never had it occurred to him, fool that he was! He reached out, clasping the square wood column at the foot of the bed to brace his trembling body. There must never be another child for his mother to use against him. Megotta was but a pawn in her game. This child she would destroy.

As she would destroy Amicia, did these strange feelings take root in his heart. He had been a fool to give warning to all in the ward. From this moment he must beware. He must never betray the least softening, lest that adder strike to maim and kill.

It would be hard for so gentle a maid, wed to a man who took neither care nor note, but she was better downcast and saddened than dead. He must trust to Enid to give her aid . . .

"My lady?"

The vinegarish distaste in the servingmaid's voice swiveled Amicia upon the stool. Her gaze lifted, meeting Enid's condemning stare. Just so had Tristan looked upon her when first he knew who she was. At least Lady Ruella, however unhappy he made her, had not also lived with the hate of the folk here.

"The hour grows late. It is needful that we begin."

Amicia stood, shivering in her light linen chemise. How bitter life was. Mayhap Mother Margaret had found moments to glory in its sweetness, but she would never know that glory. Only the weight of duty binding her to a man who had but one use for a woman—and that use made her sick with fear.

Her gaze shifted to Lady Sybilla, enthroned upon a carved oak chair an ell's length away. Her bovine gaze indolently surveyed the uproar of ladies dressing and servingmaids scurrying and lap dogs yapping. There was beauty in the flawless cream of her skin and a regal bent to the slant of her chin, but still she reminded Amicia of nothing so much as a placid cow at cud. So calm was she now, it seemed but a dream that her eyes had burned with the fire of hate when she looked upon her son.

Though she appeared indifferent to what passed so near, Lady Sybilla's shapely hand drifted from the arm of her chair. Her fingers snapped and servingmaids came running. Amicia was twisted and turned, asked to sit and asked to stand, and soon she was attired, a bride fair and fearful.

"Come, child, that I might see you," Lady Sybilla said in her low, slow, and husky voice.

Amicia did as she was bid, and stood mute while her soon-to-be mother-by-marriage studied her with the care of a cottier buying an ox at the fair. Pride, sinful pride, sent her chin climbing a notch as that expressionless gaze traveled from her green-slippered feet to the stuffed and pleated touret holding her sheer white veil in place. She was garbed in her best, and that poor enough in the midst of these costumed as brilliantly as the peacocks strutting in the king's gardens—never seen by her, but drawn in the rhyme of a minstrel come to the mountain vale. Her cotte, in a simple wool as blue as the Lord of Eden's eyes, had angel sleeves that fell from wrist to floor and a hem at the back that draped the whispering rushes as a lady's should. Her sleeveless surcoat, split at the sides, was the green of grass fresh sprouted in spring. Blue for fidelity; green for love. Would she find either in this place where hate hung in the air like dust trailing an ox-wain's passage?

"I see your father wasted no coin on you." Lady Sybilla idly fingered the sable trimming her crimson damask surcoat. "Ever was he tight-fisted as a moneylender."

Color sped across Amicia's cheeks. A titter sounded nearby and her blush burned hotter, but what answer could she give? It was her father's shame and hers that no time did she have, nor coin to spend, to garb herself as befit the day.

Lady Sybilla stood, a graceful figure of queenly bearing. Her smile spread, crinkling the smooth skin of her cheeks and betraying her years. A smile that did not warm her wintry gaze. One finger, cold as icicles hanging in midwinter, touched Amicia's cheek. "How fortunate you are, not to need the trappings of beauty, child. Yours is in your youth and in your face. No need do you have for silks and sendals, jewels and furs. I bid you welcome to the hearth of Castle Eden.''

*Welcome.* Words Amicia yearned to hear and thought never to be said. Tears welled in her eyes, hanging heavy on the rims of her lashes. ''Thank you, my lady. I hope to abide here in peace and love,'' she said, taking that icy hand in hers and bending to press her lips to its back.

''How sad that my son is as he is.'' Each word rolled sweetly soft, a jarring contrast to the woman's cool, watchful gaze. ''How sad that you, no more than she who was first wed to him, will find the peace and love you crave.''

The whisper reached no farther than Amicia's ears, but there it clamored loud and long, as unpleasant and unbearable as the rasp of steel. Mayhap Tristan's mother had reason to hate him. Her misgivings gathered force once more. Piling one atop the other like stones on a cairn, they sat low in her belly, a heavy weight of fear.

From the spine wall came the creak of the massive wooden door. Amicia's breath fled as if a blunt head had rammed into her middle. Gasping for air, she whirled and stared.

Did *he* come? Breath pent and heart throbbing, she fought the urge to flee. The chatter of the women died on echoes of whispers. Even the hounds ceased their barking and yapping, while the door scraped and screeched and groaned. It stilled with a shudder . . . and so did Amicia's heart.

The cumbrous mantle of silence was broken by feet rustling over the crisp rushes. The ladies parted, leaving a path with Amicia at its head and the yawning jaw of the door at its foot.

A figure stepped into the gaping maw. It was a small page garbed in the scarlet and black of Eden's colors—not the man Amicia thought to see. A dizzying rush of relief swept through her. The delay was a small one, but welcome nonetheless. Another thing to hold the crowding visions of approaching night at bay.

''I come bearing the bride-gift from Sir Tristan, Lord of Eden,'' the boy's treble piped into the silence.

Amicia forced a smile and nodded her head to beckon him.

His narrow chest puffed out with the importance of his task, he chanced a glance past the gold enameled casket set atop his flat hands and began a measured march that softened the stiffness of Amicia's lips into a genuine smile. Beneath the wayward shock of wheat-colored hair, his expression was as solemn as that of a worried baron counseling the fickle king, but the tiny ears neatly cupping his head were a deep and burning red. Careful steps carried him around tumbling pups and lazing hounds and traveling chests spilling costly samites and richly embroidered brocades, ever closer to completion of his charge.

He reached her and stopped, his small face splitting into an ear-to-ear grin. "Demoiselle . . ." His eyes shined up at her.

She glanced at the intricate design and bright colors gracing the lid. It was her duty to take the casket, to open it and pull forth whatever trinket resided therein, but an inner shrinking stayed her hands at her sides. To take it was to accept Tristan of Eden to husband, and her heart writhed in wild rebellion against it. Hope kindled, flickered . . . and died. To missay the vows at the church door was to fall into her father's hands and that would make this hell seem like heaven. Yet, even knowing this, she could not reach out, and so sought delay . . .

"Your name?" she asked the boy on an uncertain breath.

"Guy of Lancasterdale, demoiselle."

"You have done well, Guy. Your lord would be proud."

"Th-thank you, demoiselle." His thin chest swelled like a strutting pigeon's.

Lady Sybilla's fingers snapped. Enid hurried to take the casket and raise the lid. Guy was swallowed by the surging crowd, while Amicia waited to one side. Lady Sybilla's smooth hand delved deep and came up spilling a glittering length of necklet. Biconical gold beads reflected the firelight. Pendant garnet cabochons swayed like drops of blood in golden settings.

"See how Tristan honors his wife-to-be!" The necklet dripped from her fist, asparkle with pagan splendor. "This is old in the family Eden, won from a Saxon lord by the ancestor who came to this land with William the Bastard.''

Murmurs of admiration flowed round Amicia, but she had no ear to give them. Lady Sybilla's free hand had clamped about hers, drawing her so near she could hear the tinkling of the dangling gems. How strange the sound was. Like a distant devil's laughter. As if the necklet had a soul of its own, and that soul, evil and aware of its purpose.

"Hold fast, child," Lady Sybilla murmured. "I would link the necklet in place."

Amicia stood, her legs atremble, while the jeweled yoke of the Lord of Eden clutched at her throat with a chill that seeped through the wool of her cotte.

"I would have a moment's private speech with you," Lady Sybilla whispered. "Follow me to my chamber."

Amicia trailed blindly after her, aware of nothing but the alien weight of the necklet. Had he chosen it apurpose to keep her mindful that she would ever be his to do with as he willed? That she, who would be his wife, would dare to be no more willful than the lowest of his serfs?

"I bring you here for good reason."

Amicia's tongue skimmed across her lips, pausing at the split where her father had struck her. Mayhap not the last heavy hand she would know.

"Child"—the warm voice ill-matched the cold hands that gripped Amicia's—"I would that I need not give these warnings."

"Warnings, my lady?"

"Ay, to my sorrow. I would not see you suffer as the last who was joined to my son as wife. Mayhap, had I known . . ." Her cool, watchful gaze dropped to their entwined hands. "Alas, I did not then know to what lengths Tristan might go."

"Lengths, my lady?" Amicia questioned breathlessly, her eyes as round as a miller's wheel.

"You must have a care in his keeping. A vicious temper he has, and a heavy hand. It is needful to show him a meek face, lest you provoke him. I will protect you where I may, but even I may not intrude in your bedding chamber. And that, I fear, is where you will have most need of me.''

Sluicing cold doused the embers of Amicia's strength. She swayed and sagged, and was caught and led to a wooden chest. Her hand gripped Lady Sybilla's forearm, while her tearing eyes met that passionless, ever watchful, brown gaze.

''My lady, how may I turn aside his wrath and his . . .'' She swallowed painfully, unable to go on.

''Lust?''

The word, given voice as it was, sucked the blood from her head and set it to swirling. She dared a brief nod, swallowed the bile of terror, and clutched Lady Sybilla the tighter.

''I fear it drives him like a savage beast. Naught may you do, but gently nudge him to seek the leman in the village. She is paid to sate men's lusts. Better that he seek her than you. I would that I had more comfort to offer.''

''Nay, you have been as a true mother to me.''

Amicia raised a shaking hand to the heavy yoke oppressing her body and spirit. Her fingers shrank from the smooth garnet cabochons, curled into fists, and pressed to her pounding heart. Her gaze sought the window slit, aglow with morning sunlight. There was no escape. Yet hope scurried through the labyrinth of her mind, like a mouse fleeing the rat-catcher's ferret.

''It is time, child. We must away to the ward below.''

No escape. She stood, her shaky legs pushing against the odious weight of the necklet. Clasping her hands at her waist, she stared sightlessly at the leather curtain shielding the entryway. A single breath shuddered in . . . shuddered out. Better the cruel hand of one man than the host her father promised, a small voice of sanity whispered again and again through her silent screams.

The savory scents of baking bread and roasting meats saturated the bitter gusts of wind whipping red-gold curls about Tristan's face. He shifted, ignoring the bawdy jests flying among his guests, and worried that Amicia and Lady Sybilla had not followed the women to mount for the ride to the church. What did they do alone in the keep, emptied of all but the buttler and pantler and scullions preparing for the feast?

His riveted gaze narrowed as if he could pierce the darkness of the entrance chamber. A swirl of color, a blue so dark it near blended with the surrounding shadows, stilled the restless fingers scraping his palms. Amicia appeared, the bloodless ivory of her face set like a medallion in the draping hood of her mantle. Her chin level, her eyes staring straight ahead, she walked as if each step must be separately ordered. Tristan searched her taut features, seeking the warmth glimpsed so briefly. It was vanquished as though it had never been.

Vanquished! And he knew how! His blood burned through his veins. His hot eyes wrenched from Amicia to the regal, flowing figure of his mother.

She paused at the top of the stairs leading down to the entrance tower. Her gaze, bright with menacing triumph, plunged into the fiery blue of his.

"God rot your soul in Hell!" he gritted beneath his breath.

She smiled. The smile that some called beautiful, seeing in it no more than the arrangement of rosy lips and white teeth and smooth skin. The heartless smile that never failed to set his stomach to revolting and his thews to setting like rock.

"Tristan," the Earl murmured, "you do not join Demoiselle Amicia at the foot of the stairs?"

He could not look away! His hands balled into fists. Sweat popped on his forehead. He was bewitched by his hate.

"Tristan!" The Earl clasped his forearm.

His mother laughed, her deep repellent laugh, while her eyes said she knew what was happening to him and took joy in it. Still, he stood as if turned to stone.

"Tristan!"

She looked away, the laughter still twitching at her lips.

His shoulders slumped. His chin dipped. "My lord," he sighed, "I . . . I—"

"Begone! She is near the foot of the stairs, and you standing lackwitted! No matter how little you desire this joining, you have no cause to shame her!"

"Nay, my lord," he muttered. "I . . . I have no wish to do so. I . . ." He stopped, passing a shaking hand across his brow. There was no explanation he could give. Nothing to do but go to Amicia, and hope that whatever that fiendish devil had said would not send her screaming from his sight.

He strode forward with more assurance than he felt, slowing as he approached. "Demoiselle." He dipped a skimpy bow.

Her wide gaze lifted to his face, devoid of recognition, as if her every thought were focused relentlessly on some inner struggle. A chill rippled across Tristan's flesh. He stepped near, his eyes scouring hers for some sign of life.

"Amicia?" he whispered. "What has passed with you?"

"I come, my lord, as I am bid."

Her cool toneless voice dug beneath his heart and turned it in his chest like a spade in the earth. "Amicia—"

"You keep our guests waiting?"

His head snapped up, his wary gaze touching his mother's cruel smile and sliding away.

"Amicia, give him your hand. It is needful we begin."

"Needful," she murmured and dutifully raised her hand, waiting patiently while he slid his beneath it. She moved slowly, as if any quickness might jar her from her suspended state.

Murder found an uneasy dwelling place in Tristan's heart as he lifted Amicia to her palfrey and set the reins in her hands. He thought she might wake to life when the vows were spoken, but she said each word as by rote and moved through the Mass like one asleep. Everywhere he turned, everywhere he looked, he met his mother's malignant shine of triumph. Through the ceaseless courses of the feast, through the pauses for dancing to the tunes of the minstrels, and the entertainment of tumblers and jugglers, he could not escape the sliding brown of her eyes and the lingering humor of her smile.

The window slits dimmed and darkened with the fall of night. Rushes flared across the soot-blackened walls. The bawdy jests of the day turned coarse and crude, while wine flowed as freely as if the butts deep in the undercroft were without limit. And all the while, Amicia sat by her husband's side as still as a statue of Virgin Mary on an altar. If he offered a bite from the platter they shared, she ate it. If he offered a sip from the chalice they shared, she drank it. If he begged answer to a question, she turned a vacant gaze upon him and spoke as if each word were a silver coin not to be cast away thoughtlessly.

The night wore on. He ate little and drank much, dread perching upon his shoulder like hawks in the mews. The purity of Amicia's profile drew his reluctant gaze like a lodestone. What fear had that witch called his mother built to such fever pitch that now she must hide away, even from herself?

His hand closed about his silver chalice, his gaze drifting beyond Amicia to the Earl's gesturing hand. He caught a glimpse of the scarlet his mother wore, and saw it shift as if she prepared to stand.

"My lords," her low voice rang out, "I fear I must put end to your merriment for this little while. It is time for the bedding ceremony to begin."

Cheers rattled the rafters above. Amicia shuddered, drawing Tristan's curious gaze.

"Ay, time it is!" Bellay laughed coarsely. "Wield your rod handily this night, Tristan of Eden. I would see a grandson nine months hence, does this puling excuse for a woman last so long."

Amicia swayed and her cheeks blanched, bringing Tristan to the edge of his chair. Her face turned toward him, so slowly he thought she meant not to look upon him, but she could not stop herself.

"Ami—" As her eyes met his, her name stuck in Tristan's throat, jammed there by the terror gathering in those dark liquid pools.

"Amicia, it is time." His mother's voice belled a strangely soothing melody.

His gaze shifted upward, meeting exultant spice brown. He watched the twitch of her lips and the spread of her smile, and his blood ran as cold as the bitter wind howling outside.

# Chapter 7

The massive canopied bed dominated Amicia's thoughts while hands stripped her garments as if she were a hen to be plucked for roasting. A musty smell of mildew and neglect tickled her nostrils. The offensive odor reached beneath her shell of fear, twanging a jarring note on the chord of cleanliness honed to perfect pitch by stern Sister Catherine's wagging finger.

"A clumsy ox, my lord was!" Guinella's whisper set a finger to the chord, silencing it. "I vow the sheet looked as though butchery had been done rather than—"

"Hush, you witless goose! Must your tongue clack at both ends? She looks near to swooning now, and you dwelling on the horrors of your bedding!"

"Welaway! Listen to her!" Guinella said with a sneer. "At least *my* lord was young and comely, not a fumbling old clodpate! Who did he hide in your chamber to take the maidenhead he could not?"

"At least my lord need not shackle me with a chastity belt to assure that no other plows his field when he is from my sight! I misdoubt yours may say the same!"

"Gertruda, Guinella, cease your hissing and scratching." Lady Sybilla lazily intruded on the fray.

The voices hammered at Amicia's shell of fear, cracking it like an egg. Each of these had faced the night that lay before her. Each had lived to complain or exult as was her wont. Even the serf women had survived brutal rapine. Even . . . Lady Ruella.

Lived, and loved Tristan thereafter, though he gave no heed to her in hall and beat her in private. It made no sense, yet truth it must be. Amicia frowned. Lady Guinella was silly and spiteful, but she had no axe to grind, so no need to lie. And Eden's mother? Was it not said that a mother never saw evil in her child, unless that evil was fearsome to behold?

She must take heed of her warnings and turn a meek face to him, though meekness was not born in her. Stubborn. That she could be. Mayhap stubborn enough to outlast all he might do.

Her chin climbed a notch. Would she waste her life sunk in an abyss of fear and self-pity as she had this day? Surely there would be scattered moments to glory in its sweetness. Mayhap—her breath hitched in—they would come with a child. A child to make these cold stone walls ring with love and laughter. For that great joy she could endure anything.

"They come!" The shrill cry pierced her armor of pride. "Hasten her disrobing! She yet wears her chemise and the men near upon us!"

Amicia's lashes slid to her cheeks. Her life would be what she made of it, for good, for ill. Her will was no longer hers, but her heart and mind were left her. Her choice it was to become another such as her father, tainted by the bile of hate, or one such as Mother Margaret . . .

Hands caught the rippling weight of her hair, lifting it from her back. Hands caught at her arms . . .

"Nay"—the line of her jaw firmed—"I will do it."

Her chemise boldly stripped off, she was left bare as a babe from the womb. Bare to the prying of curious eyes. Bare to the shame that chipped at her resolve like a chisel at a stone. Her hair swayed down her back, a chestnut-brown curtain whose curling tips tickled the back of her knees.

She stared at the entry with a feverish intensity, oblivious to the fingers of icy air raising whipping currents of goosebumps. She must learn all there was to know of this man who owned her as surely as he owned the serfs working his fields. She must know what provoked him to anger, what soothed him, what his likes and dislikes were. Only then would she find a measure of safety.

The sottish slurring of a bawdy baritone song seeped around the leather curtain. "Lust and wine. A heady mix boding ill," Lady Sybilla hissed beside her, and Amicia's heart quivered anew.

Stumbling steps, jarring the oaken planks beneath her feet, coiled her hands into fists at her sides. Fear would be her undoing. She needed a cool head and steady heart. She must listen and watch and learn.

A huge hand, hazed with red-gold hair, thrust the curtain aside. Tristan stepped through. The muted fire of his eyes searched and found hers, plunging deep into her widening gaze.

*So quickly I forgot how bright his eyes are, how frightening his size is, how fear knows no master but itself.* Her mouth dried to tasteless dust.

*So quickly she learns to fear me. So easily does she believe the lies spilled by that fiend's hellish breath. Lies that I must give the ring of truth to, lest I fail me and mine.* Tristan's mouth dried to tasteless dust.

"You are . . ." A frown nudged his brows together. It was not what he meant to say, but the question slipped from his lips as if his will were not his own, "You are . . . yourself?"

"Ay, my lord," her voice cracked, and her expression crumpled in dismay. His heart panged fiercely, while she struggled to smooth the ravages of fear away. "I beg forgiveness, my lord, that I was not . . . myself this day."

Tristan watched the graceful bend of her head and hurled a hard look at his mother's gloating face. How he hated her, who once he had yearned to love and have love him, so long ago and best forgotten. He was no longer a boy lacking a man's wisdom. His mother was a woman. And women were faithless creatures, incapable of honor or truth or fidelity.

His gaze shifted to Amicia, to the wide blue eyes fearfully searching his face. Eyes, whose luminous innocence rocked his certainty. He set his jaw and frowned, and felt the quiver that raced across her lips as though it were a blow landed low on his belly. If ever he was to meet an honest woman, let it not be this one. Not now, when he could save neither himself nor her.

Behind him, the men tumbled into the mural chamber like pups at play . . . all but the last.

"Here is the wench!" Bellay stumbled to the fore, his raddled face red. "Ay, Sybilla"—he leered—"she's a lush piece to tempt a man. He will find no fault with his work this night."

Tristan's murderous look stole his loose-lipped smile, and Bellay drew himself up in offended dignity. "Whatever she is to you, Eden, she is daughter to me and do not forget it!"

"I could not, if I would," Tristan gritted, and Amicia went cold as the night howling its contempt outside.

Bone and blood of her father. He would never forget it. He would never forgive it. That, no matter how meek the face she turned to him, she could never change.

"Enough! Would you draw swords here?" Earl Simon roared, casting a jaundiced black eye Tristan's way. "Is it your intent to stand full-garbed through the night? Aimery, strip him to the skin. We need keep Lady Amicia shivering in the cold no longer."

"Ay," Guinella said, laughing, "we would see the weapon he plans to use on this tame bird."

"Ay," Bellay sneered, "a weapon to make her sing a song of his making."

"Courage, child," Lady Sybilla murmured, her hand trailing ice along Amicia's arm. "You will have need of it this night."

Courage. How could she hold it near when Tristan peeled its layers away with the clothes he shed? She struggled to recapture it, painfully aware of the lecherous looks raking the flesh that had been bared to no human eye, save her own, ere this.

He was down to his breech-clout, and stripping that away while jests flew like pigeons loosed for hawks' play. Amicia's burning gaze touched the thick slopes of his shoulders and the massive power of his arms. Arms that could snap her like a brittle twig. What strength could he put behind a blow to one half his size? No thought to linger over. Her eyes shifted to the broad sweep of his chest. A scar arched across his ribs, another puckered a line from nipple to shoulder, another sliced from waist to hip, none marring his striking masculine beauty. Every move sent layers of muscle surging beneath the red-gold thatch spreading from side to side and shoulder to . . .

Her breath hissed like water on a griddle. Pure white rimmed her midnight-blue irises. She swayed in a grip of terror so acute her mind reeled from the memory of the man-at-arms rising from the V of the serf woman's legs to the reality of Tristan's swollen rod jutting from a curling nest of fiery-red.

"Ho! He is hot for her already!" her father shouted. "Do not drop your eyes like a bashful milkmaid, daughter! Look instead upon the weapon that will spit you this night like—"

"Enough!" Earl Simon roared. "We do not gather to fright the maid! Tristan, turn that all may see there are no marks or blemishes upon you. Ay, a warrior's form with the honorable marks of battle. Bellay, speak before these here. See you aught that may be used to annul their joining?"

"Nay, my lord. Naught do I see but a man eager to be rid of all here save one."

In the burst of laughter, Earl Simon crossed to Amicia. "We must have your word. Look upon him and give truth."

She dared a shrinking glance that encompassed the fanning halves of his back dipping to the runnel of his spine, taut flat buttocks and firm horseman's thighs. Breath failed her. "Nay, my lord, I see naught ill made."

"Ay," Guinella gusted. "Could it be she is as hot for him as he is for her?"

A blush scaled Amicia's cheeks with stinging heat. Lady Sybilla's fingers snapped behind her. A hand brushed across her back lifting her hair.

"Tristain," the earl ordered, "look upon her."

Amicia's eyes met Tristan's with a shock of awareness, her fists curling so tight her fingers hurt. His hot gaze stroked her breasts and hips and thighs, rousing unsettling sensations of heat beneath icy cold fear. Was he a wizard to command her body at will while he remained untouched? she wondered, until his eyes lifted to hers with a disturbance akin to her own. A muscle leaped in his jaw and his throat convulsed, as though he swallowed a bitter brew.

"Turn, Amicia, that all may see you," Earl Simon murmured.

She flung him a pleading glance, but he shook his head in silent warning. Needs must is a hard master, Tristan had told her, and so it was. Though her knees shook and her heart pounded, she must do as bid, as she must ever after.

"Tristan, see you aught upon her that might be used to annul this joining?" Earl Simon asked.

"Nay." His voice strangled in basso depths. "Nay, my lord, I see naught ill made." He wished, God, how he wished he did! Why need she be so small, so weak, so perfectly made?

"Let all here bear witness. Neither of these may use this as grounds for annulment in the future."

It was done. Tristan watched his mother bend to Amicia with a spate of whispering. She stiffened, as if a hand dug into her back, and her eyes darted at him. She was placed abed, her hair arrayed across the goosedown pillow and the coverlets raised to shield her from prying eyes. He joined her between the cold linen sheets, lying back with every muscle attuned, as if he must leap to battle at a moment's notice. The chamber emptying, he chanced a glance and saw a single tear swoop across her temple.

He swallowed hard, a thick sucking sound that seemed overly loud and long. Ruella had been so different, even softer and gentler than this one, but with no fear of the joining to be done. She came into his arms eagerly, while Amicia lay as white as the linen beneath her and looked to swoon at a word.

With Ruella there had been the need any man had for a ready wench, while this one, all unwitting, roused a fire that spread from his aching loins to his mind. And with it, sneaking tendrils of a concern little to his liking.

Never had he thought on any pleasure but his own. Never had he wondered how it was for a wench. So why these thoughts acrowding? Was he a vainly strutting peacock to wonder if she found his body pleasant to look upon? It was a warrior's body, marked by battle and strongly made as needed. This joining was ordained by Earl Simon. Why need he care that she find pleasure? Why need he lie like an unseasoned boy with sweaty palms and misgivings?

"Tristan, Lady Amicia"—Earl Simon stood at the entry— "God grant you both the happiness I have found with my wife, Lady Eleanor. Make one where there has been two, and you will find the greatest joy man may know this side of heaven."

The rustling of the curtain scratched at Amicia like claws. She lay as stiff as a lance with her hands knotted at her breast and her eyes firmly closed. She waited for a low, lusty laugh akin to the men-at-arms'. She waited for Tristan to leap upon her and reft her maidenhead like a ram with a ewe. The bed heaved beneath her. Her heart leaped. A meek face. How hard it was when her mind was asunder and her soul rebelling. Would that this was a dream and she would wake . . .

"Amicia?"

His voice wafted as soft as a lambkin's wool. As her lashes quivered against her cheeks and climbed slowly, she stared into the high canopy at a dusty cobweb spun in the candles' glow.

"M-my lord?"

"You are so pale."

"I—I am sorry to offend you, my lord."

"You do not. Why do you lie so stiff, as if to leap away at a touch?"

"I am sorry, my lord. Such is not . . ." Her tongue skimmed across her dry lips and she shivered. "Such is not my intent."

"You are cold. A coverlet lies in the chest. I will—"

"Nay, my lord. We have here aplenty." Her eyes whisked to the corners for a quick look. "Unless you—"

"Nay," he breathed. "I need it not."

Silence ripened while the wind wailed winter's dirge. Tristan said naught but wondered much of the unwonted feelings besetting him. Amicia lay mutely questioning the softness of his deep voice and that single glimpse of hesitance in his features.

"You must be weary after your journey and the day spent here," he said.

"I—I had not thought on it, my lord."

"Must you think to know you are weary?"

"On a day such as this? Ay, my lord, I must think on it."

Silence descended. Tristan studied the flickering flame of a candle as if it were an enemy bent on conquest. He was shrinking like a boy with an unblooded sword! She was his wife to do with as he willed! Why did he not yield to the urgings of his loins and take that which was his?

Amicia, her heart jumping in her chest, stared into the canopy, waiting . . . waiting . . .

"I would give you time to grow accustomed, did I have it."

Her head turned slowly, her gaze flinching from the resolve molding his bronze features. Dare she hope the kindness she saw was more than a deceit wrought by the candlelight?

"I must join with you tonight. There must be blood upon the sheets to prove it on the morrow. In this we have no choice."

"It is custom, my lord. All would be amiss, did we not."

"Ay, Earl Simon would carry out his threat to deseisen me."

"And I would return to my father."

"Ay." A wry smile twisted his mouth. "Better the devil you do not know, than the one you do."

She looked away, her teeth gnawing her lower lip.

"I mislike this fear I feel in you," he whispered.

"I am sorry, my lord." Her eyes closed. She steeled herself. "I will seek in all ways to be as you wish."

"So meek, Amicia?" he chided. "And you the girl who told me she knew but one way to be and that as she was."

The hint of suspicion sharpening his tones pulled her eyes to him as to a lodestone. "I am wife to you now, my lord, though I know not your ways."

"My ways are as any man's."

"But I know not the ways of men, my lord. I know only the priory and the peace . . ." To her horror, tears welled in her eyes and spilled, sliding in warm streams across her temples. Her fists inched up to press against her chin. "I—I beg forgiveness, my lord."

A sob fought its way through her throat, and Tristan watched with a horror equal to hers. His gaze lifted, darting from corner to corner, as if the shadows might take form and give guidance. Were she Megotta, he would lift her on his knee and stroke her hair and mutter nonsense until her sadness was spent. But Amicia was a woman, not a child. Her tears rose from a deeper source. One he feared to soothe lest he do or say the wrong thing and be met with more and harder of the same.

He reached out a single finger to touch the ivory-white curve of her shoulder. She froze as if he had struck her, her sobs dying on a single gasp. His hand whipped back to his side, while his eyes locked with hers.

"You unman me with your tears, Amicia," he said gruffly.

"I . . . I am sorry, my lord."

A frown swept his brows together with an inaudible clap of thunder that quaked through her. "Cease with, 'I am sorry, my lord!' " he barked. "I mislike it!"

"I am so . . ." She shuddered. "Ay, my lord."

"I have a name." Irritation flattened his voice. "Say it."

"T-Tristan, m-my lord."

His eyes sliced at her and cut away, the clear blue growing stormy. She lay, daring neither to blink nor breathe, lest she draw his anger unto herself. A vicious anger, his mother said. The tiny vein beating like a tabor in his temple seemed to throb in her own breast. His mobile mouth pursed as if he thought, then thinned as if those thoughts were not pleasant ones.

"I do you no good to delay here." His eyes lowered to hers, the spent storm leaving them grimly assured. "Your fear does not lessen, but grows instead. Give me your hand, Amicia."

Her heart lurching like a sotted knight, she watched his hand rise with flexing fingers. The palm was scarred and calloused and huge, a mighty weapon to bend her to his will. Did she refuse, it could break her jaw with a swat.

What, then, could his angry fist do? Her arm shook with the effort of raising her hand, stretching it out, and laying it in his.

"So small," he murmured, his thumb rubbing gently. "Your skin is soft, as I thought it would be. Smooth, like the silk you should wear. Soonest may, I would see you garbed as those others today." His eyes lingered on the chestnut-brown curtain of her hair. "I would have you wear it down always, Amicia, with naught but the sheerest veil to shield it."

"As you wish, my lord."

"So biddable, my lady. Will you always be so?"

"I will seek in all ways to please you, my lord."

"What magic do you work that I am pleased simply by your being?"

He lifted her knuckles to his lips, and sweet content flooded her, warring with the last tenacious tentacles of fear. How hard it was to think the callused hand so gently holding hers could be raised in anger. Harder still to envision his tender gaze hardening with rage.

He lightly brushed her knuckles across his beard-stubbled chin. "There can be much pleasure in the joining of a man and woman, Amicia. Let me show you the way. Let me give pleasure"—he leaned down, his lips inches from hers—"and take my own."

Content shattered. The dark night of her eyes, starred with rising fear, watched him lower to her and blur. Would he now leap upon her and tear her asunder? His mouth touched hers and moved upon it. She lay stiff and still and waiting. Errant thoughts came on tiptoe. So warm his mouth was. So soft. Never would she have thought a man's lips could be so soft.

He moved back, releasing her hand and shifting closer with his elbow dug into the pillow and his head propped upon his palm. A smile quivered around his lips as though he yearned to break into full laughter. "I vow you will put me to much work this night, wench. Do you not know to close your eyes?"

She studied the rosy fullness of his lower lip, the arch of the upper, the tremble of humor in the corners. Where was the vicious temper? The heavy hand? Who was this man who was now hers as she was his?

"I—I have never done so in a kiss of peace, my lord."

"But this is no kiss of peace. When a man lays his mouth to a woman's he does not like for her to watch him."

To listen, to watch, to learn. Only that would protect her, and this small thing she could do. Pray, he would ever be so easy to please. Her lashes dropped to her cheeks. "I will seek to do better, my lord."

His breath flowed across her nose on a scent of wine. *Lust and wine. A heady mix boding ill.* A chill prickled across Amicia's scalp. His lips touched and moved, gently suckling hers. Ease came stealing like the rosy rays of dawn. How pleasant it was . . .

"My lady"—his smile spread to reveal the snowy white of his teeth—"did I wish to kiss a walnut shell, I would do it. Do not pinch your lips together as if you expect me to filch them."

He smiled yet. Not a glimmer of anger darkened the blue of his eyes or twitched in his cheek. Had her terror been for naught? If so, what of those things said by Lady Guinella and his mother? Things she could so easily believe were meant about another. Not this man with the smile that looked as if it were crafted by the angels.

"I am very ignorant, my lord."

"It is not displeasing to me."

"Is it not, my lord?"

"Nay, Amicia." His voice dropped to a deep strumming as he leaned close once more. "I am well pleased, and would be more so, do I find a talent for this." His mouth wafted across hers and her lashes drooped obediently. "Softer, Amicia, softer," he breathed, his teeth nipping her lower lip and tugging.

The smell of clean man and fragrant wine rose from him like a cloud. His body radiated heat that seeped deep to warm her from within. Her lips trembled beneath the gentle kneading of his. How strange it felt. How . . . pleasant.

He sucked her lower lip between his and grazed the velvety inner surface with his tongue. Her lips fulled and prickled. Her nipples hardened and tingled. She flinched and gasped, her lashes flying up. Tristan leaned back, staring down at her with the candlelight sparkling like gold dust in the stubble of his beard. His eyes were a cloudy hue, but the darkening of the blue was a shade different somehow. A shade that warmed her like a cup of hot spiced wine. His tongue slicked across his lips. His russet lashes blinked.

"Amicia?" he questioned. "Why do you stop? Does this not give you pleasure?"

"Ay, my lord," she whispered, her forearms pressing tight against her tingling breasts. "This kiss between a man and a woman is a pleasant thing. Only . . . only I feel so . . . I have never felt this way before, my lord."

"How so?"

"As if . . . as if my bones were melting like beeswax candles." She paused, at a loss for words as she searched his warming gaze. "My lord, you lay your lips to mine, but . . . but I feel the kiss in other places."

"Other places?" he questioned with a curious frown.

"Ay, my lord." She swallowed hard.

"Where?"

Heat crawled up her cheeks and burned to the peak of her forehead. His eyes dropped to the arms pressed tightly to her breasts and color stained his high cheekbones.

"Is this the way it is for a wench?" he said huskily.

"I . . . I know not, my lord. Think you I am ill made?"

His smile twitched into place. "Many things I might think, but that you are ill made is not one."

"I am glad, my lord," she whispered.

"Tristan," he corrected, and leaned close. "Say it for me."

"Tristan," she murmured against the lips that claimed hers as by right old and honored.

The kiss spun long while his fingers threaded the shining mantle of her hair. Summery winds of burgeoning passion laved Amicia's senses as Tristan tasted the virginal recesses of her mouth. Sweet yearning melted her resistance. An instinct as old as time lent a creamy softness to her lips and curled the tip of her tongue to tentatively stroke his.

His body jerked along hers as if he had been struck with a lash, then went utterly still. Disentangling their joined mouths, she pressed deep into the pillow to raise a bewildered gaze. "I have offended you, my lord?"

"Nay," he said hoarsely, staring down at her as if looking upon a fearsome sight.

"I—I know not the way of this, my lord," she whispered. "Am I not allowed to do unto you those things you do unto me?"

"Nay . . . I mean . . . ay, you are, but . . ." He swallowed hard. "Amicia, what witchery do you practice?"

"None, my lord! I know nothing of potions and philters such as those use. I am but a woman—"

"Ay, like none I have seen. How do you leech my will from me and make me forget that which I dare not?"

"I do not do so apurpose, my lord. I seek only to please you as is my duty."

"Is it duty that warms your flesh beneath my hand? Duty that makes your mouth tremble beneath mine?" A frown gathered in the depths of his eyes. "I would hear it from your lips. Is it duty that brings your body seeking the curves of my own?"

"What would you have me tell you, my lord? My body is yours to do with as you will. Must you have my heart, too? Must you hear that I have wondered this night if you are a wizard? Must you hear that the touch of your eyes is to me as the touch of a hand? What will you leave me to call my own, Tristan?"

"Naught!" he rumbled. He leaned low, his eyes claiming hers with a victor's right. "I would have it all and call it mine. If I am ensorcelled, so shall you be. Tell me, witch, is it duty?"

Amicia stared into the glittering gems of his eyes, and knew there were things worse by far than the pain of a beating or the loss of life. It was the heart and mind that gave substance to life. If they were lost, what was left?

"Nay, my lord," she whispered. "With your lips upon mine, I think naught of duty."

"And so it shall ever be," he growled, reaching out, catching the coverlets and stripping them away, baring her, a feast for his famished gaze.

The liquid rush of fear filling her as wine fills a chalice was different somehow. She did not flinch when his huge hand followed the path of his eyes and began its shaken quest at the tingling peaks of her breasts. She did not shrink when he cupped their fullness in his palm, when his hand glided from rib to rib with his eyes shuttered against the sight as if he soaked the feel of her into the center of his being. She did not suck in her breath when his thumb coasted across the valley of her navel and his hand slid lower to feather across the dark nest at the joining of her thighs.

He would cause her no pain. She knew it as surely as she knew why Lady Ruella loved him. The threat that she, too, would follow that mournful path lay in this bed. Did she allow it, he would reft her heart as surely as he would reft her maidenhead. She would have done far better to deny this joining and fall into her father's hands. He could only abuse her body and bruise her heart. Tristan could steal her soul and leave her empty.

His mouth closed about the peak of her breast and suckled. A molten flame burned into her loins and seared her mind free of all but the need to resist. His sinewy hand coaxed and her thighs parted with a treacherous eagerness. His tongue rolled in honeyed circles around her quivering nipple and flames of desire licked at the edges of her resistance. She panted, her hand climbing, hesitating over the curve of his nape.

The heel of his hand rubbed slow raptured circles low on her belly. Vaulting flames consumed her resistance, leaving ashes scattering on flurries of passion. Adrift on a sea of sensation, she knew nothing but the heat of his mouth and hand, and the supple sensuousness of the body that was no longer hers alone. Pulses throbbed where never felt before. Her hips rotated, seeking what, she knew not. Her fingers furrowed the thickness of his hair, dragging his mouth up to hers with a demand that pulled a guttural groan from him. The slant of her lips across his, the hot thrill of exploring that velvety wet recess, the pressure of his hard chest against her aching breasts, naught was enough. She scattered kisses along the corded column of his neck and sank her teeth into his shoulder. Running her hands across his chest, she reveled in the softness of the thatching of curls and the hardness of muscle beneath. The yearning grew . . .

"Amicia," he murmured, his knee sliding between her thighs. "I can wait no longer. No longer," he sighed and moved over her.

She whimpered low in her throat, and twined her arms around his neck, nuzzling her face into the curve of his shoulder. Her forearms crossed at his nape and her fingers fanned across his back, feeling the tension of muscles drawn as taut as hers. He shuddered in her arms, and there seeped in a dim awareness that his need was as hers. A force that drove him beyond his will.

Silken fire probed tentatively and her breath stuck low in her throat. He went still, as if gathering his strength. Rills of movement beneath her digging fingers gave scant warning.

The thrust came hard and fast, stretching and tearing on a burst of pain that swept away her yearning. She arched against him, gasping, welcoming the pain as if it were a lover. Her forehead pressed against his shoulder. She breathed deep, willing the pain to linger. The yearning was gone. The threat was ended. He would not steal her heart, her soul. She would not end as sad Lady Ruella, giving love where it was not wanted. It was over, this joining of man to woman. This deed promising untold pleasure and giving only pain. She was safe . . .

"Amicia?" he said softly above her. "Amicia!"

The pain ebbed and she lay back, blinking tears away. Strange tears of mourning for the untold pleasure promised.

"Only this once. No more," he whispered. "From this time, there will be only the pleasure."

"It . . . it is not over, my lord?" she asked, the fear a niggling presence, threatening to consume her once more.

"Nay, sweeting," his mouth softened for a smile that did not come. "It only begins now."

A long silken stroke inflamed her new-fledged senses, which paid scant heed to the dread clutching her heart in a grip of iron. Her entire being quivered in anticipation, setting her adrift in sun-splashed splendor. "Ensorcelled," he had said. So she was. So she would be. Yet with the promise drawing nigh, she could not care that he was molding her into an image of his own making. She could not care that this might end, if she could only reach out and touch and be given answer . . .

It came in a rush that stole her breath, and she dug her fingers deep into his shoulders. It came on his low groan, on the shuddering of his body against hers, the quivering of hers against his. It came on the sundering of her mind and heart. It left her with the bittersweet knowledge that, for good or ill, she would never be the same again.

# Chapter 8

Ever was the dream the same. Alone in the web sticking to his bare flesh like plaster to stone, Tristan struggled to reach his father's ghost shimmering against the hellish black. "Why, Papa? Why?" he cried. "For a woman! How could you?" The empty cavern of his father's mouth opened in soundless answer while his son arched against the web, the tendons of his neck jutting against his skin, his arms quivering with effort.

Ever was it the same—until now. Now another presence waited in the dark near his father's shimmering ghost. Now he struggled to form the question, but it would not come. Panting breaths tore his raw throat. Fear came with its shrinking companion, shame.

The presence moved, a shadow of blue on black. Close it came, the face a glimmering ivory medallion in the gloom of the hood. Small, pale hands reached up. The hood fell back. Amicia! Smiling, while the ravishing abundance of her chestnut hair floated out. Shiny tendrils coiled around his fingers and snaked across his palm, binding his hand tighter and tighter . . .

Tristan's eyes flew open, his body jerked, and his hand flexed to rid itself of the lovely tendrils wrapping it tight.

Amicia's head climbed from the pillow of his shoulder. Misty eyes, dazed with confusion, met his and slid away to roam his features as though a stranger she beheld. Her lips parted invitingly. Her cheeks flushed with rosy sleep's color. Taunting, tantalizing feminine curves melted along his length. The blue-mist of her gaze touched his once more. Awareness came, scalding artless confusion and leaving behind chary caution.

"My lord," she whispered, her tempting curves quickening and shrinking from him. Slowly, she drew her hand from his chest, leaving an odd emptiness within it. Shifting away inch by inch, she left the cold to caress the flesh she had warmed. Her eyes remained locked with his, as if he were a mad dog who might leap upon her if she dared blink an eye.

Rage clenched Tristan's fingers in her hair. "Be still!"

She froze, fear muddying her gaze. "Ay, my lord," she breathed softly, compliantly.

*Ay, my lord.* So meek. He watched the flutter of her lowering lashes and gritted his teeth in frustrated fury. Did she think he would use her hardly? After last night?

Deepest blue glimmered through the screen of her lashes. Blue that had glowed with sultry passion in the night. The cream of her shoulder peeking through the tangled skein of her hair was smooth as the finest silk. He could feel it still in the hollow of his palm. Her dainty fingers had fearlessly danced across his chest. Her full, soft mouth, quivering now, had eagerly flowered beneath his. The tongue timidly stroking her lips had boldly plied his, kindling a blaze whose embers now stirred in his loins.

What spell of sweet witchery did she cast that he forgot all but the need to sheathe himself deep and spend his seed in the moist welcome of her womb? No thought did he give to the secret his mother held, to the threat it posed. No thought did he give to Megotta, her life or her wellfaring. No thought did he give to Ruella, who smiled sweetly, so sweetly, even as she betrayed.

Nay, he thought of naught but the urging of his loins . . . and the yearning of his heart. He must speak truth to himself if no other. From whence came the ease that settled upon him like the mists of evening? Such ease as never felt ere this. Ease that could be his undoing and others'.

His eyes dropped to the hand caught in the lustrous web of her hair. Revulsion rose like a stench in his nostrils. So would she hold him, did he yield to this frailty of his heart. His fingers arched like talons and shining strands of brown snaked out, sinuously caressing his skin.

His mouth twisting in a silent snarl, he grabbed her hair with his free hand. She gasped, pulling away, and his hot gaze stabbed into hers. "Do you think to work a woman's wiles upon me, then think on this: better than you have tried and failed. Do not mistake my way of the night for the way I shall ever be. We are wed for duty's sake, no other."

"Nay, my lord, I would not mistake it."

"See you do not!" He roughly wrenched his hand free.

Her cry of pain brought his head up with a snap. Eyes abrim with unshed tears, she lay poised like a threatened forest creature. And like those creatures her heart raced and ran, setting her breasts aquiver.

Tristan pulled his hand to his waist and covered it with his palm, rubbing the feel of her away. Just so would he be rid of the feelings she roused, he assured himself, even as his treacherous eyes lingered on the rosy peaks of her breasts and the heat in his loins took fire. The fire spread and, with it, anger. Was he a puling boy to allow his loins to rule his head?

"Cover yourself!" he growled, his own voice hoarse and strange to him.

She snatched the shield of the coverlet to her shoulders and huddled behind it. Bright color riding her cheekbones, Amicia looked away and a single tear escaped the rim of her lashes.

The silvery orb shivered at the threshold of her lips, and a soft yearning pilfered Tristan's intentions with the deft thievery of a fingersmith. He wanted to soothe her fear and take her unto himself once more, to yield his all and lose himself in the ease she promised. Sweet surcease. So near . . . so far. A weakness his mother would use did she espy or learn of it through another. And if she did? All would be lost. Pride in the name of Eden. Honor. Life.

A distant trill of laughter intruded on the silence. A woman's laughter, where none should be. He glanced at the leather curtain. They came, and he not ready.

He uncoiled. His hand whipped out, latching around

Amicia's throat. She hissed a breath, her hands clawing at his wrist as he bore her down to the pillow and bent nose to nose with her. His fingers tightened, a choking grip that glazed her eyes with terror. "I give but one warning, Amicia of Bellay. Do you ever speak of what passes in the privacy of this chamber, I give oath that regret will be your lifelong companion."

"I—I will not, my lord. I swear. My lord, I beg of you"—her fingers dug into his wrist—"I cannot breathe."

The leather curtain crackled. "Leave off, Tristan! I vow you have the strength of ten were you at this the night through!"

Earl Simon's laugh echoed through the chamber, whirling Tristan around. He schooled his face to a lightness not found in his heart. "I do my duty as bid by you, my lord. Have you not trained me up to know that duty rides us hard?"

"Ay, Tristan, so I have. But there is duty"— black eyes danced over his crooked grin—"and then there is duty."

"Ay." Bellay stumbled in, wine sloshing over his up-raised horn. "As there are rides . . . and rides. Come, Sybilla, let us see how well your son broached this shrinking maid. I vow she looks to have taken no pleasure in it."

A satisfied smile nipped his mother's mouth before it drooped in spurious sympathy. Tristan's hands coiled into fists. Naught could he do now for good or ill. He had given truth to the lies that bitch spilled. He had taught Amicia the need for silence and fear. He had failed neither himself nor his. His weakness of the night would be forgotten in the morning's fright. So why this regret that came with the stealth of the reiver?

He set his jaw like rock. Naught could he do but rise and thrust his arms into the camelin robe offered by his squire while the giggling women and laughing men filled the mural chamber like grain in a bin. Knotting the belt at his waist, he cast a cautious gaze Amicia's way.

She settled a fragile hand in Enid's capable grip and slid from the bed in a cloud of dark hair and a flash of smooth white hip. Rushing into her plain woolen robe in trembling haste, she pulled it around her with an unsteady sigh of relief.

His mother stripped the coverlets away for all to witness the proof of their joining on the blood-smeared linen. The Earl proclaimed them truly wedded and bedded. Bellay grinned and kept his tongue between his teeth. Tristan vowed a butt of wine waited below, and the chamber began to empty, leaving the new husband and wife to dress.

All were gone, save Lady Sybilla, who paused at the entry, her chin high and her cold eyes searching her son's face. "I vow I see a difference in you, Tristan."

A chill climbed up his backbone and prickled across his scalp. "I am as I have ever been."

"Nay, I think not. Dare I plead a mother's hope that you have found more pleasure than duty in this joining?"

"Pleasure, my lady?" his voice came flat and hard, though his belly quivered with the effort to make it so. "One maid is as another when the candles burn low."

"Mayhap it is so with men," she said softly, her gaze clinging to Amicia, "but I do not think your new-wed wife can find pleasure in knowing you place so little value upon her."

So this was where she led him, all unwitting as ever. Twisting words to her own ends, forcing words from him. "I value no woman born of this earth, and well you know it."

"So I have warned her," she murmured, as if saddened.

Only he saw the smile that came when she turned to the leather curtain and languidly swept it aside. Her footsteps died away, and Tristan looked to Amicia. Her chin tilted up at a regal angle, her blue eyes meeting his steadfastly. He looked away, the color flowing hot in his cheeks. His hand climbed to his mouth and he tried to cough his tension away. Enid re-entered the room, breaking the taut silence.

"I will leave that you might dress for the day," he mumbled, then fled, the curtain crackling behind him.

Through the last whispers of swaying leather, came his wife's voice. "A bath I would have, Enid, to wash the stench of man away."

\*    \*    \*

Though her flesh itched and burned from her vicious scrubbing, Amicia failed in her intent. Sandalwood's exotic scent wafted from the rippling fall of her hair, shielded by naught but a sheer linen veil as Tristan had commanded. The scent clung to her skin like a ground-hugging mist and filtered into her mind, hinting at bold crusaders treading the sun-baked earth of faraway lands. Yet beneath it ran an ever-present thread, like wool spinning from a spindle.

Beyond the flesh, so easily bathed and perfumed, lay the dark realm of memory, and that could not be washed away. Sitting atop a low stool in the Great Hall, she applied her needle, her ears half attending the circle of gossiping women engaged as she was. The archangel's trumpet grew at the tips of her agile fingers while memories came plundering. The yellow-gold thread became red-gold hair caressing her palms like fine silk. The raveling ends moistened between her lips became the hot velvet of Tristan's wooing tongue. The eye of the needle, watched with a squint, became the blue of his eyes, passion-heated to the brilliance of a midsummer sky. The sleek sendal beneath her fondling fingers became his flesh, finely wrought silk over heavy linked mail.

The least move brought the memories plundering her will. Her saffron linen chemise glided across her fulling breasts as his hand had done. A twining curl feathered across her cheek as his lips had done. Her woolen hose hugged her thighs as his had done. New-fledged senses possessed her body, aching for more than memory to guide them. The scent of wine and man curled inside her with sweet content. A sprightly flute, singing above the babble, set her toe to tapping. The radiant heat of the nearby brazier touched her cheeks like the gentlest of hands. Each sensation trespassed with cloddish feet upon the path her struggling mind longed to take. The path back and back to the maid she had been, untouched, unsullied, unchanged.

Tristan's low rumbling voice vibrated distinctly amid the discordant clangor of the hall. One masculine voice among many, it came to her like music from afar. How did she know each time he moved and where he stood and how? She spared no single glance for him, but she knew when he stood before the hearth with the Earl at his side and his feet planted wide and sturdy like the mountains ringing Holmby Vale. She knew when he moved to a trestle table and propped his foot atop a bench and his forearm atop his knee, when he bent to offer aide to a beleaguered bachelor-knight's game of chess. She knew when he stood silent and still with his lips hard and unyielding, caught in night converse by a wayward wench who was known as a lady.

It was as if her soul had become one with his as surely as her body had done. If so, it had happened only to her. He remained untouched, unchanged. Was more proof needed than those words to his mother: *I value no woman born of this earth*.

Her eyes lifted from the wheat-colored sendal sprouting its religious theme in brilliant colors. The hall boiled with life like frumenty in a pot. Men knelt in a corner intent on rolling dice. A bardy-coat held court with a favorite tale of a shrewish scold and her shrinking spouse. Harp and fydel, gittern and flute vied for the ear. Knights gathered round the hearth, bemoaning King Henry's banning of tournaments. Children played a shrieking game of Hot Cockles, and there her gaze lingered.

Guy of Lancasterdale knelt with a blindfold knotted about his head and his hands behind him, palms up. Children darted one by one to slap his hands, giggling while he guessed who it was and shrieking with excitement when the guesses went awry. Only one hung back on the fringe of the dancing mass. The girl's nut-brown eyes stared from her thin, pale face, avid with hunger to join them. A smile trembled uncertainly along her wide mouth, as though she took joy in theirs, but was unable to find it for herself. Alone she was in the midst of many.

As alone as Amicia. Loneliness rushed upon the bride like roiling spring freshets, cold with winter's melting snow. Here her span of time would be spent, alone in the midst of many. A yearning came to see a single face look upon her with kind intent. Her father? Sitting in the window seat, whispering with Lady Sybilla under the watchful eye of Aimery? Nay, she would see no kindness in his dark eyes. None here . . . save Odo.

Despair shook her. A lady she was, born to like estate as these in hall. Yet, to none could she turn and say, *I am alone and lonely. Come, break bread with me and share a cup of wine. Look to my heart and hear what I say, as I would do for you.* Not even to him who was her husband. Nay, less to him than any. He did not want her heart and she would not give it. Never would she become another Lady Ruella. She would wrap her heart in a shroud of indifference beneath the meek bending of her head.

Beneath the meekness, deeper still than the indifference, would lie the loneliness. None here would lay the balm of a friendly hand to it. When Odo was gone, she would be bereft of even one kindly gaze.

She looked up, espying hard-faced Enid nearby, the sullen shadow that had trailed her through the long morn and longer eventide. Amicia's shaking fingers fumbled the needle into the cloth. Her trembling hands hastily folded and stuffed it in the withy basket at her side. She beckoned to the serving woman.

"My lady?"

"Enid, summon Odo, my father's master-at-arms. I would see him . . ." The uproar of the hall pressed upon her. "Not here. In the chapel. Ay, the chapel, where all is peace."

Enid's hard face cracked, melting into supple lines of loathing. "Does my lord give you leave for this . . . my lady?" The address came as an afterthought, a courtesy that choked through her thinned lips.

"Nay." Her eyes flicked toward Tristan, one of a knot of men in a circle of torchlight. Must she have leave of him for her comings and goings and speakings? Would she be ruled as a child would . . . or as one distrusted? Ay, so it would be evermore. To struggle against it would only give him reason to believe himself right. Meekness. Père Brocard, Holmby's cherub-faced priest, said the meek would inherit the earth. Before her span of time was done, she would know whether it was truth or lie. "Nay," she repeated, her fists tight at her sides, "I have not asked his leave. If you think he needs must give it, then seek his will."

"Ay, my lady, and so will I do." The woman's submissive dip of her chin was more insult than the words she spoke.

"My lady?"

"Odo!" Amicia whirled in the gloom of the window slit, and rushed into the eerie quiet of the chapel nave. Fleet, light steps carried her to him with her hands outstretched.

Surprise wrinkled grotesquely across his ravaged face, but he caught her hands and held them in the leathery hardness of his. "Is aught amiss?" he hissed between his broken teeth.

"Nay, no more so than I expected. Less even, for my father is like to find that my husband is not a man such as he."

"Then why have you sent to meet me here? Did angels reside in that priory of yours? Do you not know this will rouse a hissing and whispering among all in this place?"

"I . . . I did not think—"

"Ay, you did not!" He chastised her as he would a wayward child, his frown an ugly thing of shifting scars and folding flesh, his single eye glittering like a sleet-glazed stone. "Think you these will soon forget from whose loins you spring? Would you give them yet more cause to doubt and suspect by meeting your father's master-at-arms as if by secret?"

"I ken not the difference it could make, when all look askance at my passing. Another stick added to the load—"

"And the mule is laid flat, my lady. If naught is amiss, what womanish fancy has brought me hither?"

Amicia's eyes dropped to the gnarled hands holding hers in a painful grip. "I wished to look upon you once more before your leave-taking on the morrow."

His grip tightened. When she winced, he relaxed it, yet held her still. "To look upon me is to see ugliness beyond bearing," he said gruffly. "Why would you wish to do so?"

Her eyes climbed slowly, touching the puckered scar

splitting his brow into uneven halves, the sunken hollow where his eye had been, the bluish seams carved in his cheeks. While she looked, his one gray eye stared steadily, as if in horror-stricken waiting of the moment she would shrink away.

She pulled her hands from his. His eye dropped, the color fleeing his skin and the square set of his shoulders sinking the least bit. Her fingers feathered across his cheeks, and his eye swept up, wide and startled.

"I see only what lies behind these scars when I look upon you, Odo. The kindness that protected me from my father and his men. The strength that was lent to me that I might hold my head high. The loyalty I have not earned. Loyalty that would have withstood the ire of him I have wed, had I but given the word. I see a soul unstained by evil and a heart pure and clean."

He caught her hands, as if the most fragile flower he held. His eye, shining with a hint of tears, looked away and he swallowed hard. "None but you and . . ." His voice quivered and he stopped, raucously clearing his throat. "None but you and your father have ever seen aught but this ugly face of mine."

"My father?"

"Ay, he has looked at the man beyond the scars. How often I have thought he might be other than he is, did the devils of greed and envy not ride him. There is kindness in him, buried so deep that mayhap only I have seen it."

Amicia stared at him, seeing the sadness that softened his features. "You love him, Odo?"

"Love him, my lady?" he asked, as if shocked. Realization crept across his features. Surprise gave way to acceptance. Acceptance to wonder. "Ay, and so I do. Should there be naught in this land to hold him dear?" he asked softly. "I have had this face long and long, my lady, since a youngling when the wolves got at me. All shrank from my sight as from the devil himself, until my lord came to the village one day and raised me from the lowest estate to be man-at-arms for him. I feared him not then, nor do I now. Mayhap that is why he has raised me yet higher and kept me at his side, the conscience he can neither obey nor shed. Ay, I love him, my lady."

"He does not deserve your love, Odo," she whispered.

"My lady"—he smiled ruefully—"you have not yet learned the heart is a cross-grained ox that goes not where the mind wills."

"Nay! Nay!" Her hands trembled in his and she pulled away. "Do not say it, I beg of you. It cannot be so."

"What have I said?" he asked, alarmed.

"The heart is not an unruly child tripping to its own will. We choose where we love. Ever has it been so with me. Ever shall it be so!"

"What is amiss that you fear the way of your heart?"

"He . . . he . . ." Her throat closed.

"He has harmed you," Odo growled, his hand settling on the hilt of his dagger.

"Nay, he has done naught of ill to me. It is . . . it is . . ." Her eyes lifted to the rood above the altar. "I fear him, Odo," she whispered. "His mother says he has a vicious temper and a heavy hand. Yet I cannot believe it is so. I cannot believe he will raise his hand in anger to me."

"Then what is this fear you have?"

"I fear . . . to love him."

"You are wed to him, my lady. It can be no bad thing to find love in your joining."

"Mayhap, did both find love, but where only one knows it . . ." She looked to him, her eyes dark with pain. "Odo, I could not bear it, and there is something in him that calls to me. I know not what. I only know if I yield to it, I will be lost."

Tristan gulped untasted ale and watched the passage leading to the chapel nave. Enid should have gotten her way. He should have allowed her to hide on the chancel stair and listen, but such was a dishonorable deed and he had a squeamish belly. Honor could not be practiced at will for opportunity's sake. Even in this, it must his. Even if Enid was right and this meeting meant ill for him. What did Amicia say to Odo? What plans did they hatch like clucking brood hens?

A shadow darkened the dim passageway. The horn froze at Tristan's lips. Odo appeared, a hulking, misshapen brute with bandy legs and too-long, too-thick arms. Set atop his squat neck was that face to make a brave man cringe. Could it be yet uglier, the scowl that lowered his brushy brows on the jut of his forehead made it so. Across the width of the hall, Tristan felt that hot silvery eye coldly speaking the words of defiance and threat dammed behind Odo's pinched mouth. Words as eloquent as the gnarled hand caressing the hilt of the dagger at his waist. Words that pulled Tristan across the hall as if no other existed beneath the soot-blackened rafters.

"My lord."

Odo's voice held neither servility nor insolence, yet it scraped Tristan from shoulder to waist like a hairshirt. "You have taken leave of Lady Amicia?"

"Ay, my lord. She feared there would be no time for leave-taking on the morrow and wished to give me thanks for the aid I gave her on the journey here."

"Surely no more than your duty."

"More, my lord, for I protected her from the worst of her father"—his silvery-gray eye glittered—"as I will revenge her upon any man who does ill unto her."

"Do you threaten me?" Tristan asked, ominously soft.

"Nay, my lord. I but warn you."

Tristan slowly set the horn aside. Poised over his squarely set feet, he hooked his thumbs into the jeweled leather belt at his waist and studied Odo with a slit-eyed stare. "For what you have said here, I could take you into the ward below and have the flesh stripped from your bones. None would say me nay, did I choose to do it. Why do you take this chance for a woman who is naught to you but your overlord's daughter?"

"Because, my lord, she has looked beyond the horror of my face to see a man behind it."

"It is much"—his eyes narrowed—"but there is more."

"Ay, and so there is." Odo's gaze drifted away for the first time. "It is of moment to none but me."

"I would know what it is."

"Nay, my lord." Their gaze locked once more. "It is enough that you know she has shown me kindness where no other has and that I will avenge any ill done to her."

"Does she deal with me in honor and truth, she will abide here, safe and well."

"I pray it will be so, my lord, for her sake and—"

"Do not press my good intent to its limit, Odo. You may yet find yourself in the ward below," Tristan warned. "You have my leave to seek the Guard Hall and a stoup of ale to oil your clacking tongue."

Tristan watched the man pull his forelock, an obsequious gesture with naught of obsequiousness in it. As Odo blended into the shadows of the turret stair, Triston wondered about the woman who had touched the heart of that hard, lonely man . . . just as she had touched the heart of another hard and lonely man, giving ease where none had been.

He moved into the passage, begrudging the direction his feet took even as his pace quickened. Alabaster candlelight lured him into the chapel nave. His gaze swept the dancing shadows, and stopped on Amicia's slight figure, kneeling at the foot of the altar. An odd gawkiness shifted his feet beneath him and set his damp palms to scrubbing over his black velvet surcoat. His hands stopped abruptly, screwing into fists. Was he a callow youth to feel again that his feet were too big and his hands too many?

She stiffened suddenly. Her head rose and turned, and her eyes widened. "My lord," she said uncertainly.

"My lady." He silently cursed the quiver in his voice. God's Eyes! The wench was here but a day, and he acting as lackwitted as a stripling boy!

She shifted on the rushes, as if to rise. His treacherous feet stuttered and started toward her. One reluctant stride followed another. His hand reached out. He waited, meeting her startled gaze with one equally startled by his own actions. A moment passed, then another in brooding silence. Her hand rose, paused, and settled in his.

"I thank you, my lord," she murmured, rising with his aid.

Her hand moved in his, tugging gently. He released it, his hands falling to scrub down his sides. He frowned and put them behind him, his thumbs scrubbing the feel of her from his palms. "You, ahh . . ." He cleared the frog from his throat. "You have taken leave of Odo?"

"Ay, my lord."

His wandering gaze touched the sad droop of her mouth. "You seem downcast, my lady. Have any here—"

"Nay, my lord," she rushed to give answer.

He breathed deep of sandalwood and woman, watching the feathering tip of a curl drift on a current of air. He yearned to reach out, to brush his knuckles across the warmth of her cheeks, to bury his hand in the lush life of her hair.

"I would ease you of this sadness, did I know the way." He listened to himself say as if another, unknown to him, spoke.

"It . . . it is naught you may change, my lord. Odo must leave with my father on the morrow."

The strain in her voice pulled his eyes from the small hands clasped at her waist, as if each offered comfort to the other. "His leaving is of great moment to you?"

"He has been kind to me, my lord, when . . ."

She fell silent and Tristan waited. "When?" he prompted.

Her gaze rose and met his. "When no other has, my lord. I am left here among those unknown to me, those who despise me. I but grieve for the loss of one who has shown me kindness."

"There are those here who would be kind—"

"Nay, my lord. Kindness is a gift of the heart. These here, by your word, will do me no hurt. But kindness? Nay, my lord, I will not find that in this keep of yours."

What answer could he give when it was truth she spoke. He, too, knew what it was to be alone among many, to hunger for a kind word, a kind look, a kind deed. He had felt his heart shriveling inside him, and he a man with no need of such things as kindness and love. But she was a woman, hardly more than a maid. How keen the bite of grief must be for her, raised by the loving hands of the nuns.

"Mayhap he need not go." He listened to that other speaking with his voice, who gave no thought to danger or future. "Mayhap your father, if asked, would give him leave to stay as your man."

Her eyes rose with a sheen of hope that quickly dulled. "Nay, my lord. My father would do naught to bring me ease. And you, my lord? Would you want Bellay's man in your keep?''

''Does he stay, he would be your man,'' the fool in him said, spitting out his specious reasoning. ''I will speak to your father of it.''

Her gaze touched his and clung, her eyes bedecked with the starry light of the heavens. Her trembling mouth shed the bonds of sadness, her spreading smile giving birth to a crest of a dimple high on the curve of her cheek. Her hands reached out, and his came up to enfold them.

''My lord,'' she said. ''I will not forget this kindness of yours. Even do you fail, my heart is glad that you would think on my pleasure.''

Tristan stared down at the blithe span of her smile and ease came stealing. Beneath the ease came the curling heat of desire. A warmth in his loins. A pounding in his heart. A fire in his mind. A fire for this sweet witch and her gentle spell. A spell he would know once more before the night was done and he must set her aside—forever.

# Chapter 9

The warming breeze whispering around the turrets seemed to carry the husky murmur of Tristan's voice. "Sweet witch, sweet witch," it sighed as he had sighed in the wee hours of the night. The haunting hours that tore Amicia between terror and enchantment. The damning hours that made of her fear a reality.

What a boastful child she must seem to him, speaking of stubbornness and will when she had none. He took her will and molded it as effortlessly as a potter and his clay. He touched her soul and took her with him to that other Eden, where all was good and fair, save the snake slithering through the apple tree—the snake that spit "Fool, fool" with every flicker of his forked tongue.

A fool she was. Her own eyes had given her proof. The man who possessed her in tenderness in the night had turned as cold and indifferent as she wanted to be. His gentle ways were shed like the evil snake's skin the moment he stepped through the rustling leather curtain covering the mural chamber door. Would that she could shed the feelings he roused as easily.

He lit a fire for life that would not be quenched. Wine tasted sweeter. The sun looked brighter. Her linen chemise caressed where it had only touched. Needs, new and unwanted, prodded her. Where peace had reigned in contentment, she now needed happiness. Where kindness would have been enough, she now needed acceptance. Where acceptance would have been enough, she now needed . . . more. But what that *more* was, she dared not think.

She stood in the midst of the ward and watched the guests leaving in mass with her heart sinking lower and lower. She would be alone soon. As alone as that fey child flitting through the snarled confusion as lightly as a butterfly amid heady drifts of columbine. That lonely child with the wary brown eyes and wan cheeks. To whom among these did she belong?

Her gaze wandered the tumult. Horses neighed and asses brayed and hounds howled. Knights shifted restlessly beneath the weight of hauberk and mail. Ladies mounted and servants scurried like a swarm of disturbed ants. Soon the ward would be emptied of all save those who belonged . . . and her.

Others' hate and suspicion would be her companions, those and her fear that hovered over her like a weeping cloud. The fear that Tristan would steal her soul piece by piece until nothing was left but a pitiful heart giving love that was not wanted. Had Lady Ruella once felt this bubbling of life and hope and fear?

Amicia folded her arms beneath her mantle, her gaze sliding from the departing guests. Lady Sybilla, regal and serene, stood atop the landing before the entrance tower with Aimery at her back, a merry-lipped lackey attending his queen. His teeth twinkled white against his swarthy face, but above the easy smile, his brown eyes were untouched by humor. Worried he looked, and fearful. As fearful as Amicia felt.

Her unease deepening, she followed the direction of his gaze . . . to her father. He stood apart in hissing converse with Odo, his face red with rage, while Odo's bleached whiter and whiter, his lacing of scars standing out like the marks of a scourge. Her father's fist raised and Amicia flinched, while Odo visibly steadied himself for the blow. A blow that did not come. Instead, that heavy fist flexed upon its wrist and shook a threat beneath the flat nose that moved from side to side in denial.

"Then, begone, damn you!" Her father's raised voice lanced through the noise. That hard, hating voice she would so gladly hear the last of. "And may your soul rot in everlasting hell!"

Odo's face went whiter still. He turned heavily, his rolling, bandy-legged walk bringing him to her side.

She reached out, lightly brushing the rough russet wool of his sleeve. "What is this anger between you, Odo?"

"I am to abide here as your man by request of your lord," he said stiffly, and took his place to her right and rear as if he were a chained hound to be pulled at her will.

"I fear the fault is mine. My lord . . ." Her thoughts strayed. Was this why he left her bed so early this morn? To do this deed for her good? Tristan, her tongue caressed his name. What ill did he work all unwitting by this goodness of his?

"The stirrup cup, my lord."

Tristan's voice played its honeyed strumming melody upon Amicia's ear, enticing her gaze. His hand, big and bold and golden-hued, raised the chalice to Earl Simon, high atop his palfrey. Tristan's hand, rough palmed and gentle—touching her, gliding, coaxing, caressing. Her flesh tingled in vibrant memory.

"It is welcome, Tristan." The Earl drained the cup and pulled his hand across his mouth, black eyes canting heavenward with a frown. "Would that the cold had not broken in the night. The ox-wains will be mired to the hub before the day is done. I vow the hot winds of Gascony warm this day."

"There is still a bite of autumn in the air, my lord."

Earl Simon's struggle between fond disgust and amusement snared Amicia's curious attention. How much he knew of this man she wed. How much she had yet to learn.

"Ay, Tristan"—he grinned widely—"never do you change. A thing is what it is and naught else may it be."

"I leave it to you, my lord, to see a war-horse in a cloud."

"While you see naught but rain or shine ahead. Alas, who is to say who is better in the end. You, at least, have whiled away no time lying afield to chew a stem of grass and study that which God draws overhead."

"Nay, my lord, such is not for me."

Nay, it would not be. Amicia studied Tristan's profile, his square jaw and chiseled mouth and straight nose. Driven by duty and honor, he would find naught but guilt in lazy pleasure. Such was not the path to his heart. Pleasure would not soften it, but . . . attendance to duty might.

"Who knows what changes time will wring? Who knows what new ways a man might find in the eyes of a gentle maid?" The Earl clapped his hand atop Tristan's shoulder, a hard man's gesture of affection, while his knowing gaze touched Amicia's with a smile. "My lady," he called, "I would bid you farewell."

She moved to his side, the cynosure of all eyes save those she longed to have look upon her. Why did Tristan stand so stiffly, as if the chill breeze were a gale instead? "My lord," she looked to the Earl, "God be with you on your wayfaring."

"And with you here, my lady," he said, the solemn invocation spilled through a wicked grin. "I lay charge upon you now to teach this bold knight to take his pleasure whilst he may."

"My lord, did he not come to you as page when a youngling?" she asked softly, her gaze as guileless as a babe's. "How then may I, an untried maid, succeed where you have failed?"

"She has you there, my lord." The hint of a smile softened the etched line of Tristan's mouth and warmed Amicia's heart.

Earl Simon tossed his head on the strong column of his neck, his full laugh pealing. Would that all could be as it was at that moment, Amicia thought, watching him wipe his eyes and grin. Settling in his saddle he sucked in a chest-swelling draft of air and innocently—too innocently, she would have sworn—stared at the sun-washed sky.

"Ah, the sport this winter will be fine indeed."

"The sport, my lord?" Tristan inquired.

"No matter," the Earl sighed. "We must be away. God keep you in health and honor, my friend."

"God keep you in pleasure and peace, my lord."

The hemp-brown palfrey, dainty of limb and thick of chest, wheeled about to join the column filing through the gate. A wave of his gloved hand, and Earl Simon of

Leicester plunged into the shadows, taking with him the last hearty laugh Amicia feared she would hear in many a long day.

"So you are truly wedded and bedded, daughter."

Her father's hard, harsh voice pulled her yearning gaze from the shadowy gate passage and vanquished the remnant of her smile. She stared up at his ravaged face, lying like a blemish on the clean blue of the sky, and shuddered.

"I wish you well of her, Eden," he sneered from the saddle of his ill-tempered destrier. "Would that she proves to be of more worth than her mother, then you may get a son out of her. Think on it. My blood and yours, mingled for all time."

"A thought to curdle my belly, and well you know it."

Tristan's voice, slow, deliberate, and deadly cold, struck Amicia like the slap of a hating hand. She gasped and fell back a step, her fingers rising slowly to her quivering mouth. The honey-gold arrogance of his face was taut as a skull. Loathing burned in the eyes riveted upon her father. As once before, she had been forgotten. Nothing existed but his hatred of her father, her blood. What a fool she had been to hope he might see her as more than his enemy's daughter. Pray God, he had got no child upon her. Pray God, another would not be born to be hated by its father as she was by hers.

"Ay, as it does mine, Eden," her father growled. "I would see the wench dead first. The Earl has but delayed us here. I *will* see the end of you."

"I give you leave to try, Bellay, but hear this: do you fail, not all the devils riding out of hell will stop me from marling this earth with your blood."

"A cockerel's crow would fright me more than this threat of yours, Eden. We both know your hands are trussed by your sword-oath, while I care not what oath I disavow to reach my ends."

Her father's blue eyes turned to lie full upon Amicia, alight with evil triumph. His wolfish smile pulled over yellowing lupine teeth, and flurries of goosebumps rushed down her spine. She wanted to turn and run, but was rooted as firmly as the sturdy keep rising to the sky behind her.

"Look to your back, Tristan of Eden," he growled and slanted her a vicious look, "or mayhap you must need look to your own bed. Farewell, daughter mine, the devil be with you and yours." He wheeled his wild-eyed destrier and thundered across the ward, his mantle flapping like a vulture's wings.

Amicia stood as if struck to stone. Bone of her bone and blood of her blood and evil to the core. If ever a doubt dwelt in her heart, it did so no more. He threw her to the wolves and rode away with an ugly smile. He left her as wife to a man who so despised her and hers, he would not have a child from her. Tristan, whose touch melted her resistance, whose lips inflamed her. The raging pain of loss and disappointment scoured the yearning from her, leaving naught but anger and shame. Shame for the blood sluicing through her veins. Anger for the weakness that betrayed her in the arms that despised her.

Her eyes, glowing coals of blue, swept up to meet white-hot condemnation. "Why, Tristan?" she asked, her voice hard with anger and shaken by shame. "Why last night when the first was enough? Why take another chance of getting a child on me?"

His red-gold brows snapped together over the bridge of his nose. "I would not have the Earl think all would come amiss on his leaving," he growled defensively, color blooming high on his cheekbones. "He has much to worry over. I would not add this."

"More of a man's honor, my lord?" she asked bitterly. "Did it curdle your belly to touch me as it will curdle your belly to get a child from me?"

Her question scrubbed the anger from his face like a washclout scrubbing dirt from flesh. Remorse softened the hard line of his lips and wrinkled across his brow. He stretched out his hand to her, and she flinched away, her stubborn chin climbing.

"Amicia," he began throatily and stopped, his eyes flicking to the landing where Lady Sybilla and Aimery waited. His hand dropped to his side, curling into a fist. His shoulders squared and he stood tall with the autumn wind lightly fingering the golden fire of his hair. Arrogance, remote and cold, settled upon his features like a shield.

That arrogance, it had been no part of him in the night. Every caress, every sigh, every deed had lured her with gentle need. Lies! All lies! Yet even now the fire he lit could not be quenched. Amicia's heightened senses absorbed the aroma of bread baking in the ovens and the squeals of a litter of piglets trotting after a sow and the bathing heat of the sun.

"So, tell me, husband"—she swallowed the shameful tears pressing like stones against her throat—"how do we go from here? What will you do to keep me barren?"

His unblinking eyes stared over her head at the far distance. "Enid is even now moving your traveling chest to your new chamber in the women's solar."

Warmth ebbed from Amicia's cheeks, leaving them as cold as her heart. So very busy he had been this morn, and her witless as a headless hen. Would that she had basked less in the glow of the night's joy, and looked instead for that which she could see. She was unwanted, and would ever be so. Janus with his two faces was an apt symbol for this husband of hers. She ruthlessly crushed an upsurge of pain, and schooled her face to match his.

"I wondered where my warden had got to." Amicia silently cursed the fading strength of her breath. "Do you not fear what I may do out of her sight for this while?"

"Nay"—he stared straight ahead—"for you are in mine."

*Hate and suspicion would be her companions.* The words returned, a melancholy refrain more potent with the evidence of their truth standing before her. Her lower lip trembled. She chewed it into submission and lifted her eyes to his. "Need I wait for you to return me to her, or may I fare within alone?"

He drew a breath that swelled his chest. "You have leave to go and do as you may, until I am given sign that my trust—"

"Trust, my lord?" she scoffed, while her damned and damning heart wept tears of sorrow. "For Bellay's *seed*?"

Tristan's darksome gaze dropped to her face, racing lightly from the flushed curve of her cheek to the tender line of her mouth to her tear-spangled eyes. It was a gaze filled with those scuffling rivals, rage and pity. The rage was of no moment. She could meet it with her head high, but the pity . . .

Amicia swept up the heavy wool of her cotte, her fingers white against blood red, and whirled to flee him and herself and the pity she could not bear. His hand clamped around her arm like a smith's vise, a painful grip that jerked her up short and hauled her against his heaving chest.

"I am not done with you, Amicia of Bellay," he gritted between his teeth, while the fiery blue of his eyes halted the protest that rose to her lips. "I would know if your father spoke the first truth that ever passed his tongue."

She stared up through a haze of unshed tears. "If I spoke truth to you, my lord, would you know it?"

His grip on her arm tightened. "Play me no riddles, my lady. My life and yours are the stakes in this game."

"High stakes they are, though of worth to none but us. My father would as gladly see the end of me as you. Nay, my lord," she whispered, "I am no part of his plan."

One red-gold brow arced it suspicion over his searing stare. "So, you know his plan."

"That he has one, though what it is, I do not know."

"And if you knew?"

The question came soft, husky, hesitant. Amicia blinked the haze from her eyes and saw the ghost of that other Tristan. The Tristan that made gentle, tender, and passionate love to her.

"I do not," she breathed, and saw the ghost shimmer and vanish beneath the face tautening with anger. The face of the man who climbed from passion's tender bed to coldly set her from him, as if he had never whispered "Sweet witch, sweet witch" in the night.

"Ay, you may not, but"—his eyes shifted to glare a threat over her shoulder—"*he* does."

He? She swiveled on the pivot of Tristan's hand and saw Odo standing near with his ungainly arms hanging loose at his sides and his scarred face unmarked by fear of the threat that faced him. A fear that exploded inside Amicia like a catapulted stone shattering against a keep wall. Tristan had worked his way of her and kept Odo here that he might torture her father's plans from him! And she had given him thanks for it!

Her breath rasping, she swiveled back and raised a defiant fist that did not quite dare to thump his chest. "Do you harm one hair on his head, I will see your end if it means my own!"

He wrenched his suspicious glare from Odo and leveled it upon her, his clenching fingers biting to the bone of her arm. A muscle ticked wildly in his jaw. Suspicion blazed into a rage that sucked the strength from Amicia's thews and the defiance from her heart. Just so had her father looked at her, setting the hand of loathing to her shoulder to press her to her knees. A suppliant stance she would gladly assume would it save Odo, but this Tristan of Eden was not like her father. He would take no sick pleasure in abject pleading.

"Let him go from this place now!" she demanded, though her heart battered her ribs unmercifully. "He is loyal to my father and will tell you nothing, no matter what torture you devise to loosen his tongue."

"My lady!" Odo gasped.

"God's Blood, wench!" Tristan snarled. "What foolishness do you speak?"

"My lady!" Odo groaned and scrambled toward her, his small feet slapping the hard-worn earth.

"I tell you, Tristan of Eden," she said, her voice low and hard, "do you ever want a peaceful moment, you will—"

Odo's hand clamped over her mouth. "Hush, my lady! You set all amiss with this wicked tongue! My lord, she is but a wench and knows not of what she speaks. Give me leave to set all aright."

"Do you make sense of this womanish fancy?" Tristan rumbled low in his throat, his hot eyes boring into Amicia like a carter's auger into wood.

"Ay, my lord. If you would release her?" he asked, gently detaching Amicia from Tristan's grasp, while keeping one hand clamped over her mouth.

She stumbled backward a step; his hand fell away and she breathed deep of air and anger. "What do you here,

Odo? Will you not leave me to make good of the evil I have done?''

"Hush, my lady!" His rough voice scratched. "You have done no evil. I am as safe here as I would be at Castle Bellay.''

"Nay! He will torture my father's plans from you!"

*"Peste!"* Tristan gusted. "The wench is mad!"

"Only fearful, my lord," Odo informed him. "My lady, your lord has given me leave to stay as one of his. He is honor-bound to do me no hurt whilst I am in his keeping.''

"Honor?" Amicia spit the foul word, her eyes shifting to Tristan. "Odo, do you trust him in this?"

"God's Wounds!" Tristan roared, taking a threatening step toward her and bending to give her stare for stare. "You dare question my honor?"

"Ay!" Amicia hurled at him. "When the life of one I love is forfeit do you fail in this honor you claim! I would have oath of you that Odo will be safe here!"

He fell back, his jaw agape and his eyes round with amazement. "You would have oath . . ." The words dwindled on a gust of air. A vein throbbed wildly in his temple as his face flushed a dark ruddy red. "Do you know that I would kill any man who spoke to me as you have?" he asked softly, as if louder speech might jar his tenuous hold on his temper.

"I care not what you would do to man or maid! I want oath of you that Odo will not be harmed by you or yours!"

"My lady!" Odo moaned.

Tristan's jaw knotted and writhed, his color darkening to an alarming hue of red. His mouth opened, closed and opened once more. "You have it," he gritted.

"Sword-oath, my lord!"

"Wench, you try my patience to its limits!"

"Sword-oath, my lord," she repeated icily.

His huge fists flexed at his sides. The blue of his eyes paled to the white-heat of unchecked rage, and there came to Amicia the shriveling thought that she pushed him too far. His right hand swept across his body, clenching around the quatrefoil hilt of his sword. Metal scraped and hissed, and she stepped back onto Odo's foot. Tristan tossed the sword and caught it by the blade, holding up the cruciform hilt and quillons.

"I give sword-oath that Odo of Bellay will be done no harm by me or mine so long as he remains in my keeping." He grunted each word as if fighting for breath, then touched his lips to the hilt. Scraping the sword into its sheath once more, he angled a savage look her way. "Say no more, wench, lest I do you a hurt despite my good intent."

His attention shifted to Odo. "I would have word of you—"

"Ay, and you will have it," he said quickly. "I will give you neither help nor hindrance, my lord, for either would betray those who have my trust."

Tristan's narrowed gaze studied him. "Villein you may be, Odo of Bellay, but I trust your word sooner than some lords I know. You will stay here in peace and health so long as you prove no hindrance to me."

"I thank you, my lord."

Tristan grunted and turned away. His broad back rigid, he strode with the stiffness of roiling anger.

Amicia caught Odo's hand and gripped it tight. "His sword-oath we have," she whispered, "but may we trust it?"

A whir of sound jerked her head up. A brilliant shaft of sunlight winking from a blade stabbed into her eyes and a dagger twanged in the dirt at her feet. The leather hilt, polished by hard use, quivered scant inches from her toes. The leather hilt that could so easily be quivering over her breast. A daunting thought, it doused her last ember of defiance. Her wide gaze lifted to Tristan's face, bronzed by fury—a fury the more frightening for being so tightly leashed.

"Do not question my honor again, do you value your life," his voice came soft, gentle, and terrifying.

# Chapter 10

The wench was mad! Tristan, watching Amicia fly up the stairs to the entrance-chamber door with Odo hard on her heels, yanked his dagger from the earth and wiped the blade on his tunic. She heedlessly defied him! As if he were a hoary toothless hound of no worth or cause for alarm! By the Mass! She needed lessoning in the proper respect for her lord! Did her tongue always rattle so, he would have no peace at bed or board.

The thought gave him pause. Nay, he would have peace at bed. She would not be sharing his with him. There would be no soft body following his through the night, seeking heat like a winter wayfarer seeking a fire.

He thrust the notion aside, spun around, and set off. Long strides eating the distance, he fought a leaden sense of loss. Earl Simon had the right of it. Women could do more to break a man's peace than aught else he knew. The wench tweaked his nose and he twisted like a skein of wool. She dared to defy him, demanding—*demanding!*—her liege man's safety! As if he would give the man leave to stay and use it to his own ends. Did she know nothing about honor?

"My lord, I beg a moment with you."

Tristan slewed to a halt, his belly churning with rage and his face twisting in a scowl.

"Alas, my lord! I fear this is not the moment for this—"

126

"Why would it not be, William?" he growled at his huntsman, sending the man's long head slinking into his shoulders.

"I beg pardon, my lord. You are sore overset. I—"

"You wanted a moment. You have it. Speak up, man!"

"My lord, it is needful that you know . . ."

*Bold and brave as a warrior she is*—Tristan's thoughts wandered—*but she knows nothing of a man's honor! I should expect no more! She is but a woman, and women spill lies as easily as truth. Can any man espy the difference?*

". . . the West Wood, my lord. Fires were laid . . ."

*Lies. Did she give truth or lie when she said she knew naught of Bellay's plan?*

". . . in the ashes, my lord. Their stay has been long . . ."

*Does she lie and I trust, all will come amiss here. My head will be forfeit, my oath to the Earl broken, and Megotta left to my mother's mercy. A thought not to be borne.*

". . . a troop of men. Reivers, mayhap."

Reivers! Tristan's eyes dropped from a puffball cloud to the longish, leathered face of his huntsman. "Where?"

The man's tawny brows lifted. "The West Wood, my lord."

"Say again what you have told me," Tristan commanded, cursing himself for the folly of dwelling on that irritating, fascinating wench he had wed.

"We found sign of a troop making camp. So many as would make my fingers and toes."

"Scots? Do they come thieving out of the north again?"

"Nay, my lord. No sign they were Scots. We followed their trail west to the mountains and lost it there."

"West. Bellay's land?"

"Nay, my lord. They skirted his boundary."

"Do you find that odd, William?"

"Ay, my lord."

"So, it begins." Tristan's thoughtful gaze rose to the keep. Bellay's daughter. His wife. The wife he dared not trust. His narrowed eyes shifted to the huntsman. "Assign two of your best trackers to keep watch on Lady Amicia and her man, Odo. They are not to leave the outer ward without being followed and their doings reported to me. And, William, they are not to know.''

The orders given, Tristan drew an expansive breath in preparation for the relief he expected to feel. A breath that choked to a thread of air by a nettling unease. He would not be snared by another woman's lies, he told himself, but the vexing unease persisted. This new frailty of heart had not misled him. He had set the wench from him and had withheld his trust from her. The ease she gave him had no great hold on him. He should be relieved that his will had triumphed, and he was. He was, he assured himself. He was his own man as he had always been.

Ignoring a prickle of foreboding, he clapped a too hearty hand over the huntsman's shoulder. "Come, William. We are away to the West Wood. I would see this reivers' camp for myself," he said, scowling when his betraying eyes strayed to the keep.


"I vow your father's blood runs hot in you!" Odo huffed up the gloomy turret stair, trailing Amicia.

"Do not speak to me of him!" She spun so quickly her mantle spiraled about her. "I am no part of him, nor he of me!"

"Nay?" Arms akimbo, Odo glowered up at her. "Had your lord set his hands to your throat and choked your tongue to silence, I would have been sore tempted to cheer him! What madness possessed you in the ward below?"

"Madness!" Amicia mimicked his stance, firmly quelling the suspicion that it had truly been madness to fling Tristan's oath back in his teeth. "Fear for your well-faring possessed me!"

"God save me from more of your aid!" he growled. "You were more like to get my head spitted alongside yours!"

"You cannot believe he would do you no harm were he not bound by his sword-oath!"

"Believe? No belief was there to it, my lady! I know it!"

"You know it?" Her voice climbed in disbelief. "When he is as changeable as the wind? You dare not trust what he says!"

Odo propped a foot on the stone tread and clapped a hand on his knee. "In no way is he changeable. He has a healthy suspicion that might keep his head firmly joined to his neck."

Amicia stared down at him, her delicate jaw adroop. "You sound as though you respect him!"

"Ay, that I do," he affirmed to her utter disgust. "He is a man whose honor sits heavy on his shoulders."

"Honor!" Her fingers curled into claws. Even Odo, afflicted with this plague of witless devotion to honor!

"Ay, the honor which is my protection and yours! Did they teach you naught of the ways of men in the priory?" He leaned forward, his gray eye slitted. "It was no light speech he gave you, my lady. The man who tried him as you did would be lying now, a bloodied corpse ready for his shroud."

"Had I not, *you* might be that bloodied corpse!"

"Nay, my lady." His head shook. "What is this need you have to see the worst of him?"

"I see what is there!"

"You see that which you wish to see," came his stolid reply. "Ill will it go for us do you follow the path you tripped down this day."

She drew herself up, her slim nose lofty. "Does he have this honor you claim, then—"

"Even an honorable man may be pricked beyond sense by a needle-tongued wench! And *that* I know as surely as I know you are your father's daughter!"

"A kinship I claim not." Her voice broke, and with it, her anger. "How could he do it, Odo? How could he plant that seed of doubt in Tris—my lord's mind and ride away laughing?"

"My lady," he sighed, the flush of anger draining from his face. "A devil rides him hard. Betimes peace may be his."

Her gaze clouded with doubt. "Do you believe that day will come?"

"I hope it will, my lady."

She studied his scarred face, lit by the dim glow of the lancet window. "It cannot have been easy for you to defy him as you did in the ward below."

He shifted uneasily. "He was willing that I stay, my lady."

"So much I could see. It is his reason that besets me. What did he ask of you that you would not do, Odo?"

"Naught that need concern you, my lady."

His shifting weight and sliding gaze stressed his evasion of her question, but the reason for it eluded her. "I would not be as like to set a foot amiss in the tangle of their hate, did I know what he might do."

"Ay," he agreed, and heaved a sigh. "He asked that I spy upon all here and send word of their doings, my lady."

"You did not fear to say him nay in this?"

He stared down the dark stairwell. "No worse would befall me than a buffet, and I am used to such."

"Yet he is your lord. Such is his right to ask. Why, then, did you refuse?"

His chin climbed, his single eye staring at the moisture-seeping walls. "Were I caught, none here would believe you innocent of my deeds. The danger was too great."

Her gaze followed his to the gray stone patched with moss and dampness. "And he did not care," she murmured into the silence, stricken anew by her father's hatred of her.

"My lady, he is—"

"Ridden by a devil? Nay, Odo, he is steeped in evil to the marrow of his bones. Your love blinds you to that truth. Make no more excuses, for we ever see a different man." She descended the steps to him, her hand outstretched. "Lest we begin to squabble like younglings at play once more, I would ask you now to forgive my earlier ill temper."

His leathery palm covered her hand, his grip offering comfort. "Naught is there to forgive," he said, and hesitated. "More that I should seek your forgiveness for trespassing upon your kindness and rising above myself to—"

"Nay, do not say it. You are much more to me than liege man, Odo." Her wondering gaze traced his scarred features. "What is this tie that binds us? You a villein and me a lady, yet I trust you with my life and give to you the hand and heart of a friend. In these few days, I have learned the blood tie to my father means nothing to me, while this strange kinship between us means more than I can say."

"You do me too much honor, my lady." His whisper scratched unsteadily.

"Such, my friend, would not be possible," she murmured, turning to climb the stair. "Come, you may wait for me in the Great Hall while I go above to put up my hair."

"Put up your hair, my lady?" Bewildered confusion lightened his rough voice.

"Ay." She paused, and bent a humorless smile upon him. "You see, my lord has asked that I wear it down."

"My lady!" Odo groaned. "Can you not please him in this small thing that our heads may rest easier on our shoulders?"

"Nay." Her mouth turned grim. "It is only in this small thing that I dare defy him."

"What do you call that which you did in the ward below?" he asked in wide-eyed disbelief.

"That was for you," she said softly. "This is for me."

It was done. The coiled rope of her hair hung heavy in a plain caul of linen cord. Not a single burnished strand peeped from her frost-white wimple, but the eyes staring from Amicia's silver mirror held not a glimmer of satisfaction. Instead, they mocked her paltry defiance.

She slapped the mirror face down on the massive bed, where she would sleep alone, in this chamber where she would live alone. This chamber where no masculine voice would override the incessant wind wailing around the turret like a lost soul.

The echoing emptiness of the years to come rimed her heart with a forsaken chill. The years that would be hers to make of what she would, for good, for ill. So she thought at the bedding ceremony, unaware that her husband so despised her he would set her from him, denying her the child she craved; unaware that her arms would remain empty of any blessed swaddled weight; unaware that her breasts would shrivel with age, unsuckled by a babe. A woman was born to serve God or bear children, so she had been taught. But what of those who could do neither? What purpose was left to them? To her?

Amicia moved swiftly, as if to leave that barren chamber was to leave the question and its answer behind. Distant laughter, rousing, haunting reminders of the giggling girls fostering with her, pulled her through the narrow passageway into the solar.

At the far end sat a circle of women spinning and weaving, gossiping and laughing. Amicia watched them with a growing hunger. Hunger for the companionship and love left behind at Holmby. Hunger for the idle chatter and laughter that brightened monotonous tasks. Hunger for a woman with whom she could share her sorrow and fear.

Someone like the buxom apple-cheeked woman sitting at the far side of the circle, now lifting her spindle and running deft fingers along the tufting wool pulled by the cone-shaped weight. Her pale eyes watched a nearby speaker, her lips quivering with incipient laughter. A laughter that quickly spilled from her, joining that of the others. Her chin bobbled and her eyes climbed, meeting Amicia's. A spark of recognition, a dimming, and her laughter died. She nudged the woman next to her, and so it went around the circle until silence claimed cheer. The round row of faces raised condemning stares, then returned to their tasks. The *clack-clack* of the loom and the whir of spindles marked their disapproval and Amicia's humiliation.

Only Enid continued to stare with pinch-lipped suspicion. A sight that kindled a fire in Amicia's cheeks and sent her gaze fleeing to restlessly roam the solar.

The age-darkened wainscoting was clean, scrubbed free of soot from the smoking hearth. The walls, stretching to the distant rafters, were newly whitewashed. The clean smell of lime lingered in the air. Amicia's gaze sharpened. The rushes strewing the oak-beamed floor were new and crisp and sprinkled with herbs that smelled of mint and sweet flag and lavender. The candles, flickering in wall niches and dripping from wall brackets and iron candlesticks, were all of fragrant beeswax. All other rooms, the Great Chamber opposite the thick spine wall and the Great Hall below, made do with resin torches, cresset lamps, and pungent tallow candles. In chamber and hall, the rushes were old and dry and trampled to dust and the walls were blackened by smoke. Surely this was a thing to be set aright. Amicia quickened to this evidence of the need for her skills and herself.

Yet there was one who should have seen to such work. Lady Sybilla's duty this was. A duty she obviously had no taste for, was her own comfort not at risk. Mayhap that was why all was amiss below and the Great Hall as odorous as a midden heap deep with the kitchen's offal.

At Holmby—the vision of Sister Catherine's stern finger awagging gave birth to a rush of grief—Amicia was taught there was no shame greater than poor housewifery. Did she live in the poorest of circumstance in the solar, all else need come first. It was honor to her lord and herself to see that he and his were housed and fed and bedded as befitted their state. It was her duty as lady. It could be her way to make her own place among these who . . . despised her.

*In time, if you are not another such as your father, my people will see it. They are kind and good, and respond to kindness and goodness.* Tristan's words returned to comfort her.

Time. She would have that. Weeping and wailing would gain her nothing. Wishing that all was different would not change the fact that she was hated by all in this place and might never be accepted as their lady. Only she could change their hate to respect, if not love, and only in time.

She dared not struggle to assume her rightful place. That would put spurs to their resentment. Nay, instead, she must move among them with her head high. She must look ahead to life, no matter how bleak the years appeared now. She must find some task that would keep her hands and mind busy, else she would surely go mad. Did she ever hope to have a place here, she must make her own, one small step at the time.

Only one here could help her, if she would. Amicia moved rapidly toward the turret stair, her steps as firm and sure as her resolve. Behind her the pad of her warden's feet rustled across the rushes.

"My lady." Odo leaped to his feet, his knife in one hand, a block of whittled wood in the other.

"Rest this while." Amicia hurried passed.

Dissipating puffballs of dust—rising with her every light footfall— followed her down the rows of trestle tables covered with dirty linens and the remains of the morning meal. Acrid resin torches and the odor of cast-off food rotting in the rushes flared her nostrils and hurried her steps to the hearth, where Lady Sybilla sat in a high-backed chair, her feet propped atop a yawning hound. Aimery was hovering, as ever. His earlier worry and fearfulness had been replaced by the sagging appearance of a chastised child. His chin resting on his forest-green tunic, he dug a toe in the rushes, unearthing a half-gnawed bone.

"You are a fool!" Lady Sybilla's hiss traveled to Amicia. "He has a strong arm, well used by the Earl of Gascony. With that arm goes the hottest head the length and breadth of this land, and a passion for honor as mad as your father's and Tristan's. Does he return from France to find Lady Guinella with child, he will roar before this gate, demanding your head!"

Amicia faltered. This was no time to be intruding. She began to turn away.

"I will not have my plans set amiss by your wenching!" Lady Sybilla's low tones sharpened, stopping Amicia.

Wenching? Gentle Aimery and Lady Guinella? Surely that shrew-tongued lady led him astray, and not the other way. Amicia stared at his drooping head and pouting lower lip, and tried to imagine him indulging in adulterous intrigue. It stretched her imagination to the snapping point to see him in amorous, flirtatious play, whereas the sight of Tristan so engaged came all too easily. Tristan had made her own body a stranger to her, and then so easily set her aside. His needs were many and strong. They would not go unattended while she slept in her lonely bed. Why should that thought bring this deep gouging pain?

Aimery rocked his barrel-chested body from side to side, his swarthy face sallow above his saffron surcoat. His dark eyes slid away from his mother, touched Amicia, and widened. He fanned a gesture of silence to Lady Sybilla and a smile sprang to his mouth. A smile whose forced and false twisting reminded Amicia that she listened where she should not.

"I—I was looking for Lady Sybilla," she stuttered, heat scalding her cheeks.

"Join us." He walked toward her with outstretched hand, his thick legs pumping the embroidered skirt of his surcoat.

Unable to meet his uneasy stare, she looked at his thick hand with spatulate fingers. "If I am intruding—"

"An intrusion that is welcome, as you no doubt have guessed," he said smoothly.

A glance askance caught a twitch of strain in his smile. Her discomfort heightened. The last thing she wanted was to be caught in a battle of wills between mother and son, but there was no graceful way to retreat. Her hand climbed to rest atop his, her laggard steps matching his to the hearth.

"I fear she has learned the worst of me," he admitted to his mother in his light singsong. "Sin it might be, little sister, but I cannot resist a ready wench. Can you forgive this middling weakness of mine?"

"Do not plague her, Aimery."

The sharp warning pulled Amicia's gaze from the dusty rushes to dart from mother to son. Their rich spice-brown eyes were locked with expressions more like foes than kin. Mayhap it was so, if Lady Sybilla's *plan* was an advantageous marriage and he was threatening it with his wenching.

"You must learn to do as I do, Amicia, and ignore Aimery when these fey moods are upon him." Lady Sybilla wrenched her gaze from her son. "Sit, child." Her white hand lazily waved at the canopied chair reserved for the lord. "I hope you have suffered no ill-effect from your . . . talk with Tristan. I fear he has ever been hot of head and short of temper. Though I must admit, never have I seen a woman rouse his ire as you have. I am curious. What did you say to him?"

Amicia perched atop the thick velvet cushion, acutely aware of the current of tension tautening between Aimery and his mother. "I fear . . ." she began, her voice fading beneath the stunning realization of the folly she had committed. Anger and fear had truly driven her beyond all sense. The wonder was that Tristan had not choked her to silence as Odo had said. "I fear I questioned his honor, my lady."

"His honor?" Lady Sybilla's thin brows scaled her forehead. "You are braver than I, child. The men of Eden are mad for honor. They hew to it through trial and travail at the risk of their heads and lands. They clasp it to their breasts as a lover to hold above their wives and offspring." Her voice thinned, becoming brittle and bitter. "No pain, no loss is too great can they cling to their honor. It is beyond my ken."

"And mine, my lady." Amicia's voice hardened at thought of Mother Margaret suffering for Robert of Eden's honor. Did Lady Sybilla know of the woman her husband had once loved? "Too often the cost of a man's honor is a woman's pain."

"So it is, child." Lady Sybilla's cool gaze warmed with the balm of approval. "How wise you are for one so young. I look forward to your company through the long winter to come."

"And I yours, my lady," Amicia said softly, wondering how that balm of approval could leave her so untouched. Her gaze wandered the woman's perfect features, her milk-white brow and large eyes and small mouth. She should warm to this kindness, but somehow she could not.

"You were looking for me, child. How may I help you?"

Her dainty mouth tilted in a smile that appeared to Amicia more of a smirk. Truly, she was evil-hearted to think it so when Lady Sybilla was being kindness itself! Shame lowered her eyes. "I hope I may help you, my lady. Will you allow me to ease you of some of your burdens?"

"Burdens?"

"Ay, my lady. There is much to do in a keep such as this, and I am unused to idleness. Surely, I could relieve you of much that has grown wearisome for you."

"So"—her smile thinned—"you wish to assume your place as lady here."

Amicia's blue eyes met hers squarely. "My lady, I am naught but the seal to an oath made by my father and your son to Earl Simon. I am not and I may never be the true lady of this keep. You are that, while I am a stranger hated by all. But, my lady''—she leaned forward, urgency in her voice and in the hands clasping prayerfully together—''I cannot be ever idle. I will go mad with naught to do. I beg of you, give me those tasks that are wearisome for you. I will gladly do them, best as I may.''

''Poor child.'' Lady Sybilla leaned to place an icy hand atop Amicia's, a comforting gesture at jarring odds with the shrewd gleam in her eyes. ''Gladly would I yield to you my place as lady of this keep. It is your right to have it, but my son has given an order that I cannot disobey.''

''Your son?''

''Ay. Tristan. Alas, was ever a woman burdened with a more ungrateful son!'' She leaned back and heaved a forlorn sigh.

Amicia squelched the budding thought that her words and sigh lacked sincerity.

''He cannot see what you, sweet child, have seen so quickly. That I grow weary and would gladly yield my place.''

''But, my lady, it is the way of things that you should rest while I take up these endless tasks. Can you not make him see—''

''Nay, child. I fear he gives no thought to any comfort, but his own. He has given me order that all should not come awry while you are learning the ways of the keep and folk within it. I am to keep the household keys in my possession, and all is to continue as it has been.''

''I see,'' Amicia sighed amid the ashes of her hopes. How would she fill the emptiness of her days with naught to do and none but Odo to talk to? How could Tristan be so cruel!

''Fret not, child. All is not lost,'' Lady Sybilla said. ''My son has given many an order that I have found a way around. Together, you and I may find a solution to this boggle.''

Amicia's melancholy eyes climbed from her lap. ''My lady, if you can give me aid in this, I will be forever in your debt.''

''Speak not of debt between us, child. You are my

daughter-by-marriage and so daughter to me, a welcome change from these ill-bred sons of mine." She leaned back in her chair, her eyes narrowed and sly. "Let us see what we can do. Do you know the ordering of kitchens and cooks?"

"Ay, my lady," Amicia said eagerly. "I have been trained well in all tasks that would fall my lot."

"Then from this day, you will have charge of that task. Together, we will show that son of mine that you can do all to his liking. Then I may begin my well-earned rest."

"My lady, I thank you with all of my heart. Never can I repay this kindness, though I give oath that I will try." Prodded by shame at her distrust, Amicia leaped from her chair and knelt before her mother-by-marriage, the woman who was acting as true mother to her. She took Lady Sybilla's icy hand in hers and pressed a kiss to the back, her heart full to overflowing with gratitude and hope.

"There, there, child. No need is there for this. I but give to you what is your right. Now, hurry about your task."

"Ay, my lady," Amicia sang. Rising lightly to her feet, she rushed away in a flurry of skirts. "Odo!"

"My lady"—he stood, thrusting his dagger into its sheath—"you are as bright as the sun of a sudden. What brings this smile to your mouth?"

"Lady Sybilla! She has been kindness—"

"Lady Sybilla? What has *that one* done?" he asked with withering scorn, a scowl puckering the scars on his brow.

Amicia's smile ebbed beneath the surge of persistent doubts. "Why do you frown so? She has given me a much-needed task at the risk of angering my lord—"

"How do you know this?"

"She told me." Amicia's mistrust returned full force. She told herself the mistrust was baseless, that none could have been kinder to her, but it remained to chafe her with uncertainty.

"Ah, she told you." He jutted his jaw and folded his arms over his chest. "I vow they kept you innocent as a babe in the priory! *That one*"—he jerked his head toward the hearth—"is not to be trusted. Does she tell you that the sun has risen in the morn, you should look to see that it has! She is so filled with hate, she spits lies for the pleasure of it.''

Lies? Like the lies she told of Tristan? Amicia wondered. *He had a vicious temper and a heavy hand,* Lady Sybilla had said. *It was needful to show him a meek face, lest he be provoked. His lust drives him like a savage beast.*

All lies! A temper. Ay, he had that, though no heavy hand to enforce his will. If ever he was going to strike her, he would have done it when she questioned his honor. As for his lust driving him, it did. But no savage beast was he. Nay, instead he was gentle. So gentle . . .

Amicia's fingers curled around the scratchy wool covering Odo's thick forearm. ''You must tell me what you know of her that I may not set my neck in any noose she hangs for my lord.''

He looked away, discomfort shadowing his face. ''I can only tell you to put no trust in her. Tell her naught of what is in your heart or your thoughts, and do not cross her, my lady. She makes a deadlier enemy than your father.''

A chill slithered across Amicia's shoulders. Odo was refusing to tell her more. Odo, who gave warning where he could . . . where it did not conflict with his loyalty to her father.

Her father and Lady Sybilla. The pair cavorted through her mind like gleemen in hall. Her father and Lady Sybilla, whispering in the window recess under the watchful eye of Aimery. She had given no thought to it when she saw them, but now she remembered all too clearly the unshrouded urgency in their faces. What unholy alliance had they formed? They shared naught—but their hatred of Tristan.

They joined to destroy him! Had Amicia been privy to their council, she could not be more certain. She would go to Tristan! She would tell him she was no willing part of their plans. She . . .

The fire for action dwindled to embers. She could do neither. She was her father's daughter, and so suspect in Tristan's eyes. She was a woman, and he thought women were creatures with no understanding of a man's honor. Without his trust, naught could she do.

Had he really given order that all should not come awry while she was learning the ways of the keep and the folk within it? Or was that another of Lady Sybilla's lies?

She could not go to Tristan nor expect truth from his mother. She must order the kitchens, the cooks, and the meals, despite her fear that she was being used for some unseen plan.

# Chapter 11

Lady Sybilla might take joy in seeing Tristan vexed by chaos at table, though it seemed to Amicia a childish spite. One that she would thwart, if she could. Just as she would thwart any deed more dangerous to him, could she see the way. Whether he wished it or not, he was husband to her in the eyes of God and man. She had been given oath to cleave unto him, and that oath could not be taken lightly. However little faith he put in a woman's honor, hers was as important to her as his to him.

Determination squaring her shoulders, Amicia crossed the lively ward with her two companions, purse-lipped Enid and her hostility. Ripples of silence spreading in her wake left no hope that she would be allowed to rule with love and kindness. She would meet with resentment and hate and, mayhap, a sullen resistance to following her orders.

At the scullery adjacent to the wattle-and-daub kitchen, a spindle-shanked lad sand-scoured an iron pot and followed a buxom maid with a lovelorn gaze. The maid scrubbed pottery with a grimy washclout and flirted with the fletcher, whose attention was sorely divided between the laughing maid and the goose honking a protest at the loss of her best feathers. Hard by was a stump, brown with dried blood; at its foot, trussed hens were clucking. The earth all about was strewn with innards and offal and swarms of flies, a sight that offended Amicia's nostrils as

141

well as her sense of order. Such would never be allowed at Holmby—nor would it be allowed longer here.

Amicia swept through the kitchen door with the swish of the washclout, the gritty scouring of sand, and the honking of the goose trailing her.

She stood in the square of light spilling through the door, staring in dismay. Pots dangling from hooks were caked with burned-on tallow. If ever the filthy tables had been sand-scoured, it was long, long ago. Yellowing kale leaves, parsnip tops, bones, and innards strewed the earthen floor. Rose hips browned in a withy basket. Haws dried to husks in another. A scullion beating a loaf of sugar with a mallet sent chunks in all directions. Almond milk scorched atop the iron grate over the center hearth and a haunch of venison burned on the spit, unturned by the plump scullion leaping after flying chunks of sugar.

How right stern Sister Catherine had been. A lax lady bred lax servants. There was no need for her to summon icy arrogance; it came on a rush of anger at the filth and waste. "Who, among you lack-witted wastrels, is cook?" her sharpened voice cleaved the babble as deftly as a knife through butter.

A red-faced rascal, triple-chinned and paunch-bellied, bestirred himself from his stool and set aside a bowl of hanoney. Wiping pudgy fingers on his tunic, he ambled toward her. "I am Thomas the Cook, *lady*," he used her title as if a serving maid had taken on airs above herself.

A petty tyrant as little liked by these as she, Amicia thought and would have wagered all she owned on her quick summation. He had been too long without the steadying hand of the lady. He would respect nothing and no one, but he *would* be bent to a will stronger than his. Her chin firmed and tilted up, her cold gaze sliding to the mound of his belly and back up to his slitted eyes. "More like Thomas the Glutton. You stink of onions and idleness."

The chirping laugh of a scullion, quickly stifled, sent the cook's head swinging around like a dog-baited bear before it swung back to jut at her. "The lord has given no complaint and it is him I answer to."

"Nay, Thomas the Cook. From this day, you answer to me."

"Bellay's get." He spat on the floor at her feet.

Amicia went cold as a winter morning's sleet. She expected hatred and resentment, but not arrant insolence and threat. No villein would dare such an act, did he not know himself secure from the lord's vengeance. And the promise of that vengeance, where love did not rule, was the only surety of obedience. Did all here know their lord had set her from him, and so believe that he would not come to her aid?

Yet Tristan had said her honor became his when they wed. This insult was the same as if directed at him. She could not believe he would allow it to pass unavenged—unless he, as these, would delight in seeing her shamed. And that was what would happen here, she feared. Could she not bend Thomas the Cook to her will, she would be forced to retreat like a craven hound with its tail between its legs.

"My lady, have you a problem here?"

Odo's rough voice came to Amicia like the song of angels. He dallied in the doorway like a sluggard, his shoulder canted against the frame and his knife drawn. The tip rested against one callused finger, spears of light stabbing from the honed edge.

"You were to await me in the Guard Hall."

"I thought you might have need of me." His gray eye dropped to the blade twisting slowly on the pivot of his finger. "Shall I slit his throat for you?"

The question was so casually spoken Amicia was not sure it was meant in earnest. Thomas the Cook had no such reservations. He gobbled and choked, as if he swallowed his tongue. "My lady," he bleated, and sank to his knees at her feet. "Do not set him upon me! I beg of you, my lady!"

"I have no . . ." The words *such intent* died on her lips. He would see kindness as weakness. Even a stronger will would not rule him here where he had worked his own way for too long. Only fear would do. "I have no reason not to. You have offered me insult here . . . in my own keep," she emphasized the last and saw his terror check with a spark of anger. "Odo!"

Every step her man made widened the cook's round

raisin eyes until they bulged from folds of flesh. "My . . . my lady, I beg forgiveness that I have . . . have spoken rudely to you."

"It is given. You may rise," she said icily. "I will return before prime on the morrow. There will be no filth upon the tables, pots, or floor. There will be no waste such as that scullion does with the loaf of sugar. There will be none eating when they should be working. Do I find anything to my misliking, Thomas the Cook, it will go hard for you."

"Ay, my lady! All shall be as you wish, my lady!" he squawked to her retreating back.

In the gray light of prime with the sun peeking over the eastern tors, Amicia found Thomas the Cook mincing obsequiously about his cleaned and polished domain. She gave scant praise and orders for the evening meal and left with a niggling worry over the sly gleam buried deep in his small eyes.

In the gray twilight of the day, Amicia sat at table. The sly gleam had born the fruit of a meal not fit for the lowest serf's hovel. Her burning gaze resting on her slice of leathery venison, she listened to the laughter snickering across the trestle tables below. Arrant insolence and threat had yielded to mockery, and the shame of it bit deep.

Neither her position or Odo's threat had availed her. What did Thomas and these others know that she did not? No lord with any pride in his estate would allow such insult to his lady. Even Tristan, little liking her as he did, could not allow this to pass—or could he? Did he so despise her, he would allow his villeins to mock her?

While Amicia asked herself that question and shrank from an answer, Tristan dismounted at the keep steps. His mood was surly at best, for two days of hard riding and a night on the cold ground had favored him not. The reivers tracks had vanished among the rocks with no hint of their identity or purpose.

Weariness pressing at his shoulders, he climbed the steps with his belly gnawing his backbone. The nearer he came to the Great Hall the more his steps quickened. He told himself it was the ripe aroma of herring pie that sent him flying the last steps to burst into the crowded hall, but his searching gaze no sooner found Amicia on the dais than he knew he told himself a lie.

During his night away, he had lain beneath the reproachful blue of the night sky wrapped in his mantle and memories. He had tried to clutch his rage close, but felt it oozing through his fingers. Were Amicia as faithless as all women, she would have looked to her own skin and left Odo to his mercy. That she dared his wrath for her liege man's sake proved that she was not without honor, even if it was adulterated by what she called *sense*. A disturbing thought to dwell upon beneath the stars twinkling as gently as her smile. But far less disturbing than the wind whispering through the beeches, *What will you leave me to call my own, Tristan?* Even less disturbing than his reply murmuring through a rocky crevice, *Naught. I would have it all and call it mine*.

He watched Amicia now, sitting so still at the lord's table across the length of the hall, and studied her features one by one: small determined chin, rose-hued defenseless mouth, and downcast eyes. And while he looked his hungry fill, the ease came stealing. His surly mood vanished. His mouth longed to smile. Peace draped his heart like a sheer sarcenet veil, whose shimmering folds parted for a soul-searing glimpse of the wondrous world he might have known, if only . . .

If only. Words for minstrel's songs and weak-kneed wenches. He was a man firmly rooted in what was, not what might have been. The surly mood claimed him once more, darkening his brow.

"My lord!" Giles beckoned him with a thumbless hand.

Moving along an aisle between trestle tables, Tristan caught the eye of his kennel-ward, a man ever ready to give the last detail of the latest litter of pups, but all he got was a weak grin before the man stuffed his nose in his bowl. Tristan frowned and listened to the rumble of voices with laughter scattered here and there. Laughter with an edge of malice to it.

"Giles"—he thumped his man on the back and peered over his shoulder into a full bowl—"your potage goes awasting. Are you sickening of a fever?"

"Nay, my lord. I hunger, but this swill I cannot eat."

"Does Thomas the Cook—"

"Nay, my lord. Our new *lady* has taken over the ordering of the kitchen, and this"—he waved a hand over the bowl— "is what we are served. It swims in tallow and, if ever there was a gobbet of meat in it, I cannot find it. Does she seek to weaken us by starvation, so that her father—"

"Enough, Giles! She is your lady," Tristan barked, and walked away, scanning the close-packed tables. Of all the places for Amicia to begin her duties, why did she choose the kitchen? Thomas the Cook was hand in glove with Lady Sybilla, as cocksure and insolent as any villein dared to be.

He found Enid watching him and shifted his eyes to the garderobe passage. Stopping to speak to his farrier about a new shoe for Vainqueur, he marked every moment until the serving woman had been gone for some time.

In the dank passageway, he came upon her. "What goes here, Enid? Why did you not warn my lady that the kitchen was no place to begin her duties?"

"I had no chance, my lord. Lady Sybilla's fine hand stirred this brew."

"I should have expected some such from her." Tristan set a shoulder to the stone wall and folded his thick arms across his chest. "Tell me what has passed that I might be forewarned of the trouble she plots."

Enid rapidly recounted all that occurred. Tristan listened carefully, without interruption, though his eyes narrowed and a low oath hissed beneath his breath when she told of Thomas the Cook's spitting at Amicia's feet.

"I vow, I could hardly believe the sight of my eyes, so clean the kitchen was before prime this morn. I fear, I should have known he was up to no good. Thomas is not so bright that he can remember a thing long, even fear. He chose to do this so that all could see her humbled in open hall. My lord, what will you do?"

"Naught," Tristan said grimly.

"But, my lord, all will laugh behind her back and some to her face. You must—"

"I must not. It is for her good as well as my own that I

take no part in this,'' he said, wondering at Enid's determination to see Amicia protected in this.

''But, my lord—''

''Fret not for her, Enid.'' A humorless smile twisted his mouth. ''Another will take this charge where I cannot.''

''Odo? My lord, you cannot allow it! You did not hear him. I vow I went cold as the winter's snow. My lord, he will do it!''

''Nay, Enid. He will not endanger her life or place her by slaying Thomas, though he may give him a fright he will not soon forget.'' The humorless smile vanished and a deadly look hardened his face. ''And, if ever I am free to do as I will, Thomas the Cook will live long to regret his insolence to my lady.''

That oath given, he made his way to the dais. A hush descended on the hall. Tension sharpened the air. At his approach, Amicia rose from her seat. Tristan looked into the strained and shamed blue of her gaze and locked his throat to keep from roaring indiscriminately for heads to roll. A hard, hating look slashed at his mother, sitting beyond Aimery and watching all with her stingy smile.

''My lord, you are welcome.''

The greeting was so soft Tristan bent to listen and breathed deep of the scents of sandalwood and woman. Scents that added the pungence of desire to his turmoil. If only they were alone and all different . . . His own futility ate at him.

''I hope you found success in your faring after the reivers,'' Amicia breathed into the awkward silence.

Suspicion pierced the compassion that tugged at his heart. ''How did you know I was after reivers, my lady?''

She stared for a moment, as though she felt that suspicion as keenly as he. ''Enid got it from a serving maid, who got it from the wardcorne, who got it from the gate-guard's son. You are the head and heart of this keep, my lord. Where you go, eyes and ears follow.''

There was no complaint in the silvery cadence of her voice, but Tristan felt he had been gently reprimanded, and rightly so. Had he not growled more times than he could remember that his least sneeze was fodder for gossip? An apology rose to his lips and froze at sight of his mother's smile.

Amicia's luminous gaze moved across his face with a touch as palpable as her hand. Her eyes warmed with a look of such concern that Tristan could almost believe she worried over him.

"You look wearied unto death, my lord," she said softly. "Come, sit and rest . . . and eat. You must be sharp-set, though I fear there is little here to tempt any but those empty of belly."

She beckoned to Guy of Lancasterdale and the small page came to her eagerly, his face shining with the adoration usually reserved for saints in chapel. "Guy, go above and order water heated that my lord may bathe when he is ready. Find Enid and tell her to look in my chest. There is a leather pouch tied in a strand of red wool. In it are soothing herbs. Take it to my lord's chamber that he may use them in his bath."

Tristan listened to those orders given for his good. The first given by a lady in this keep of his. He caught a broader glimpse of the wondrous world that might have been, and suffered a fierce longing for the haven of peace it promised.

"My lord?"

The fleeting touch of her fingers on his arm yanked him from his maunderings with a start. A touch that burned beneath the thickness of his sleeve, searing him like a brand. He mumbled a word and saw Amicia to her chair. So much he could do beneath his mother's eye. It was the impersonal courtesy of any lord to a lady. But the word of comfort he yearned to give must remain forever unspoken.

He took his seat in the full glare of his watchful villeins, bathed his hands in the basin held by his squire and dried them. A deep breath and he turned to the plate he shared with Amicia. Upon it lay a single slice of leathery venison and a wedge of herring pie with a single bite gone.

"You do not hunger, my lady?" he asked, and heard a low ripple of laughter roll through the hall. Her pale face colored, and the dark eyes that flickered toward him were filled with a bitter shame that hardened his vow to see Thomas the Cook get his just reward.

"Nay, my lord," she whispered, and lowered her head.

Tristan beckoned his squire to fill his half of their plate and took a spoon to his pie, aware of the silence, more acute now, as if all awaited his first bite. Steeling himself, he slipped the spoon in his mouth and out, leaving the pie to bite his tongue with an excess of ginger and cinnamon. His nostrils flared. He braved the grind of his teeth through near raw crust and chewy, salty herring. Another grind and he swallowed, his eyes watering and his hands groping for the cup of wine. A long draught sluiced down his salt-and-spice-coated throat, and his belly gnawed his backbone, not in hunger, but in protest. The cup thumped to the table, his hand clenched around it, while a frosty stare raked the tables below and forced rows of eyes to drop to their bowls.

He set to with a will, and heard a concerted sigh of disappointment sing through the hall. Good and kind, his people were, he brooded. So he had told her, though he could see no evidence of it now. They waited like slavering louts at a dog baiting, while she sat in silent dignity with never a complaint voiced. Stolidly chewing his way through his meal, he awaited the moment his mother would spit her sticky skein to ensnare him. His last draft of wine swallowed, he reached for an apple . . .

"We have here a meal not fit for the lowest serf's hovel," Lady Sybilla's voice rang out, bringing all to the thin-lipped silence of agreement. "You must take issue with Thomas, Tristan. I fear he has no liking for following the orders of your lady. Surely you will not allow her to be humbled so in open hall."

Expecting this as he had, Tristan was still unprepared. If he rose to Amicia's aid, his mother would know he gave a care to his wife and would use her against him. If he did not, Amicia would be hurt and might turn against him, if she had not already. A fine brew that bitch had stirred, and him with no way to win, no matter what he did. Always, always, it was the same.

His hand clenching the weapon of the apple, he leaned back in his chair. He dared not speak with the bile rising in his throat, so he pulled his knife from its sheath and began paring thin strips as red as the haze of rage and frustration that clouded his vision. When sure he could act as he must, he slanted an indifferent gaze Amicia's way.

"I have no time for the trifling day-to-day care of the household, nor for enforcing her will upon my servants," he said, as if she were not sitting there beside him and he not acutely aware that the last vestige of color was fleeing her face. "If she cannot see to her duties, mayhap all should be left in your care, my lady." He set the apple aside and thrust back his chair, rising. "I care not who sees to the ordering of all here so long as I am not discomforted by it."

His mother's face sagged with disappointment, and Tristan knew that, whatever the cost, he had chosen the better of the two evils she offered. Mad as she was, she plotted well and wisely. She wasted no effort in lashing out at any that she could not use to hurt him. Amicia would be safe now.

He started to turn away, but a movement caught his attention—Amicia's face tilting up. Tristan stared into her eyes, blue bruises battered into the pallor of her face. A swift, unexpected, unwanted pain knifed through him. He wrenched his eyes from her and spun on a heel, leaving the dais and traversing the length of the silent hall.

The pain lingered in the region of his heart. He assured himself it was his belly's revolt at the meal forced into it. The pain persisted, and he told himself he misliked seeing any small, weak thing hurt apurpose.

At the foot of the hall Odo sat alone, as if a leper with bells clapping. There was a curious expression in his silvery gray eye. Had Tristan given thought to Amicia's liege man, he would have expected a threat to glare its promise of vengeance. What he saw was understanding and approval, each laying a soothing balm over his pain. If Odo could feel so, then he knew much of what passed here, and so could offer more aid to Amicia.

Tristan sketched a nod of greeting, hoping the man would read into it his sanction to take the action he could not.

On a day long ago, when burgeoning spring urged her to the wayward thoughts of innocent youth, Amicia lay upon the greening grass of the mountain vale and dreamed of the day she would be the lady of a keep of her own. She dreamed of a knight, bold and brave. She looked ahead to a life where she would love and be loved, need and be needed. The memory of that day came to her now. A bittersweet memory rising like a ghost from the ashes of that dream.

"An ungrateful wretch, my son is," Lady Sybilla's low voice whispered unpleasantly. "Ever has he been heedless of others and given no thought to any comfort, save his own. Fear not. I will summon Thomas on the morrow and see that he heeds your rule."

Amicia murmured something appropriate, though what it was, she could not have said. Her blue gaze followed Tristan across the width of the hall. He paused at the entry to the turret stair, as if he might look back. If he did, would she see in his eyes a mockery to match that of his retainers?

"What man was ever cursed with a brother so thoughtless," Aimery lilted and stroked her hand. "Much have I forgiven him, but this I cannot."

Amicia, repulsed by his insinuating touch, detached her hand from his hot grasp. She waited for Tristan to turn. She waited for a glimpse of an answer in his wintry gaze, but he plunged into the darkness and vanished, abandoning her to the ardent comforting of his mother and brother.

# Chapter 12

The moon was a sliver of white hanging low on the horizon when the first inhuman scream shattered the peace of the night. Guards patrolling the parapet atop the keep leaped to the square-toothed battlements to peer into the shadow-draped ward. Guards patrolling the curtain wall turned white-eyed stares from the threat of an enemy without to the threat of one within. The second scream scrabbled aloft, and the master-at-arms bolted from his pallet with a bellow that roused the guard room. Rush lights winked in the hovels crowded around the kitchen and bake-house tower. Torches sped across the dark ward like falling stars streaking through the sky, all converging on the source of the screaming.

In the Lord's Hall, Tristan left the window seat, where he had kept vigil through the night. A vengeful smile tilted the corners of his mouth and lit his eyes with the devil's own satisfaction. Thomas the Cook would be long in giving insult to his lady again. Would that he had been the one to slip from shadow to shadow with the stealth of a Scots reiver.

The noise, lightly penetrating the window slits, did not disturb the retainers sleeping on pallets against the walls. Snores, snufflings, and restless shiftings accompanied Tristan to the hearth, where he knelt to stoke the fire. The warmth was welcome after his chilly vigil, as welcome as the knowledge that Odo had made it safely back to the Guard

Hall before the alarm was sounded. Now there was naught to do but wait and see if he was as wily as Tristan thought he was. If so, Amicia would be safe here, and protected, even if it was not by his own hand.

His own hand. Tristan set the poker aside and curled his hand into a fist, staring at the back liberally coated with hair that blazed as red as the fire. The red of his wild Scot grandfather's hair, so his mother had told him as a child, when she spoke to him at all. The red that had set her against him from the day of his birth.

Unfurling his fingers, he stared at his palm. Callused by the quatrefoil hilt of his sword, it was lean and hard and strong. It had served him well in battle; but for all the good it did him now, it might as well be as thumbless as Giles's hands. What use was he to any here, when he could not raise this hand in defense as he was pledged to do. His palm settled on his cross-gartered knee, scrubbing across rough leather thongs and soft close-woven wool in a vain effort to scrub the feeling of worthlessness away.

He stood slowly, his reluctant gaze probing the darkness swallowing the rafters. What was this nagging ache he had not known before Amicia came? He shifted uneasily, one hand kneading the thick column of his nape. Was Enid right? Was there a first time for everything under the sun? Even his bewitchment by the soft lips of this one woman? He wanted . . . what?

Love? his heart whispered.

Fool, have you learned nothing? his mind railed.

Love! he scoffed bitterly. What woman was capable of giving it? None that he had known. He would be fortunate did she not turn to his mother and conspire against him.

The mutter of myriad voices flowed from the turret stair at the far corner of the Great Hall, drawing Tristan's wary gaze. He must be careful to show none of the revulsion he felt for Thomas, none of the sympathy he felt for Odo. None must know this was done with his sanction, else all would be for naught.

"My lord!" Rolf, his master-at-arms hurried ahead, trailed by two guards roughly yanking Odo along. Behind them, butcher, baker, scullions, and grooms poured across the Great Hall, through the arcaded spine wall, and into the Lord's Hall, ringing Tristan about like wolves slavering for blood.

He assumed a look of surprise and lifted an arm to point a finger at Odo. "Why is my lady's man bloodied and beaten and trussed like swine for butchering?"

Rolf slapped a hand to the hilt of his sword and spit upon the rushes. "I fear we have near seen murder done this night. The lady's man has slit Thomas the Cook's throat."

Misgiving flared in the questioning gaze that slid to Odo. A misgiving that was allayed by the twinkle in that unwinking gray eye.

Rolf's horny fist jabbed a goggling scullion's thin chest. "Stand aside that my men may pass!"

The muttering crowd parted. Two guards stumbled beneath the cook's heavy weight, unsupported by the thick legs that wobbled and wandered under him.

Tristan studied the filthy tunic pulling tight across Thomas's heaving paunch, then angled a cool look at his master-at-arms. "Surely a small slit, Rolf. I see no blood upon him."

"Ay"—his square face, leathery and rough-hewn, grimaced with a hardened soldier's disgust—"for all his womanish screeching, you would think worse was done."

Thomas the Cook tumbled to the rushes at Tristan's wide-braced feet, though whether he tumbled voluntarily or was heaved there by the panting guards was in question. Rolling raisin eyes fastened on the cold blue of his lord's.

"Never will I sleep peacefully again! Waking to that hand over my mouth and the knife at my throat!" Thomas shuddered and raised his pasty pudding face. "Look what he did to me!"

He canted the ball of his head on his thick neck, revealing a thin red line etched from the bulbous lobe of one ear to the bulbous lobe of the other, so shallow it bled no more than a drop.

Tristan's lips twitched. Resisting the urge to look at Odo, he sucked in a corner of his mouth and chewed mercilessly. Had he given order of his own, he could not have chosen a vengeance more fit. Could he save Odo from this none would risk his wrath in fear his knife would

bite deeper the next time. None would insult Amicia as
this one had done. All impulse to laugh died.

"A vicious act, indeed, Thomas," he intoned dryly.

"Ay, my lord!" The cook bobbed his head, oblivious to
both Tristan's sarcasm and the deadly glitter in his eyes.
"He did it and your lady gave him order! When the guard
brings her down—"

"Guard?" Tristan's hot eyes stabbed at Rolf.

"Ay, my lord. If she is behind this—"

"You gave order to have my lady brought from the
solar?" Tristan growled.

Silence scuttled to the outer edges of the gaping crowd.
Rolf stretched his corded neck, as if he could feel
fingers digging into his throat. "I thought—"

"You do not think, Rolf! You obey my orders!"

"Ay, my lord!" The master-at-arms snapped straight.

"Send a man to—"

A noise, coming from the entrance to the near turret
stair, snapped Tristan's head around. The furied blaze of
his eyes hewed a path through the crowd like a scyth
through wheat. Amicia, flanked by guards, each with a
grip on her arms, was roughly hauled forward. Her sleep-
mussed plait, thick as Tristan's wrist, draped across her
shoulder and bounced against her knees. Her feet, bare and
small as a child's, peeked from the skewed hem of her
robe, barely skimming the floor. Her face was so pale it
had a bluish cast and whitened lips. But it was her eyes—so
big and confused and frightened they seemed to swallow
her whole face—that struck sparks of rage in Tristan.

Reason murmured, let it go, leave it alone. What better
proof could Lady Sybilla have that you give no care to
your wife. Yet, even as he thought it, he was roaring,
"Unhand my wife!"

The guards' faces, pink with youth and health and exertion, slackened with astonishment. Their grips loosened
and they stutter-stepped backward.

His roar echoing around the hall, Tristan stared into
Amicia's eyes, which stared up at him as if she had
stumbled upon Satan himself. Acutely aware of the ears
straining to hear, more acutely aware that he should not,
he still found himself bending closer to her and his lips

moving against his will, "This was done by no order of mine."

No order of his? Amicia stared up at him, searching for truth; searching for the reason she was pulled from her sleepless bed and hauled to him before the cock could crow the morning's awakening; searching for the reason the guards laughed as they yanked her down the stairs and promised she would regret what she had done—though what it was, they would not say. Her tongue eased out to wet the surface of her lips.

"What passes here, my lord?" she asked, as aware as he of the silent hostility ringing them about, but unable to tear her eyes from his frowning features. She watched every shifting of muscle beneath his taut skin, every flicker of emotion in the blue wells of his eyes, and what she saw confused her all the more. Regret, pain, anger, frustration— all jumbled together like potherbs in potage, and none to give her warning of what was happening. Could she believe him when he said this was by no order of his? Distrust gathered in faint lines between her brows and quivered across the velvety fullness of her lower lip.

Distrust. No more than Tristan expected; so much less than he wanted. He drew himself up to his full imposing height. "Odo has been accused of slitting Thomas the Cook's throat."

Amicia's eyes widened. The hostility pressing about her took on a new breadth—the turgid heat of bloodlust. Her knees trembled and folded beneath her.

Tristan swept her into his arms and strode to the cano-pied chair. "Wine for my lady!" he bellowed in a voice that brooked no slackness, and sent his buttler leaping a foot from the floor and whirling in midair to race away on winged feet.

Amicia, settled on the velvet cushioned seat with Tristan kneeling before her, tried to gather her scattered thoughts into some semblance of order. None could save Odo but Tristan, who had shown so recently as the night past that he would lift not a finger to aid her or hers.

"Odo would not, my lord. I know him well, he would not," she whispered, and silently prayed she was right.

Tristan, frightened by her pallor, lifted one small cold

hand and began to chafe it. She winced. He turned it palm up and stared at the bleeding patches scraped of skin. "What happened here?" he asked hoarsely, dully aware that his temples were throbbing and his temper rising. His effort to appear untouched by her plight was dissolving rapidly.

"Naught of import, my lord." Her eyes clung to him, revealing the desperation that scoured fear away. "Odo—"

"It is of import to me."

Scraped hands? Of import to him? When Odo's life was at stake? She studied the strong fingers circling her wrists and saw the light flickering like fire across the whorls of hair on his knuckles. "I—I fell on the stair. I was not fast enough—"

"Rolf!" Tristan barked, and shot up. "I want those two"—his pointing finger unerringly found the two guards, huddled together like sheep in a fold—"put in the dungeon now!"

Amicia gaped, her delicate jaw adroop. Were there any who could understand the man! Up and down he went, like a child's merry-totter! He could shame her before all in hall with his indifference, but a scraping of her hands was cause to set his guards in the dungeon!

"My lord, they but followed my orders." Rolf stepped forward to defend his men—and a jiggling lump crawled across the rushes to root against the back of his legs.

"Do you wish to join them?" Tristan's voice cut like a winter wind. "No lady will be mistreated in my keep!"

It was not her he defended, but all ladies through her. Ignoring a twinge of sorrow, Amicia stared around Rolf's legs to get a better look at the suspiciously familiar lump. Vaguely aware of the pounding of approaching feet, she stared at the pudding face peering fearfully around the master-at-arms' knee. Thomas the Cook? He with the slit throat? She shot from her chair at the same moment the gasping buttler leaned down to offer the cup of wine. Her forearm slammed into his hand. The cup flew. Wine sprayed. Thomas the Cook squealed like a lance-struck boar and dove for Tristan's legs, wrapping his arms around them.

"My lord, I beg you! Save me! She will set him upon me!"

While Tristan rocked and righted himself, a familiar rough voice sounded a low note of warning. Amicia whirled around. Odo's bloodied mouth quirked in a gap-toothed grin and his single eye winked. A grin and a . . . surely it was a blink! Amicia stared transfixed. Had all in hall gone mad this night? Odo must know the danger he faced. And, Tristan! Offering kindness, coldness, anger, and sympathy until she was dizzy!

Behind her, Tristan knotted his fist and boxed the cook's ear. ''Unhand me, you scurrilous knave!'' he shouted over the man's abject howl.

''My man has been beaten!'' Amicia spun and settled a frown on the trembling cook. ''Beaten, and for what? I see neither bruise nor blood upon this villein!''

''Raise your head, Thomas! Show your lady the grievous wound you have been dealt,'' Tristan ordered, watching the man's raisin eyes roll in folds of flesh, as though he would refuse. ''Do it!''

''My man has been beaten for this scratch!'' Her hard gaze jerked from the cook's quivering jowls to Tristan. ''I have suffered worse at my stitching! Why are we called here?''

''We are here to find the truth, my lady,'' he said repressively. ''Thomas claims Odo cut him at your order.''

The flush of anger that had warmed Amicia's cheeks now fled them. Her eyes, prickling with tears she refused to shed, lowered to her clasped hands. The menacing grumbles of the hostile crowd assaulted her shaky defenses, threatening to topple them one by one. She was not surprised that these angry, hating people believed this of her, but Tristan? Why did it hurt so much to think he believed it?

Her chin climbed, her eyes sweeping up to boldly meet his. ''It was by no order of mine, husband,'' she said deliberately, and saw his mouth tighten, ''nor do I believe my man had any hand in this. Who saw him do this deed?''

Husband. He was that by his own oath, yet he could not raise his useless hand in her defense. He could not shield her from the hate weighting the air like a thick fog. Tristan lowered eyes holding hell's own fury. "Thomas, did you see him?"

"Nay, my lord," he whined. "It was dark. I woke with a hand over my face and the knife at my throat. He knocked me witless, slit it, and escaped."

"Did he speak that you might know his voice?"

"Nay, but I know it was him!" he shrilled. "Ask any in the kitchen! They heard him threaten me!"

"So, there is no proof that my man did it," Amicia said. "It could have been any here with spleen to vent upon you. Any who saw this as a chance to have it blamed on my man."

"Odo, what have you to say to this?" Tristan intervened.

"My lord!" Thomas screeched, his small eyes shifting between Amicia and Tristan. "He will lie! Why do you not mete out swift justice to him and her that we will all rest easier henceforth?"

"Because justice is what I would give! None in my care will be punished without proof! Odo, what do you say to this charge?"

"Only, my lord, that I was sleeping as peacefully as a babe when the guards pulled me from my pallet."

A truth split so finely it left not a hair between it and a lie. Tristan suppressed a twinge of distaste at being forced to tread the knife's edge of dishonor. How long would it be before he was so bathed in the muck of lies and deceit that he would not see dishonor when it raised its scaly head?

"My lord," Thomas wailed, and climbed on his knees to raise imploring hands, "he could have come back to the Guard Hall long before I woke!"

Revulsion for all he had been forced to do and all he might be forced to do in the future twisted Tristan's mouth in a snarl. "None here has proof that Odo did this deed, and I will not hang a man for a threat! Begone, all of you! The cock has crowed and here you are, slavering like wolves for blood when you should be about your tasks! Begone!"

The last command rolled like thunder, startling Amicia as much as it did the retainers packed around them like herring in a cask. Jaws dropped, eyes widened, spines snapped straight, and they turned to flee like rats from a fire. All but Thomas the Cook, who huddled on his knees in slack-lipped dismay. The last back with a flying-tailed tunic was vanishing through the far archway when Amicia turned to Odo to untie his hands and the cook began to gather his feet under him.

"Not you, Thomas!"

Tristan's thundering command stilled Amicia's fingers and pulled her eyes to him. His big hand slammed into the cook's round shoulder, gripped it with fingers like steel, and hauled Thomas up to grapple for the floor with the tips of his toes.

"If I am given another meal like the last, you will hang from the turret until the meat rots from your bones," Tristan growled. "A warning to all that I will suffer no man of mine to do his work ill."

"Ay, m-my lord," the cook stuttered and danced.

"I have a hunger, Thomas. Get you to the kitchen—"

"My throat, my lord. I cannot—"

"Cannot?" Tristan asked softly. "You prefer the burn of a rope to that puny sting?"

Beads of sweat popped on the oily surface of Thomas's brow. "Nay, my lord. Tell we what you want and it will be done."

Tristan stared deep into the man's bulging eyes, giving every appearance, to Amicia's curious gaze, of relishing the moment. "My lady will give you order. Lest you forget that her order is given for my comfort, I will post a warning. Look for the noose dangling from the turret, Thomas, and remember what I have said."

He thrust the shivering cook away, who wobbled, caught his balance, and rolled white-rimmed eyes at Amicia. A stare that grazed her to settle on Odo. "My lady, your order?"

Amicia's eyes, wide with surprise, met Tristan's hard stare. However the order was couched, it was done for her good. A blush of pleasure warmed her cheeks. "I will come to the kitchen later, Thomas," she said softly, her eyes never leaving Tristan's as she waited for the cook's scurrying steps to fade.

He stood in the full glow of the fire with an expression

that invited no word from her. An expression that seemed to accuse her of betraying him in some way. She moved slowly, her eyes locked with his and her head tilting back. "My lord, I thank you for what you have done for Odo and for me. I—"

"My lord," Odo interrupted, his rasping intrusion strangely neutral, as if he wanted to give warning, but dared not.

Tristan's gaze slanted toward him, angled toward the near archway, and hardened. "I assure you, my lady" —his face congealed into a cold, arrogant mist—"had I been given proof, Odo would now be hanging from the turret and you would be barred in your chamber to stay until you are too old for sly trickery—"

"Sly trickery!" she gasped, all gratitude vanishing.

"Do not think I believed you over my own man," he ground on icily. "I did no more for you than I would for any here."

"Nay, my lord." Her shoulders squared. "I would not expect you to believe me over your own man, nor would I expect more from you than any other here."

"For shame, Tristan. Your own wife, and you abuse her so," Lady Sybilla's husky scolding neared. "Come, child. Come above to the solar, where you may be treated as is your right."

Tristan's dark umber lashes quivered. Hate so thickened the air Amicia felt she was sucking it in with every breath. She looked to Odo, and saw him staring at Lady Sybilla as he might at an adder sliding silently across autumn-brown leaves. Lady Sybilla, who offered her comfort, where Tristan had offered insult. What did Odo know of them? Lady Sybilla, her father, Aimery, and Tristan: what ties of hate and deceit bound them one to the other? What deeds of yesteryear and plans for the morrow were whispered in the cold passageways of this keep?

"Come, child." Lady Sybilla draped a comforting arm around Amicia's shoulder.

It was a touch that gave her everything but comfort. It was a reminder of Lady Sybilla and Aimery leaping to her side too quickly, pressing solace upon her too ardently, berating Tristan too much, even as their eyes betrayed them with the same smug expression Lady Sybilla wore now. A satisfaction that warned all was not as it seemed.

Yet what else could it be? Tristan had condoned Thomas's insult to her in a manner that was an insult of its own. He saved Odo and her, not from either tenderness or trust, but because of his own sense of justice.

She longed to pull away from the grasp that, gentle as it was, left her feeling sickened and smothered. "I—I must see to Odo's wounds, my lady," she insisted.

"Go!" Tristan commanded with a look that said he could not be rid of her soon enough. "I will give order that he be tended."

"He is my liege man. I—"

"And you are my wife," he said with a steely glint. "You will obey me no less hastily than the least of my serfs."

*All was not as it seemed?* Oh, but it was! He was a hard, cold, cruel man with no love or kindness in him!

"Tristan, your wife is neither serf nor hound to be ordered to your bidding," Lady Sybilla said tartly. "Come, child, let us leave him to his distemper and spite."

In the solar, Amicia was cosseted like a beloved child. Lady Sybilla's snapping fingers sent serving maids flying for hot wine and warm crusts of bread, for hot water and herbs to perfume her bath, for unguent to spread on her scraped palms. Arrayed on the canopied chair with Amicia on a stool at her feet, she spattered her lazy delight over having a daughter at last with sly snipes at Tristan's unkind nature. And all the while, her large brown eyes gazed from beneath long, heavy lashes, empty of all but the same speculation that had marked Tristan's gaze.

The morning was full-ripe before Amicia escaped with her belly churning and her mind a whirry of grating thoughts. The kinder Lady Sybilla had been, the more distaste she felt. The more her mother-by-marriage tried to do for her, the less she wanted from her. The more the woman sniped at Tristan, the stronger Amicia's desire to defend him grew. Defend him! A man whose actions were indefensible! He was everything she said he was: hard, cold, cruel, with no love or kindness in him! So why did the hair on the back of her neck rise and tickle her nape with every verbal knife's thrust his mother made?

Harried by her own thoughts, Amicia fairly flew across the dusty rushes. She burst through the vaulting arcade into the Great Hall with Enid huffing at her heels. A sweep of the room and she found Odo, sitting on a bench with his back braced against the wall and his whittling at hand.

"Enid, I wish to speak to my man, alone," she flung over her shoulder, and hiked her skirts to run.

Odo lifted the dainty carving of a doe, pursed his lips to blow the shavings from it, and saw her. "My lady"—he jumped up—"what is amiss?"

"Naught . . . for now, but . . ." She set her hand to her heaving breast and sank to the bench, pausing to catch her breath. "Odo, I fear there is great evil in this place."

"Ay," he said, grimacing, "you went above with it this morn."

"Lady Sybilla?" He nodded, and she reached out to touch his hand and pull him down beside her. "Odo, she was so kind to me. Naught she could do was enough, it seemed. Yet, I felt . . . it was all to some purpose I could not see. As if she wanted to use me to further some plan of her own. But what could it be? I am nothing here, less than nothing. My lord does not give me the care he would give the least of his serfs, so what use could I be to her? Odo, you must tell me what you know, that I might—"

"Do not ask it of me, my lady. Much would I do for you, but this I cannot. I can only give you warning that Lady Sybilla—"

"Is set on the destruction of my lord and has joined with my father in that aim," she said, watching his face closely, but seeing no more than a telltale twitch of surprise.

"How do you know this, my lady?" he asked cautiously, as if even to ask was to betray his knowledge and his lord, her father.

"I have eyes to see and a mind to think. Enemy they are, one to the other, yet they drew near as boon companions in the window seat yonder. For what other reason than the one tie that binds them—their hate of my lord." She waited for some reply, but his gaze settled on the carving in his hand, and the puckered blue scar ridging his jaw worked with the clenching of his teeth. Amicia sighed and leaned against the wall, closing her eyes. "You will tell me nothing."

"I cannot, my lady," his voice roughened with regret. "I can only give you warning to believe naught that Lady Sybilla says and do naught that she heartily desires that you do."

"Does *he* know?" she asked softly, her eyes opening and turning to him.

For a moment she thought he had not understood what she was asking, then thought he would not answer. At length, he nodded. "Ay, my lady, Lord Tristan knows."

"Why does he not put her in her dower castle and be rid of her? It is his right."

"Mayhap, he cannot." Odo bent to his whittling with a decisive air that told her he had said all he had to say.

Cannot? Amicia watched his thick hands wield the knife with a deft touch that etched an alert eye in the doe's head. Because Tristan's mother held something over his head? It could be nothing else. As much as he hated her, he would have set her in her dower castle long ago. As much as she hated him, she would have gone did she not have a purpose here.

Amicia sighed heavily and laid her head against the wall, closing her eyes once more. She did not want to be caught in this battle between mother and son, but she could see no way to avoid it. She must tread with care, ever mindful that a misstep could tip the balance against Tristan. No matter how indifferent he was to her, she would not be the one to bring about his end.

Eager to escape the gloom of her thoughts, she straightened and watched Odo at his whittling. "I could swear the doe would breathe at any moment. She looks as if she sniffs the air for a hunter." Amicia leaned forward to look closer at the carving. "What will you do with her when you are done?"

"I make her for Megotta, the lord's daughter, my lady."

Amicia's eyes streaked to Odo's face, widening with a startled question. "The lord's daughter? Is she his . . ." A strange reluctance stilled her tongue, settling in a knot of apprehension beneath her breast. "Is she his natural child out of some . . . woman here?"

Was this why he had set her from him? Had he given his affections to . . .

"Nay, my lady. She is his child out of Lady Ruella."

The relief that loosened the knot of apprehension was one whose source Amicia would not seek. She had heard Guinella say that Lady Ruella had died in childbed, but had assumed the infant had died, too. Why else hadn't she met her husband's child? "Why did my lord not present her to me?"

"Gossipmongers say he gives no thought to her, and she runs wild lest there be guests for Lady Sybilla to impress with her care of the child."

"Do you mean that no one here sees to her care?" Amicia asked, her voice rising.

"Enid's daughter is given as servant—"

"A servant! That is all?" Her voice climbed higher. "Does no one see that she eats as she should, that she garbs herself warmly, and . . . and . . ." Breath failed her. "Where is she, Odo?"

"There"—he nodded—"in the lord's chair before the hearth. If you watch carefully, you will see her peep out."

Amicia's head jerked around, her eyes searching. The grubby white of a dirty wimple eased around the dark oak stile. One brown eye cloaked in sooty lashes slid into view, blinked, and whipped out of sight like a mouse scurrying back to its hole.

It was the child she had seen in hall! The lonely child that hung back to watch the other children play. The lonely child flitting through the chaos of the ward. Amicia surged to her feet, hurrying along the narrow space between trestle tables.

The child peeped once again, her eyes widened with fear, and she vanished, reappearing on the opposite side of the chair, her skirts lifted as she fled.

"Megotta! Do not run away! I wish to speak to you!"

The child skidded to a halt, flung a fearful look over her shoulder, and darted down the row of trestle tables near the dais, where Enid sat. Flinging herself into the serving woman's broad lap, she was enfolded in thick arms. Moments later, Amicia reached them, and the child's small head burrowed into the thick cushion of Enid's breast.

"Megotta," the serving woman scolded gently, "arise that you might greet the lady." She raised a distrustful gaze, and Enid clucked softly. "Do you forget the courtesy due a lady so soon? Your pa—"

The woman paused, and Amicia watched her curiously. Surely, she almost said *papa*. Why did she not finish it?

"Your *grand-mère* would be displeased."

"Do you think so, Enid?" the child asked nervously.

"Ay, now, give the lady your best curtsy, that none will be shamed by you."

Megotta eased from her lap, caught her skirt with the tips of her fingers, and dipped an awkward curtsy, never raising her eyes from the floor.

Amicia knelt on the rushes. "That was well done."

Megotta's small face, thin and pale, tilted up, her nut-brown eyes shining. "Was it, my lady?" she breathed. "*Grand-mère* says I am as clumsy as a village lout."

Amicia's gaze strayed to Enid, noting the grim set of her mouth, before returning to the intense expression wrinkling the child's brow. "A curtsy is no easy thing to learn. What does your papa say?" she probed gently.

Megotta's dark eyes glided to the corners, exchanging a cautious look with Enid. The small bud of her mouth quivered. "Papa says naught to me, my lady."

Amicia studied the thick fringe of sooty lashes lowered to shield Megotta's eyes. Her gaze roamed over the small, pinched face with its nubbin nose sprinkled with freckles. *Papa says naught to me, my lady.* A hard, cold, cruel man! Ay, Tristan of Eden was that and more!

No frivolity or comfort would rise to her lips, despite her desire to set Megotta at ease. Amicia wanted to pull the lonely child into her empty arms and offer the maternal love welling in her heart, but it was too soon for a lavish display of affection. She must go slowly. It would take time and nearness, and she would have them—if Tristan would give his daughter into her keeping.

She reached out to tuck a fine raven curl beneath the dirty wimple. When Megotta did not shrink from that touch, Amicia dared to draw her fingers lightly across the child's smooth cheek. "Did you know that my man is making a gift for you?"

"He is, my lady?" Megotta's gaze rose to stare past Amicia's shoulder to where Odo had taken a seat at the far end of the row.

"Ay, would you like to watch him? He is not so comely, I know," she said, speaking to the fear and hesitation she sensed, "but he has a loving heart and would be a friend to you if you let him. Go to him now, and see the dainty doe he carves for you."

Megotta inched her way down the row while Amicia watched and wondered. Could she, a lonely woman, be a mother to this lonely child? Could the emptiness of her days be filled with this child who needed the love she had to give? If Tristan gave no care to his daughter . . .

"Where will I find your lord this morn?" she asked Enid.

"In the ward, my lady. Mayhap, at the kennels or the mews."

The mews it was. Amicia marched through the bustle of the ward, oblivious to the villeins scuttling from her path. Her eyes were riveted upon her target with the concentration of a knight at the joust. Tristan stood hard by the weathering post, where a peregrine falcon perched. His face more at ease than she had ever seen it, he stroked the raptor's slate-colored head with a gentle finger. Every stroke—given the falcon, denied Megotta—inflamed Amicia the more. Flags of heat burned on her cheeks. A heat she dared not give vent to, did she hope to have her way of him.

"My lord, I would have speech with you," she murmured as she drew nigh, so as not to disturb the falcon's uneasy temper.

Tristan left the weathering post and approached, his face as cold and forbidding as it had been when last seen in hall. Was this the face he turned to his daughter? Mayhap her own raising in the priory had not been so bad. At least she had known love there, and not the hatred of her father.

"My lord, I have asked naught of you in this benighted marriage of ours—"

"But you will ask what of me now?" He folded his arms across his chest and tilted a brow in a derisive red-gold arch.

Her mouth tightened. Her eyes dropped to his sturdy, wide-spread feet. She would not allow him to anger her beyond sense. This was too important to her and the child. She struggled against the accusations that screamed for a hearing, raising her eyes to meet his once more.

"I ask that you put your daughter in my keeping. Allow me to be mother to her."

The derisive arch of his brow flattened and lowered over blue eyes gone blank with surprise. His locked arms snapped apart and plunged to his sides, and his hands balled into fists. "You would be mother to another woman's child?"

"Ay, my lord, gladly," she said, shivering beneath the intensity of his stare.

"Why?"

"For many reasons." Her gaze held his. "She runs wild and untended. The serfs in yonder village give their younglings more care than she has. I, with little else to do here, can devote myself to her. I could teach her and . . . love her."

He searched her eyes until she thought she must look away or have every secret of her heart stolen from her. "Do you wish so heavy a burden?"

"Ay, my lord."

Her firm response was near drowned out by the ward-corne's cry from the parapet. "My lord! There is smoke rising from the village!"

Tristan looked up, shielding his eyes from the sun with his hand. "Can you see what is amiss?" he shouted.

"Men ahorse, my lord, where none should be! Reivers, mayhap!"

"Rolf, prepare your men to ride!" Tristan bellowed, and started to turn away. He paused a moment, looked back at Amicia, and frowned. "You may have your wish, my lady. I care not who sees to her, so long as the burden does not fall to me."

# Chapter 13

The reivers, armed like a troop well paid and provisioned, laid waste the village and fled into Eden Chase, pursued by Tristan and his meinie of men in a circuitous route skirting Bellay's boundary—a route that set his men to muttering of treachery and roused his own suspicions to new heights.

His suspicions grew by the week as the reivers struck and vanished in the rocky scarps of the western mountains. Tristan set up a three-tiered ring of defense. Huntsmen were scattered on the far rim of the wood. Green-clad foresters, accompanied by brutish lurcher hounds, patrolled the somber heart of the chase. Men-at-arms, grouped by fives, were set nearest the keep, to be summoned at need. The reivers slipped by them as easily as they avoided every trap laid.

With a sinking sense of foreboding, Tristan accepted the fact that he sheltered a traitor within his keep. The reivers were Bellay's men, of that there was neither doubt nor proof. But who among his own kept them so well informed?

His mother. So much he knew, though his spies among hers reported no ill doing. Someone gave her aid, but who? Aimery, now basking in her graces for the first time since his birth? Mayhap, Tristan thought often, he should look to his brother as spy, but he had not the heart for it after the youth they spent with none to cleave to but each

169

other. Nay, he could not believe it of Aimery, for there was another with far more to gain . . .

Winter returned on All Souls' Day. A freezing fog muffled the chink of armor and the snuffling of horses. Tristan, weary shoulders borne down by the weight of hauberk and mail scarce removed in weeks, sat atop his destrier cursing his luck. First the fever, felling his men-at-arms until there were none but a few hearty village lads to fill the ranks. Now the weather.

"We are done, my lord," Rolf whispered, though the rolling banks of white would have swallowed a shout within an ell's length. "If the promise of silver does not draw them out, naught will do it."

Robin, the swineherd's son, shrugged aside a hemp sack and raised his head over the high wooden side of the oxwain with an ear-to-ear grin. "Fear not, my lord." Fog spun from his mouth like a hoary beard. "While they try to decide how a chest of silver became a meinie of men, we will take them."

Tristan settled his forearm on the cantle, a weary smile softening the stern mold of his mouth. "Take care to keep your head attached to your shoulders, Robin Fairface, or I will be a brace of weeks soothing grieving maids from one end of the village to the other."

"Ay, my lord." The boy's grin broadened.

"Rolf"—Tristan beckoned his man—"whatever the cost, I want a reiver taken. Can we put him to the question and find Bellay behind this, I will be free of the oath that binds me and I will know who among mine betrays me."

"Ay, my lord," Rolf said with a rare thin-lipped smile, and hoisted himself onto the oxwain bed to slip beneath the sacking.

"God go with you," Tristan called softly, and thumped the high side with his mailed fist.

The oxwain lurched on the frozen track and settled into a plodding pace, accompanied by its mounted guard of four. Eerie shadows, they were soon engulfed, leaving only the strident *squeak-squeak* of the wheels to drift back, softer and softer until muffled to silence.

"My lord"—Tristan's rose-scented squire, not so sweet-scented after weeks in the saddle, cantered to his side—"do you think they will attack?"

"With my *aid* to Earl Simon as bait? Can they find their way in this fog, they will not let that prize go untried. Did you bury the chest?"

"Ay, it lies beneath the forked oak."

"I would that I could see their faces when my men rise like dragon's teeth, where they expected naught but plunder. Come." He wheeled his destrier up the track and whistled the *two-thri* call of the partridge to gather his personal guard. "We are away to the keep, where I will take my ease within sight of all."

Could he have found humor in anything, Tristan would have laughed at that. No ease would he find with so much at stake and he sitting with his strong sword-hand clasping a cup of wine.

At that moment, Amicia sat slumped in a chair before the hearth in the Great Hall, soaking in the heat that warmed her flesh, but left her heart cold and untouched.

Her potions, plasters, and poultices went for naught. The fever raged. The young, the old, and the weak died, and she was helpless to do more than bathe fever-flushed faces and whisper futile prayers. Had she not been so worn, she would have wept or raged. But weeping and raging, as she learned in the first week of this pestilence, did no good. And, now . . .

"My serving woman tells me Megotta is abed! Why do you do naught, while she is ill?" Lady Sybilla glided from the shadows.

Amicia shifted, struggling against the limp exhaustion of bone and sinew. Her curious gaze touched the woman's wringing hands. Welcome as this concern was for Megotta's sake, Lady Sybilla's interest after weeks of indifference was suspicious.

"She was overwarm, my lady, not ill. Enid and I thought she should rest, though it may be no more than her excitement."

"Excitement? What excitement could she find in this cursed keep of my son's?" Lady Sybilla's voice came thin and high, while a vein pulsed an agitated rhythm in her ivory-hued temple.

Aimery stepped into view. One smooth palm slipped beneath his mother's elbow in an offer of support. "Amicia loves the child well." His light singsonged phrase comforted, though his expression betrayed a deeper worry than his mother's.

Amicia wondered about that worry and remembered how he ever watched Megotta with a wistful gaze, as if he loved her well. Yet, he never approached her or gifted her as an uncle would. Instead, he watched from afar, as though he dared not approach her.

"She would not rest, was there so much to worry over," he continued. "Come and sit. You fret for naught."

Lady Sybilla settled in the chair, retaining a grip on Aimery's hand. This son, ever at her side, but never touched nor smiled upon, lest that smile be tinged with malice for another. Amicia watched him kneel beside his mother, the brown of his eyes lit by his ever-present worry. Worry for his mother? Himself? His brother? Nay, not for Tristan, else Aimery would join the relentless pursuit of the reivers rather than cling to his mother's side like a tame lap dog.

"Excitement?" Lady Sybilla prompted, accusingly.

"Megotta was here when the runner came to give warning that our lord follows to take his ease with us," Amicia said.

"Tristan comes? This pleased her?" Lady Sybilla's tawny brows rucked up in surprise.

"Ay, my lady," Amicia said, unable to keep the distaste from her voice. Much could she forgive Tristan. Beset by her father's quest for vengeance on one side and his mother's hate on the other, he led no easy life. But knowing the pain of a child spurned by a parent, how could he do the same to his daughter? How could he be so cold and indifferent, when Megotta's warm eyes followed him every moment she thought none watched? Ay, Amicia vowed, much could she forgive him, but that, never.

"So Tristan returns, while his aid makes its unprotected way to Earl Simon. What a fool he is!" Lady Sybilla burst out. "My Robert would have had the reivers strung from the turrets by now. He would not have let them overrun his demesne.''

Amicia suppressed a sigh. So much for the woman's concern for Megotta. Her granddaughter was easily shunted aside for the pleasure of lashing Tristan with her envenomed tongue and lavishing her dead son, Robert, with the traits of a warrior-saint. A good man he might have been, but Amicia doubted any lived with the perfection his mother endlessly claimed for him.

'Do not think I failed with all of my sons. My first-born, Robert, was not the fool these two are! *He* was a man such as they may not aspire to be. A man like my *grand-père*, a Norman untainted by the base blood of this land. Had Robert not been slain in Gascony—''

Aimery vaulted to his feet. Firelight burnished his swarthy skin and gleamed on the frothy ringlets spilling across his brow. A comely figure he made with his rich apparel, but that comeliness was marred by the bitterness twisting his full lips. A bitterness that chilled Amicia, and not for the first time. If she felt the urge to flee at the mention of Robert, how much more would Aimery and Tristan despise their brother's name on their mother's lips?

''I beg leave to be on my way,'' he said stiffly, drawing an irritated glance from his mother and a languid dismissal.

''You would have loved Robert, Amicia,'' Lady Sybilla continued, as if Aimery was not waiting and she had not said this over and over again in the last weeks. ''All who knew him did, even your husband.''

''He was his brother, my lady. It is only natural that he would love him,'' she murmured, watching the angry knotting of Aimery's jaw. Sensing, too, an untimely need in the earthy darkness of his eyes—a child's need for a mother's love.

''Natural?'' Lady Sybilla's indolence yielded to anger. ''Mayhap, but neither of my living sons is natural! Always they coveted that which my Robert had. Always they clamored for their father's time, leaving little to him. Now''—a glint, hard and unforgiving, sparked in her eyes—''he is dead and they live.''

Aimery wheeled about and strode away, while Amicia

breathed, "My lady, it is no fault of theirs! You sound as though you wish them dead in Robert's stead."

Lady Sybilla's virulent look sheathed Amicia in ice. She knew Tristan's mother worked for his end, but she thought that end to be his fall from grace with his lord—not his death.

"My lady"—a serving woman came near—"the lord arrives in the entrance chamber now."

"Ay, Maida, I come." Amicia spared her a distracted glance that was pulled inexorably back to Lady Sybilla. "My lady," she said softly, "Tristan is your son as Robert was."

"Born of my body, not of my heart. From the moment he came squalling into the world, he began stealing from me all I held dear. I curse the day I gave him life."

Evil resided in the spice-brown eyes staring intently at Amicia. Evil and its remorseless twin—madness. She stood slowly, as if a rapid move would spring that trap of madness. The effort it took not to turn and flee brought a sheen of sweat to her brow. "I must see that all is prepared for my husband."

Lady Sybilla's thin smile did not reach her eyes. "He will not thank you. He is like his father in that. No woman will rise high in his esteem, no matter how great her effort."

"I but do my duty," Amicia murmured, and escaped to hurry the length of the hall with her mind scurrying to and fro like a hare caught in a snare. Though she stretched the rope tight, she could go only so far, and that not far enough to escape the pricking of a sharp blade of fear—for Tristan.

She was as mad as his mother to fear for him! He was cruel and cold and unfeeling. But how else would he be, a softer voice whispered, raised by a mother who hated him from birth? Would Amicia rather he be like Aimery, sweet-tempered and kind, but softly womanish with it? Nay, Tristan was a knight as brave as Earl Simon himself. She would not have that changed.

He stepped through the archway, a militant figure with his helm beneath his arm and his wine-red mantle swirling around his ankles. Crowding behind came his two squires and a trio of bachelor-knights, swathed in dampness and gloom and solitude. Amicia gave them a cursory glance, her full attention riveting on Tristan's sober gaze, which strangely lightened her step and set her heart aflutter, as if she were a true wife greeting a husband dear to her.

She firmly quelled that flutter. She was no true wife and he was no husband dear to her heart. Even so, her life was bound to his. If he died, she would be returned to her father's care. A thought to make her skin crawl. Her steps hastened. Tristan pushed his mail coif back to dangle at his nape and lifted the quilted arming cap from his head—and Amicia forgot all, but him.

"My lord, welcome," she murmured, her shocked gaze racing across his drawn features. His cheekbones, ever bold, now jutted above his hollow cheeks. His eyes, ringed in lavender circles, burned with exhaustion and suspicion. Worry and anger etched patterns on the golden patina of his skin.

Stripping his mantle from his shoulders, Tristan handed it to a serving woman, while his eyes drifted across Amicia's face. Eyes that seemed to ask why she came to greet him, when she had avoided his presence until now.

"You look weary, my lord," she said softly, suppressing the urge to reach up and stroke the lines of worry away.

"As you do, my lady," he said in a low rumble, his eyes lingering on her mouth.

His steady gaze raised a welt of sensation. Amicia's teeth nipped at her lower lip, while the back of her hand brushed straggled curls from her face. "I . . . I spent the night in the village at the woodward's wife's bed. I fear she—"

"The village? Alone?" he asked alertly.

"Nay, my lord. Enid and Odo were with me." She paused, her good intentions yielding to the prick of anger. "And your huntsmen, of course. I fear they had a chill night, huddled behind the broom bush beside the croft. I sent them hot porridge at Matins and Lauds, because they refused to warm themselves by the fire. They seemed to think you would not approve."

"They follow for your protection," Tristan said stiffly.

"Do they?" One brow tilted skeptically. Waiting for no answer, she gestured to the stair. "I fear I fail in my duty. Come above, my lord. I have ordered all for your comfort."

She sailed by him, stately as a queen, leaving him no choice but to follow. The dark and drear spiral stair echoed with the heavy steps of his trailing men, steps that in turn echoed the sickening thuds of Tristan's heartbeat. He watched the sway of Amicia's hips and the pride squaring her shoulders, and wondered if the day's end would see his suspicions confirmed. If they were, what would he do with this wife of his?

Above, all was a bustle of servants stoking the hearth fire and warming wine and meats over braziers. Heady aromas mingled with the scent of fresh rushes perfumed with winter savory. The wainscoting gleamed with a bees-wax shine and the walls glowed from a coating of limewash. Tristan faltered, his eyes roving from the clean wall hangings bright with color to the arms polished to sparkling. A wondering gaze settled on Amicia, who had stopped to order his bath readied.

His men-at-arms, those few recovered from the fever, sang her praises as an angel of mercy. The villagers, so Robin Fairface had been eager to tell him, lit candles in the church to thank God for her coming. Even thumbless Giles, greeting him at the gate, gave grudging praise for her tireless physicking of the sick. Still, she found time to see to this.

He watched her with the serving woman, Maida, and listened to the melody of her voice. The servants looked to her, not with the fear they held of his mother, nor yet the love they gave to him, but with a respect she had obviously earned. It was a good day's work he and Odo had done for her. Ay, a good day's work that gave her time to make her place here.

"My lord," she turned, raising the sapphire blue of her gaze, "if you will give your men leave to take their ease, I will see to your disarming and bath."

The suggestion of a smile softened his mouth. "My hauberk alone would send you staggering."

"I am sturdier than I look, my lord."

"Then, I am yours to command, my lady," he said, the

gallantry of his tone belied by the steely glint in his eyes. Why on this day did she see to his comfort herself, rather than ordering all as before? Mayhap did he follow her lead like a witless ox on a tether, he would learn more of her than she hoped to learn of him.

His mural chamber, like the Great Chamber, was vastly changed. Busy brooms had banished draping cobwebs. His floor was covered by a plaited reed rug, his bed draped with new hangings in a thick wool the blue of his eyes. He noted all but said nothing as he tossed his helm onto the bed and leaned a shoulder against the thick endpost.

One thumb hooked into his leather sword belt, the other hand kneading the tension from his nape, he watched Amicia's stately dance of housewifery. A dance as sensually disturbing as it was unstudied. Small and neat and efficient, she moved about the chamber with a sway of hips and skirt. A slender hand lifted the lid from a platter of meats warming over the brazier. She looked into the ewer of wine and lifted the swatch of linen covering bread and butter. A smile of approval dismissed the hovering servants, and she leaned over the huge wooden tub, dipping her fingers to test the water's heat. Tristan's warming gaze touched the slender ankles exposed beneath her skirt and lingered on the gentle swell of her hips.

She stood and turned to him. "All is ready, my lord. If you hunger, water heats to warm your bath after you eat."

If he hungered? Ay, his belly was empty and grumbling, but that hunger was naught beside another. He had had no woman since her and his loins ached with the knowledge that they were alone and she was his wife and the bed was waiting.

"My lord?" she questioned.

"I will bathe first," he said abruptly. Mayhap the heat of the water would leach the heat from him.

She moved to him, slowly, as if she were as aware as he that they were alone. The first gentle tug of her working fingers on the ornate gold buckle of his swordbelt stroked Tristan with fingers of desire. He studied the thick brush of her lashes, the smoothness of her cheeks, the tiny frown of concentration, and struggled against the surge of his hot blood.

He must remain alert for the return of his men. He could not succumb to this seduction, if that was what it was. His hand swept up, trapping hers over the icy cold buckle. Her downcast eyes lifted, wide and startled, locking with his.

"Why do you do this?" The question burst from him.

"You . . . you are my husband. Should I do less for you than I am trained to do for any knight who comes to this keep?"

He wanted to believe she had no other purpose. Almost, staring into the limpid depths of her eyes, he could believe she spoke the truth. Almost, but not quite. His doubt was keen . . . but not so keen as the needle-sharp claws of jealousy.

"And have you done this for others?" he asked.

"Nay, my lord. I was trained to disarm a man and bathe him." Her gaze dropped, and a wild-rose blush stained her cheeks, "but I have never done so."

"And you will never do so for any but me," he heard himself say, as if he had no will to choose the words spilling from his mouth. "You will train the maids to see to my guests and men."

Her eyes, wide with innocence and surprise and questions, searched his. "My lord, it is the custom for the lady—"

"You will do as I say!"

"Ay, my lord," she answered compliantly.

My lord. His eyes lingered on the moist corner of her mouth. The soft, sweet mouth that had once flowered eagerly beneath his. The mouth that might now be whispering his plans into his enemy's ear. Faithful or faithless? He knew not, and for that moment, cared not. His hand climbed to cup the downy column of her neck, his thumb tilting her chin up.

"My name is Tristan. Say it," he commanded, his thumb gliding down her throat to nestle against her drumming pulse.

"Tristan," she whispered.

Her breath flowed, a zephyr of sweetness, across his lowering mouth. For a moment, her lips lay passive beneath his impassioned demand. For a moment, she stiffened against the arm embracing her waist and pulling her hard against him. For a moment, he thought she would resist and feared her resistance would incite him to brute force.

The moment passed with the hesitant movement of her mouth on his. The pliant molding of her body against him was muffled frustratingly by his heavy mail hauberk and chausses. Tasting the heady nectar of surrender, his mouth slanted across hers, urgent, demanding. His tongue charted the quivering fullness of her upper lip, the tender moistness of the corners, the hot velvety crevice behind her lower lip. His hand foraged beneath the wimple, winnowing long fingers through strands of chestnut silk.

He forgot the oxwain trundling its way through the fog. He forgot his plans for the reivers. He forgot his suspicions. He knew nothing but Amicia. He felt nothing but the scourge of desire. He wanted nothing but the tempting woman in his arms.

"My lady." Maida's voice, calling from the other side of the leather curtain, snapped Tristan's head up. "I bring the herbs to sprinkle—"

"Leave us!" he roared.

A frightened squeak sounded. Slapping footsteps receded. Amicia's head drooped against his chest like a windflower bowing on its stem. Tristan, his breath rasping through the arid channel of his throat, raised his eyes to the shadowed rafters, spitting a volley of silent curses.

His swollen loins pressed painfully against his linked-mail chausses. His heart pounded painfully against the ribs bound by his hauberk. His mind spun painfully with the realization that it was he who had so nearly surrendered, not she. A witch she was, draining his will, and leaving nothing but the hot pulsing of his loins. A witch, untouched, while he . . .

His hands curled into claws and clamped around her upper arms, pushing her back. Her head rose as by an effort. Her eyes, dazed and guileless, sought his. Her mouth, rosy and swollen, parted for the slow slide of her tongue across her lips, as if she sought the taste of him still.

"Tristan," she said breathlessly, her hands lying limp on the woolen surcoat covering his hauberk.

Not untouched. Desire held her in its talons, as it did him. A fierce exultation gripped him. He could take her to his bed and have his way of her. He could ease the painful heaviness of his loins and spill his seed and . . .

. . . get her with child.

Desire vanished. His whirling mind focused, relentlessly, mercilessly. "Leave me." The growl he planned came out as a ragged plea.

"Tristan—"

"Leave me!"

"I cannot, my lord. You hold me still."

His hands peeled from her arms and she backed away, one hand pressed to the base of her throat. Her luminous gaze searched his with a disturbance akin to his own. She opened her mouth, as if she would speak, closed it, and whirled to flee through the crackling leather curtain.

Tristan, his knees bled of strength, sank to the bed and dropped his head into his hands. Was she faithful or faithless?

Amicia fled the Great Chamber as if the devil snapped at her heels. The sweet melting in her loins lingered. The urgings of her reawakened body paid no heed to the cautions of her mind. Ignoring the servant stationed by the great oaken door, she lifted the heavy bar, set her middling strength to pull the door open, squeezed through, and pulled it behind her, as though the least crack would give Tristan entry to her heart. She listened for the bar to slide into place with a thump, then sagged against the door.

Her fingers trembled against the lips that felt the pressure of his still. What had happened that he could touch her and set to naught all of her anger and disgust? She forgot his suspicion. She forgot his cruelty to Megotta and to her. She forgot all but this new need clamoring for fulfillment.

A need he felt as strongly as she, though he set her from him. Had he remembered she was Bellany's get? Had his blood curdled at the thought of holding her in his arms, of taking her unto him as wife to husband? Ay, naught else could it have been.

She struggled for anger, but it eluded her. She chased

after it with willful determination, and stumbled headlong
into a morass of fear. Tristan looked so weary. More than
weary, worn beyond bearing. As if he had not slept or
eaten in all of these weeks. He needed rest and comfort,
but could seek neither while the reivers ravaged his demesne.
Food he would have to assuage his hunger, but sleep to
ease him? Nay, he would not get that—not without aid.

She moved swiftly to the small mural chamber where
Megotta slept and Enid sat with her stitching in hand.
Amicia paused at the door, studying the serving woman's
stern profile. During these weeks they had worked together,
weeping over the many deaths and exulting over those who
lived, it seemed that Enid's hate had softened. Betimes she
was even kind. Had she come so far as to give her trust?

Amicia moved into the chamber. "Enid, your lord has
come. He looks . . . so worn and weary, I fear he will fall
to this fever does he not take his rest. I would make for
him a drink to help him sleep, but I know he will not
. . ." She paused, her eyes dropping to the hands twined
at her waist. "He does not trust me enough to take it from
my hand. I ask that you come with me, watch me prepare
it, and take it to him as coming from you."

The woman gazed thoughtfully in mute silence, and
Amicia's heart sank to her toes.

"My lady, I will gladly do as you ask, but there is no
need for me to watch you make the drink," the woman
said softly, in deference to the sleeping child. "I have no
fear that you would do ill to my lord or any of his."

Amicia's heart drifted up as light and free as her smile.
"Thank you, Enid," she said, swiftly turning away to hide
the tears of gratitude misting her eyes.

At lauds, the ninth hour of the night, the oxwain came
*sqreak-sqreak*ing beneath the portcullis with its burden
of men-at-arms and one battered and buffeted reiver, trussed
and gagged. Rolf, the hard-faced master-at-arms, bounded
up the stairs and woke Tristan's squire. Together, they
tried to wake their lord—to no avail. He slept deeply,
peacefully, dreamlessly.

The reiver, still trussed and gagged, was dropped through
the trap door into the lightless dungeon below the Entrance

Chamber off the Guard Hall. He would be put to the question on the morrow with the Lord of Eden hard by.

But, in the morning, the porter was found on his pallet with his throat slit. The reiver was gone.

Tristan prowled the space before the hearth like a wolf on a tether. One hand was wrapped around the hilt of his sword as if he awaited only the presence of an enemy to draw it. The other hand dug impatient fingers through his hair, leaving it standing out in tufts and curls.

"You sent for me, my lord," Enid said.

Tristan whipped around and glared at her. "What was in the drink you gave me last night?"

"I . . . I know not, my lord."

"You did not prepare it with your own hand? Who, Enid?" Tristan took a threatening step toward her. "Who has set all of my plans to naught?"

"My lord, she would not do it apurpose. I have been long at her side and never have I seen her do a thing against you or yours. I would swear she is—"

"Amicia," Tristan breathed, and spun to shield the pain twisting his face from Enid's sight. What curse followed him that he found betrayal at every turn?

"My lord, she wanted only to give you ease and rest. It was a potion to help you sleep, no more than that, I would swear."

"Make me sleep? Ay, it did that!" He turned to her, the pain coiling sinuously behind a face sheeted in iron. "Where is my lady this morn, Enid?"

"She . . . she was called to the village in the night. Odo went with her."

"Guard!" Tristan shouted to the man-at-arms posted beside the archway. "Send a troop to the village. Tell them to bring Lady Amicia and her man to me!"

"My lord"—Enid moved to his side—"what will you do to her?"

Tristan stared at the soot-blackened rafters. What would he do? He could not beat her into submission. The thought of laying a hand to her in anger brought the bile surging into his throat. "If she is guilty of this deed," he said, swallowing a lump of pain, "I will send her and her man back to her father."

Within the hour, Tristan sat on the dais, an avenging lord in his place of honor. Below stood Amicia and Odo, ringed about by his full-armed men. None had dared lay hand to his lady, but they held Odo straightly. Neither had said a word in the moments they stood staring up at him, as if he had gone mad. The silence had grown so acute that the scratching of a hound sounded like the distant rumble of thunder.

"The reiver we captured in the night has escaped," Tristan said heavily. "He could not have done so without treachery from within."

Amicia stepped forward, flinging back the hood of her mantle. Her face tilted up to him, her eyes flashing with anger. "And my man and I are the first you suspect of the deed?"

"Ay, my lady!" Tristan leaned forward, slapping a hand to his knee and bracing an elbow on the armrest. "That the reivers are your father's men, I have no doubt. Did you and your man slit my porter's throat and spirit my prisoner away?"

"Nay, husband! We did not!"

The acid bite of bitterness rose to Tristan's tongue. "Is truth ever to be had from Bellay's kin and kind?"

Color fled Amicia's face, leaving it white to the lips. "From the lowest in this hall to the greatest, we who are of Bellay's kin and kind are met with hate and distrust!" Her soft voice shook with the anger that blazed in her eyes. "We are not fools, my lord! We know that we are the first suspected of every foul deed committed by any on your demesne. If you cannot believe me, then call your huntsmen! Those watchdogs you have set upon me! Ask them what my man and I did during the night!"

"I am here, my lord." The huntsman stepped forward. "It was I who came for Lady Amicia. My sister's daughter was ill of the fever. She asked me to beg succor of the lady. Neither she nor her man were out of my sight from the time we left the keep until your men came for her."

"My lord," a guardsman spoke, "the men-at-arms did

not bring the reiver to the keep until lauds, long after the lady left for the village.''

She was innocent. Relief flooded Tristan. Sluicing behind it came a bitter regret for his hasty actions. ''My lady—''

''Release my man,'' she ordered.

''Release him and return to your tasks,'' Tristan said, stepping down from the dais, while they scattered. ''My lady—''

''If you are done with me, my lord''—Amicia bent deep and mockingly—''I will take my lying tongue from your presence.''

''But I am not done,'' he said stiffly, reaching out to catch her forearm as she moved to pass him by. ''Why did you mix a potion to make me sleep in the night?''

Her gaze, as bitter as his own, lifted to meet his. ''You looked wearied unto death. I feared you would fall to this pestilent fever did you not find rest.''

She pulled away and Tristan's hollow gaze followed her proud passage from the hall. Why was she not another such as her father? Then he would not have to fight these strange feelings she aroused.

He shrugged those disturbing thoughts away, his eyes moving to the guards leaving the hall. If it was not Amicia and Odo, then who—among these he trusted—aided the reiver's escape?

# Chapter 14

Both anger and pride deserted Amicia the moment she stepped into the dark spiral stair. With none to watch with suspicion or, worse, pity, she slumped against a moisture-seeping wall, oblivious to any chill but the one abiding in her heart.

*Is truth ever to be had from Bellay's kin and kind?* Tristan's question tormented her. Was trust, she despaired, ever to be had from Eden's kin and kind?

Aware of the tears running down her cheeks, but too dispirited to summon the effort to wipe them away, she trudged up the stairs to her lonely turret chamber. She lay abed, listening to the mourning wind and yearning for the peace of Holmby, where all was love and prayer. What wise counsel would Mother Margaret give, were she here to offer it?

Amicia slept on the thought, her question unanswered.

"My lady! Wake! I beg of you!"

The dagger's edge of fear in Enid's voice plunged deep into Amicia's restless slumber. She woke, wide-eyed and panting, to stare about the night-darkened chamber, lighted only by the candle trembling in Enid's hand. "What? What is amiss?"

"Megotta, my lady! She is taken by the fever!"

Megotta! The dregs of sleep vanished in the blink of an eye. "You should have awakened me!" Amicia accused, flying from the bed and snatching up her robe.

"I had not the heart for it, my lady. So weary you were after the night in the village." Enid wrung her capable hands uncertainly. "I hoped Megotta had escaped this pestilence."

Amicia paused in whipping the belt around her waist to lay her hand atop Enid's. "We will do all we can for her. Do not fret so. She will need your strength, as I will."

"Ay, my lady." Her muscular hands turned beneath Amicia's to grip them tightly. For a moment their eyes met, not as lady and servant, but as two women joined by a common fear.

"Bring my chest of herbs," Amicia said gently, tugging her hand from her servant's lingering grasp and hurrying toward the solar.

In the small mural chamber, Megotta's jewel-bright eyes rolled toward Amicia, staring from the setting of sooty lashes. "Papa," she whispered. "Where is Papa?"

"Shh." Amicia brushed sweat-dampened ebony strands from the child's fever-flushed face and laid her palm against her brow. Her hand flinched from the dry burning heat. Fear took root in her heart. Her gaze locked with Enid's in mutual concern and misgiving, as it had so often in these weeks while, shoulder to shoulder, they stood in death watch over young and old alike. "Have water drawn from the well in the ward." Amicia's whisper cracked, and she swallowed hard. "Honey. I will need honey. Have it brought soonest may."

"Papa," Megotta whispered again. "Where is Papa?"

"Your papa is below, sweeting," Amicia murmured, and wondered at the strength of a child's love for a parent. She, knowing her own father's cruelty and hate, still cherished a secret hope that someday he would see and love her as a true daughter. A hope as forlorn as the one Megotta now cherished. Her heart heavy, she dipped a washclout in a bowl of water and wrung it out.

"Papa," Megotta's thin hand struggled up and fell weakly against Amicia's wrist. "I want Papa. I want Papa."

"Sweeting," she pressed the cool, wet cloth to the childish brow, "your papa is very—"

"How is she?" Lady Sybilla glided into the chamber and came to the bed to stare down at her granddaughter.

"It is the fever, my lady." Amicia watched her, surprised to see her smooth skin crinkled by lines of worry.

"She must *live!*" Lady Sybilla cried vehemently, her gaze shifting from the child to Amicia. Her eyes were filled with anger and irritation, as if she thought Megotta had taken the fever apurpose to thwart her in some way. "She must live!" the woman repeated on a guttural command. "I have use for her still."

"She is your granddaughter, my lady," Amicia protested.

"My granddaughter?" The woman smiled her secretive smile. "Ay, that she is."

Amicia watched her glide away on a swish of samite and silk. What *use* could she have for Megotta? The question plagued her while the girl's fever raged unabated. Amicia, Enid, and her daughter, Wilda, a broad-faced girl made in her mother's image, worked tirelessly over the tossing, turning child. Watered wine and broth were forced between her unwilling lips. Lips that dried and cracked and bled as the fever ravaged her tiny body. A potion of powdered feverfew and honey was spooned into her mouth again and yet again. Braziers warmed the icy air.

"My lady," Enid whispered often, "you must take your rest. Naught can you do here if you fall ill as she."

Rest. It was beyond her. Amicia's feet dragged in an endless round from the bedside to the prie-dieu to a stool where she sat with wilting shoulders and sagging hopes. Megotta grew weaker; the fever grew stronger. All of her potions, plasters, and prayers went for naught, just as they had for the village folk.

Lady Sybilla came frequently to stand near the entrance, like a mourner beside a flower-strewn bier. Yet no look of mourning or sorrow found a dwelling place in the depths of her eyes. Depths as cool as the deep waters of a mountain tarn. Her wimple crisply fresh and her surcoat emblazoned with jewels, she waited with an irritable tap of her foot and an angry twist to her mouth. One minute there, the next gone, another and she returned, as if she could bear neither to go nor stay.

Megotta, burning with heat, pushed the coverlets away with a thin spidery hand whose every vein showed blue beneath her drying skin. "Papa! Papa!" she wailed.

"I cannot bear it!" Amicia burst out. "I will get him—"

"Nay, my lady!" Enid caught her arm in a grip of steel. "You know not what evil you will brew. Do not, I beg of you!"

"She is his daughter!" Amicia protested. "He cannot give so little care to her that he would—"

"My lady, I beg of you! Do not do this to my lord!"

"Do not do this to your lord?" Amicia gasped in disbelief. "It is not he that lies . . ." Dying. She could not say it. "Does he know she is ill?"

"Ay, he knows. He stays in the keep—"

"But does not come to her, when she calls for him as if he were a true father, dearly loved?" Every word dripped with the acid of bitterness.

Enid's eyes dropped. "Nay, my lady. He . . . cannot."

"Cannot? Why?"

Enid, her wimple askew and her formerly spotless cotte spattered with watered wine and beef broth, folded her arms across her ample chest and tucked her upper lip into the lower. Though Amicia questioned her straightly, the only answer was a stubborn shaking of Enid's head. To the plaguing question of what *use* Lady Sybilla had for Megotta was added the question of why Tristan *could not* come to comfort his daughter.

It was morning. Amicia knew because her untouched bowl of potage sat cooling on the floor. The days had resolved themselves into portions divided by the meals delivered and scarce touched. She dragged herself from the stool and cast a single pitying glance at Wilda, who was sitting on her pallet with her back braced against the icy wall, sunk in a stupor of exhaustion.

"Enid, go and rest. I will do for Megotta now." Amicia watched the serving woman stumble away and collapse on the pallet beside her daughter. In these weeks while the pestilence raged, she had learned much of Enid, a woman Mother Margaret would have loved and admired. Would that she might someday earn the serving woman's respect. It was lonely in the women's quarter with none to laugh with or talk to. Though she tried to overlook the silence that fell with her every entrance into the solar, it grew harder with time, not easier, as she had hoped.

Sighing dispiritedly, Amicia lifted the washclout and squeezed the water from it with hands that were dry and peeling and cracked. Megotta moaned and struggled weakly, her lashes climbing to reveal a red-rimmed lusterless gaze. "Papa," the plea croaked from her dry throat. "I want Papa."

"How cruel my son is, not to come though his daughter calls," Lady Sybilla confided, approaching Amicia from the rear. "His servants say he sits in the Great Chamber deep in his cups, while the reivers ride unchecked. The beeward and his family were found in the ashes of their cottage deep in the wood yestereve, and what does my son do? Sends his seneschal while he sits and sips wine at his leisure."

Megotta's cracked lips formed the word *Papa* without sound, wrenching Amicia's heart with pity.

"How strange that she calls for him," Lady Sybilla said thoughtfully. "I would swear he has no use for her, so why would she call for him?" The speculative look she rested on Megotta's pinched face roused ripples of uneasiness in Amicia.

"Papa," Megotta whispered.

Her ripples of uneasiness vanished beneath a surging wave of determination. No matter what evil she brewed, she would see Tristan brought to his daughter! "My lady" —Amicia raised a challenging gaze—"go to your son. Tell him that Megotta calls unceasingly for him. Plead, if you must, but bring him here."

"I will go, but pin no hopes upon his coming. He has no use for the child," Lady Sybilla warned.

A strange warning it was with that hint of satisfaction oozing in her low voice. Amicia watched her leave, her steps regal and unhurried.

"My lady, my lady," Enid mourned from her perch on the stool, "what have you done?"

"He must come," she said firmly.

Minutes passed like hours while she spooned broth between Megotta's cracked lips, urging her to swallow. The spoon weighed heavy in her weary hand, but not so heavy as her heart. The soft pad of footsteps pulled her around. Lady Sybilla stood alone in the dark passageway through the thick walls, a gaze of peculiar intensity fastened upon Amicia's face.

"He refuses to come."

"Why?" Amicia cried.

"He says he has work to attend and cannot spend his time at the bed of a wailing child."

Amicia went cold as the snow swirling on the wintry winds outside. The incessant winds moaning a lament of loss and betrayal. "She might die!" Her voice climbed in disbelief. "Did you tell him that?"

"He says children are easily made. There will be others to take her place."

*Others to take her place.* Amicia summoned a vision of Tristan's face in all of its masculine arrogance. She tried to put those words into his mouth, but could not imagine him saying them. Yet, he must have. What reason did his mother have to lie? The cold crusting her heart in layers of ice melted beneath the hot flame of rage. A rage that blurred her vision and brought color flooding into her ashen cheeks.

"I will go to him! I—"

"Nay, my lady!" Enid caught her arm. "Nay, my lady. It will do no good. He will not come."

Amicia saw in her tormented eyes a need to say more. Yet neither explanation nor excuse rose to her lips.

Lady Sybilla hovered in the entry, her speculative gaze lingering on Enid's face. She nodded briefly, and turned to go.

Naught could Amicia do but return to Megotta. The child, who was of *use* to her grandmother and abandoned by her father. This child, the only one who would ever fill the emptiness of her heart, which now welled with pity and love, while a small empty chamber filled with a festering hate for Tristan.

Tristan slumped in the canopied chair in the circle of light dancing from the Great Chamber's hearth. His long chausses-clad legs were stretched out to the fire. At his side was a stool topped by a wooden tray and a ewer. In the hand hanging limp over the armrest was a cup of wine. In the heart pounding his ribs as a carter's hammer pounds a peg was a festering hate for his mother.

He should have put his hands to her throat and choked the life from her. Would any blame him if he did? Even merciless God in Heaven?

He lifted the cup and drained it dry. Rolling to the side to grasp the ewer with an unsteady hand, he poured wine until it sloshed over the rim. Leaning back, he pulled greedily at the wine of forgetfulness.

He had done what he had to do. He had said what he had to say. Knowing he could act no other way, he still felt the icy breath of damnation. "Megotta, Megotta," he whispered through numbed lips. A numbness that would not, no matter how much he drank, spread to his mind.


"Enid! Feel her brow! I vow she is cooler!" Amicia whirled eagerly, waiting while the serving woman dragged herself to the bed and laid her trembling hand atop Megotta's translucent blue-veined forehead.

"Ay, my lady!" Enid's cheeks wrinkled in a broad smile. "Think you the worst is over?"

"We should know before morning."

Never had she awaited anything so eagerly. Never had hours passed more slowly. The candles burned low. The braziers hissed in the dark, quiet hours before dawn. Each time she woke Megotta to force watered wine and broth between her cracked lips, Amicia felt a new disappointment and a keener fear. Dawn was easing fingers of light through the deep window slit, when she trudged to the bed with her hopes at low ebb. Her hand trembled against Megotta's brow—a brow damp with sweat.

Distrusting the evidence of her damp hand, she swept up the candle set in a dish and held it over the bed. The flickering light revealed the boniness of Megotta's small face, the dark circles beneath her eyes, her cracked and swollen lips—and droplets of sweat welling on her brow and trickling into the dull wisps of hair at her temple.

"Enid! Wilda!" she cried joyously. "The fever has broken!"

"My lady! She will live!"

"We must keep her dry and warm. Wilda, bring a clean sleeping rail. Enid, clean linens."

The morning fled in a haze of happy labor. Aching backs and aching hearts assuaged by Megotta's cooling flesh, they changed her sleeping rail and linens again and again until the fever was sweated out. Wilda sank to her pallet, closed her eyes, and began snoring. Enid and Amicia hung over the bed, gorging themselves on the sight of Megotta sleeping peacefully.

"My lady, you should rest. I will stay with her this while to see that all goes well."

"Ay, but first"—Amicia's expression hardened—"there is something I must do."

The women were at work in the solar. Looms and tongues clackety-clacked. Spindles whirred to the fragile music of a psaltery. Amicia, accustomed to the silence that fell when she entered the chamber, took no note of the dying tune or the faltering voices, and moved purposefully toward the huge oak-planked door in the spine wall. Festering within her was a hate that had built to such strength she thought she would die if she did not give voice to it.

"My lady," a woman called. She did not slow, and the voice called again. "Lady Amicia."

She paused with a jerky movement, as if the massive door and the man opposite pulled her beyond any will to resist. Her brooding gaze turned to the circle of women. Why would one speak to her now after these weeks of silent disapproval?

A plump apple-cheeked woman stood with spindle in hand. "The child, my lady. How does she fare?"

"The fever has broken. She sleeps peacefully." Amicia turned to go.

"You must be weary after your labors, my lady. If Enid stays with the child, mayhap you would like for us to see your bath readied and meats brought to break your fast."

Amicia turned back, her luminous gaze searching the circle of faces. They all watched her. They all smiled awkwardly. "I—I must see the lord first," she said hesitantly.

"Then we will have all readied for your return, my lady."

"Thank you," Amicia said softly.

"Nay, my lady. It is we who thank you. The child is much beloved among us, and there are others whose lives you have saved. Kin of ours, who have never ere this been given any care by the . . . the lady of this keep. We have spoken much among ourselves in these days you have labored so. It is to our shame that we have treated you—"

"Nay," Amicia said with a smile, "do not speak of what is best forgotten. Let us begin anew."

"Thank you, my lady. See you to our lord now, and all will be readied on your return."

The warmth of loving friendship offered lasted Amicia the few moments it took her to cross the solar and knock on the massive door. No sound bestirred opposite, and she set her weight against it. It gave easily. No servant greeted her. No others moved about their work. The dark and vast chamber was empty of all save Tristan. Slumped in the canopied chair, with his long legs stretched out to the fire, he held a cup of wine in the hand dangling over the armrest.

Wine. He sat and sipped wine at his leisure, while Megotta's life hung like the thread twining from a spindle. He would not come to her. He asked for no word of her. Disgust and hate shook Amicia. One halting step, another, and her feet found a steady pace.

She trod on a lump in the rushes. A hound yapped and scrambled to his feet, his lean head swinging around to chew the bruised tip of his tail. Tristan rolled his head on the back of the chair, his eyes widening on sight of her. The cup fell from his hand, clattering and rolling and spilling its blood-red liquid. He bolted upright and swayed unsteadily. His shaking hands balling into fists at his sides, he stared at Amicia with eyes filled with such anguish the spate of harsh words trembling on the tip of her tongue was stillborn.

"She is dead!" he cried out like a wounded animal yielding its lifeblood to the sharp thrust of a hunter's lance.

A cry that gave new life to Amicia's bitterness. "Nay,

my lord. She lives. Though what could it matter to you? She is but a child, and children are easily made.''

His face twisted with torment and rage. He leaped at her so quickly Amicia had time to do no more than gasp before his hands clamped around her arms and yanked her, thumping, against his broad chest. It was as hard and unyielding as his heavy mail hauberk. Her toes stretched for the floor, but found only air. Her eyes locked with fiery blue.

''What foolish words do you spill, wench?'' he grated.

''Your own words, my lord,'' she whispered, ''spoken to your mother.''

''Do not use the title *mother* for that fiendish bitch!'' he thundered, and dropped her.

Shivering, Amicia watched him stumble to the deep hearth and reach up, clutching the stone edge with white-knuckled hands. One knee cocked, his eyes staring blindly into the fire, he breathed deep, his back swelling above the broad leather belt cinching his narrow waist.

''Did . . . did she lie to me, my lord?'' As she did once before, Amicia thought, for it had been a lie Lady Sybilla told on the day they were wed. *A vicious temper and a heavy hand*, she had said of Tristan. Temper he had aplenty, but his hand had never struck her in anger. And Ruella? Nay, she could not believe it had beaten her, either. But if not Tristan, then who?

''Nay,'' he snarled, and spun around. ''Nay, she did not lie! I said it! Got rot my soul and hers!''

*I beg of you, my lady. Do not do this to my lord*, Enid had said. *Do not do this to my lord*. Enid knew that he was here alone . . . and suffering. Ay, suffering. His eyes were dark with it. His face was carved by lines of pain. Then, why did he not come to Megotta?

*I have use for her still*, Lady Sybilla's voice whispered, ugly and threatening. Was that it? Did she use Megotta against Tristan? But, how?

''You . . . you love the child, my lord,'' Amicia said with little conviction, though it was growing within her. There was no other reason for him to act as he was.

''Ay, I . . .'' He stopped suddenly, his chin climbing. His nostrils flared like an animal scenting danger, and his eyes latched onto her with an intensity that thrust her back a step and sent fear scrabbling down her spine. A look of death and determination darkened the summer blue of his eyes. He took a step toward her, reaching out.

"M-my lord," Amicia gasped, "I beg you . . ."

What she begged for she did not know. She only knew that the look in his eyes terrified her. His hand closed around her wrist, grinding bone against bone. He pulled her toward him, though she pitted her puny strength against his in futile resistance.

"My lord, I—I—"

His hand at her throat choked her to silence, and slid around the shrinking column of her throat to dig fingers beneath the caul holding the heavy weight of her hair. Fingers that gripped her hair, pulling it painfully at the roots and forcing her head back. He bent to her, so close she could see the reddish cast of his russet lashes and the vein throbbing its maddened rhythm in his temple.

"Do you ever speak a word to any of what has passed here, I will cut the tongue from your mouth."

Amicia wrenched back and fled from that threat.

Later, when she was alone and her mind not numbed by fear, she bethought herself of Tristan and Megotta and Lady Sybilla's *use* for her granddaughter.

Round and round her thoughts chattered like the squirrels raiding clusters of acorns in the chase. Loving Megotta as he did, Tristan refused to comfort her. Only fear would have kept him away. Fear for Megotta's sake. He cared not that Enid or she, herself, knew. He cared only that it be kept from his mother.

Amicia heartbeat quickened, her chest drawing so tight she could not breathe. Was this then the *use* Lady Sybilla had for Megotta? To bend her son to her will? If she wanted Megotta alive, the threat could not be to the child's life. What threat then was so powerful Tristan dared do naught, though his mother plotted against his life?

Bedeviled by that question, Amicia could move no closer to an answer. If the threat was not to Megotta's life, why would Tristan hide his love—unless the threat would become such did his mother espy that love. A love so great, he would forfeit his life to protect his daughter.

Cold and cruel she had thought him, but no longer. What would it be like, Amicia wondered, to be so dearly loved by a father . . . or a man?

# Chapter 15

The month was old and the pestilent fever ended, marked by raw graves around the village church and new faces attending old tasks. The Martinmas feast was a waning memory of groaning tables, full bellies, and heads spinning with wine and ale. The undercroft, cleaned of vermin by the rat-catcher's ferret and of dust by the serving maids, was full to bursting with the winter's stores: bins of nuts and earthen jars of honey, casks of brine-cured meats and chests of candles and tallow-dipped rushes. The reivers had stopped their raids as abruptly as they had begun. Though Tristan had fretted and fumed and wondered what it could mean, tonight he lazed by the fire in the Great Hall, wanting naught but pleasure and peace.

Amicia, sitting hard by in the lady's chair, looked more girl than woman with her lower lip sucked between her teeth and her stitching near her nose in the poor light of the candles. Were he a true husband to her, Tristan thought, he could stretch out his hand and feel hers slide warm and trusting into his. He could bid her rise and lead her to his bed and have his way of her.

He shifted uneasily on his seat, cursing the fulling of his loins. A swish of her skirts, a glimpse of her smile, a whiff of sandalwood and woman, and he was as hot as a stallion after a mare in season. What spiteful devil pricked him that he could not ease himself on the leman in the village, but must instead yearn after that which he could not have.

Yearned, even in that moment when he choked her to silence and spoke the threat that glazed her eyes with terror. What accursed star reigned in the heavens on the day of his birth? Always, he wanted and was denied.

Russet lashes flirting with the blue of his eyes, Tristan watched Amicia set her stitching aside. She knuckled her eyes as though they ached, and leaned to rest a graceful hand atop Megotta's head, nodding against her knee.

"Sweeting," her soft voice whispered lovingly, "the hour is late. It is time you were abed. Rise and go with Wilda."

A yawn popping her jaw, Megotta struggled from the stool. "Good eventide, my lady." She obediently slipped her hand into the serving woman's. "Good eventide, Papa."

He grunted low in his throat and studied the pointed toes of his leather shoes. Got rot his mother! He could not even take Megotta in his arms and kiss her cheek and bid her pleasant dreams as a true father would.

"She grows stronger by the day, my lord." Amicia spoke low and soft, as if aware that she must use caution.

He scanned the head of the hall with a shuttered gaze. His mother sat on the dais watching the minstrel strum his harp. Aimery, at her side as ever, watched Megotta leave the hall. His gaze was soft with yearning, as if he longed to call her to him, and Tristan wondered why he did not. Though Aimery often followed Megotta with a wistful gaze, never did he approach her or speak to her.

"The fever has left her with no ill effects," Amicia said beside him, drawing Tristan's attention from his brother. "She eats heartily. Her cheeks are filling out as you can see. And her hair, though it is hidden beneath her wimple, grows soft and shiny once more. I . . . I have said naught to any, my lord, nor will I ever."

Her eyes climbed from the golden griffin's wing her handy needle plied. The glistening blue held a tenderness Tristan had seen often this last month. Her lips had spoken no untoward word, but her eyes, those eyes lit with gentleness and faith, sent silent messages of kinship that weakened his resolve.

He swallowed hard and looked away, wondering why his heart beat so fast and his thews grew weak. He told himself he had need of a woman to ease the heaviness of his loins, but he feared he had need of Amicia to ease the black despair of his heart. It was a strange feeling, this need of a woman for other than a bodily urge. Why? Why only with her and no other?

"My lord!" A guard, his face pink with cold and exertion, pounded up and sketched a bow amid a clanking of arms. "There is a meinie of men before the gate. Stephen, Lord Avon—"

"Stephen?" Tristan stood with lithe grace, a smile wreathing his mouth. Any guest to break this unwanted mood would be welcome, but this one more than others. As bold and brave a knight as ever served Earl Simon in Gascony, Lord Avon would bring news and cheer and, mayhap, a chance to break friendly lances on the jousting field. A more fitting way to while away a winter's day than yearning after his wife like a moonling boy, he thought as he strode from the hall.

No thoughts of Amicia lingered to prick him when Tristan returned to the Great Hall. Nay, instead, he thought only of Aimery. That brother loved by him, but never understood. So hard they had cleaved unto each other as younglings and youths. It seemed then that naught could ever split them apart. One heart they had. One mind. One love for their dour father. One sorrow for the mother that did not love.

That had all changed with Robert's death, when Lady Sybilla reached out to her younger son. A change whose sad effect was never more apparent than now. Tristan did not want to believe what he had been told. He did not want to believe that Aimery was utterly lacking in honor.

His face black with wrath and his wine-red mantle snapping behind him, Tristan strode to the dais and stopped. Poised over his wide-spread feet, he curled one fist about the hilt of his sword and pressed the other palm against the dagger at his waist. Those tools of his knightly trade offered comfort in this moment when he had need of it.

Frowning up at Aimery, he drew breath. "Lord Avon

returned from France to find his wife, Lady Guinella, with child! A child she claims is yours! Is it?''

Aimery slunk down in his chair, settling his chin on his thick neck like a child awaiting chastisement. It was an answer that gouged a scar of disappointment deep into the love Tristan bore his brother. His heavy gaze moved to his mother, stting at leisure with a smug smile and a skewed brow that seemed to say she had won once more, destroying as ever a thing he had loved.

''She had an itch that any could have scratched.'' Aimery's sullen gaze slid away from Tristan's flushed face. ''Who knows whose child she carries.''

''Did you lie with her, Aimery?'' he asked roughly, knowing even as he asked what the answer would be.

''She was a ready wench! If it had not been I, it would have been another!'' he blustered as he had when a child and hurt.

How often had Aimery brought those childish hurts to him for soothing? Tristan wondered, his heart misgiving him. But this was no child's hurt. It was a man's ill-starred treachery, which would not be forgotten without the letting of blood.

''A ready wench with a husband! God's Wounds, Aimery! You know how hot of head Stephen is! He will not, nay, cannot for honor's sake, allow this insult to pass!'' Tristan burst out. ''He demands that you meet him in trial by single combat!''

'Tristan''—Lady Sybilla sat forward—''you know well that King Henry does not approve of—''

''Do not interfere here! This is a matter of honor and no sport for a woman's mouthings!'' Tristan shouted, bending a baleful eye on her. God! How he hated her, this mother of his. This woman driven by her passions of love and hate to destroy, to twist good into evil, to yoke her younger son to her by fetid strings. ''Even King Henry, soft as he is, would say naught of this! I have given Lord Avon leave to camp in the outer ward for the night. On the morrow Aimery will meet him—''

''Nay, I will not.''

Tristan turned a disbelieving stare upon his brother. Surely, he had not heard aright. Yet Aimery stared back with that mulish jut to his lower lip that said now as it ever had that his way was set and not to be changed.

"Have our mother's claws sunk so deep you no longer know right from wrong?" Tristan asked in a strained whisper.

"Lord Avon is the best swordsman in the land, as you have said yourself, brother. With this temper upon him, I would have no chance."

"You would have the chance of redeeming your honor," Tristan whispered, laboring beneath the rising temper that swelled the veins in his temple and brow.

"What good does honor do me if I am dead?"

"What good?" he choked out, his eyes racing across Aimery's square face, as if a stranger be beheld. "Did you learn naught from our father? Better dead than dishonored!"

"You would see me dead for the sake of a wench—"

"There is not a wench alive that is worth a single drop of a man's blood. An adulterous wife deserves naught of any man but his contempt. She is nothing! Less than nothing!" Tristan's disgust lent a scathing note to every word. "We speak of the stain you would place upon the name of Eden. Will you make our name a hissing and spitting for gossipmongers the length of this land? Will you have them say Eden is name for a . . ." He broke off abruptly, his face twisting with pain and anger.

"Coward? Is that what you would say, brother? Is that what you think I am?" Aimery climbed to his feet, his thick hands clenched into fists. "Then think it, for I will not make my head forfeit for a night's dalliance with a ready wench!"

"Then I will meet him as your champion!" Tristan thundered. "I will not allow our name to be dragged through the muck and mire—"

"Tristan," Aimery began, his face lighted suddenly by love and fear and shame, "do not—"

"Nay, Aimery." Lady Sybilla's fingers slid sinuously along his arm. "Does he wish to act the champion for you, let him do so." Silky voiced she was, and smiling a smile that lent a vicious twist to her mouth. "He is well matched with Lord Avon. No better sport could we have for a cold winter's day."

"Trial by combat can hardly be judged as sport," Tristan said through clenched teeth, and moved away.

At the corner of the dais, Amicia stood with her hands knotted beneath her breasts and her white face turned up to him. He paused, staring at her wide eyes, brilliant with fear. He waited, frozen, while she walked the few steps to him and reached out. Her hand, cold as ice, touched his.

"I will pray that you be preserved to m—us, my lord," she whispered, and stepped closer still. Climbing on tip-toe, she raised her lips and gifted him with a fleeting kiss. "Have a care to yourself, husband. There are those who need you here."

She spun and fled, leaving him staring after her, his forefinger lightly brushing the lips that tasted hers still. Before he moved away, he chanced a glance at his mother and found his greatest fear confirmed in the speculative gaze that searched his.

Long into the night Amicia shivered at her prie-dieu. One moment, she raised tear-glazed eyes to the rood and implored a good and gracious God to spread His mantle of mercy over Tristan. The next, she dropped her forehead atop her clasped fingers and prayed for understanding of this thing called *honor*.

The dishonor was Lady Guinella's and Aimery's, Amicia railed in frustrated silence. Yet Tristan and Lord Avon would let blood one of the other. In the name of honor, one would live and one would die, and both would believe themselves bathed in glory. But dead was dead, and what honor was there in that?

It was a belief more akin to Aimery's, but she spared no sympathy for that base knight. Ay, indeed, she thought him the coward Tristan had so near proclaimed him. A man-child, wielding his rod handily, but refusing to reap the bitter fruit he had sown. Nay, he left that to his brother.

Her knees aching and the cold seeping through the mantle Enid quietly set about her shaking shoulders, Amicia wondered at the fear quivering through her belly. If Tristan died, she would be returned to her father. Surely that was cause enough for these misgivings. If Tristan died, Megotta would be left to Lady Sybilla's care. Surely, that was further cause for misgiving. Yet, there was something more. A fear for Tristan that had naught to do with herself or Megotta.

Amicia could not bear to think of him lying in the cold earth, his strong body moldering and his eyes dimmed in death. He would never know she had come to . . . honor him as a man. That word again! Was there no escape from it?

Tristan was right. She knew it now. No woman could understand honor in its full meaning to a man. Even less she, who loved life at its worst. So why did she feel this sneaking sense of pride?

She promised herself she would not be witness to Tristan's trial by combat, but dawn found her and Odo on the alure of the curtain wall staring into the outer ward, where the combatants gathered.

New snow had fallen in the night. The broad sward was untouched by any track, a glistening white, stained pink by the rosy rays of the rising sun. Soon it would be trampled by the destriers' great hooves and speckled with knightly blood—no pink, but the vibrant red of life.

Tristan, too, studied the virgin blanket of snow. A cursed danger at the joust where a keen eye, a steady hand, and a steadier mount were needed. Did ice lie beneath and Vainqueur's hooves slip, he could be skewered like a pig on a spit.

He gave no heed to the herald crying Stephen's defiance and his own acceptance. He knew what the charges were and what the combat would be. Three passes with the lance and, if both survived, a duel afoot with sword in hand. A duel to the death.

No less would avenge Stephen's honor, though he himself had seen the sickness blanch his boon companion's face when he entered the woolen tent to say he would be acting as champion. Far into the night he and Stephen sat, dredging up memories both fair and foul of their warring in Gascony. And Stephen, as ever, torn by changeling moods, first solemn, then gay, thoughtful and fey. Two men of an age they were, sharing wine and laughter and honor's reward of kinship with a like mind—and all the while knowing that on the morrow one must die by the hand of the other.

The morrow that had come with a red-streaked dawn and a crisp cold that nipped at fingers and steamed breath. The castle folk, solemn and silent, lined the stone heights of the inner curtain wall. At one end of the lists Lord Avon's men ranged in neat ranks, their bucklers painted the white on green of his colors. At their head was his mounted squire, holding a lance topped by his banner, a black eagle in a lozenge of white on a green field. And before them all, Stephen, Lord Avon, mounted atop his white destrier with the sunlight glinting from hauberk and helm. At the opposite end, Tristan's men stood shoulder to shoulder, row upon row. At their head was his mounted squire, holding a lance with banner affixed. The black head of Janus whipped on its scarlet field, snapping in the wind like biting jaws. To the fore was Tristan, mounted on dapple-gray Vainqueur.

His forearm thrust through the straps on the back of his heater-shaped shield, he carried its weight easily as an extension of himself. The shaft of the heavy ash wood lance hugged to his side by his elbow and held firmly in his mail-clad hand, he controlled Vainqueur's eager dance with the pressure of his knees. Would that he could control his thoughts so easily.

Willful as a headstrong child, they moved as they would—to Amicia. Why had she kissed him? Why had she whispered those haunting sweet words: *Have a care to yourself, husband. There are those who need you here.* Even now he could feel the pressure of her mouth on his. His eyes moved to the stone curtain wall, searching, until he found the ivory medallion of her face in the dark blue of her hood. So pale, so still. What unquenchable fire had she lighted that the life he had born as a curse now seemed a pleasure to be eagerly won and held dear?

The trumpets sounded the clarion call to battle, jerking Tristan from his musings with a start. Stephen was no untried boy that he could attend with half a mind. He straightened in the saddle, shifting the weight of his shield and focusing relentlessly on the task at hand.

"In the name of God, do your battle!"

The herald's shout traveled clearly to Amicia. She watched the destriers leap forward as one, thick-muscled beasts with spread nostrils and steaming breath and sleek hides. Thundering hoofbeats quaked the earth, gouging scars in the virgin snow. Tristan crouched in the saddle, his flat-topped helm near touching the top of the shield swung to cover his body. Guiding Vainqueur with his powerful legs, he dropped the lance, aiming just off center of Lord Avon's shield. How often Amicia had heard each detail told in a minstrel's tale. How often she bethought herself it would be a fine and glorious sight to see. But never had she thought to watch with her heart throbbing and her head swimming and her hands drenched with terror's sweat.

Each lance struck fair in center field. The crash echoed across the glittering white landscape. The impact rocked the men back on their high cantles and threw the destriers back on their haunches. The horses whinnied. Men and maids sent up a shout. The cooing pigeons roosting atop the keep rose, clattering, into the air. Lord Avon cast his lance aside and gripped the pommel to stay ahorse. Tristan clung to his lance, but swayed drunkenly in the saddle. The steeds clambered upright and cantered back to the head of the list. All to be done again—and Amicia's knees buckling before a drop of blood was spilled.

"My lady, you look to swoon!" Odo slipped an arm about her waist. "No good can you do here. Await him in the keep."

"Nay! I must see!"

Another charge with clods of earth flying. For good or ill, Amicia did not know, but even she could see the two men were well matched in strength and skill. The pointed tips of the lances struck fair once more. The thick lengths of ash bowed and broke with a splintering of wood that echoed from the curtain walls. The two men reeled in their saddles, desperately gripping the pommels.

Another pass to make. Amicia knotted her hands beneath her chin and sought to say a prayer, but no prayer came from her lips. "One more, my lord," she whispered. "Ay, drop your lance and wipe your brow and be steady. Steady, my lord, that you may win the day and return to me. Tristan, Tristan," she said so quietly only she could hear, "your mother will not have you as fodder for a lonely grave. Together, my lord, we will best her cruel game. Trust me. Trust me, my own dear lord. Trust me."

On the field below, Tristan grasped a new lance in a hand so numb he had to look to see he held it. Blood trickled warm from a gash in his jaw where his shield had bounced back to bruise and cut. His ribs ached where the truncheon of the broken lance had hit him. One pass more, and then afoot. His knees squeezed his destrier's thick shoulders; his mount turned and galloped down the field. Sweat, trickling into his eyes, blurred the black eagle painted on Stephen's shield. A worthy opponent, but this no mere breaking of friendly lances as he had hoped. Nay, a duel to the death with a man he called friend. All for honor's sake.

He crouched low, blinked his eyes, and struggled to aim the lance. His blow struck first. A fair hit, to the right and above center shield. Stephen rocked back, his lance hitting a split second later. It was a dangerous inside blow, angling Tristan's shield, allowing the point of the lance entry toward his vulnerable belly. He thrust with his shield, his muscles screaming with pain in his shoulder, and leaned to the side, watching . . . watching the metal tip career toward him. A desperate lurch, and the tip bounced against his side, ripping the black silk of his surcoat and catching in the links of his mail. His ribs shrinking away, he felt the mail tear and, with it, his skin before the lance tore away.

The last pass was done and he was alive. The clean scent of the air rushed into his heaving lungs, but he had no time to savor it. He threw himself from the saddle and pulled his sword from its sheath, spinning around to give good greeting to Stephen with the ring of metal on metal.

A worthy opponent. A friend. A man with a bold heart. Sickness churned in Tristan's belly. To slay Stephen like a butcher or be slain by him, all for the wayward ways of a worthless wench. Could he bring himself to do it? Even for honor's sake?

Above, Amicia's fingers dug into the icy stone wall, her eyes following Tristan's every move. Rays of sunlight shattered across his flat-topped helm and shone from the ragged links of mail exposed by the tear in his surcoat.

Blow upon blow rang out, dull when sword met shield, sharp when sword met sword. Toe to toe, Tristan stood with his opponent, bludgeoning with his shield and battering with his sword. No dance of grace and wit, but a battle of strength and will. And the men so evenly matched neither could win the day.

On and on it went—and Aimery huddled by the hearth nursing a stoup of ale, Amicia thought bitterly. Safe he was, and warm, while his brother fought his battle for him. By the Mass! She could not ken the ways of a man's honor—nor of her own heart, swelling with pride for this man who was hers.

Tristan's shield hung lower and lower. Lord Avon's fierce blows lost their power. Tristan took a blow to the shoulder that sent flecks of blood spraying across the trampled snow. Lord Avon was pricked in the side and a steady stream of blood darkened the green of his surcoat. Chests heaving, they backed away from the battle, each resting upon his sword.

"Is it over?" Amicia asked.

"Nay, my lady. They but rest this while."

She dared to look away and found the sun high in the sky. "How much longer can they last?"

"Until one is dead, my lady."

The battle was joined once more. Cut. Thrust. Slash. Parry. On and on it went.

Tristan's chest burned with every breath sucked into his starving lungs. The weight of the shield dragged at his shoulder; the weight of his sword dragged at his arm. Stephen's shield hung as low as his own, yet every slash was met with the edge of his sword, every thrust speared naught but air.

Tristan summoned the waning reserves of his strength and brought his sword up and over for a downward sweep. Stephen's sword met it with a power that shuddered Tristan's arm to his shoulder. He thrust with his shield, Stephen wavered on a slippery patch of ice, and fell full length.

Tristan stood over him, the tip of his sword pressed to Stephen's throat. He studied his friend's flushed, sweating face, meeting the steady gaze as blue as his own, and knew that, even for honor's sake, he could not slay him.

"Honor has been well served here." Tristan's deep voice carried in the hushed silence. "Yield to me, Stephen, and I will spare your life."

"Strike hard and fast, Tristan of Eden," he rasped, "for I will yield naught to you or any man."

"Stephen, I beg of you," Tristan pleaded raggedly, "for the love I bear you as boon companion and bold knight, yield to me!"

"You dishonor us both with this squeamishness of belly."

"It is no dishonor to either give or accept mercy," he said, stepping back. "Rise, Stephen. I will not have it said over the whole of this land that I beat you with the aid of treacherous ice. Do you wish to fight on, I will do so."

A twinkle entered the tired blue of Lord Avon's eyes, and Tristan breathed a sigh of relief. "Will you admit to all in hall that I was not bested by you?"

A slow smile curved Tristan's mouth. "Ay, I am not so proud that I would deny it. God's Wounds, man, you are too strong for me. Another moment and I would be where you are now, with no ice as good excuse."

On the alure, Amicia gripped her hands so tightly her bones ached. What did they do? Those foolish, prideful men. She watched Tristan stretch out a hand and clasp Lord Avon's and give him aid in rising. She waited for the battle to be rejoined, but saw them throw their arms around each other, clattering and clanking as each pounded the other's back. Her jaw dropped. Her eyes wide, she turned to Odo.

"It is over," he said with the hint of a smile.

"Over?"

"Ay," he nodded. "They fought hard and well. Honor has been served and mercy given."

"But—but," she spluttered, "they now cling to each other as boon companions, as if no battle had been joined!"

"And why not?" Odo's single eye widened in surprise. "They fought for no hate of one another, but for honor's sake."

"Men!" Amicia gusted. "Has the woman been born who can understand them!"

\*   \*   \*

An hour later, she knelt on the mural chamber floor with her chest of herbs at hand and gently spread a healing unguent on Tristan's sorely bruised and scraped ribs. He sat silent and frowning, indifferent to her presence as he had been since she entered. She had stitched the cut on his jaw, and bound his ribs and shoulder. Though his eyes had sparkled with tears of pain, he had made neither move nor sound.

She finished and sat back on her heels, wiping her hands on a wet washclout. Her gaze roamed his features. The red-gold curls drying soft and springy from his bath. The straight length of his nose. The hard set of his mouth. The chiseled square of his jaw. Her heart swelled with pride for his courage and his mercy.

"I am done, my lord," she murmured.

"You have ordered the night's feast to honor Stephen?" he asked, not looking at her.

"Ay, all is done as you requested." She climbed slowly to her feet, clenching her hands to prevent their reaching out to smooth the frown from his brow. "You were right, Tristan," she said softly. "No woman can understand honor in its full meaning to a man."

He drew a deep breath that swelled his massive chest. "Nor can some men," he said, his voice thick with pain.

She reached out, hesitating, before her hand touched his brow and smoothed curling ringlets back. "Aimery is not as other men, my lord. I think he loves you well, but he has a . . . need for your mother's love that comes before all else. Do not judge him too harshly. All men cannot have your courage and strength."

His eyes, palest blue, brightened by surprise and curiosity, wariness and disbelief, shifted up to her. He said nothing, so she moved away, busying herself with her chest of herbs. "My lord, what will happen to Lady Guinella?"

"If Stephen is merciful she will be locked in a room of her dower castle for the rest of her life."

Amicia's fingers stilled in the act of tucking a linen bag of touchwood into a corner. "If he is not?"

"She will die, very slowly."

"Should he not leave her punishment to God's will?"

"It is not her sin he punishes, but the stain upon his honor that he rights."

"But the sin and the stain were hers," Amicia protested.

Tristan's gaze, darkly brooding, ensnared hers. "The sacrament of marriage makes them one before all, as it did you and I. Her honor is his as yours is mine. Her strain of dishonor becomes his as yours would become mine."

"Is there never forgiveness for such a sin, my lord?"

"Never."

"No matter the circumstances?"

"No matter. Does a woman cling to her man, she would fight to the end and die before allowing herself to be dishonored so."

"Do you believe that I would sin so against you, my lord?" Amicia asked softly.

"Who," Tristan said, his eyes turning from her and bitterness curling along his mouth, "can say what any woman would do."

# Chapter 16

*Who can say what a woman will do*. Amicia had expected some such reply from Tristan. Yet, expecting it, she was still strangely hurt by it. A deep and personal hurt that lay like a stone in her breast, weighing heavy on her spirits.

During the weeks that followed, winter storms enshrouded the castle, keeping the folk pent within and surly. The cold nipped at noses and stiffened aged joints. The damp seeped through wool and linen, and all huddled before the nearest fire. All save Lady Sybilla. Draped in her black velvet mantle she reclined in the capacious lady's chair on the dais, warming herself with endless tales of her dearest dead son, Robert. Amicia thought she must grow as weary of singing his praises as all else did of hearing them. Certain it was that Aimery did so. Seldom was he at his mother's side during the snail's crawl of those days. Instead, he sat away to himself, as if he could abide neither care nor comfort. Ever was his nose thrust in a stoup of wine. Ever did his red-rimmed eyes follow Tristan's restless pacing through the hall. Where once Amicia had seen worry and fearfulness bestir the brown of Aimery's gaze, now she saw naught but sullen envy and despair.

She tried to shrug her forebodings away, but they grew stronger each day. It seemed that all around her waited, patiently or impatiently as was their wont, while the Yule season approached.

\*     \*     \*

On a foul day lashed by wind and sleet the wardcorne's horn sounded a feeble note. A wayfarer was before the gate, and that wayfarer none other than Eustace of Bellay. Amicia was in the hall when the guard came arushing, his eyebrows crusted with ice and his mantle dripping. Tristan, on a stool before the fire with his sword flat upon his knees and an oiling cloth in hand, grunted a greeting to his man.

"My lord"—the guard knuckled a salute—"the Lord of Bellay stands before the gate begging entry."

Amicia, guiding Megotta's thin fingers through an intricate stitch, paused and looked up to find Tristan's brooding gaze full upon her. "Nay, my lord," she murmured softly, her gaze locked with his. "I have sent no word to my father nor asked him to come. I told you once that he had given me no cause to make his enemies my own. Yet, you would not believe me then . . . or now," she added.

Tristan slanted a bedeviled look at his man. "Give order to Rolf that the guard be doubled and all to keep a sharp eye and keen wit. When it is done, open the gate and grant Bellay entry."

The guard hurried away, his mantle slapping wetly against his pumping legs. Amicia waited in silence.

"Why do you speak of this now?" Tristan asked, his heavy-lidded gaze stabbing into hers with the distrust that came so easily to him.

Her lips parted to speak the soothing platitudes that came so readily to her tongue. More half truths to add to the lies and secrets that filled the dark corners of this keep like ghosts, she thought with revulsion. Would a freshening wind of truth sweep those ghosts away? Naught could be worse than this endless dance upon the hot embers of suspicion.

She nudged Megotta from her lap, sending her on her way with a loving kiss pressed to her smooth cheek. Standing, Amicia walked the few steps to Tristan, dropped gracefully to her knees, and laid her hands atop his.

"My lord, I know that my father and your mother seek your death," she said, and saw his eyes widen with surprise. She bethought herself that truth was indeed rare here in this keep of his. "I would see you live, Tristan. I am no part of his plan or of hers, nor will I be, am I given choice.''

"What plans, my lady?'' His brows came together over his eyes.

"I am no fool, my lord,'' she said softly. "This keep reeks of plots and plans.''

"Why do you tell me this now?'' The roughness of doubt rasped in his voice.

"I grow weary of balancing on the cliff's edge, never knowing what to say or whom to trust.'' She sat back on her heels and stared up at him. "My lord, I would help you, if I could.''

He set his sword aside and frowned down at her, the red of his hair shimmering in the firelight and his eyes bright as gems polished by use. On his jaw was the ragged scar, scarce healed from his battle with Lord Avon, and on his face, a battle now waged between belief and disbelief. He leaned toward her, reaching out with the callused pad of his forefinger to tilt her chin up. "Why?'' he demanded of her.

Amicia's eyes searched his. "I will not lie and say it is for love of you, my lord,'' she whispered, and wondered that the words clutched at her throat as if refusing to be spoken. "Each of us knows there is no love in this marriage of ours, but neither is there hate. I would not see you slain by such as those two. That is a part of my desire to help you.''

"And the other part?'' he asked, his voice low and deep.

"If you die, Megotta will be raised by your mother and I will be returned to my father's keeping. I would see that such does not happen.''

"If ill befalls me, Megotta will be safe in my mother's care, though not happy, I have no doubt. And you, my lady,'' he said, then paused, his gaze lingering on her mouth. "Your father will use you in another marriage for lands—''

"Nay, my lord. He will not.'' Amicia lifted her chin from the tip of his finger and wished that he did not look upon her so intently. It was shameful, what she must confess. Summoning her courage, she thought it no won-

der that it curdled his belly to think of joining his blood
with hers. Needs must is a hard master. Ay, it was. She
was weary of waiting. Such had been her lot at Holmby.
Such was her lot here. No more. Her lashes climbed, her
glistening gaze seeking the strong contours of his face.
Surely, did they join together, making one where there
was two as Earl Simon had said, they could best her father
and his mother in this cruel game they played.

"Do you know why my father was so eager to see our
vows taken, my lord?" Her gaze meshed with his, darkest
blue to palest blue, passionate to dispassionate.

"Nay," he began.

"I beg you, my lord." She reached up, her hand pressing lightly upon his wool-clad forearm. "Let us speak
naught but truth here. You thought my father set his spy
within your keep. Do you yet think so?"

"Nay." His eyes dropped to the slender fingers resting
upon his arm. "Nay, I do not."

"I am glad, my lord."

His eyes lifted at that, meeting hers, darkening, aswirl
with an emotion that set her heart to tripping. "So, why
then," he asked, his gaze falling to the hollow of her
throat, "was he so eager to see you wed to me?"

"He told me you would slay me, and my death would
give him leave to seek your end without let or hindrance
from any man."

"For all he hates me as he does, he knows me well,"
Tristan said with a frown. "Why would he believe I would
slay you?"

"I know not, my lord. I know only that I came to this
keep believing I came to my death."

He sat back at that, his elbow on the broad oak arm of
the chair and his knuckle pressed to his lower lip. His
thoughtful gaze touched her face, then shifted away, seeking his mother who took her ease on the dais amid a bevy
of maids.

Amicia's eyes followed Tristan's. "Do you think that
she—"

"Ay," he said flatly.

"But why? What gain could there be for her—"

"To prick me with your fear and shrinking would be

enough, but I think there was more. This way she has Bellay as ally not enemy. Left to his own, your father would see Aimery's end as well as mine. That would not suit her, for she would be left as ward to Earl Simon, and so pressed to make a marriage of his liking.''

"But my father will see me alive and well. He will know it for the lie it was and be wroth with all here.''

"She will have a plan. Always, she has been as wily as a serpent with her plotting and planning. A woman's gift she has for treachery,'' he said, his bitter gaze lingering on his mother's face.

"Not all women are so, my lord. Some—''

"Are they not?'' His head whipped around, his eyes hot upon hers. "I could tell you much of women and their ways. You, fresh from the priory and innocent as a babe, yet still a woman and wily. If you thought you came to your death here, why did you not take sanctuary in the church when I offered you the chance?''

"A woman and wily!'' Her chin climbed. 'If I were, your head would be forfeit these many times I have put a cup of wine in your hand and again when I tended your wounds after battle. You missay me without cause as you ever have, as you ever will.''

She made to rise, but his hand clamped over the curve of her shoulder and his face loomed near, suspicious and hard. "You have given no answer with these womanish mouthings of yours,'' he said roughly.

Her eyes met his. Steady they were, betraying naught of the sorrow wrenching her heart, naught of the anger fermenting in her thoughts. "Think you, my lord, that only you have known betrayal and despair. Think you that only a woman may hold hate in her heart and lash out to hurt. A man you are, holding your honor above all. But all men do not do so, and my father is one of those. He told me that not even the church would halt his vengeance if I destroyed his plans. He said he would take me to his keep and give my body to any man, even unto the dogboys in his kennels. I thought it better to yield to one than to many, my lord. So thinking, came I to your bed.''

Tristan's eyes filled with sick disgust and pity. The hand clamped over her shoulder loosened its grip, gentling for the wafting touch of his thumb on the smooth white skin of her neck. "Even he would not dare—"

"Ay, my lord. He has hated me long for the death of my mother. He would dare hell itself to see me suffer." Amicia's gaze sharpened with urgency. "Tristan," she said, using his name apurpose, "the day must come when you give your trust to someone, even if it is not to me. You think me but a woman without honor, and such is your right. Mayhap you have reason good and strong for placing no trust in a woman, but think on this, my lord. Can you not believe that I would cleave to your side for that you are my husband and a man I esteem, then believe that I would do so for my own protection. If you die, I will be returned to my father and I will die, too. Mayhap not in body, but my soul will shrivel and blacken. I will be a thing used by men, no better than a leman—"

Again, his hand clenched painfully around her shoulder. "Speak no more of this!" he growled, and released her. Sitting back in his chair with his fist at his mouth, he stared beyond her to the flames crackling and dancing. "Arise and see to your duties. Our guest will hunger and thirst."

It was a dismissal, simple as any, but one Amicia could not accept. She stayed on her knees to search his face for any middling sign that he gave her either care or trust. There was naught but the tiny vein wildly beating in his sweat-sheened temple, and that could betray naught but his loathing of her father. She thought to feel anger that he could so easily dismiss her and her offer of aid, but anger's molten presence lay far beneath the stony weight of sorrow.

"Leave me," he said.

She paled at that, her heart beating heavy and her spirits sinking. Ever did she fail to touch him, his mind, his heart, his soul. So easily he had set her aside and given no thought to her. So easily he refused to see the woman she was, blinded by those faithless women he had known. Naught could she do that she had not done. He did not trust. He would not trust.

He remained, as ever, untouched, unchanged, while she . . .

What change had time wrought that her fears were more for him than herself?

She climbed to her feet and paused, her worried gaze caressing his rigid features. She took a step and paused once more, her hand moving with a will of its own. It settled atop the powerful slope of his shoulder, feeling the strength of bone and sinew through the thick wool of tunic and surcoat. She offered comfort with a gentle squeeze, sighed softly, and moved away.

It was only when she was gone that Tristan dared allow himself to move. His head fell back against the carved wood of his chair. His umber lashes sagged over his eyes and his hand climbed to his shoulder, squeezing the spot she had touched. Tart bile burned the back of his throat and he swallowed uneasily. So small Amicia was, and so earnest. So softly she spoke, unknowing of the burden she laid upon him.

He had accepted the fact that Megotta's well-faring lay in his death. Though he had no wish to yield himself too easily to the sacrificial altar of his mother's hate, he had long known that when the time came he would die for Megotta's sake. A child she was, with her life before her, and that life, for good or ill, to be chosen by him. Did his mother tell all she knew, Megotta, for no fault of her own, would be shunned as a leper.

Then, too, there was that other, where once his father had wavered. The letter he had written so long ago, now secreted by Lady Sybilla and used as a bludgeon to force Tristan to her will. Should it be bruited about, it would place a stain on his father's memory and honor, and he would not see that happen.

Nay, for reasons good and plenty, he had accepted that he must die at a time of his mother's choosing. But now Amicia had come all earnest and gentle to offer him aid, and in that offer she had swung wide a door to hell.

As page and squire, and later, knight and liege man to Earl Simon, Tristan had seen much of men both faithless and cruel—but none worse than Eustace of Bellay. A festering pustule on God's good earth. Ay, he was that, and more. His own daughter, Amicia was, yet he would see her brought to the lowest state a woman could know.

And that man, better fit to be a worm crawling through a midden heap, was come here to foul Tristan's own hall.

His hand fell to his waist, seeking the dagger's hilt, worn smooth by hard use. A single thrust and Bellay would be no more. The thought roweled Tristan with spurs of regret and anger. Would he become another such as Bellay? Inviting the man into his own hall and sinking to treachery? Nay, he could not do it. The end, however gladly sought, could not justify the means. A sneaking coward's way that would lay worse stain upon his name than any other.

Yet, what was he to do? To live would be to save Amicia and doom Megotta. To die would be to save Megotta and doom Amicia.

Surely, there was a way, could he but see it . . .

The clatter of men striding into the hall pulled Tristan from his chair. His fingers arched, taut with strength and rage, but naught could he do. Bellay was a guest in his keep, so safe from harm. He walked forward, summoning half-hearted greetings.

Bellay, his sodden mantle dripping, stripped coif and cap from his head. "Foul weather we have for faring out," he said, his eyes searching the head of the hall.

"So why did you?" Tristan asked.

Bellay's dark gaze shifted to meet icy blue. His raddled face crinkled in a chilling smile. "The Yule season approaches, Eden. I come to gift my daughter as is a father's right."

"For that and more, I have no doubt."

"You would missay me?" Bellay asked, his mobile mouth arcing down at the corners.

"Would I missay a guest in my own hall?" Tristan parried, his voice cool and crisp. They were like hounds snarling and circling and looking for the weakest spot, he thought. And like hounds, they would be at each other's throats the moment a weakness was espied, mayhap even here in the hall, where guest and host were bound by rules of courtesy.

"Nay, ever do you practice the knightly courtesies that make you so welcome at Earl Simon's board," Bellay said with a disparaging frown, as if he were privy to Tristan's thoughts.

"Mayhap it is not knightly courtesy that makes one welcome and another . . . endured." The shaft struck home. So much, Tristan could see the fury kindled in Bellay's eyes, which shifted away to search once more. Tristan studied the man's strong features, which were marked by envy and greed and dissipation. "My wife prepares all for your comfort," he said, his eyes narrowing. "Mayhap you would like to have speech with Lady Sybilla while you wait."

Bellay's searching gaze stilled and climbed, meeting Tristan's with a glitter of displeasure. "You are your father's son, Eden," he said gruffly, and smiled without humor. "He, too, thought honor a magic mantle to shield him from harm."

"Will you say it was not, Bellay?" Tristan asked. "He lived to a ripe age and died abed, full honored by all."

"Ay, so he did, but will his son?" Bellay's lip lifted away from his teeth in a silent snarl. "Will his son?"

He waited for no answer, but strode away. Stripping his sodden mantle from his shoulders, he tossed it at a serving maid and approached the dais. Tristan watched him bow to Lady Sybilla, stretch out his arm, and lead her away. They had been long cloistered in the dark of a window recess when he felt a gentle tug on his arm.

"They do you no good, my lord," Amicia said softly. "Why do you not try to keep them apart?"

"Did they not meet here openly, they would meet in secret. Did they not meet in secret, they would send more messages between here and his keep. Now, at least, I will know to guard myself well. Otherwise . . ." He shrugged.

Her hand lingered on his arm, gently stroking as a mother with a babe. A soothing touch, it filed the rough edges of Tristan's temper and gave rise to a strange tranquillity. Ever did she affect him so, this gentle maid he had wed. What life might he have known with her had not all been as it was? In that moment he longed to lift her in his arms and make away with her, to ride to the ends of the earth where peace might be found.

Her blue eyes, lighted as by a candle within, lifted to

Tristan's and melted his thews with the weakness of desire. There was danger in that, here in the open hall with eyes all about. Yet, for life's own sake, he could neither frown upon her nor speak with gruff intent.

"My lord," she said, her voice mellow and soft, sweet music to his ear, "I have long wondered why my father holds such hate for the house of Eden."

He shifted uneasily, a frown pleating his brow. "It is a long tale and ugly, my lady."

"I would know what it is, my lord."

He led her away at that, seeking the privacy of a window recess. All was dark and gloom within, lit only by the feeble torch around the corner. Sleet beat sharp and strong against the scraped skin covering the window, and wind, cold and wet, eased through cracks. He seated her and sat beside her, feeling the warmth of her small body and the glow of her gaze.

"Your father was squire to the Old Earl of Chester when my father joined him as page," Tristan began. "From the first they took a misliking for each other, and often it was that your father used his position to do ill unto my father. This much I had from the old Earl when once we met. Men were harder in those days and he did naught to protect my father, saying he learned much from Bellay's baiting and held himself as a man even then as a child." Tristan paused, lost in memories of his sire, a man difficult but fair, and loved by him. "My father was fifteen when he was betrothed to Lady Margaret of Castle Rydding."

"Betrothed, my lord?" Amicia sat straight at his side. Mother Margaret had not told her she was to wed her beloved, she thought. She wondered what more there was and how her father became a part of it.

"Ay," Tristan glanced at Amicia and away, caught up in the tale. "She must have been the most comely of maids, for my father dwelt on it long when he told me of this. He loved her dearly from his first sight of her, and she him. Mayhap it would have been better had she not been so comely and sweet tempered, for Bellay came to love her as well."

Amicia stilled at that, her lips parting, her breath huffing. Her father had loved Mother Margaret! Always as a child she had held a thought close—that her father had known but one true love and that, her mother. It eased the pain of his yearly visitations to remind her of her guilt. It allowed her to think he was driven mad by grief, and so could be pitied, not hated. Hated and reviled with the depth of passion Mother Margaret felt for him. Amicia closed her eyes, dreading to hear what was yet to be told.

"They were to have been wed in the year the Magna Charta was signed at Runnymede," Tristan continued, "but war came, neighbor against neighbor and brother against brother. The barons, revolting against King John, offered the crown to Prince Louis of France, who brought his army to ravage the land. Lady Margaret's father joined the barons' revolt. My grandfather remained loyal to King John. He met his death and my father became lord of this place, swearing fealty to the Earl of Chester and his king."

"My father? Where did his loyalties lie?" Amicia asked.

"With our rightful king. Whether a blessing or curse, my father long wondered. He was in the midlands when Bellay was given order to invest Castle Rydding and take it for the king. Her mother dead, her father slain, and her brother given as page to Prince Louis, Lady Margaret held the keep alone. Bellay took it by guile, coming as friend and man known to her."

Tristan stopped, his eyes dropping to the hands clenched over his knees. So much he could tell, but that most shameful of deeds . . . that he could not. Not even to tell of Bellay holding Lady Margaret hostage or his threat upon her life, though that would not surprise Amicia, knowing her father as she did. Nay, he could not tell that, for then he must tell all. How Bellay had sent a messenger to seek his father out. How Bellay had demanded that his father dishonor himself by forswearing his oath to the King and writing a letter to prove it. How his father wrote that letter, but could not send it. How his father chose his honor on a bitter day and lost the woman he loved.

Now, thinking of the pain and sorrow in his father's eyes when he spoke of those days long past, Tristan felt an odd sympathy for him. Sympathy, where once there had been naught but shame and confusion. Death before dishonor, his father had taught him from a child. Yet, once for a brief space of time he had placed a woman above all. Nay, never before had Tristan felt sympathy for his plight nor thought to understand how . . .

He stood abruptly, shooting to his feet and moving away from the taint of Amicia's presence. What softness crept upon him that he could think to understand how any man might hold a woman so high in his esteem? He turned and gazed upon her smooth ivory brow, wide eyes, and beguiling mouth. His frown etched its displeasure beneath the tumble of red-gold curls.

"My lord," Amicia breathed, "what happened then? What did my father do when he took Castle Rydding by guile?"

Tristan shifted uncomfortably, needled by awareness. Awareness of the music of her voice, the tenderness of her gaze, the gentleness of her hands, the softness of her mouth. So much he might know in any woman. What was it about this one that brought understanding and sympathy where once there was . . .

"My lord?"

Tristan tore his gaze from her, jammed his thumbs in his leather belt, and set his feet wide to brace against buffeting emotions. "None but your father knows what happened there. Lady Margaret escaped him and vanished on the wilds of the high moors, never to be seen again."

Amicia rose slowly, moving to the window. There was another who knew all that occurred at Castle Rydding. One who had hidden herself away, seeking the solace of worship, but never forgetting the man she had loved. Amicia sifted the seeds of the tale. A shameful deed, Tristan had called it. It could be naught but the letter Mother Margaret held dear. The forswearing of an oath to a man who deemed death preferable to dishonor. Ay, that was the way of it. And when he could not bring himself to do it . . .

A chill, unbidden by the cutting cold, crawled across her flesh. Mother Margaret escaped, but did not seek her beloved. Instead . . .

*I came here broken in body and spirit*. The Prioress's words haunted Amicia. *Holmby was a haven from despair*

*where I could hide from myself and . . . another. I came
with no calling and no desire to serve God. I stayed
because I had no where else to go.*

No where else to go. Why? Amicia struggled against the
answer that came all too readily. Mother Margaret had
been dishonored. Raped and soiled by the Lord of Bellay,
she could not go to her beloved, so stern and saintly in his
mantle of honor. That man who bred himself again in his
son, her husband.

*Does a woman cling to her man,* Tristan had said, *she
would fight to the end and die before allowing herself to be
dishonored so.*

Amicia turned and settled a distant gaze upon Tristan.
"Your father, my lord? When Moth—Lady Margaret vanished, what did he do?"

"Naught could he do with the Prince's men pressing
hard at every point, but later, when the warring was done,
he searched, but found her not. He grieved for her his life
long and, when he lay dying, called her name and asked
her forgiveness. Forgiveness"—Tristan shook his head,
staring blindly into the hall—"for doing naught but his
duty. I ken it not."

"Nay, my lord, you would not." Sadness plumbed the
depths of Amicia's voice. "Life is precious and love even
more so, little of it as there is in this world of ours.
Mayhap your father learned that too late."

"Honor is all that makes a man a man," Tristan said
harshly. "It is all that distinguishes a man from a two-
legged beast like . . ." He broke off and looked away.

"Like my father, my lord?" Amicia's question laved
him with sorrow, but she gave him no time to answer. "I
can see where your father would hate mine for the ill done
unto him, but why would my father hate yours and all his
issue?"

"Envy, greed, and more," Tristan said. "You are young,
my lady, and have seen little of men and their ways. It
would seem that the man who has been hurt by another
would feel the greatest depth of hate, but often it is the
man who has done the hurting who later hates the hardest."

Tristan's gaze strayed to the hall, where Aimery sat with
cup in hand, and a sullen frown wrinkling his broad face.

# Chapter 17

Mother Margaret's secret was old and well kept. Amicia could not betray it, though she longed to tell Tristan the woman his father loved had returned his love full measure and more.

Heavy eyed and heavy hearted, she watched her father's ill-tempered leave-taking the following morning. His time- and temper-ravaged face red, he bid a curt farewell to Lady Sybilla, eyed Aimery with a measuring look, and summoned his pock-marked squire to lay the linen-wrapped Yule gift in Amicia's hand. She held it with a squeamish distaste, knowing it was no more than his excuse to come and plan a further attack on Tristan.

Her gaze strayed to her husband, standing to one side. His hair was damp from an early foray into the rain-drenched ward. His gaze, flat and impenetrable, betrayed naught of his thoughts, though his mouth did. Tightly drawn and crimped at the corners, it spoke mutely of a distaste equal to hers. Taller even than her father, he stood straight as a lance. Dressed simply in an unadorned tunic and surcoat in contrasting blue and green—the colors of fidelity and love, Amicia remembered with a painful twinge in the region of her heart—he yet looked more richly appareled than Aimery with his vibrant colors and gay embroideries, or Bellay with his costly fabrics.

Mayhap, she thought, it was because Tristan was a man such as those two would never be. He needed no outer trappings to bedeck his inner strength. Was this the kind of man his father had been? The man Mother Margaret had loved? Tristan, like his father, would ever choose his honor above all, even above the life of the woman he loved, could he ever trust enough to love. And she, Amicia thought with a start of surprise, would be as Mother Margaret—unable to blame him for choosing so.

*I loved him for the man he was,* the prioress had said. *Being that man, he had no choice.*

Ay, no choice would he have. Amicia's gaze caressed the bold contours of Tristan's face. He was neither a two-legged beast like her father nor a weak-kneed boy in man's garb like Aimery. What, she wondered wistfully, would it be like to be so greatly loved by such a man that he would choose her above all else?

The question nagged at Amicia through the Yule season and into the new year. The weather continued foul and cold, sequestering all in the gloomy keep.

Lady Sybilla sat as a queen in the lady's chair, looking at naught, but seeming to see all. Betimes her cold gaze would follow Amicia, as if she easily discerned the resentment growing in her daughter-by-marriage's heart.

Tristan braved sleet, snow, and cold to ride his borders with his meinie of men. When pent in the keep he sharpened his sword and dagger, muscles rippling across his broad shoulders and bunching in his brawny forearms. On occasion he would stare into the fire with a frown wrinkling his burnished brow, then his eyes would seek Amicia's with a fretting question and a deep-seated yearning that melted her loins like the beeward's thick honey.

Aimery captured Amicia's attention more often with each passing day. Huddled before the great hearth in the Lord's Hall, he stayed muffled to the eyes in mantle and furs with a brazier at his feet, as if he could not get warm enough. Ale and wine were his companions. Those, and the sweat on his brow. What was in his heart, no one knew, not even, Amicia thought, Aimery himself.

She busied herself easily, for there were tasks aplenty that cared not what the weather was. Meals must be ordered and stitching done. Unruly servants must be lessoned.

Sniffles and coughs must be physicked. So, her round of days passed with restful times by the fire and Megotta at her knee, but always Amicia was aware of the brooding air of time waiting . . .

Waiting. Tristan chafed and paced and planned as much as he could. None greeted the clearing weather with a gladness greater than his. Heavy frosts outlined branches in traceries of ice, and withered brown bracken sparkled in the wood while he set up his defenses with huntsmen, foresters, and men-at-arms.

Plow Monday came and went. The calving and lambing began. A recently abandoned camp was found in the chase, evidence the reivers had returned. Tristan's blood heated and sang through his veins. The waiting would be over soon.

On a day cold and clear, he paused atop Vainqueur to watch the rapturously swinging tails of suckling lambs. Overhead, shiny black starlings flecked with winter's white wheeled through the brilliant sky and rasped discordant songs. On the brow of the near hill, a shepherd tweetled a tune on his pipe. In the distance, villagers plowed their strips of land with bony-ribbed oxen. The season was changing with the promise of spring. Life's age-old rhythm was renewing itself. A life that seemed of a sudden sweet and strong.

Tristan watched Amicia, small and childlike atop her palfrey, trot from the village, trailed by her two minions, Odo and Enid. What gentle way had she worked upon him that the life he would have given gladly so short a time ago, he now yearned to live to its fullest? Naught had she done, but go her way with dignity and grace. No complaints had she offered, though he treated her not as a wife or companion. Instead she had given a mother's love to Megotta and a lady's care to his folk. Even they, hating her father, were bewitched by her.

As bewitched as he was? His unruly thoughts ever strayed to her, as now. Would that he was not haunted day and night by the knowledge of what would become of her upon his death. Better that he should take her with him to a cold grave than allow her to be returned to her father.

Though he had worried and wondered the winter long, he was still no closer to an answer. Surely, there was a way to save her, could he but see it.

He waited on the crest of the hill, watching Amicia's approach. He saw Odo lean toward her to speak, and heard her dulcet laugh, a light sound of merriment as mellifluous as the shepherd's pipe. A thought nagged, incomplete and obscure. Odo was the answer, but how?

Longing stole upon Tristan. A longing to take Amicia to yon low hill, to sit beneath the single spreading oak and lay his head in her lap, to chew a stem of grass and watch the plump clouds sail overhead, to know peace and . . .

Earl Simon! His hands tightened on the reins and Vainqueur tossed his great head, snorting and prancing. Soothing the destrier with soft murmuring words, Tristan's mind spun with relief. Ay, the Earl would give him aid in this.

Amicia drew near, her nose pink with cold and her eyes ashine. "My lord," she said, her smile twinkling the dimple high on her cheek, "the swineherd's wife was brought to childbed with twins in the night. A boy and a girl, squalling when I left."

Tristan's heart leaped into his throat, leaving an empty, yearning space in his chest. "You will go no more to the village with naught but these two," he said gruffly. "There is sign in the wood that the reivers return. I will leave men to accompany you in the future."

"Ay, my lord," she said compliantly, though her smile dwindled to naught and her cheeks lost their color.

Tristan ground his teeth and stared at a far hill. "I would have speech with your man. Begone with Enid. I will send him to you as soon as I may."

"My lord—"

"Begone, my lady!" He cut her off abruptly. "Odo has done no ill unto me, nor will I unto him."

"I have no fear of that, my lord."

Her voice was sweet and soft, but her gaze was heavy with sorrow. Heavy, too, with a yearning akin to that churning in Tristan's own chest. Through the winter she had watched him so, until he thought he must sweep her up and carry her away and discover for himself what the yearning was, what these new feelings besetting him were.

"I will fare to the keep and await you within, my lord," Amicia said, and urged her palfrey into a gallop that carried her rapidly away.

Tristan ordered his squires to follow her, and watched the flutter of her dark blue mantle and her grace atop the dainty steed. Whatever happened to him, she must be protected. She must never know a moment's sorrow, a moment's pain.

He settled a measuring look upon Odo. "I must know," he began, his eyes narrowing, "if it came to a choice between Amicia and Bellay, where would your loyalty lie?"

Odo's single eye widened, its gray hue turning wary. "I hope, my lord, never to face such a choice."

"But you must, and now," Tristan commanded. "Amicia has told me her father has vowed he will return her to his keep and give her body unto any man who wants her. If I die, such will be her fate. Could you stand by and watch it?"

The thick knob in Odo's throat bobbed beneath his blanching face. "Nay, my lord, I could not," he said, looking away and frowning. "I wish I could believe it was an idle threat, but he has hated her long and hard. I fear—" he began and stopped, his scarred face twisting. "I fear he would do it."

"I would have word of you now that your loyalty will lie with Amicia. Do you betray me in this, you betray her and yourself as well."

Odo looked away, his thick hands clenching the pommel of his saddle. "You have it, my lord," he said, his voice scraping low. "What would you have me do?"

"I have four men, good fighters and strong, who know the way to Kenilworth as well as I. I will leave them in the keep as guard for my lady's faring, but will give them secret order to follow your bidding. At first word of my death you are to leave here by stealth, taking Amicia to Earl Simon. Take naught that you do not need and ride fast as you may. Tell the Earl I have asked naught in the years I have served with him, but now I ask that he take my wife as ward to protect her from Bellay. Have Amicia tell all she knows. The Earl will see to all else.''

''Megotta, my lord—''

''Is to be left with Lady Sybilla. Tell the Earl I would have him seek no vengeance against my mother nor remove Megotta from her care. Should he do so, all I have done will be for naught. It is only Amicia I dare send to him.''

''Ay, my lord. Think no more upon it, for you may trust me in this.'' Odo's gaze moved to stare beyond Tristan's shoulder. ''Your squires return with all speed.''

''My lord!'' the youngest bellowed. ''The reivers attacked the woodcutters in the chase.'' He pounded up, flushed with excitement, as once Tristan had been, eager to blood his sword and prove his worth in battle. Words tumbled from him, while Tristan sat grim and silent. ''Only one escaped to tell the tale, and he is wounded. Lady Amicia tends him now.''

Tristan stared at the broad gate in the distance, watching his meinie of men pour out with Rolf in the lead. It began anew. This time to be no test of strength or will, but a battle true. His mother grew weary of games. He had seen it in her eyes. And Aimery? What of him? Was his brother truly lost to him, or was there left some portion of the love they shared in their youth?

''Odo''—Tristan bestirred himself—''I will send the four men back to the keep. You will not forget your vow.''

''Nay, I will not. God keep you, my lord.''

*God keep you, my lord*, Amicia's silent prayer unwittingly echoed Odo as she wrapped a linen cloth around the last of the woodcutter's grievous wounds. She gave him an infusion of powdered feverfew and honey, and left Enid at his side.

Climbing the stairs to the Great Hall in hopes of finding solace in the chapel, she thought of small things. The way the wind whipped the single red-gold curl escaping the confines of Tristan's arming coif. The power of his hand gripping the hilt of his sword and the gentleness of that hand exploring her flesh. The blue of his eyes, hot in anger, smoky with passion, pure in his few moments of peace. The frailty of flesh beneath the slash and stab of sword and dagger. A danger he faced now in his faring against the reivers.

She paused in the light of a torch, trembling and wondering why she trembled so. Tristan was a man to hold high in her esteem, but no more than that. Surely, her breath caught in her throat, it was no more than that.

"My lady," Aimery called out from the hall adjacent, his light voice roughened by wine and disuse, "come and sit beside me and share a cup of wine."

Amicia moved slowly, reluctant to do his bidding, reluctant to sit in his presence. Resentment tugged at the corners of her mouth and wrenched the knot of apprehension beneath her breast. He was a man, burly and strong, with a good right arm his brother could use. Yet here he sat the day long, deep in his cups like a hoary warrior beyond his prime. She sat in the chair, folding her hands neatly, and shaking her head at his offer of wine.

His thick hand, short fingered and smooth, lifted the ewer and poured a generous draft, blood red in the firelight. As red, Amicia feared, as the blood Tristan might spill. She watched Aimery tilt the cup high, greedily sucking it dry, and longed to dash it from his hand and demand that he rise as a man and ride to his brother's aid.

"Where have all gone?" he asked, gazing into his empty cup.

Amicia, her nostrils flaring with distaste, studied his thick jaw and small nose and lips slack with wine and weakness. "Tristan has been called away. The reivers attacked the woodcutters in the chase."

His eyes lifted at that, meeting hers with a look of fear that dried her mouth and set her heart to pounding. She wanted to ask what he knew and why he feared, but her tongue would not move to speak.

"The reivers," he repeated. "So it is today," he added, as if to himself.

"Today?" The single word pulled Amicia to the edge of her seat to watch his working face and paling skin. Sweat beaded and oozed down his forehead, as if his body wept tears his eyes could not shed. "Aimery," she began, but fear sucked the breath from her lips. "Aimery, what do you know?"

"Naught!" He sank deep into the shiny furs like a child seeking to hide. "I know naught."

It was firmly said, but there was a quiver to his mouth and a furtive look in the eyes that refused to meet hers. Amicia slipped from her chair and sank to her knees at his feet. Her hands pressed together in an attitude of prayer, she raised a pleading gaze to him. "He is your brother. He loves you well, and your mother loves you not at all. Aimery, you must see that, between them, you must choose the better. I know you hope to gain her love, but even you must see there is no love in her to give. Tell me, Aimery. Tell me what you know."

His brown eyes shifted to hers, as if drawn by the force of her will, and she saw in them a torment that roused her fear and trembling. "I cannot." His voice dropped low, a husky whisper. "It is better this way. He will never know what I have done."

Her every thought focused relentlessly on Tristan and the danger he faced, she had no time nor thought to give to what Aimery had done. "Why?" she demanded. "Why will he never know?"

He looked away, his lower lip jutting. "Ever was he good to me." His lilting voice sheered up the scale into maudlin self-pity. "It was always Tristan who belayed our father's harshness and wiped my tears when our mother made me weep. It was he who played games with me and listened to me and brought a candle to light my chamber when I was afraid. It was he who made my first wooden sword and taught me to use it."

"Was?" Amicia caught his wrist and leaned close. "Why do you say *was?*"

His gaze moved from the fire to touch her face and linger. A gaze empty of all save a child's bright memories. "You must see that it was for the best. Now he will not learn what I have done and hate me for it."

"A trap," she said. "The reivers have set a trap for him and you have let him ride into it!"

"If I had not, *she* would have told him," he said, frowning. "It is better this way. He will suffer no more, nor will I."

Amicia stared up at him, her eyes bright with tears and

her heart torn between pity and hate. "Aimery, can you not see the evil your mother has worked? You think to earn her love with Tristan's death, but you will not. She has no love to give. Only he has loved you, and when he is gone, you will be alone."

"Nay, you are wrong." The sly look in his eyes sent a chill slithering down Amicia's spine. "She will love me then as she loved Robert. I will be her only son."

The odor of madness was in the air. A rank odor that drifted on the heated air perfumed by the scent of winter savory rising from the rushes. An odor ripened by old betrayal and thwarted love and a child's unmet needs.

Amicia stood, backed away, and whirled to race across the hall. Mayhap—she could only hope—mayhap, all was not yet done.

In the Guard Hall she rushed upon Odo. "You must ride out with men," she babbled in her haste. "My lord rides into a trap set by the reivers. Hurry, Odo! Hurry! He is like to be slain all unsuspecting!"

"My lady," Odo protested, "I may not lead his men! And did I ride out, your lord would have my head for it! He has laid a charge upon me—"

"I care not what he has said or done, nor what he will do! It is a trap!"

"My lady, you must—"

"Then *I* will go with yon huntsman who plays my shadow!"

"My lady!" Odo said, aghast. "You cannot—"

"Then go for me! Take his men and ride to his aid. Odo, I cannot bear it! I cannot bear to think of him dead!"

The few men-at-arms taking their ease about the hall, leaped to their feet, throwing aside whittling, meats, and oiling cloths to gather round, rumbling and growling.

Amicia turned to them, her face white as parchment and her eyes dark with fear. "Go to him," she pleaded. "Go to give warning should the trap await or to fight at his side should the trap be sprung. My man will lead you, or one of you, if you trust him not."

"We will follow your man, my lady, and fare out to save our lord can he be saved," said one man gray with years, but sturdy and true. "Fear not," he added, then looked to Odo. "We await your order."

"To horse," Odo commanded, and turned a wry gaze upon Amicia. "The lord will have my head for this."

She watched him go, then flew to prepare. Water was heated, and sand. Needles were laid out with silken threads. Linen cloths were torn into narrow lengths. Herbs were set to brew. She looked for more to do, desperate to keep her hands busy and her thoughts occupied. Naught was left, but prayer.

The chapel was dimly lit by spears of light lancing through the window slits. The dry smell of rushes and the dampness of seeping walls filled Amicia's nostrils, as fear filled her mind. She folded her hands and tilted her chin and gazed upon the rood, a wooden cross agleam with a beeswax shine.

"Oh, good and gracious Lord," she prayed, "guard and protect him. Turn aside sword and dagger. Strengthen his arm. Preserve him to me and all here who need and love . . ."

Her prayer stopped abruptly. Love? Was it true? Did she love him? Ay. Oh, God! Ay, it was so. Her shoulders sagged and her heart grew heavy with dread. Love had crept upon her unawares. Her esteem of Tristan as a man had changed to that emotion, so strong, so soft. Was this what love was? Courage and fear? Hope and despair? Joy and sorrow?

For the first time in weeks Amicia thought of Ruella, first wife to Tristan of Eden. That poor lady who was looked upon but not seen, who gave love where it was not wanted, who died calling a man who would not come. When first she had heard of Ruella and her sorrow, she thought she understood the bitterness of that lady's life. Amicia knew now that she understood naught, for now she knew the same bitterness . . .

The spears of light lancing through the window slits faded, and still Amicia knelt at the altar awaiting Tristan's return, reviling her own weakness and praying for his life. So long he had been gone and no word yet. She feared the worst.

The wardcorne's horn sounded a firm note. She leaped to her feet and fled the chapel, unmindful of her sacrilege in her need to look upon Tristan and know he survived. She arrived on the landing of the outer stair, breathless and disheveled, with her wimple askew and her face flushed. Her heart threatening to burst the bonds of her ribs, she hung there by the hardest effort. She would not be as Lady Ruella was. She would not look upon him with her heart in her eyes. She would not run to his side, as if she wanted to be nowhere else. He had a man's pride, and she had a woman's.

Tristan's squire, holding his rippling banner aloft, was the first through the inner gate. Behind him came Tristan, sitting rigidly in the saddle. Swathed as he was in his wine-red mantle, Amicia could see no wound upon him, but the sweat shining on his pallid face told her he had not escaped unscathed. His destrier, sweat flecked and ribs heaving, plodded wearily across the ward, cleaving a path through the gathering folk.

Amicia spared a glance to search for Odo in the wounded men following and found him hail and hearty. Her eyes returned to the lodestone of her lord, her love. A current of pain swept across his face and her woman's pride deserted her. She lifted her skirts and ran down the stairs, hurrying to his side.

"My lord," she said, reaching up to touch his knee, "you are—" The words dried to dust in her throat. Her palm was wet. Wet with blood.

"It was a trap, well baited and sprung," he said, his eyes bright with pain. "Had Odo not come with his men howling like a horde of ravaging Scots, we would be dead to the last man."

He set his hand to the high pommel—a hand glistening red with blood—swung his leg over his mount, and crumpled at Amicia's feet. She cried out, a wild cry that brought his men running. On her knees, she cradled Tristan's head and stroked his brow.

"My lord, my own dear lord," she murmured incoherently.

His lashes climbed from his cheeks. His eyes found hers, his gaze a rueful one that seemed to jest at himself. "I wanted to come to you in victory on my own two feet," he said and went limp in her arms.

As terrified as Amicia was, she knew it was a blessing.

Though his men-at-arms took care with him, Tristan was buffeted unmercifully on the long climb up the spiral stair. The men remained in his chamber, more hindrance than help in stripping him down to his loincloth. Enid shooed them out, flapping her arms and clucking like a hen, while Amicia hung over the bed, her heart misgiving her for the task ahead.

Tristan lay as one dead with his sweat-sheened face as pale as the linen beneath him. Gone was the arrogance, the manly pride, the power of a knight bold and brave. Instead, he was as an overgrown boy with his hair tumbling wild and his strong hands limp and weak. On the cap of his left shoulder was a gash dug deep, and in it, iron links broken from his hauberk. On his right thigh another gash, long and ugly and oozing the bright color of his life. On his side, the long slit of a dagger turned by his ribs.

Her heart ached to see him brought so low, but there was time neither for her rage at Aimery's treachery nor for the fears that set her atremble. "Bring me the touchwood, Enid. We will stanch the flow of blood at rib and thigh that we might attend his shoulder first."

An hour passed and another, a blur of time awash in the red of blood. So long had Enid and Amicia been together, so practiced were they by the plague of fever, they worked as one with few words spoken. It was a blessing, for often in those hours Amicia could not have spoken had there been a need.

Tristan's every low moan pulled a moan from her own aching throat. Every careful stitch linking his torn flesh felt as though it was made on her own. At the end, when the last stitch was taken and the healing unguent was spread over the raw scars, her hands shook too much to help Enid wrap the linen cloths around the wounds. She sank to her knees by the bed, her shaking hand smoothing sweat-soaked strands of hair from Tristan's brow.

"Fear not, my lady," Enid said. "He has survived worse than this. Stay with him, and I will go to tend his men."

The candles burned low in the aging night, while Amicia remained on her knees at his side. No thought of sleep came to her. No heaviness of eyes beset her. She waited for him to wake, waited for the moment she could look deep into his eyes and see that he would live.

He stirred restlessly in the wee hours, awakening by slow degrees. His lashes fluttered and climbed. His eyes, blank at first, turned to her. A smile played at the corners of his mouth. "I have surely died and gone to heaven to wake with an angel at my side."

"No angel, my lord," she said throatily, attempting to blink back a rush of tears. "Only a woman as weak and sinful as any."

He studied the single tear slipping from her lashes. "Why do you weep, Amicia?" he asked, his voice deep.

"For joy, my lord," she whispered, her tears spilling unchecked. "For joy that you are brought back to me."

The candlelight captured a look in his eyes. A look of surprise and pain and gladness. A look that beckoned Amicia to rise, to lean down, to press her lips to his. Gently, she moved her mouth upon him, and felt his hand slide around her nape, while the kiss deepened. Fiercely, he shaped his mouth to hers, as if he took that which he had long yearned for . . .

"I see you are well."

Lady Sybilla's cool dry voice parted them as effectively as yanking hands set to their shoulders. Amicia gasped, straightened, and spun to stare at her mother-by-marriage, as if an apparition she beheld. The woman stood in the doorway, a gloating look in her eyes.

"I am not done yet," Tristan said heavily.

"Nor am I," Lady Sybilla responded in her husky voice before leaving. "Nor am I."

# Chapter 18

Lady Sybilla's vow hung in the air of the mural chamber, as chimerical as the shadows cast by the candlelight, but no less real. Amicia listened to its dying echoes and watched Tristan lying so still and silent. He was in pain, but he neither moaned nor moved. She longed to go to him, to nestle his head against her breast, and whisper words of love. She longed to take his pain from him, to suffer it herself, to offer him a brief respite from the horror of his days.

The leather curtain rustled in the doorway and Amicia spun about, her eyes hard and her lips drawn back in a snarl, but it was not Lady Sybilla who peeped around the edge. "Megotta, what do you here, sweeting?" She hurried forward. "You should—"

"I want to see Papa!" The child stepped through the doorway, her small chin jutting and a mutinous look lighting her eyes.

There was danger in this, though Amicia knew not why or what. Only that Tristan had so carefully shielded his love of Megotta from his mother. Surely this once it could not hurt. He was wounded and none but God knew whether those wounds would fester and he would live or die. How bitter it would be if Megotta was turned away and never saw her father again.

Amicia looked to Tristan. He had risen on an elbow and leveled a solemn gaze on her. A questioning gaze that sent her heart sinking into her toes. Would he never trust her?

"Enid," she said briskly, "go to the head of the passage and stand guard. Tell any who seek entry that your lord sleeps and cannot be disturbed. Megotta"—Amicia moved to the doorway—"you may stay a few moments only. Your papa needs to rest."

Megotta tiptoed into the mural chamber and paused, as if afraid to approach the bed. "Papa?" she asked tentatively, her nubbin nose wrinkling and her sooty lashes blinking.

Tristan lay back on the deep-piled pillows and stretched out his good arm. "Do not fear, heartling. Come."

The child flew to him, the hem of her skirt billowing and her black plait bouncing, but at the side of the bed she stopped abruptly. "I would not hurt you, Papa," she whispered.

"You could never hurt me, Megotta," he said, reaching out to gather her to him.

Amicia, standing in the doorway, saw the sheen of sweat glistening on his brow, the pain crinkling the corners of his eyes, and knew the effort it cost him to hold his daughter close. Megotta's anxious questions and Tristan's assurances followed her through the curtain into the dim passageway. There she waited, listening to a child's adoration of a father and a man's love of a daughter. She bit her lip and blinked her hot dry eyes, and wished she could find a dark corner to spill the tears she longed to shed. This was what she had missed as a child. A father's loving inquiry about how her days were spent, his worry that she ate not enough, his pride in a new tooth crowding her baby teeth.

Unable to intrude on their happiness, Amicia waited long before realizing that Megotta would not tear herself from him nor would Tristan send her away. She drew a bracing breath and entered. "She must go, my lord."

Amicia thought Megotta would weep and wail, but she did not. Instead, she eased from the bed and reached out with her tiny child's hand to touch his brow and smooth his hair. "I love you, Papa," she murmured.

"And I you, heartling," he said, and reached to take

her hand and press it to his lips. "Do not return here,
Megotta. Whatever happens, do not return."

"But—" she began, her breath hitching in and out.

"I would have your word!" he commanded.

"Ay, Papa, you have it," she said, and turned and
walked out like a woman grown and worn with care.

Tristan lay back, staring into the canopy, the white of
pain—his price paid for the time spent with his daughter,
Amicia thought—riming his mouth.

She could offer naught to ease the agony wrenching his
heart, but that throbbing in his wounds she could physic.
The black of night lay against the window slits while the
embers hissed in the brazier and corn-rose hips steeped
atop the grate. He did not speak, nor did she, and time
passed slowly. A time laden with his unknown thoughts
and her own, known too well.

Her hands tensely cupping her knees, Amicia sat on a
stool where she could watch him. She studied the shell of
his ear and his tousled hair and the curve of the lashes
lying against his cheek. The fitful light of the candles
molded his jaw in light and dark. It revealed the taut line
of his lips and plunged them into darkness.

Love had come upon her unawares, giving her heart to
him who would not take it. If Mother Margaret were here,
what advice would she give? Amicia closed her eyes,
remembering: *And if you find love, Amicia, fight for it with
every breath in your body*. She had found love where she
had never expected to find it. She had given it, all unwilling as she was. But how could she fight for it when her
love wanted neither her nor her heart?

How wise Mother Margaret had been to question her
vocation. Truly, it had been her shrinking fear of this
unknown life. God forgive her craven reasons for wishing
to serve Him. God forgive her for wishing, even now, that
she could return there where the love and peace of the
order could fold her to its breast. Would that she had never
been torn from it. Would that she had never learned the
pain of loving a man.

Sighing, Amicia stood and poured the steeped brew into
a cup. "My lord, drink of this. It will ease your pain."

He eyed the steaming cup with a misgiving that told

Amicia how futile her love was. He did not trust her. He never would, and where there was no trust, love could not find a dwelling place. Her lip quivered and she chewed it into submission.

"I will drink of it first, my lord," she said unsteadily, "that you might know I intend no ill—"

"Nay, there is no need of that." His voice was a hollow husk robbed of the strength shining in the thoughtful gaze that met hers and sent it fleeing. "I have hurt you, though I know not how," he said. "What have I done?"

He reached out, clasping her wrist, and Amicia felt the heat of his palm, a heat that foretold the fever to come. Her hand trembled and his moved to the cup, taking it from her. Tears prickled at the back of her eyes, threatening a deluge.

"My lord," she whispered, and stopped to swallow before she could say more. "You must know after all of this time that you can trust me. I—"

"Amicia, it is no distrust of you that makes me shrink from this brew. Enid has long given me such, and more often than not, I would rather the illness than the cure. I vow she steeps the foulest potions in the land."

A smile lurked at the corners of his mouth and a look of truth sheened his eyes. Amicia reached out, the back of her fingers trembling against a coppery curl fanning across his brow. "You are sure it is naught else, my lord?" she asked softly.

"Ay, my lady. You have seen more here today than any in this keep have seen, save Enid whom I trust above all others."

Amicia looked deep into the blue of his eyes and knew he spoke truth. Was there hope for her in this? Did she dare press for more that she might aid him where she could?

"Tristan, can you not tell me why you and Megotta must hide your love, one for the other?"

"Nay, I cannot," he said flatly.

"I—I see." She turned away, but he took her arm, gently tugging her back. Her gaze met his, questioning.

"It is for no lack of trust, my lady. I have learned much of you in these months, and the first that you are not a wench whose tongue wags at both ends. You have seen much and kept your own counsel. You have taken Megotta and loved her as your own, and for that you have my thanks.''

"She . . . is an easy child to love, my lord. I have been glad to call her my own. But, it is you I fear for. Can you tell me nothing?''

A frown wrinkled his brow. Amicia thought he would say naught, for the moments stretched long. He sighed heavily, wincing as if a shaft of pain had struck, and she suffered a deep regret for pressing him so.

"Lady Sybilla holds a secret that could ruin Megotta's chance of a good marriage and a happy life." His gaze probed hers, as if he doubted his wisdom and hers. "That secret is the goad she uses to force me to her will. Should she, also, learn that I love Megotta and would do anything to keep her from harm, her hold upon me would be strengthened as would the threat to Megotta. That is why we must play this game.''

"There are games aplenty within these walls, my lord," Amicia declared. "Is it another part of this game that you have set me from you and treated me not as a wife?''

The warm hand encircling her wrist clenched tight about it. His russet lashes fluttered and fell, shielding his eyes from her sight. "There is danger for any here who show kindness to me. I would not draw you in and make you pawn for my mother's hate.''

"My lord"—Amicia's voice quivered with pain—"do you think I would allow myself to be used against you?''

"You may not be given a choice. It is best for you and those whose memory and life I must protect, that you hold yourself from me.''

"Tristan, have you ever been thus?" Amicia asked, softly sorrowing. "So alone?''

His chin tilted and firmed. "It is a way old to me and known," he said stiffly.

"But I am your wife. Made one with you before God and man. I beg of you, share this with me. Give me leave to help you where I may.''

"Amicia, could I share this with any, it would be with you." His voice came deep and throaty, while his eyes

searched hers with a wary tenderness. "But, I cannot.
Where you seek to give aid, you will only bring harm."
He released her wrist and reached up to cup her cheek,
trailing his thumb across her lips. "Do not look upon me
so, sweet witch. You rouse a fire for life, where I must
needs have acceptance of my fate."

"I will never accept it," she vowed.

"You must, and so must I."

By dawn Tristan's fever was rising. By twilight his flesh
was so hot it burned against Amicia's palm. By the following morning she had to summon two burly men-at-arms to
hold him down while she and Enid tied him to the bed.
Still, he thrashed and struggled, shouting orders to troops
and fighting battles that existed only in the fevered recesses
of his memory.

Amicia would have wept in fear, but there was no time.
He struck out, opening the oozing wound in his shoulder.
He kicked out, opening the wound in his thigh. All was to
be done again. Her voice thin and high, she gave order
that the door be taken from the kitchen, scrubbed clean
with sand and soap, and brought above. By the nooning
Tristan was strapped to the padded door like a swaddled
babe, unable to move anything but his head.

She hung over him, crooning low, stroking his hot
forehead, and aching when his wild eyes turned to her,
blue flames of agony in dark sunken sockets. "I am here,
my own dear lord," she murmured. "None shall harm you
while I am by, and I shall not leave you while you suffer
so. Nor later"—her voice broke and tears welled in her
eyes—"should you want me by your side. Tristan, you
must live and grow strong again. God could not be so
cruel as to take you from me now."

It was a plea Amicia made again and yet again in the
days that followed. Tristan's fever, now burning, now
cooling, but never breaking, ravaged his body. Weight
melted from him. His lips dried, cracked, bled. His skin
lost the sheen of health. His red hair lost its golden luster
and assumed the texture of hay. She forced wine and broth
down his throat, drop by precious drop. She ordered
blancmanger and frumenty and fresh venison cooked and

pounded to a paste. She fed him more by the force of love than the force of will. He would live, if she had to snuff out her own life with lack of sleep, lack of food, lack of rest.

She knew she should not push herself so, but she could not stop. She cared not that her cotte hung about her thinning waist like a sack nor that her hair grew as dry and dull as Tristan's nor that her eyes burned as feverishly as his. It mattered only that his pain be assuaged, that he be fed and bathed in cooling water, that he live.

During those days Lady Sybilla came again and again. Gliding in like a hungry bird of prey, she waited, silent and smiling as she looked upon her son. Each time, Amicia reminded herself what Tristan had said: *Where you seek to give aid, you will only bring harm.* Each time, she swallowed the rage that was building inside her.

"My lady, your hand shakes so you cannot feed him." Enid took the spoon from Amicia's hand. "Go and rest. Naught may you do here if you fall as ill as he."

"He will eat from no hand but mine," Amicia's voice came, a whisper hoarsened by exhaustion. "Enid, I cannot bear to see him so low."

"Your tender heart misgives you, my lady. His fever is not so bad now and a crust forms on his wounds. We win the battle," the serving woman said with a brisk assurance Amicia envied. "If you will not rest, then sit abed and stroke his brow. Mayhap he will sup, if you do."

Amicia crawled into bed, set her elbow above Tristan's crown of straw-red hair, and laid her lips lightly against his hot, dry brow. His eyes, a brilliant blue betraying both weakness and need, followed her every move as they had for days.

"You must sup and grow strong, my lord," she crooned as to a babe. "Open your mouth. Ay, just so. Swallow now, my lord. Ay, you are weary, but you must. Good, my lord. Now another."

Just so did she talk him through the last spoonful of broth and the infusion of corn-rose hips sweetened with honey. At the end, his lashes sagged low and he eased into sleep.

Enid stared down at him, her gaze softly wondering. "Ever before has my lord been a surly sickling, foul of temper and hard of head. I know not what skill you use upon him, but never has he been so easily led."

"Mayhap," Lady Sybilla's husky voice sounded from the entryway, "it is because a mother's wish has been answered and he has found joy in this new wife of his."

Amicia's head whipped around, a gasp strangling in her throat. Her heart raced with fear and loathing. She should say naught. She should ignore Lady Sybilla's presence and swallow her rage . . . but the hypocrisy of the woman was Amicia's undoing. She slid from the bed in a flurry of skirts, her flaming temper raising flags of heat on her cheeks and the weariness trembling in her thews burned away by a surge of energy.

"A mother's wish to see him find joy!" Amicia railed bitterly, knowing that she should not. Tristan had given a warning that she should heed, but her anger had been too long held in check. "No mother have you been to him from his birth! Always he has been alone to fight your hate! But no more, my lady! I vow to you this day that he stands alone no more!"

A silence fell, so thick and full of hate Amicia thought she could extend her hand and part it like a curtain. Lady Sybilla stood rigid and regal, the ivory of her skin bleaching to a cold white as chilling as the deadly look in her eyes.

"Do you, puny child that you are, think you can fight me where he, a man grown, cannot," she said sharply. "I give but one warning, Amicia of Bellay. Do not thwart me, lest you seek his fate."

"Ami-cia." Tristan's voice cracked and faded.

She spun to the bed. He stirred restlessly, his hand plucking at the coverlets, and she bent to him, laying her palm atop his brow. His fever-bright eyes searched for and found hers. "I am here, my lord. Rest. Sleep. Naught is there for you to do but grow well and strong."

He sighed heavily and slept once more, and Amicia canted a glance over her shoulder. "Begone, Lady Sybilla, and do not darken this door again."

"Ay, I will go and gladly." Triumph glittered in the

murky brown of her eyes and a vicious smile twisted across her mouth.

Amicia, her heart pounding with dread, watched Lady Sybilla glide out as silently as she came. Shivering, she shifted her uncertain gaze from the door. "Why, Enid? Why did she smile?"

"I know not. But surely it bodes ill for my lord."

"All she has done has boded ill for him. Why does she hate him? It is no fault of his that he is the image of her Scots father."

Enid, her wimple abandoned and her hair skinned back in a generous knot on her nape, tucked a stray wisp behind her ear and sank to a stool. "It is far more than that, my lady, though that was the beginning. The old lord was a good man, hard but just. He was patient at first, but when she would not take Lord Tristan to her breast as a babe or hold him in her arms, he began to hate her for it. She, in turn, gave all of her love to Robert, her first-born, a sweet and loving child. He grew to manhood in the old lord's image, unspoiled by his mother."

"Was he as perfect as she claims?" Amicia asked.

"Nay, my lady." Enid smiled. "He had faults as all men do, but he loved his brothers well and tried, where he could, to ease their lot. He had a merry way about him that misled many into thinking he could be bent to their will. He could not, and so Lady Sybilla discovered after the old lord died. Lord Robert took himself a wife. A meek and mild maid, comely and gentle. Lady Sybilla made her life a misery from the first, but she would say naught to her lord of it, though many a tear she shed when alone. It was Lord Tristan, newly knighted and come on a mission for the Earl, who saw the way it was between his mother and his sister-by-marriage. Having suffered the lash of his mother's tongue his life long, he could not stand by and watch the maid suffer. He spoke to his brother of it, little knowing the evil he brewed for himself."

"His brother was angry?" Amicia asked.

"With Lord Tristan, nay. With his mother? Ay, that he was. She had misjudged him as ever, thinking herself well loved. But Lord Robert had a mind of his own and she had worked her last wiles on him. The maid, young and shy as she was, had taught Lord Robert much of love and the way it should be. He came roaring into the hall below and told his mother much that was better left unsaid. The bitterness of years spewed from him, and before he was done, he had cast her out of his keep and sent her to her dower castle, there to remain the rest of her life.''

''And she blamed Tristan for it,'' Amicia said softly.

''Ay, so she did. She would not see that it was her indifference to Lord Tristan that set the old lord against her or her cruelty to his wife that set Lord Robert against her.''

''Why did she return here, Enid? Why did Tristan allow her to stay?''

''Ah, my lady, no one knows but the lord and his mother. When his brother died without issue, he came to take his rightful place as Lord of Eden. One cursed day Lady Sybilla arrived, took him aside for private speech, and has been here ever since.''

''A cursed day. Ay, Enid, it was that,'' Amicia said, looking upon Tristan and stroking his thick hair. *What hold does she have upon you, my lord,* she wondered, studying the shadowed hollows beneath his cheekbones.

''My love,'' she whispered, and leaned down to kiss his brow. ''Could I but see the way, I would save you from her. Then, my lord, I would do as your brother's tender-hearted maid did for him. I would teach you much of love and the way it should be.''

In the days that followed, while Tristan lay limp and unmindful of who he was or where he was, Amicia feared she might never have the chance to teach him of love. She thought often of the rueful gaze that seemed to jest at himself and his words: *I wanted to come to you in victory on my own two feet.* They became for her an amulet against despair, a hope that transcended the frailty of body to nourish her spirit and will.

It was only later, when his fever broke and he eased into a deep sleep, that fear and hesitancy returned to haunt her. Then she remembered Lady Ruella and the love Tristan had not wanted. She remembered how easily he had set her from him, how it curdled his belly to think of having a child of Bellay's blood.

A warming sun bathed the rain-soaked land when Tristan opened his eyes and knew where he was. He tried to lift his head and could not. He tried to speak, but his voice came in a harsh croak. The sound, unpleasant as it was, brought Amicia to his bed.

"My lord," she breathed, the deep blue of her eyes searching his, "do you return to us at last?"

Staring up at her, Tristan licked his dry lips and suffered a fear that shook him to the solitary depths of his soul. He had seen ancient crones with more flesh on their bones. The small fist knotted anxiously at her throat was traced in blue beneath ashen flesh. Where once her eyes were lighted as by a candle within, now they were dull and red-rimmed.

His hand struggled off of his chest, an effort that brought a sheen of sweat to his brow. He tried to capture her wrist, a useless attempt, as he was too weak to grasp. "Am . . . Ami—"

"Do not try to speak, my lov—lord," she said, her voice shaking and her face crumpling. Tears fell freely across the sharp planes of her cheeks. "Enid! He wakes and knows me!" she cried, taking his hand in hers. A hand once so fair and soft, now spidery thin, red and rough.

Enid came, her plump cheeks sagging with weariness. "You have been ill of your wounds long and long, my lord. It is good to have you back with us."

Tristan watched her place an arm around Amicia's shoulders and saw the love in her eyes, shining for this maid he had wed.

"My lady," Enid said, strangely gentle, "you must rest now that he is well, else you will end as ill as he. Tell her, my lord, for she will not leave your side do you not."

"Rest. Go and rest," he urged, his voice weak and trembling like a leaf in the wind.

Amicia breathed a faint protest, but Enid insisted, leading her to the nearby pallet and pulling the coverlets over her. The serving woman returned to Tristan, a smile softening her mouth and a steely glint in her eye.

"I have nursed you much in times past, my lord, and know you for a surly sickling. Your lady has not left your side these many weeks. She needs rest, not the bite of your temper."

"Ay, Enid. She will have it," he vowed and closed his eyes, but failed to sink into the oblivion he courted. The sight of Amicia so worn and thin was etched into his mind. The fear still wrapped choking fingers around his throat. The fear that she might have sickened and died and vanished from his life. Why that terrible fear? he wondered. She was naught but a woman. She was naught but his wife. She was naught, naught to him.

Tristan quickly came to regret his vow to hold his temper. When he grew weary from so simple a task as spooning potage from a bowl, he longed to bellow his irritation and discontent, but how could he with Amicia at his side, so pale, so earnest, so gentle. When his legs trembled and his chest heaved from a short walk to the window slit, he longed to kick a stool, to shout or snap, but somehow his brutish anger melted away at a single word of encouragement or praise from his wife. When his strength began to return and the two women joined as one to confine him to his bed, he longed to pound his fist against a thick endpost and demand his freedom, but always, always, Amicia was there to kindle a mood strange to him.

Though his body itched to return to his active life, to feel Vainqueur beneath him and the sun on his face, his soul fed on the tranquillity perfuming the air of his chamber as herbs perfume a bath. He grew to love the early mornings and listened eagerly for the rustle of the straw-stuffed pallet that heralded Amicia's awakening. He would watch her then, mewing like a kitten, stretching like a cat, and rising all woman in a sheer linen chemise. Most of all, he liked watching her comb her thick chestnut hair, frowning only when she coiled it on her nape, secured it with a caul, and covered her glory with a wimple.

There came a day when he knew he was strong enough for Amicia to abandon her pallet and return to her chamber. She did not, and he could not summon the strength to send her from him as once he had. There came another day when he knew he was strong enough to leave his chamber, to seek the Great Hall and feast among his folk. Amicia did not suggest it. He did not mention it. He remained sequestered with her in the peace of his chamber. Day by day, he watched the hollows in her cheeks fill out, her blush of health return, and the luster come to brighten her gaze.

It came to him then that he was happy. He enjoyed having Amicia near and speaking of wifely things while he honed his sword or dagger. He enjoyed the twinkle in her eyes when she teased him, the gentle touch of her hands when she changed the linen wrappings on his wounds, and the sound of her voice drifting through the blackness of night with a soft, "Good eventide, my lord," as she settled on her pallet. He enjoyed the peace she gave him, the most precious gift he had ever received. A peace that receded with the resurgence of his strength.

He had no need to wonder why it happened. He knew only too well, for with the strength warming his thews came desire to warm his loins. He told himself he should send her away, but the thought brought such pain he could not do it. He told himself he could bear to have her there, so near, so far, and knew he lied. He told himself that she was his wife before God and man, and none would blame him did he take that which he so dearly wanted. He knew then that he was lost, for he would blame himself.

One chilly morning when aging winter seemed to be winning its battle with spring, Tristan watched Amicia's slender arms moving in a graceful woman's dance. By twist and turn and tuck the glossy length of her hair shortened and the coil on her nape fattened and his frown deepened.

"Do not," he said, his voice soft, softer than he intended. Low, napped in silk, and cross-grained with pleading, it pleased him not at all.

Amicia paused, her elbows high and her hands splayed across the thick coil of her hair. Peering around her raised arm, she studied Tristan with a questioning gaze. He lay abed, propped atop an elbow with the coverlet draping low across the flat furred plane of his belly. His skin was the palest honey tone and he was thinner than he had been. Still, he looked the bold knight he was. For a while—such a short while, she thought with a pang of sorrow—he had succumbed to the strands of peace she wove around him like a weaver at a loom. She longed to ask what had broken that peace and why he watched her so intently, but she feared what he would say and what she would betray.

"I asked you once to wear your hair down," Tristan said.

Amicia's gaze fell, her cheeks brimming red with shame for the defiance that had taken so mean-spirited a revenge. In all of these months he had asked but this one small thing of her, and it she would not do. She hesitated a moment, feeling oddly like a bride preparing to reveal her all to her new-wed husband.

Tristan sensed her hesitation and saw the flaming of her cheeks and wondered what it could mean, until her hands released the coil of her hair. It fell in heavy hoops and deep waves and feathering curls, a glossy curtain of chestnut-brown that tumbled to the pallet at her hips. The flickering light of the candles, now bold, now shy, frolicked in a playful game of hide-and-seek, highlighting with a deep red sheen and leaving behind a dark, rich brown.

He longed to lift it in his hand, to feel it clutching his fingers as once it had done. He knew he should not, could not, yield to the yearning that churned in the pit of his belly. She was a woman, and women were faithless creatures, he told himself, purposefully summoning the thought like a shield. But it quavered like a battle-scarred knight, hoary with age, still claiming the power he once knew, power long since fled.

The shield crumbled bit by bit, leaving Tristan bare before the knowledge that this woman was not as others. He could not take her unto him and then dismiss her from his thoughts. He could not lie to himself any longer. He could not resist her.

She sat so still with her eyes downcast and her head bent and her hands cupped together in her lap. Her shoulder, clad in the autumn-leaf brown of her camelin robe, peeked through the curtain of her hair. Her breasts thrust against the soft, silky fabric, as if consciously, purposefully tempting him.

"Amicia," he called her name in a voice as soft as fleece, as rough as rubbled stone.

She looked up slowly, the screen of her hair sliding across her shoulder and baring the ivory column of her throat. Her eyes, huge and dark, met his. Her thick lashes fluttered. Her mouth parted, as if she would speak, but no words came.

Tristan stared at her lips, softly pliant lips that seemed to offer themselves to him in sacrifice. His throat convulsed. His heart hammered. His every thought fled. Naught was left but need. A need he could no longer deny.

His gaze meshing with Amicia's, he slid from the bed and felt the cool of the air wash across his bare flesh. He walked to her and stood over her and stared down at her, resisting the insistent tug of temptation. Her face tilted up like a flower in search of the sun. Her eyes glistened like jewels, as dark as night, as bright as day, as sweet as the song of desire humming through his veins.

His yearning took on a fierce quality, a clutching at his vitals, a freeing of his soul. He knelt slowly, wincing at the sharp painful tugging of the scar on his thigh.

Amicia winced, too, as if she felt his pain. She reached out, her hand hesitating a knuckle's width from his chest, curling into a fist, and drawing back to press against the hollow of her throat.

Tristan sat back on his heels and studied her face. The lashes shielding her gaze. The small nose, so straight and proud. The lips quivering from an indrawn breath. The hair springing away from her temples and brow, thick and shining and alive. He followed its waving length to the deep bed of curls spreading across the pallet.

Reaching out with both hands, succumbing to temptation with a sudden greed for the feel of it, he scooped up the soft mass and felt it seize his fingers and arms with sinuous tendrils—just as he longed to have Amicia seize him and never let go. Dipping his nose into the froth of brown, he breathed deep of sandalwood and woman.

"Why do you wear it up?" he asked, his voice plunging to guttural depths, his breath setting fragile curls to quaking.

Her head turned slowly, her eyes rising to meet his. Tristan saw in them a bitter shame, a hesitation, and something more. A softness, a yearning, a need that matched his.

"I fear to tell you why, my lord," she said, each word a broken thread of sound. "I would have you think well of me, and surely you will not."

"I begin to think, my lady wife, that I could not think ill of you did you plunge your dagger into my chest with your own hand." He stopped, lured by a beckoning curl to brush his cheek against it. "Why, Amicia?"

He watched, fascinated by the rapid rise and fall of her breast, more fascinated by the dipping of her chin and the dropping of her gaze.

"I was hurt, my lord, that you could so easily set me from you. I was hurt to know that you so despised me and mine that you would not have a child of my body to make my blood one with yours. I—I had no way but this to thwart your will. It was a childish spite," she whispered.

Her hair tumbled from his hands, cascading to the pallet. He reached out and touched her shoulder, his palm cupping it and rubbing gently. "Truly you are a wonder to me, Amicia," he said. "Some, in your place, would have found far worse ways to show their spite. Some would have joined with Lady Sybilla—"

"Never, my lord!" Amicia's head snapped up, her eyes searching his. "Never would I sink so low as she has sunk, nor would I join with Aimery in—"

"Aimery?" Tristan's eyes dimmed. Aimery. Ay, it was so, though it wrenched his belly to admit it. His brother had become one with his mother, and this wife of his knew it. Always, Amicia kept her own counsel, and helped him where she could.

"I beg forgiveness, my lord. I should not have said—"

"Nay, naught is there to forgive." His hand cupped her shoulder, feeling the fragile bones. She was still too thin and worn by her effort to save him. Guilt gouged him hard.

'But there is, my lord. I should not have—"

"Shh, Amicia. Do not summon them to this chamber to break our peace. Not yet, for I would have this moment

and take its memory with me when I leave.'' He leaned
down and pressed a kiss to the cap of her shoulder, feeling
the warmth of her skin, soaking in the scent of her. His
head tilted, his lips a breath from hers. "Did you save me
for this moment, sweet witch?''

His lips touched hers. They trembled beneath his and
opened willingly, eagerly. His heart lurched in his chest.
Warmth flowed through him like hot spiced wine, at odds
with the chill of his thoughts. He should think . . . think
of himself, of Amicia, of the child he dared not sire upon
her. The child his mother would destroy did he give it life.
He should think on that.

Always it had been so for him. Never could he take the
moment's joy for fretting over the morrow's penance.

Just once . . . just this once . . .

Tristan drew back, leaving Amicia's lips caressed by
naught but the chill of the air, leaving her heart caressed
by naught but the chill of defeat. So close she had come to
seeing him succumb to his need, to her. Her eyes searched
his, watching the battle waged between his mind and
heart, watching his terrible struggle, seeing the moment he
lost and she won. A moment that held for her as much
sadness as gladness.

His mouth swooped upon hers, slanting desperately,
demanding that which she gave freely. An impassioned
demand, an impassioned need that shuddered through her,
resonating in a sonorous harmony with her own need, her
own demand. Sadness fled, rushing before a buoyant surge
of joy. He was hers. For this moment, no matter what
happened thereafter, he was hers.

Reclining against the strong forearm he set about her
shoulders, Amicia felt its steely strength, a strong guard
against all harm. She raised her arm and threaded her
fingers through the thickness of his hair, and breathed in
the earthy male scent of him. A scent that had haunted
nights she spent in sleepless longing. A longing now realized with the seductive invasion of his tongue and the
heady exploration of his hand, and the potent power of his
desire.

His callused palm, gentle and eager, cupped the arched
line of her throat. He dipped a questing thumb into the

hollow where her pulse raced, then his hands smoothed down and down to the belt cinching her robe about her waist.

His nose nuzzling her cheek and his heart pounding against her shoulder, he fumbled the knot free with shaking hands. His fingers eased beneath the robe, the tips touching the indentation of her waist, trembling, trembling against her bare flesh, before he folded the soft silky camelin fabric back to reveal the curve of one pale ivory hip and the full swell of one breast.

His breath shredded in and out, flowing moist and hot across her cheek. His eyes, twin flames of passion burning brightest blue, met hers with raw hunger. A hunger for more than the mating of man and woman. A hunger for those things that transcend desire of the flesh—love and caring and sharing. A hunger she knew he had, but he did not, could not, recognize in himself.

She slid her fingers across his nape, feeling the silkiness of his hair and the heat of his body. "I am yours to do with as you will, my lord," she breathed against his lips, offering that which he thought he wanted, hoping that he would see his need for more. "Take me unto you. Make me one with you."

He shuddered, a sound purring low in his throat. A sound of defeat, of triumph, of desire. His mouth descended on hers to punish and adore. He laid her back on the pallet with her hair tumbling in wild disarray. His lips brushed with a sweet seductive warmth down the arched line of her neck to the swell of her breast to the aching peak. His breath purled around the nipple sending shards of sensation spearing through Amicia.

She forgot his need and knew only her own. His questing hand roused firestorms of sensations. His worshiping mouth pushed her to heady heights of rapture. His quivering response to her every touch, her every sigh, trailed ribbons of fire through her.

Poised on the brink of rapture, she waited in taut suspense. Slowly—so slowly Amicia's throat ached from the pressure of holding back a cry of joy—Tristan filled her with the throbbing proof of his need. Her fingers dug into

the sinewy hardness of his back. She waited . . . waited
. . . and felt him move . . . and joined with him as one
in the elemental rhythm that was as old as time, as new as
the love that burned in her heart.

# Chapter 19

Defying Tristan's gruff command that she not leave the safety of the outer ward, Amicia sneaked through the postern gate, fled down the grassy slope, and plunged into the willow brake. She was being willful. Sinfully willful, she thought with a merry smile that revealed her utter lack of repentance.

She flung herself down on the cool of a mossy bank and watched the crystalline blue spring. It bubbled from porous, pitted limestone hung with swags of fern. The somnolent day spoke in nature's disparate voices: the hum of bees raiding the willow catkins; the gurgling laughter of the water; the murmur of the breeze through the gaunt branches budding green overhead.

Alone, she sat with her knees updrawn and her deep blue gaze misty. Alone, she thought her private thoughts, smiled her private smiles, and dreamed her private dreams. Alone, she remembered the heated caress of Tristan's hands, the shredding of his breath against the curve of her neck, the passion that made her one with him in gentleness, tenderness, and . . . love?

Dare she hope it was love that kindled the fire of need within him? Ay, she dared greatly, not only to hope, but to believe. Yet, hoping and believing, she also knew him, mayhap better than he knew himself. He, who was so honest, who would die before lying to another, would lie to himself. He would say it was naught but a man's need of a ready wench. He would deny the aching of his heart, the loneliness searing his soul, the desire for more than the joining of his body with hers.

Mayhap she should be downcast. It had been four days since Tristan had risen from her side and sent her from him; and, in those days, he had neither looked upon her nor spoken a word he need not speak for courtesy's sake. Try as she might, not a single pang of discouragement could penetrate the bliss that enwrapped her. No matter what warnings her mind summoned, her heart sang that she would be the victor in this war for Tristan's heart, his soul, his mind. She would not have to wage a single battle. She would only have to wait. Time was friend to her and foe to him.

Time, Tristan thought, padding through the willow brake as silently as a cat. So little time and so much to do.

Not a twig snapped underfoot, not a branch swished in passing, while he stalked along Amicia's lightly trodden path and cursed her willful disobedience. He flexed the ache from his shoulder, knowing it would soon stiffen. He had not had time to work it out in the swordplay with his knights before the huntsman came to tell him of Amicia's flight.

Tristan could easily have sent his man after his errant wife, but chose, instead, to sheathe his sword and find her himself. He told himself only he could impress upon her the need to obey without question. He believed that was his intent, until he approached the edge of the sun-dappled glade and saw Amicia sitting on the mossy bank. She was safe—and alone.

His fingers unfurled from the hilt of the dagger at his waist. Sluicing relief left him limp-kneed. The desire to fling himself down beside her and take her into his arms turned him angry. "What do you here, my lady?" he growled, digging his thumbs beneath his belt and setting his feet wide and sturdy.

Amicia gasped and swiveled about, her face rising to him and her hair tumbling around her. "My lord!" Her hand trembled against her breast. "I fear you gave me a fright!"

"Better I than another sneaking up ill intentioned!"
Each word fell on the air like an ingot of lead. "I gave you
order to remain within the ward. Why have you disobeyed
me?"

She gazed up at him. Dappled sunlight stroked his hair
in bands of fiery red and captured the sparks of anger
leaping white in his eyes. Her gaze fell to the linked mail
hauberk, the sword at his side, the mail chausses hugging
his muscular legs. He was garbed as if for war. Always,
he must be ready to draw sword at a moment's notice.
Could he never rest or know peace?

Her gaze climbed slowly, meeting his. She longed to
tell him why she had come to this secluded spot. She
longed to tell him of her love, growing stronger hour by
hour and minute by minute, but he was not ready to hear
such from her. It would send him bolting into the safe
haven of anger like a stag bolting into the thick heart of the
chase, and she could not bear to see anger despoil the
beauty of the day or the beauty of her love.

"I beg forgiveness, my lord," she said compliantly. "I
thought of none but myself and my desire to be alone to
take joy in the day."

"We know not when the reivers will return nor where
they will strike," Tristan said, clinging to fast unraveling
threads of irritation. His eyes lifted, carrying with them a
vision of her sweetly earnest face. "We should be away to
the keep."

He said it flatly, adamantly, yet he did not urge her to
her feet or turn to leave himself. Instead, he stared into the
distance and saw naught but the pale perfection of her
features and the warm blue of her eyes.

"Is the danger so great, my lord, that you may not take
your ease beside me this little while?"

"Only a fool tempts the fates when he need not,"
Tristan said harshly, knowing that he blustered like a weak
cockscomb. Had he grown so spineless he could be led all
unwilling by this tantalizing wench?

"Do you not feel the need to play the fool betimes, my
lord? Do you not grow weary of ever doing right and
being right?"

His gaze fell at that, meeting hers with a twinkle of

amusement. "My lady," he began, a smile twitching at his mouth, "I am so seldom right, I thought you must have taken note of it."

It was not a full smile. Only a suggestion of what might be, but it sent a shock of pleasure shooting through her and tilting her own lips, full merry and laughing. "Ah, my lord, no good wife would ever admit to such. I must needs now give assurance that you, my husband, can do no ill, only good, can do no wrong, only right. Come, my lord." She patted the cool moss beside her. "The meadow is aquiver with cowslips and the wood bright with gorse and the robins are anesting. It is spring and time for all to take their ease, even you who bear the burden of our lives. Come, Tristan, and sit beside me."

"Just so did Eve tempt Adam in the Garden," he said, his voice roughened by the desire stirring in his loins. "And look what he lost for the yielding."

Her eyes met his steadily, plumbing their depths with sadness. "His innocence, my lord, but yours was lost long ago."

"Ay, and so it was," he said, moving slowly, dropping down beside her and sitting stiffly.

Amicia fell silent, basking in this small victory, taking pleasure in having Tristan near. She breathed deep of the cool air, damp and clean from the spring. A thrush sang a series of reedy spiraling notes and was answered by the croak of a frog. Serenity came like a mist rising from the water; awareness burned it away like the first rays of the rising sun.

Did Tristan remember every touch, every sigh, every word spoken on the pallet in his chamber? Would that she could forget. She was haunted by his tenderness, his gentleness, his passion. She was haunted by that glimpse of what might have been.

Beside her, Tristan silently fought his own demons of remembrance. He sat cross-legged and uncomfortable on the cool earth. The accouterments of war were meant for moving afoot or sitting astride a saddle, not for lazing on a mossy bank in the company of a fair maid. The hilt of his dagger dug into his ribs. The long leather sword sheath lay across his lap with his forearms braced atop it and his hands gripping his knees.

Those physical discomforts were the least of his worries, for he was inured to them by the real miseries of war. He was far more distressed by his emotions, surging and ebbing like the waters of the Narrow Sea. The pleasure of having Amicia near with none to espy his mood. The liquid fire of desire that set his blood to humming and his loins to throbbing. The memory of her offering the rose-tipped peak of her breast to his suckling mouth, of the feverish movement of her small hands on his body, of the joining of male to female, hard to soft, wanting to accepting. The guilt that scarred him with sharp talons of shame.

A shame that came like a dousing of icy water. He told himself he was only a man, weak and sinful as all men were, but he knew that few sins could reap the bitter harvest of his actions. He had wanted her as he had never wanted anything in his life. He had taken her, knowing that if he got her with child he would not be here to protect her or the babe born of his flesh. He could only hope and pray that his seed found no fertile field. Not now, when his mother had lost all patience with making him suffer.

Lady Sybilla had done nothing and said nothing, but he knew her plans were drawing nigh. He could see it, a sheen of triumph in her eyes. She had found a weapon to use against him, and Aimery was a part of it. Aimery, who could not or would not see her for what she was. Mayhap, Tristan thought, he should hate his brother for cleaving to their mother's side, but he could do no more than pity him. He, above all, knew what Aimery had suffered as a child.

He thrust away those heavy thoughts and dwelt instead on Amicia. The scent of sandalwood perfumed the air. The scent of woman seeped deep within him, an uncomfortable paradox of disturbance and rest. He chanced a glance and found her watching him. She smiled and, though her smile asked for naught, his gaze jerked away studying the pitted limestone glazed with water. The need to speak set him to shifting restlessly, while he suffered a keen regret that he had never practiced the art of conversing with a lady.

He cleared his throat and stretched his chin.

"You look weary, my lord, and pale. So soon from your bed, you must take care not to overdo."

He sneaked a single glimpse of her through the screen of his lashes, then settled his gaze on the bubbling spring. "I must regain my strength and work my shoulder that it does not grow stiff and useless."

She shifted closer, her cotte whispering across the moss, and Tristan suppressed the urge to rise and run like a callow youth. "I have an unguent to use on the scar," she murmured. "It will keep it supple and soft."

He cleared his throat and stretched his chin once more, wishing she was not so near and he not so weak. "Thank you, my lady. That will be welcome."

"You frown so, my lord," she whispered, so close her sweet breath fanned his cheek. "Have I made you angry?"

"Nay, m-my lady."

"Amicia," she breathed softly. "I would hear you say it."

There was in her voice a huskiness, a need, that sent chills rippling across Tristan's flesh. His gaze moved slowly, reluctantly, leaving the crystalline blue of the water to plunge into the deeper blue depths of her gaze.

"Amicia," he whispered, his head dipping, his mouth finding hers. Sweetly, so sweetly, her lips yielded to the pressure of his, her breath becoming one with his. Tenderly, Tristan cherished her mouth, the moment, the new and fragile feelings set aflutter in his chest. Feelings as hotly desirous as the blood pounding through his veins. Feelings as softly yearning as the melting of his heart. Feelings as enchanting as they were frightening.

He shifted back and gazed down at her. A delicate tremor raced through the rosy contours of her mouth. Her lashes climbed, revealing the misty blue of her eyes. She sighed, a soft blissful sigh, and smiled up at him.

"Have I learned to please you in this, my lord?" she asked.

"Ay, you please me well," he answered, his voice a broken husk of sound. "I begin to think you lured me here apurpose, as a siren lures sailors at sea."

"Nay, my lord." Her smile widened, the tiny dimple

winking at the crest of her cheek. "Though had I given thought to it, I would have."

"Sweet witch," Tristan murmured, and stopped fighting himself and her. A growl of laughter thrumming low in his throat, he bore her down to the cool mossy bank. "You are a saucy wench this day, Amicia of Bellay. Mayhap you must needs have . . ."

The wardcorne's horn pealed across the land, sliding from the bottom region of the scale to the thin upper range, once, twice, thrice—a warning.

Tristan stiffened in Amicia's arms. His head climbed, his gaze sharpening, as if it could pierce the crowded willow brake by force of will. "The reivers," he said hoarsely.

"You do not know that, my lord!" Amicia's fingers dug into his rigid shoulders so fiercely a nail snapped against an iron link of his hauberk.

"Ay, it is the warning I ordered given for naught else." He vaulted up, his hauberk scraping link against link, and his sword sheath clattering against his thigh.

Amicia saw him wince and roll his shoulder as though it ached. She saw the corded strength of his thick neck, the muscles bulging on his clenching jaw, the hand he stretched out to her.

"Rise, my lady," he said impatiently. "We must away to the keep."

She set her hand in his and felt it close warm about hers. His hand, nicked and scarred from battles old and forgotten, pulled her to her feet in a single lithe move. Amicia was heart-stoppingly aware that he was too soon from his bed and not as strong as he thought.

"Come," he said, moving at a rapid pace.

Unable to move, she watched him go. Watched the sunlight dapple his hair with its warming rays. Watched the powerful long-legged stride carrying him away from her. Watched, and suffered a terror unlike any she had ever known. It crushed her chest in a vise of pain. It brought tears flooding her cheeks. It leached all warmth from her, leaving her teeth chattering despite the balmy breeze.

Her mouth moved but no sound disturbed the tomblike

hush. "Tristan!" she found her voice and cried out. "Do not go! I beg of you, do not go!"

He stopped as if struck between the shoulders by a blow, and turned upon her a look so incredulous she pressed her knotted fists to her quivering lips. "Do not go?" he asked, frowning mightily. "Would you make of me a mincing milksop shivering behind a woman's skirts while my folk are slain by these reivers?"

"Nay, my lord," she whispered, her fists inching down to her chin while she blinked the tears from her eyes. "It is only that I am afraid."

His expression softened. The rigidity of anger left his taut body. He walked back to her, holding out his hand. "Naught do you have to fear, Amicia. You will be safe in the keep, for they will not attack so strong a fortress."

He spoke as to a child, soothing, comforting. Every word tightened the knot of apprehension in Amicia's breast and fed a growing anger. "You are a great fool, my lord!" she burst out, her cheeks flaming and her chin tilting to pride's sharp angle. "Can you not see that it is not for myself I fear? It is for you!"

One thick brow scaled his forehead betraying his displeasure. "They are but reivers, however wily and strong. This is naught I have not done many times ere now."

"But this time is different, my lord!"

"How so?" He settled an impatient frown upon her.

She should say naught. She knew it, but the words bubbled from her as the spring bubbled from the limestone outcropping. "Because I love you, Tristan, and I will die moment by moment for fear you will be hurt!"

His eyes widened, the azure blue growing dark and wary. "Do not," he said woodenly.

"Do not fear for you? Tristan—"

"Do not love me!" he thundered.

Amicia did not shrink from the blazing anger contorting his face. "Tristan, the heart cannot be cautioned like an unruly child! As well it would be to tell birds not to fly—"

"You have seen my mother and her hate! Do you think yourself safe from it? Does she espy this love you claim, she will make of your life the living hell she has made of mine!"

"I will take care, my lord," Amicia vowed.

"Better you should scourge your heart free and live with me as other wives live with their men. We were wed to seal a bond for peace, not for love."

"Tristan," Amicia faltered, "do you know so little of love that you believe it can be scourged from my heart?"

"I have loved no woman, nor will I!" he said harshly. "I would as soon clasp your father to my chest and call him friend!"

Naught else could have forced her to see so clearly that he would never love her or any woman. There was comfort in knowing it was not only her. Scant comfort that did little to soften the ravages of defeat. Amicia stared up at him, her eyes welling with tears, her lips trembling, her heart aching and desolate.

"Amicia, do not," Tristan began, his voice thick with pain. "Do not look at me so."

"Forgive me, my lord," she choked out. "I do not mean to make this harder for you."

He cursed, a low vicious sound that held more frustration than anger. He reached out, his hands clamping around her arms, yanking her to him. Savagely, he slanted his mouth across hers, punishing, demanding, giving. "There is naught of love in this," he murmured raggedly against the tender corner of her mouth.

"Nay, my lord." Amicia's fingers threaded his silky curls and pulled his lips hard against hers. "I would not mistake it."

He yielded then. She could feel it, the moment his resistance broke, the moment his need overwhelmed him. His arms wrapped her tight, crushing her against him, as if he wanted to hold her always, to never let her go from his side.

"I must go," he moaned against her mouth, yet held her still, kissed her still. "I beseech you," he breathed, "let me go."

Awhirl with pain and regret, Amicia knew that she must help him. Did she hold him here he would never forgive her, never trust her, and for him trust must be as strong as love. Yet how would she forgive herself or forget, should he lose his life in this battle?

"Ay, my dearest lord," she murmured. "Have a care to yourself. I would have you return to me."

He wrenched away and stared down at her, his expression rife with tormented longings that even he did not seem to understand.


The ward clamored with children gathering and women wailing and men-at-arms leaping to horse. Dogs barked. Vainqueur whinnied and pranced with Tristan firmly in the saddle. Amicia watched him twist about to see that his men were ready, saw him turn and settle a darksome gaze on her.

"My lady," he bellowed over the noise, "should ill befall me you will go where Odo leads."

"Ay, my lord," she called out. "Think not of me, but of yourself. Take care, Tristan."

He wheeled Vainqueur about and sped for the gaping mouth of the gate. "For Eden! The right is ours! For Eden!" he shouted above the thunder of hooves.

Amicia waited until the last man was through the gate, waited while the portcullis creaked down and the drawbridge creaked up. Only then, when the ward was silent save for the grunting of swine and clucking of hens, did she move slowly toward the gloomy gray keep. There was naught for her to do but wait and hope and pray that Tristan would return to her. Loving or unloving, she cared not, only that he came whole and hearty.

She trudged up the outer stair, oblivious to all but the fear that dampened her palms with sweat. Entering the cool archway of the entrance tower, she was rudely jostled aside by a serving man carrying a woven willow pannier. He said naught, though he cast her a white-rimmed glance before hurrying on his way. She noted the swollen red of his newly boxed ear and the hunch of his shoulders, as though he had taken a painful blow. A thoughtful frown wrinkling her brow, Amicia moved through the archway onto the stairs and met there a procession of heavily laden servants that sent her shrinking against the chill stone wall.

"Maida," Amicia hissed, plucking at the woman's thick wool sleeve and pulling her out of the scurrying line, "what passes here?"

The serving woman cast a furtive glance toward the Entrance Chamber door and turned back to whisper, "Lady Sybilla goes to her dower castle of Carrickmuir and takes the child with her."

"Megotta?" Amicia frowned. "Did the lord consent to this?"

"I think not, my lady. We were warned we would have the tongues cut from our mouths did he learn of her plans." Maida leaned near, her whisper a mere sibilance of breath. "I think she knew that the reivers were going to attack. She set us to packing before the sun rose this morn."

Ay, Lady Sybilla knew, Amicia thought bitterly. She had planned well with her partner in evil. As cruel as it was, she saw a single ray of hope. If Tristan had been lured to his death, then his mother would have no reason to leave. He was being lured away to some other purpose, though what, she could not see. Mayhap Odo would know.

Amicia lifted her skirts and raced up the stairs, dodging retainers until she reached the Guard Hall. Searching frantically, she called Odo again and again, but found him not. Neither the guards at rest nor the servants at work had seen him.

She hurried up the spiral stair, her breath catching, her heart pounding. Enid. She would find Enid, but the serving woman, too, had vanished. All was quiet in the solar. No maids sat at their stitching. No hounds sank to the rushes heaving a sigh. No servants moved about to set new candles atop their sticks, to heap new logs atop the fire.

Amicia stood in the center of the vast chamber feeling alone as she had never felt before. Odo gone, none knew where. Enid vanished, none the wiser. Lady Sybilla leaving with Tristan's daughter. Tristan riding through the warm spring day in search of the reivers her father sent—to what purpose?

"You should be below." Lady Sybilla's husky voice came stealing from the shadows. "Naught is there for you to do here."

Amicia spun about. Her mouth dry with fear, she probed the shadows. Lady Sybilla moved forward, her mantle swaying about her, her face pale in the folds of her hood.

"The lord would not wish his daughter gone!" Amicia burst out.

"The lord," Lady Sybilla said smoothly, "has no say in the matter."

"Why must you hate him so for naught but that he looks like your father?" Amicia cried, the injustice of it forcing caution from her.

"For that and more do I hate him!" Lady Sybilla said venomously. "It was not enough that his father loved another and so had nothing left for me. Nay, then Tristan was born and took what little love there was left in him. For more do I hate him! For that he lives and my Robert is cold in his grave in Gascony!"

"He is your son!"

"Ay, and for that I do spit on the day of his birthing!"

Amicia shivered with revulsion. "I will not allow you to take his daughter from here! If I must gather the men-at-arms myself, I will stop you!"

"His daughter?" Lady Sybilla's laugh oozed like oil on a platter. "His *daughter* is no daughter of his, and well he knows it." She paused, her eyes glittering feverishly, her smile lingering, as if to relish the stunned incomprehension with which Amicia regarded her. "His wife, that puling weak thing who looked at him with the eyes of a moonling, played him false, albeit against her will. He returned from the Earl's side to find her in childbed with the child no chance of being his, though none but he and she and I and . . . one other . . . knew that. Is that not so"—her eyes lifted to stare past Amicia's shoulder—"Aimery?"

Amicia whirled around. He stood in the portal of the great oaken door, his shoulders squared, his feet spread, and a look in his eyes that sent shards of fear lancing through her. A look of lust and lechery unmasked. She reached out for support, but found none. Trembling, she drew herself up. A thought came, an assurance, a knowledge that she rejected even as she knew it was true. This, then, was what he never wanted Tristan to know. This ultimate treachery against his brother.

"Yours? Megotta is yours?" she said with a gasp. She saw him smile, a loathsome smile so like his mother's Amicia had to quell her need to retch. "You played him false, Aimery? He, who has loved you well and risked his life for you? He, who has been kind to you, even knowing this thing you have—"

"But he does not know that I was the man, Amicia," he said in his light singsong. "He will know soon though, as he will know about me and . . . you."

"Nay," Amicia whispered. Backing away, she whirled to flee, but Aimery caught her in a vicious grip that yet caressed and turned her belly.

"Ay, Amicia, you will do all I say, else Megotta will be told all."

# *Chapter 20*

Only a fool would join in battle with half a heart, half a mind. As squire to Earl Simon, Tristan had been relentlessly drilled to set all but one thought aside when he drew his sword. Yet, clattering across the drawbridge and pounding down the slope toward the opening gate of the outer ward, he thought not of the battle to come, but of Amicia waiting behind.

The gray stream of Vainqueur's mane became, instead, the rich and glossy brown of her hair. The pale blue of the sky darkened to the deep and mysterious blue of her eyes. The warm wind rushing against the square of face exposed by his helm gentled to the sweetness of her breath flowing moist across his lips. The beating of hooves on the hard packed earth became her voice, her words: *I love you, love you, love you . . .*

Tender words that plunged like a dagger into his chest. The sweat of fear pearled on Tristan's brow and dripped into his eyes. A fear no physical danger could wring from him. Nay, only those words spoken by this woman . . . words once spoken to him by another who said them as earnestly, who smiled as sweetly, who then betrayed him.

Ruella, the wife he had taken reluctantly, and for the reasons all men wed; for children of his body, for lands to leave to his heirs. It was only after he wed her that he knew he had erred. He had hoped to be kind, if not loving, but his mother ended that hope. Her cruelty to Ruella grew apace with his kindness, and dwindled with his studied indifference.

It was not until he returned from Gascony and found his wife brought to bed with another man's child that he knew the bitter harvest of his indifference. Ruella's death was a blessing and the child, Megotta, a curse—until the day she toddled away from Enid's strict care and under the milling hooves of his destrier. He had leaped from the saddle and lifted her in his arms, soothed her tears and watched the smile that followed. In that moment he lost his heart just as surely as he lost it when . . .

Nay! Tristan straightened in the saddle, bringing his shield up, as if to ward off his own thoughts. Nay, he had not lost his heart again. He had given it only once, and then to a child who was innocent of her mother's misdeeds and her father's, whoever he was. Nay, he had not lost his heart again. Amicia was naught to him but a burden added to all of the burdens he bore. A wife he did not want; a woman he would not love.

Ahead, the village seethed with a terror that banished all thoughts but those of the task at hand. Smoke, thick and black and flickering with hellish red sparks, boiled from blazing thatch roofs. The reivers, well mounted and laying about with their bloodied swords, cut down the villeins fighting with scythes and flailing hooks.

Tristan's sword rasped from its sheath and he thrust it high in a brawny hand. "For Eden! The right is ours! For Eden!" he bellowed in mounting rage, and behind him, his men raised an answering shout, "For Eden! For Eden!"

On the greening grass at the edge of the village lay a fat swine writhing in the red slick of its own blood. Farther along, a woman lay sprawled in a bed of periwinkles, her chest gaping red and her eyes staring blindly through a tangle of chestnut-brown hair. It was a sight like many Tristan had seen in his years of warring with the Earl. Neither blood nor death could make him flinch, but the sight of that hair so like Amicia's scraped down his spine like the needle-sharp talons of a hawk.

He breathed a silent prayer of thanksgiving that she was pent within the keep and safe. A fervent vow to see that she never came to harm hissing from his lips, he struck the first blow. His blade sliced through a mail-clad arm, leaving a spurting stump and a screaming man to topple from his horse. Vainqueur swept on by, but Tristan found no foe to meet him.

The reivers, ten strong less one, raised a concerted shout, wheeled their steeds about and fled, leaving Tristan and his men-at-arms to give chase. Clucking hens flew from beneath the horse's hooves. Geese honked and waddled away. Squealing swine trotted drunkenly about, barriers fleet Vainqueur sailed over.

Tristan gained on the slowest of the fleeing thieves, vaguely aware that all was not as it should be. None were encumbered with sacks of grain or squawking hens or oddments of value gleaned in the village. Nay, instead, they came for naught but slaughter and rapine, and slewed away to the cool embrace of the wood without standing to fight as they had when last he met them. That time they had but one desire, and that his life, his blood. Yet, now they turned tail to run, almost as if . . .

The thought vanishing, Tristan leaned across the high pommel, swung with his sword, and felt it strike deep and true. The reiver screamed, a high womanish scream that echoed through the twilight of the wood and sent birds shrieking into the air. Vainqueur pounded on, Tristan feeling a keen satisfaction that he could meet his enemy at last and know the sweet taste of victory.

The wood grew thicker, darker beneath the canopy of limbs woven as tight as linen. The pace slowed and slowed still more, with Tristan and his men dodging the broad trunks of oaks and the thinner trunks of hazel and lime. The reivers fled on, careless of low-hanging limbs, of vines and thorns and thickets.

"My lord!" Rolf pulled alongside, his chest heaving, his face sweating. "We approach the boundary to Bellay Chase! Do we follow, should they flee across it?"

"Ay, we follow them to hell if need be!" Tristan slanted a hard look at his man. "I will lose no more of my folk to them."

"Ay, my lord!" Rolf knuckled a smart salute and fell back to warn the men.

Tristan, his bloodied sword in hand, galloped through

the dank gloom speared by moted beams of sunlight. All was not as it should be. The thought fretted him. The reivers were fewer than they had been and less daring. They fled now in a neat row, straight for Bellay's lands. A trap? he wondered, his blood simmering hot and ready. Would he, at last, have a chance to meet his enemy, pitting sword-arm against sword-arm, strength against strength?

He caught a glimpse of the reivers ahead, a flapping of mantles, blood red against verdant green. They angled away from the boundary of trees blazed with black scars burned deep into the bark, and Tristan knew a keen frustration. If he could prove Bellay gave them succor, he would be free to act as he would.

For one hour, then another, the reivers skirted the boundary, always within sight, but frustratingly out of reach. The shadows grew darker with the sinking of the sun. If he did not catch them soon, Tristan fumed, they would be gone once more and he outwitted again. It was almost as if they led him on this chase apurpose.

A chill wormed its way the length of his spine. Apurpose? What reason could they have? Why would any want him drawn away from the keep? Amicia! Megotta! Nay, it could not be! He had taken such care! His mother would not dare . . .

She would dare anything! *Anything!*

He yanked on the reins to wheel Vainqueur around, stood in the stirrups, and shouted, "To the keep! As fast as you may! To the keep!"

He rode hard and careless in the waning light of day. Vines whipped at him. The rich odor of damp earth and rotting leaves filled his nostrils, and brought a bright memory of the glade and Amicia. A memory of her hair flowing like silk across his hands, of her mouth clinging to his, of her body pressed against him.

He sweated hard, not the clean sweat of exertion, but the oozing sweat of fear. So small she was, so dainty and gentle. If any had dared to hurt her, he would cry defiance before the gates of Heaven itself. No vow would hold him. No man would stop him. Amicia, Amicia, he whispered her name like a prayer.

\* \* \*

The pure white of the sickle moon rested on a jagged peak of the eastern mountains when Tristan pounded up to the outer gate, shouting for entry. The gate-guard, an inky silhouette against the star-spangled sky, gave order to the gate-wards, then lifted a horn to his lips. The single note belled across the cool night air and was answered by the wardcorne's horn high atop the keep.

In the inner ward, Tristan flung himself from Vainqueur's back, leaving the destrier with his head hanging and strings of foamy sweat dripping from his heaving sides. Running as fleetly as an unburdened youth, he raced up the outer stairs, taking them two at the time. Nothing so rational as thought could penetrate the bubbling stew of his mind. Fear mingled with dread; hope meshed with despair; visions of Amicia smiling and happy yielded to nightmares of her screaming in pain. And, rising above it all, a dim awareness he could not explain—an awareness that she was gone from this place.

The scrape of footsteps and the high note of worried voices brought Tristan to a wavering halt. He looked up and saw Odo and Enid hurrying through the entrance door. They stopped in the full light of the torches, Enid's face haggard and Odo's twisted with fury.

"She is gone, my lord! And the child with her!" Odo burst out. "Lady Sybilla and Sir Aimery have taken them away!"

A hole so vast as the sky overhead yawned in the place where Tristan's heart had been. His shaking hand groped for the cool stone, gripped a corner with fingertips digging into the mortar, and supported his quivering legs. He had known it while deep in the wood. He had felt Amicia's absence while riding into the ward. Why? What hold did she have upon him that he could know that now she rode like the wind with fear as her companion?

The answer came with the shattering of his last feeble resistance, the crumbling of his last tenacious delusions. He loved her. That knowledge sucked the strength from his thews and left him trembling like a reed in the wind. When had it happened? he wondered, and knew it did not matter. Somehow she had leached the bitterness of old pain from him; she had revived the hope he had lost; she had given him the gift of love; and, now, she was gone and in danger because of him.

An agony of grief and regret tore at him like the sharp beak of a vulture tearing at its prey. If only . . . the words, heavy laden with remorse, whispered again and again. If only he had recognized his love sooner. If only he had held her close and whispered that he loved to feel the silk of her hair clutching his hands with eager tendrils, that he loved the softness of her voice and the sweetness of her smile, that he loved her as he never thought he would be able to love any woman. If only he had protected her as he should have.

His gaze lifted, meeting the worried silver of Odo's eye. "You . . ." His breath wheezed out. "You did not stop them?"

"He could not, my lord!" Enid wrung her hands and wept. "Odo and I were barred in my lady's chamber and released but moments ago by a serving maid who came above and heard us pounding on the door."

Death? Was that what awaited the child he loved, the woman he loved? Nay, he would not allow it. He would do anything, *anything,* to keep them from harm!

"Where?" he asked, his voice low and hard. "Where have they taken them?"

"No mention was made in our presence, my lord," Odo answered. "We were ordered to tell you a letter awaits you on the High Table."

The letter was there, a black scrawl on white parchment pierced through by the dagger pinning it to the table. Tristan stood on the dais, his shoulders hunched, the tips of his fingers spread to touch the smooth worn wood. One finger lifted, stretched, touched a curling edge of the parchment, and trembled. He had ridden into the whirring path of crossbow bolts with more courage than he felt now. He had risen from his bed of illness with more strength than he felt now.

"Leave me," he rasped to Enid and Odo, who were waiting beneath the dais.

"My lord," Odo began.

"Leave me!" Tristan shouted, his head snapping up, his hot gaze sweeping the hall. "Begone! All of you!"

His voice echoed from plastered walls and soot-blackened rafters like a deep threatening thunder rolling down from the hills. Servants spun to stare and whirled to flee. Enid and Odo hurried away.

The Great Hall was empty and Tristan was alone. His eyes glittered in the blanched white of his face, studying the haft of the dagger and the curling missive beneath. His nostrils flared. Was it naught but dreamery, or did an odor of evil linger in the air? Ay, no dreamery, but truth. The evil of his mother. The woman without a conscience, without a heart, who would use any to see her ends met.

Tristan reached for the dagger, clenching his hand around the leather-wrapped hilt. He yanked it from the parchment and buried the sharp point deep in the wood, wishing, wishing it was his mother's heart instead. He pulled a candle near and spread the parchment and stared down at Aimery's thick and splattered script.

*Brother,*
  *You have ever loved unwisely, Tristan. You who have claimed to love not at all. Do not fear for Megotta. She is mine. Yes, brother, mine! Now that your end is near, she is of no further use to our mother, and so is safe.*

A giddy sensation of unreality set Tristan's head to whirling. He went back to read again, *She is mine. Yes, brother, mine!* He blinked and read it over and over . . . *mine . . . mine . . . mine,* but still could not force himself to accept it or believe it. Not of Aimery. Not of the brother who had loved him with a worshipful adoration as a child; the brother he had in turn loved and shielded from the worst of their mother's hate.

Yet, it was written in Aimery's own hand. He had to accept it, believe it. His brother had formed an adulterous liaison with his wife and she had born a child of it. Megotta, the child he had so slowly accepted and come to love. The child he now thought of as his own. The child who believed she was his.

Tristan's head sank to the carved back of the chair, his

lashes sliding to his cheeks. Had they told her? he wondered, his heart wrenching with pain. Had they shattered her innocence with a truth that would scar her for life?

"Megotta," he whispered into the emptiness of the Great Hall, feeling that emptiness in the hollow spaces of his soul, "it shames me now that I could not bear to look upon you as a babe. It was only later that I grew to love you. No matter what they tell you, will you remember that? Will you know that I loved you as a child of my own flesh?"

The parchment crackled in Tristan's clenching hands and he leaned forward, holding it up to the flickering candlelight. Dread knotting his throat, he focused his blurring eyes and read on. A jolt of shock as strong as the crash of a lance against a shield in the joust rocked him back in his seat. Even his mother could not demand this of him! Tristan's eyes raced across the sprawling script once again. Aimery could not demand this! Yet, there it was. He was to sign over his title, his lands, and his rights to Aimery in return for Amicia's life. So much Tristan could do. She was worth that and more to him, but Aimery had gone on to twist treachery's knife. He would, as the new Lord of Eden, take all and pay homage to Eustace of Bellay—thereby breaking Tristan's sworn oath to Earl Simon to hold all for him.

*Do you see our mother's hand in this, Tristan? A fine vengeance, indeed, for now you must face the same test our father faced. Which will you choose, brother? Your honor or your love? Do not seek to follow. Should you, I will kill your beloved Amicia and so make the decision for you. A runner will come on the third day from this for your answer.*

The parchment slipped from Tristan's nerveless fingers and scraped across the wooden table. He sank back, limp as a washclout, his hands dangling over the carved armrests, his head resting against the oaken back.

His honor or his love. A fine vengeance, indeed. Sweat trickled down Tristan's temples. How often he had wondered what his father had felt so long ago. He thought he must have foamed at the mouth with rage, stomped about, cursing and threatening. He knew now that there were calamities so sinister and far reaching that rage was not only useless, it was impossible.

Rage would not make Aimery the man he once was. It would not bring Amicia back or protect Megotta. It would not even relieve the agonizing ache that had become his heart.

What a callow fool he had been all of these years. Never had he understood how his father could have considered the choice he was given any choice at all. Never had he understood how he had come so near to choosing a woman over his honor. Never had he thought of it without feeling a pang of shame. After all, honor was all that made a man a man. It was all that distinguished him from two-legged beasts like Eustace of Bellay.

Had his father's Lady Margaret of Castle Rydding been a woman like his own Amicia of Bellay? Had she been comely and sweet tempered, gentle and loving? Had she touched him in a way no other woman had ever touched him? Had he felt that life without her would be no life at all?

Tristan climbed to his feet, slowly, heavily. He could not stay where the ill-omened presence of his mother permeated the air. He needed to get away to some place uniquely his . . . uniquely Amicia's.

Within minutes he was slipping through the postern gate and striding down the slope, oblivious of the weight of his hauberk and mail chausses, oblivious of the sweat that oozed across his flesh in spite of the cool night breeze. The sickle moon bathed the land in opalescent serenity. The tattered black shadow of the willow brake was framed against a sky as blue as Amicia's eyes. He moved through the trees more by instinct than sight, drawn by the green smell of moss and the chuckling of the spring.

The white of the moon glazed the wet limestone and danced atop the water. The black of shadows, as dark as those falling across his soul, lay round about. Tristan dropped down onto the mossy bank and breathed deep. He smelled the fertile odor of leaf mold, the clean mist of water, the sweet scent of violets, and, eerily, impossibly, an essence of sandalwood and Amicia.

He saw her as he had seen her that day, reclining on the mossy bank with her hair tumbling around her. He saw the sweetness of her smile, a sweetness that roused an ache of yearning in him. He felt the pressure of her mouth upon his, the throbbing of her heart against his, the sinuous lines of her body molding to the hard lines of his.

Then, he saw her shrinking from Aimery's dagger, calling for help that did not come, screaming in terror and pain. He saw her lying as the woman in the village had lain, sprawled out, her chest gaping wide and red, her eyes staring blindly through the tangle of her hair.

Could he live with himself if he condemned her to death as the price of his honor? Could he live with himself if he did not?

His fingers rubbed restlessly over his seal ring, feeling the intaglio of the two-headed Janus. Honor or dishonor? He had given oath to protect Amicia from harm. He had given oath to the Earl that he would hold his lands and title of him. No matter which he chose, he would be dishonored.

The Earl's claim upon him was stronger. Amicia was but a woman with one life and that life of less importance than his ties to his lord, his king. Should those ties be broken and Aimery swear to Bellay, then the Earl would come with fire and sword to ravage the land and beat his rebellious subjects into submission. The village folk would be slain, the crops and kind burned, and the keep taken down stone by stone. Naught would be left. The name of Eden would be whispered in infamy throughout the land and he, himself, would be put to the horn as an outlaw.

This was what his father had faced. This cruel agonizing choice. One life weighed in the balance against many. Yet, that one life more dear to him than all of the souls in the kingdom. How, Tristan wondered, had he done it? How had he condemned the woman he loved to a painful death in the full knowledge that he had not loved her enough?

Tristan stared up through the willow branches, clicking like old bones in the breeze. If only it was his own life at stake, he would gladly choose death. But it wasn't his, it was Amicia's. Amicia, who had come to his keep so proud in her fear. Amicia, who had given a mother's love to Megotta and a lady's care to his folk. Amicia, who had loved him and taught him, all unwilling, to love.

He would be but little loss to this land, while she, who gave so much, would be bitterly missed. Was it honor to make her life forfeit for his honor? Nay, he could not think it was. Yet, he feared he was splitting hairs because he could not bear the thought of her dying alone and afraid.

If he chose her life above his honor, would he ever forgive her or himself?

If he chose his honor above her life, could he live with the knowledge that he had slain her as surely as if he had plunged the dagger into her breast?

*Have you ever been so, my lord? So alone?* He heard Amicia's voice as if she stood beside him and whispered in his ear.

Ay, he had ever been alone, but never had he felt that loneliness as he did now. He sat on through the night, listening to the crickets chirp and the mournful hooting of an owl. Morning came. Twinkling stars merged into the azure-blue sky, and still he did not know what he would do. He knew only one thing that stayed rock-solid and unassailable: a man without honor was nothing.

# Chapter 21

Amicia's dower castle, the shell keep of Byly, squatted on the brow of a hill in barren moorland heights honeycombed with narrow limestone valleys. No towers protruded above the ancient curtain wall scabbed with lichen. No square keep climbed from the open center ward. Instead, the decaying domestic buildings backed onto the crumbling circle of the outer wall.

In spite of the fire blazing in the hearth, her chamber was dreary and cool. Plaster flaked from the walls, cobwebs festooned the ceiling, and the oaken floor groaned with her every pacing step. She had a bed and a stool, but no stitching to occupy her hands, no prie-dieu to kneel and pray. She had only her thoughts to while away the hours, and those no fit company.

She worried about Megotta, now in the Scottish lowlands with her grandmother. She worried about Tristan, returned to the hall to find them gone and Aimery's letter skewered to the High Table with a dagger. She worried about what he had read on that curling parchment. Had Aimery confessed that he was Megotta's father? Had he said that he was taking her, Tristan's wife, away to make her his? Was he, or did he have a more sinister purpose for her?

Her hand trembled on the stone sill of the window, an arrow slit designed for defense with a width less than a man's foot. Mortar sifted to the floor in a granulated rain.

A stone came loose and Amicia jumped back, watching it thud to the floor. Her gaze climbed, wide, alert, brightening with hope. Escape? Could she escape and return to Tristan?

She forgot all but the need for him, a sick yearning that grew by the hour. Leaping at the window as if it were a living foe, she scrabbled at the joints, searching for weaknesses, finding them, digging, digging at the gritty dust of the grouting. A fingernail snapped at the quick. She gasped with pain, but ignored the welling blood and snatched her eating knife from its sheath at her waist. If she could loosen the stone and send it tumbling after the other . . .

She plunged the knife into the joint, but saw, instead, Aimery's dagger stabbing into the parchment. Her lashes squeezed shut. She saw him as he had been at that moment—his face flushed with a febrile obsession that routed every sign of weakness and confusion. He had turned from the High Table and frowned down at her.

"Do you hope to escape me, then think on this," he had said. "Megotta's life will be forfeit. My mother has awaited her vengeance for too long. She will have it now, however she must take it."

Amicia's grip on the knife slackened. Her shoulders drooped, her head bent, and she leaned to rest her brow on her forearm. She did not wish to remember more, but the memories came as relentlessly as the reivers . . .

"You will use Megotta's well-faring as a goad to force me to your will, as your mother used her to force Tristan," she had said. "How can you do it, Aimery? She is yours, flesh of your flesh, bone of your bone, blood of your blood."

Had she imagined the wavering of his gaze? The slight hesitation before he squared his shoulders and smiled a smile so like his mother's she grew lightheaded with revulsion. A smile she had once thought was merry. How could she have mistaken it so?

If he had any regrets, they were buried deep, for he boasted, "Ay, she is mine. One thing, this one thing, I have done before Tristan."

"Your mother said . . . said Ruella was . . . unwilling."

He looked away then, his hesitance more pronounced. "Ay, she thought herself in love with Tristan and claimed that he would love her someday. She was a fool to cling to him as she did," he said, and Amicia heard in his voice the strange love-hate-envy-admiration he felt for his brother.

"It was you who beat her at Carrickmuir!" she cried, furious that Tristan had been blamed, sorrowful that Ruella had suffered so for her love.

"How do you know that?" Aimery scowled so fiercely her knees threatened to buckle. "None from Eden were with us to carry the tale. None knew—"

"Lady Guinella spoke of it, believing Tristan—"

"But my dear brother would never lay a hand to her or any wench," he said bitterly. "Was he the man he should be our mother would now be locked in a tower or cold in her grave."

"And if you were the man you should be," she flung at him heedlessly, "you would cleave to your brother's side, for he loves you well and gives you his loyalty!"

"Loyalty!" Aimery growled. "I have suffered a lifetime of pain because of him! Always, *always*, I have lived in his shadow. First with my father, so consumed by his love of Tristan that he had nothing left for me. Then with my mother, so consumed by her hate of Tristan that she had nothing left for me. Do not speak to me of loyalty!"

"Nay, I would not, for you ken not its meaning! You cleave to your mother like a youngling in hopes she will give you her love, while she knows nothing but hate. You should fear where that hate will turn when she is done with Tristan."

"And you, my lady," he said so coldly Amicia felt the skeletal fingers of death caressing her nape, "should fear for yourself . . . and Megotta. Do not think I will be as weak willed as my brother. Do you not do as I wish, I will see Megotta dead."

Now, remembering that threat, Amicia shuddered and lifted her head from her forearm. The window slit framed a slice of mud-bottomed moat, rank with weeds, and rolling green moor patched with heather. In the distance gritstone cliffs clawed at the sky; and, beyond them, three days of hard riding through mountain and valley and wood, lay the vast demesne of Castle Eden.

"Tristan," Amicia whispered. Was it possible for one heart to reach out and touch another far away? Now she knew how he had felt all of these years. She knew the frustration, the desire for action, the fear for Megotta's life and happiness, the guilty wish to act for her own happiness, for her own well-faring.

It would be so easy to move one stone and another until she had space enough to squeeze through this narrow span, to drop to the ground and wade the moat in the dark of night, to run free toward the cliffs, toward Tristan.

A tempting stone shifted beneath her clutching fingers and her heart soared with hope. A hope whose wings were abruptly clipped by reality. She could not win her own happiness with Megotta's life. She must wait and hope that somehow Tristan would find the answer to save them all.

She pulled her knife from the mortar and slid the shaft into its sheath. Turning away, she heard the stone slide from its setting and crash to the floor. She flinched, but did not look back. It would do no good. She could not leave. For Megotta's sake she must stay.

The thinning shadow of the gritstone cliff was reaching for Amicia like a beckoning hand when the rusty hinges of her door squeaked. It scraped across the bare oaken floor, and a gaunt serving man entered, the first of a procession of hollow-eyed, hollow-cheeked servants that moved mutely about the task of arranging a small feast.

Watching them, Amicia suffered a swift misgiving. Though Aimery had acted the gentle knight on the journey, there had been times when his gaze lingered upon her. A hot gaze holding nothing so clean as the honest desire of a man for a woman. Honest desire she could understand. What she saw in his eyes made her flesh crawl.

Would Aimery now abandon his role of gentle knight? A guise that, she thought, fooled not even him. Or would he come to her, smug lipped and boasting? Pray, the latter. Then she might learn why he had brought her here and how he hoped to use her against Tristan.

The servants gone, she waited near the elongated strip of light pouring through the window. Cinnamon spiced steam curled above a venison stew thick with currants. Mushrooms and leeks floated in a broth colored with saffron and smelling of ginger. Apple fritters drowned in almond milk lay on a platter. Amicia's mouth watered and her belly growled, reminding her of how long it had been since she sat at table. The oatcakes Aimery had given her on their journey had staved off starvation, but little else.

The rusty hinge squeaked a warning and Amicia's hunger dwindled to naught. She moved into the glowing nimbus of candlelight. She would not escape, but she had few means to best Aimery, and the crumbling sill was one, should she need it.

Closing the door behind him, he stopped to stare at her as she stared at him. Her fearful gaze traveled over the black of tunic and chausses, the scarlet of his thickly embroidered surcoat. She sensed a difference in him that had naught to do with what he wore, and much to do with what he was.

His feet planted firmly apart and his thumbs hooked into his jewel-encrusted belt, he studiously wore a new aura of confidence. Amicia studied the square set of his shoulders and the assurance of his gaze with a growing apprehension. She saw no chink in his armor of pride, no hint of the maudlin man sunk deep in his cups and mourning for his brother.

"You are a comely wench," he said, his lilting voice deeper toned and stronger.

"I am your brother's wife," she reminded him.

"So was Ruella."

It was said neither in challenge nor threat, but simply stated. And that simplicity was more frightening than aught else he might have done. It suggested a determination new to him, and she feared that, weak as he was, he would hew to it senselessly.

"Come," he said, "you must be sharp-set after the journey and your night of rest."

He moved toward the table, his great square body a commanding presence. As if, Amicia thought, he had found a new power in his mother's absence. What manner

of man might he have been had his life been different? A
fruitless thought. She must deal with this one, and he so
changed she knew not how to begin.

He pulled out the stool. Amicia hesitated. The idea of
sitting at table with him as boon companion made her sick
with disgust. She swallowed her pride, her anger, her
disgust. Just as he thought to use her against Tristan, so
she would use him to learn what she must.

She moved slowly and sat uneasily. Aimery's soft swarthy
hand daintily caressed the slope of her shoulder, but she
dared not flinch away. His thumb feathered along the side
of her neck and chills scrabbled down her backbone. She
waited with pent breath, but he did nothing more than pat
her arm, sigh, and move around the table.

He attended her with the flair of a courtier: pouring wine
in her cup and filling her wooden bowl with the choicest
gobbets of venison from the stew. And all the while his
eyes stroked her, lingering on the fragile hand clutching
her cup, touching her lips, the peaks of her breasts.

Her legs trembled with the need to leap up and away, to
escape his fulsome gaze. Quelling that need by the hardest
effort, she concentrated instead on her hunger. She set her
spoon to her stew, but her belly threatened to revolt. She
sipped wine to wet her dry mouth, but dared not drink
deep with her throat knotted so tight it ached.

"You do not hunger?"

His swarthy face betrayed a deep concern that affected
Amicia little. She set her cup aside and laid her hands in
her lap, where they clutched at one another, offering what
poor comfort was to be had. "Nay," she said softly, and
leaned forward. "Why, Aimery? Why was Megotta sent
north with your mother and I brought here by you?"

His gaze wandered from her to the darkening window
slit. "We had no assurance Tristan would not follow. If he
does, he will go north and find only Megotta. We will still
have you."

"For what purpose?" she asked, her voice sharp and
demanding.

His head swiveled, his eyes narrowed, piercing. "For
my mother's final vengeance upon him!"

"The letter, Aimery? What was in the letter you left him?"

His dark and lightless eyes held hers, almost, she thought, as if he dared not look away. "I told him Megotta was mine."

His voice resonated with boasting, but the words were no sooner said than his gaze fell to his steaming stew. Flurries of movement agitated his fleshy cheeks with twitches and tics and tremblings. One thick spatulate finger grated the shaft of his spoon to and fro along the rim of his bowl.

Did he fear what Tristan would do? Amicia wondered as she watched his confidence crumble before the onslaught of apprehension. She caught a glimpse of the tormented man who let Tristan ride into the reivers' trap and remembered Aimery saying, *Now, he will not learn what I have done and hate me for it.*

"Once you would rather have seen Tristan dead than have him know you sired Megotta on his wife," she said, and saw his gaze shift up to her and slide away. "You said he would have to suffer no more, nor would you. Why do you now tell him?"

His nostrils flared and his thick chest swelled, rippling the intricate black embroidery over the field of scarlet red. His eyes, capturing the swaying light of the candles, gleamed with a fanatic light. "Megotta is mine! Mine! Yet I dared not claim her! I could only sit by and enjoy Tristan's plight. He could neither reject her as the child of his faithless wife nor love her as his own. How often I watched them in hall, and never did I see a sign of love between them."

He stood abruptly. His stool crashed over, the sound bouncing from the walls of the chamber. His agitated hand plowed through his hair and his face twisted with a pain that roused Amicia to pity. A pity that vanished when his pain was replaced by a flush of rage.

"It was a trick!" His light voice assumed a shrill, womanish whine. "They tricked me! My brother and my daughter! She loved him as a father, and I never suspected it!"

He stared down at Amicia, his pain-glazed eyes holding a plea. Almost as if he asked how those he trusted and loved could have betrayed him so. Was it true? *My daughter*, he had called Megotta with a trill of pride in his voice. Did he . . .

He shook his head and the dazed look of pleading vanished. Naught was left but anger. An anger that stilled Amicia in midthought.

"I never suspected it until *you* came to change us all! God's Wounds! Who would have thought it possible?" He threw his head back, staring into the sagging rafters thick woven with cobwebs. "Bellay's daughter and Eden's son. I have seen him follow you with his eyes. I have seen him struggle. I have seen his love for you grow day by day."

"Nay, Aimery," she choked out. "You are wrong, for—"

"You, the daughter of his enemy!" he said, as if she had not spoken. "He loves you where he would not love Ruella! Ah, God! God! Ruella!"

He cried the name as if calling Ruella to him, and Amicia froze, her eyes wide, her heart pounding, her mind reeling. She watched him stumble toward the bed and clutch the endpost, rolling his flushed brow against it. His breath came in sobbing gasps and tears rolled down his anguish-contorted cheeks.

"I loved her," he moaned. "By the rood, I do swear I loved her. But she . . . she had eyes for none but Tristan. Even when he turned from her, when he went to her bed no more, when he paid no heed to her, still she saw none but him. My mother vowed that Ruella would turn to me when he returned to Gascony. So we went to Carrickmuir where naught would remind her of him and I could woo her as I wished. I can see her still, standing on the parapet with the wind blowing her black hair while she watched the south. Always the south, in hopes Tristan would come."

Amicia's lashes slid to her cheeks. The scene Aimery drew was so potent she, too, could see the solitary woman standing beneath the summer-blue sky. She knew that woman's heartache, her loneliness, her need of the man she loved. It was the same heartache, the same loneliness, the same need that she felt now—and for the same man. Tristan of Eden, who loved neither of them, though they gave their hearts to him fully and without question.

"I bought her gold thread from a chapman traveling with his wares. I picked wild flowers for her to weave through her hair. I did all to woo her as a lover, but the more I did, the more she shrank away." He looked up, his gaze empty and hollow. "I went to her on bended knee and declared my love. She touched me. So gentle a touch. I feel it still," he whispered, his thick finger trailing lightly along his tear-wet cheek.

"She said that I must not. It was a sin, for she was my brother's wife. She said that even if it was not, her heart was given to him." Aimery turned to Amicia. "I knew that. Why did she not stop there? Why did she go on to say more?"

Amicia stood slowly, her legs trembling beneath her. "What did she say, Aimery? What did you do?"

His mouth, so easy to curve into an empty smile, now quivered like a child's. "She said . . . that I did not really love her, that I only wanted her because she was Tristan's wife. She said . . . I must not envy Tristan all he had, when he had so little." His quivering mouth stilled and firmed into a hard angry line. "So little! All I wanted! All I needed! All that had been denied me! That was when I hit her! I hit her again and again, and then I . . . I . . ."

He swallowed hard, a sound Amicia could hear across the chamber. A sound at one with the sick convulsion of her own throat. She sank slowly to the stool, her heavy head finding a resting place in her palms.

"Always, always, Tristan has had what I wanted. All came so easily to him. My father's love, Ruella's love, Megotta's love, and now . . . yours."

The last soft sibilance whispered into silence and Amicia trembled. Her head climbed slowly, her gaze rising to meet Aimery's. His harrowed expression revealed the deep and lacerating suffering of years. A suffering he now shrugged off visibly.

"He loves you as he never loved her, and I will see that love destroy him," he said with a steely resolve. "We have planned it well, my mother and I."

"What have you done?" she whispered.

He smiled through his anger, and a premonitory thrill tingled through her. She straightened, waiting.

"We have given him a choice," he said softly, his glittering gaze plunging deep into hers with a malicious humor. "Your life for his lands, his title, his honor."

She stared at him, too stricken to breathe. The same choice her father had given Tristan's father. *Tristan, Tristan,* she wailed mutely. *What will you suffer before your decision is made? What sorrow have I brought to you all unknowing?*

"You have given him no choice, Aimery." Her gaze held his with unwavering conviction. "Tristan holds naught dearer than his honor."

"Ay, but I have. If he chooses his honor, your lifeless body will be returned to him to mock his choice." Eyes alight with evil triumph, he dropped his hand to the jeweled hilt of the knife at his waist.

Cruelly fascinated, Amicia watched his fingers stroke the glittering stones. Blues and reds and greens sparkled, the colors of awakening spring, the colors of life. She wrenched her eyes from them, looking up into Aimery's face, into his eyes. Eyes that held not a glimmer of mercy.

"You will wait, as I do," he said softly, then swiveled on his heel and left her.

Amicia stood slowly, feeling the strength of her thews, the pulse of life at her wrists and throat, the smooth caress of linen. She moved to the window and stared at the vast heaven strewn with twinkling stars. A curlew screamed in the distance. An owl glided silently over the moat. The cool breeze lightly fingered her hair.

She savored it all, sight and sound and scent, knowing that soon it would be hers to savor no more. Tristan would choose as his father had. Being the man he was, he could do naught else. And she, like Mother Margaret, could not blame him for that choice. How could she, when she loved him for the man he was.

Though she could not blame Tristan for his choice, she feared it. She feared the moment of death: the pain and loss of life. She wondered if Aimery would use his jeweled knife and how. Her knees buckled and she knelt before the window, her hands clasped for prayer.

She begged forgiveness for the sin of loving life too well, of clinging to it too hardily. She pleaded for strength and courage, and wondered if Mother Margaret had once knelt to pray as she did now. Had she suffered the same fear? Had she mourned all she would lose? Knowing the choice her beloved Robert would make, had she felt her heart breaking and bleeding for herself and him?

Her faith should be stronger. This knot of terror should not have taken up permanent residence in her breast. For two days the loose stones tantalized Amicia with the knowledge that freedom could be hers.

Her fingers resting lightly on the cool stone, she spent hours staring at the moors while her disjointed thoughts wandered at will. She suffered for Tristan and the decision he must make. She grieved for Ruella, that poor lady who had suffered for her love. She feared for herself. She wondered if Aimery was capable of killing Megotta.

*My daughter*, he had said with that undercurrent of pride. Did she but imagine that his eyes softened on mention of Megotta's name? Was it love, or a frenzied obsession with possessing what was his? An obsession akin to her father's? If only she knew Aimery loved his daughter and could not hurt her, then she could flee. But who could say what he would do, teetering on the edge of madness as he was.

A madness that had sunk its claw deep. He often came to her chamber, his lumbering body pacing to and fro while he gloated and spoke at random. One moment she would swear he loved Tristan and regretted his part in this villainy. The next, he cursed his brother with a virulence that chilled her. Another time he spoke of Ruella, dwelling long on her beauty and gentleness of spirit in a voice sunk low with pain. Again, and his hot gaze swept her with a lustful look that stripped her bare. A lustful look that grew stronger and more frequent by the hour.

Her nerves stretched taut, Amicia pondered the peril that faced her while watching a twitchy-nosed hare nibble on the lush grass bordering the moat. Looking up, she saw a lone man running in the distance. Slowly, he grew larger, a nearly naked figure glistening with sweat—a messenger. She had no need to see the length of split cane he carried in his hand. She had no need to guess what his mission was. Aimery would have his answer soon.

It was done, not to be undone. Peace, the same peace she had once found at prayer, dissolved the knot of terror in her breast. Her gaze lifted to the sky, the azure sky as bright as Tristan's eyes. Love warmed her where she thought to feel naught but death's cold breath. Flooding through her was a fierce gladness that Tristan had not found a love as she had found. It would make his decision and its consequences easier. He would not live with the painful regret his father had suffered.

She moved to the stool and sat as she had once sat beneath the yellowing leaves of the apple tree. With her small feet neatly aligned, leather-clad toes peeping from the hem of her cotte, and her fragile hands reposing in her lap, she was the image of composure. An image that was disturbed by a single sobbing breath.

Sooner than she expected, she heard the creaking of her door and saw Aimery step through. A strangely subdued Aimery, whose swarthy face mirrored an inner battle.

"I told you he would not do it," she murmured, torn between sadness and pride, an odd pride in Tristan's strength and his honor. Mayhap, she thought, it was because she could see what a man without honor became. A creature like Aimery, adrift on the tumultuous winds of his emotions, tossed thither and yon like an autumn leaf with no will to choose the direction it would take.

He stood before her, staring, frowning, his small mouth pinched at the corners. "Read it," he commanded, tossing the parchment into her lap.

She touched it gently, the smooth surface so late in Tristan's hand, still gritty with the *pommes* used to dry the ink. She closed her eyes and saw his hand, long fingers tufted with red-gold hair on the knuckles and the muscular palm thick with calluses. She could feel it touching her, an imperious finger tilting her chin up, a gentle palm gliding over her breast.

"Read it!"

Aimery's rude intrusion on her sweet reverie sent her lashes sweeping up. He stood over her, arms folded, feet spread, and his face black with growing wrath. Surely he had expected Tristan to choose as he did. Why, then, was he so angry?

She spread the curling sides and held the missive up to the candlelight. " 'Be it known to all that I, Tristan, Lord of Eden,' " she said, reading the bold steady script aloud, " 'do forswear my oath . . .' " Her breath seeped out on a broken thread of air, while her eyes leaped back to race over the words once more. . . . *do forswear my oath to my lord, Simon de Montfort, Earl of Leicester* . . .

Impossible! What did it mean? Amicia's stunned gaze jerked up to Aimery. Tristan forswore his oath. He chose . . . her life!

The parchment sank to her lap, her fingers lax around it. It made no sense. He loved her not. So he had told her in the shadow of the willows with the spring bubbling behind them. *There is naught of love in this,* he said. Yet, remembering his savage kiss, the desperate way he had held her, she knew now there had been more than the need she recognized: a love so deep and abiding he would save her at the cost of the honor he cherished above all.

She would not die! She would live to rush toward life with outstretched arms, to fold it to her breast and glory in its sweetness. Never had life tasted sweeter than now. Never had Mother Margaret's words been so richly significant as now. Tristan loved her. He loved her so much he would . . . give up the one thing that gave his life meaning— his honor.

What would become of him without honor to sustain him? Amicia's buoyant bubble of joy popped with a shattering finality. He would become less than a man. Their love would be tainted by the guilt of his treachery toward his overlord, toward himself.

The cost was too high! She could not allow him to do it! Her fingers curling protectively around the parchment, she watched Aimery's face, alert to the angry flush brightened by the flickering fire.

The fire! What would Aimery do to her if she destroyed Tristan's letter? She could not think about that. It would be better to watch this parchment, her one slim hope of life, shrivel and blacken than to watch Tristan shrivel inside, to watch his love for her die inch by inch.

Her tongue slicked over her dry lips. "You . . . you have won," she said, rising with the parchment in her hand.

"Why?" Aimery burst out. "Why did he do it?"

Anger sharpened his question, but beneath it ran a scalding disappointment. The disappointment, Amicia thought, of a child who finds a hero to be nothing more than a man, with all of a man's frailties and flaws. Aimery had not wanted Tristan to yield. He wanted him to stand firm, to cleave to his honor.

"You said he loved me. You expected him to choose as he did." She played for time, slowly dropping her hand to her side.

"Nay! It was my mother who thought so, who hoped so! I knew he would do as our father had done. I knew he would . . ." Aimery's hand raked through his hair, his eyes darting about. "Always he pleased our father and I could not. Always he was strong and I was weak. He was good and I was not."

He stared blindly, his heavy brows knit into a solid line. Amicia edged away, slowly moving around the end of the table. The heat of the fire warmed her back, beckoning her to its devouring flames. She dared not look away from Aimery's face, and so saw the curious twists and turns of his changing expression. A chilling transmutation from anger to laughter.

His eyes sparkling, he threw back his head and set his hands to his hips. His laugh spilled out, high pitched and mirthless. "God's Eyes! I would that our father was here this day! Here to see how Tristan betrays all he was taught to be. Another Roland our father thought him to be. I would that he could see this!"

Listening to the acid jealousy in Aimery's voice, Amicia backed around the end of the table, closer to the fire. If only he would not notice what she did, and it seemed he would not, for he propped a foot on the stool and leaned to brace his forearm atop his thick thigh. Another sliding step and she breathed deep of burning peat.

"I was raised on his perfection." His eyes narrowed. "None could throw a lance as far as Tristan. None could joust as well as Tristan. None could hew to the path of honor as Tristan did. Ay, my father thought . . .''

Amicia eased back another step and Aimery frowned.

"What are you doing?"

Spinning around, she leaped for the fire and tossed the parchment into the heart of the flames.

"Nay!" Aimery screamed.

She heard the stool crash over and his foot slap against the floor. Her hand closed around the hilt of her eating knife and she yanked it from the sheath. It was a puny defiance for a man trained in the arts of war, and none more aware of that than she, but she had only to hold him off until Tristan's letter burned.

He came at her like a maddened ox, roaring his fury. Though her pounding heart threatened to burst the bonds of her ribs, she stood steady. The honed edge of the blade fragmented the light into shards as sharp as its points. Shards that stabbed at the huge claw of his hand. She slashed out, drawing blood.

He paused, poising lightly over his wide-set feet. His breath whistled in the deathly quiet, while his cunning gaze appraised her. "You are but a woman and weak," he said slyly.

"You will not destroy him," she gasped, her breath tattered by fear.

"But I will!"

He feinted to his right. She followed, and felt his left hand clamp viselike around her wrist. He wrenched once, and pain speared the length of her arm. He wrenched again, and the knife fell from her nerveless fingers. He shoved her, and she flew backward. Falling, she saw him plunge to his knees and reach into the flames. Her hands hit the oaken planks and she sprawled on the floor. An agile twist of her body and she was up, bending, running with outstretched hands. She caught him at the shoulder and bowled him over and fell atop him. Clutching at him, her gaze streaked to the fire, to the parchment shriveling and burning. She had done it! It was useless now!

His elbow sank deep into her belly. Air whooshed from her lungs and pain exploded inside her. He slammed her into the floor, pinning her shoulders while he, too, looked to the fire. "You have destroyed it," he said incredulously.

His eyes lowered to hers with a fury that killed her burgeoning triumph. She had won, and in winning, she had lost. His hands clamped around her throat, his fingers gouging her tender flesh. Her eyes widened as she clawed at his wrists and beat at his arms, but the pressure was unrelenting. She struggled for air. Her head drummed with an insistent cadence: *Tristan, Tristan, Tristan.* Her lips tingled and her throat ached. Her vision blurred at the sight of the hate ablaze in Aimery's eyes. She was dying . . . dying . . .

"Tristan thinks he has saved you and himself, but he has not," he growled, his voice sounding faint and far-away to Amicia. "Two messengers have gone forth. One to Tristan, telling him to come and claim his wife. The other to your father, telling him to come with all haste to take Tristan prisoner. You have done nothing, for I will have him still!"

The pressure on her throat eased and she gasped for air. It rushed painfully through her bruised throat and burned into her lungs, but not half so painfully as the knowledge that her short burst of courage had all been for naught. It did not matter what she did, Aimery and her father would kill Tristan. She should have suspected it, she cursed herself. She should have known better than to expect honor from them.

"I will not kill you yet," he said above her. "I may have use for you, but when I am done, Amicia of Bellay, you will suffer for what you have done."

She saw his raised fist blur into motion, felt a burst of pain, and sank into oblivion.

# Chapter 22

Amicia woke abruptly, her head pounding to the chant of *Save Tristan! Save Tristan! Save Tristan!* She struggled to a sitting position on the floor, every muscle screaming with pain. Waves of weakness lapping at her resolve, she sank her head into her hands and remembered Aimery's eyes ablaze with hate. She heard his voice, coming as if from far away, *Tristan thinks he has saved you and himself, but he has not.*

The messengers were on their way, summoning Tristan to a trap! Steeling herself, Amicia scrambled up, clutching at the table and swaying until the dizziness passed. She must warn him! She must not allow him to ride unknowing into her father's hands!

She stumbled to the window and gaped in disbelief at the sun hanging low in the east. It was morning! A day and a night she had slept . . . nay, not slept. She touched her jaw and winced with pain. Her fingers trailed across her lip, feeling the roughness of dried blood. She was bruised and aching, but alive.

Resting against the sill, Amicia stared at the green moor, scintillating with the mating of morning dew and sunlight. The magnificent sight failed to touch her. It would take at least three days for the messenger to make the trip to Eden, and as long for Tristan to arrive for her. A week. Tristan could not come in less time than that. Dare she wait to escape? Nay, for Aimery's mood was as treacherously changeable as a peat bog. If she could only make it through the day, then tonight she would slip away in the darkness.

To do what? She dared not go far, lest she miss Tristan and fail to warn him. Her gaze lifted to the distant gritstone cliff. Striated by rain and polished by wind, it gleamed in the sunlight. At its base there would be pitholes and caves. Ay, she would go there, conceal herself, and wait for him.

Shuddering at the memory of its last use, she spied her knife on the floor and returned to the window. She would not dwell on Aimery's rage or the blood that had dripped from his hand. She would think only of Tristan and his danger. Her teeth sinking into her lower lip, she stabbed the sharp point into a joint and began scraping the crumbling mortar.

By dusk her fingers were blistered and bloody, and she was wet with sweat for fear her task would not be done in time. The last thick stone, bordering the outside, was proving more stubborn than the others. Though her belly rumbled with hunger, she breathed a silent prayer of thanks that none had brought food to break her fast. Of greater concern was the rising moon, a translucent disk of white that would brighten with falling night.

Time was measured by the granules sifting away from the point of her knife. The leather hilt rubbed blisters in her palm, blisters that burst and bled. Full night came. Tears of pain streaming from her eyes and the hilt slick with blood, she worked by the silvery moonlight. A light that glazed the land with a semblance of daylight. Pausing to draw the back of her hand across her sweating brow, Amicia glanced at the moor.

Her hand froze, her fingers clenching into a fist. It could not be! She leaned forward, blinked her eyes, and stared at the file of horsemen, black shadows moving slowly through the darkness.

Her father? So quickly? It could not be! Yet, if not him, who? She could not leave while they rode toward the keep. She must time it perfectly. When they rode through the gate, she would slide across the sill and slip away.

She worked feverishly, digging at the mortar, pausing to set her shoulder to the stone, digging again, and all the while those menacing black shadows loomed larger and larger. They were so near she could hear the jingling of harness and the snuffling of the horses when she felt the stone shift.

Not daring to wait, she set her shoulder to it and prayed that the thick tussock of grass below would deaden the sound of its fall. Surely the guards patrolling the parapet above would be intent on the riders and would not hear it scraping from its seat. Her feet braced against the floor, she strained and pushed with shoulder and hand. It gave an inch, two. She stopped, gasping for air, then set to once more.

The stone teetered and rolled out so abruptly Amicia, unable to stop herself, lunged after it. She heard a man's pained grunt and the muffled thud of the stone as she slapped a hand against the rough side. Dangling half in and half out, she gaped down at Odo's upraised face.

Odo! Here? What could this mean? Where was Tristan?

"My lady?" he whispered, as if doubting the sight of his eyes as she did hers.

"What do you here?" she squeaked in witless confusion.

"I might ask the same of you, my lady," he hissed in a tone of accusation. "Hie yourself back through that window. I will come to you."

He waited no moment to see that she complied, but padded quietly along the wall. Amicia watched until he rounded the curve and vanished from sight, then slipped to the floor in a boneless heap. Odo was here! And Tristan?

A surge of energy propelled her to her feet. He was hard by and safe. Even she, knowing as little of war and its ways as she did, knew that this keep and its handful of men-at-arms would hold out against no man determined to take it. She rushed to the door and pressed her ear to it, but heard nothing.

Time stretched as malleable as well-kneaded bread dough. She paced and fretted and paced more, until the door creaked and began to slide open. Odo slipped through.

"The postern gate is never guarded," he said by way of explanation. "The castellan here was ever a poor one, but so loyal to your father he would not send him forth."

"Tristan," Amicia breathed. "I fear treachery—"

"Fear not. The craven cowards who guard this place are diving into their rat holes. I misdoubt one will be left to say nay to Lord Tristan's demand for entry."

"Odo, how did he know to come here?"

"The lord did not trust Sir Aimery." Odo spat, as if the name fouled his tongue. "He ordered two huntsmen to follow the messenger. They left a trail for us to follow, and early in the day we took the two messengers sent out from here. Lord Tristan is a wily one, my lady. He sent his own man to your father with the letter from Sir Aimery. While we are faring away from this place, he will be coming to it."

"Thank God!" Fearful her trembling legs would not support her, Amicia sank to the stool. "Tristan, Odo? How is he?"

"He keeps his own counsel, my lady, but there is a rage in him that makes all walk softly. Do naught to cross him, whatever he says," he warned, and turned to the door. "I must see that the drawbridge is lowered. These all know me as your father's man. They will not dare to say me nay."

He was gone, and Amicia was left with a chill settling around her heart. Rage? Did Tristan blame her for the choice he was forced to make? Had that choice slain the love he felt for her?

Had Tristan dared allow any emotion to pierce his iron guard, he would have felt relief when he entered the eerie silence of the ward and found that Aimery had escaped through an underground passage with the castellan of Byly. He was not sure he would not have slain his brother on sight, and so would have added the sin of Cain to further blacken his name.

In the days since reading Aimery's letter, he had learned how fine the line was between man and beast. In the empty wasteland of the nights, when he was alone with none to gauge his mood, he had crossed that line and discovered a dark side of himself. Sweat pearling on his brow and dripping down his sides, he had howled his festering hate in a mindless rage. He had cursed his mother and Aimery for their treachery. He had contrived punishments of such cruelty they made him shudder with disgust when morning came and sanity returned. He feared that dark side as he feared nothing else, for it, once released, threatened to consume him with its unquenchable fire for vengeance.

Was this what his mother and brother felt? Were they what he would become did he lose the battle he waged against himself? Was he his mother's son more than his father's?

Nay, he was not! He would not allow himself to be! Yet the struggle was so bitter, even he did not know whether the dark side would triumph in the end.

A flaming torch in his hand, Tristan paused at the foot of the stone stairs leading to Amicia's chamber. She was alive and well and waiting. For a moment his heart escaped the iron rule of his mind to float in his chest as light as thistledown. It was a fleeting escape. One that lowered his brows over his eyes and clenched his hand around the hilt of his sword.

If only he knew why he had chosen her life, mayhap he could accept it. If only he knew he had done it for honor's sake, then he would not feel he had betrayed his father, himself, and all he believed a man must be.

He knew but one thing. If Amicia had been slain because of him, he would have become that untameable merciless beast. He would have forgotten the sanctity of his father's memory, and that other letter secreted somewhere by his mother. The bludgeon she used upon him to make her home at Eden Castle when first he became its new lord. He would have forgotten Megotta, her future and her well-faring. He would have forgotten all but the beast's rage and the man's grief.

A grief he knew now full measure and more, not for Amicia waiting above, but for himself, for the man he thought he was. The man who would not have hesitated to choose honor's way. The man who took pride in the decision his father made long ago. The man who believed there was honor and dishonor, and naught between the two. Now, that man of surety was gone forever, leaving in his place a new man whose full dimensions for good or evil Tristan did not know.

All because of his mother and his brother! Sweat pearled on his brow. One drop, another, and another, until it rolled in rivulets down his temple. Rage grew within him, clawing for release. He fought it, struggling for the man he had been.

Above, Amicia listened to the footsteps slowly approaching her door. Not the leaping, light steps of a man eagerly joining a loved one he thought lost, but heavy deliberate steps, sounding full of ominous resolve. She stood, her body quaking with tension.

The door swung open, grating across the floor. The glow of a torch spilled into the chamber. Her gaze climbed the unrelieved black of Tristan's surcoat to the scarlet tunic tied at the base of his corded throat, and up to the lips that looked as though they had never smiled and the brow that looked as though it had never known peace. His every feature seemed molded of unrelenting iron, but it was his eyes that sucked the strength from her thews and leached the last hope from her heart. His eyes, lighted by an inner fire that consumed all of the man she knew. Naught was left but a cold and deadly rage.

Fearing her legs would fold beneath her, Amicia locked her knees and swayed like a slender beech in the wind. "My lord," she said, breathing uncertainly into the tomblike still of the chamber.

"My lady," he said in a voice as flat and unleavened as a wafer served at mass.

Tristan knew it was a poor greeting, that hers had been more question than aught else. He knew he should allay the fear that trembled in her voice, but he could not have said more on threat of death. Not with his heart writhing wildly in his chest and his throat wracked by painful spasms. Not with this stunning knowledge bursting in his mind, the knowledge that his choice and been no choice at all. He could never had chosen honor without Amicia existing to give that honor meaning.

His eyes roamed restlessly over her, seeking every change, every nuance of expression. She was as white as bleached linen and as scruffily dirty as a village lad. There was a smudge on her nose and another on her chin; above them, her eyes were round as the moon and dark as the night. Her hair, cascading down her back in an abundance of waves and curls, was powdered in gritty white. She had never been more comely, more desirable.

His inner rage, so painfully controlled, drained away bit by bit, leaving him achingly empty, as if that rage had been all that gave him substance. In that emptiness flickered the terror of a man wandering alone and lost.

A terror that shimmered unmistakably in the bright blue of his eyes. Amicia, seeing it, forgot her fear of his rage, her fear for herself. All was submerged beneath an overwhelming need to comfort him. Moving quickly and surely, she placed her torn and bloodied hand on his arm and raised her face to him.

"Tristan," she pleaded, "I beg of you. Share this pain with me."

Her voice played upon his ear like a harp, but it was the gentle touch of her hand that banished his terror. A sweetly haunting warmth welled within him, filling the emptiness. A warmth that laved his battered heart and purged him of old sorrow, old pain. There was room left for naught but the love he could no longer fight, no longer deny.

Once, before she came into his life, it had been filled by naught but duty and honor. He had thought it a rich life and full. Only now did he realize how barren it had been. Only now, with Amicia gazing up at him, her eyes dark with tender concern, did he glimpse the promise of untasted, untold riches ahead. Riches he had so nearly lost, as he had so nearly lost her.

Could he find words to tell her of the love he had found dwelling unknown in his heart? A love she had planted like the most tender husbandman, nurturing it with her gentleness, her love, her loyalty. Nay, he was no minstrel, silky tongued and smooth.

He hurled the torch into the cold ashes of the hearth and pulled her into his arms, crushing her against his heaving chest. "Amicia."

Her name came as reverently as a prayer, singing through her like the *tempus perfectum* of a pastorale. The power of his arms sheltered her from all that was ugly and evil. The strength of his need met and matched hers. Her arms slipped around him and her body trembled against his, as his did against hers. A trembling that had naught to do with weakness or fear, but much to do with love's eager fervor.

Tristan adored the downy warmth of her temple with his lips. Breathing deeply in a quest for her scent, her soul, he touched her cheek to cheek. "I love you, sweet witch," he murmured. "I know not how it happened or when. I only know I cannot bear to think of a life without you."

His full and final yielding, it was what Amicia wanted to hear, needed to hear, in order to believe it true. Her head tilted back, her hands inching up to slide around his nape. Her gaze sought his, snaring it in the tenderest of bonds. "Nor I without you, my dearest lord," she whispered. "Oh, Tristan. I love you so much. I have loved you for so long."

Tears welled in her eyes and plunged down her cheeks. Fat shimmering droplets that seemed to be wrenched like drops of blood from Tristan's own heart. "Do not weep," he rasped. "I beg of you, do not weep."

"May I not weep for joy, my lord?" she sighed, and pressed her nose to his chest. "I am sorry for the . . . the pain I have caused you," she babbled and sobbed. "I am sorry I wore my hair up to . . . to spite you. I do swear I will be a good and dutiful wife. I—I won't—"

"Shh," Tristan murmured, his lips threatening a smile. "You are perfect as you are. I would change naught should I be given the choice."

Her face tilted up, her lashes wet clumps framing her glistening eyes. "But I am not perfect, my lord. I am stubborn and willful and spiteful, though you did not notice—"

"I noticed."

"You said naught, though I put it up each day and wore the darkest of my wimples."

"I dared not then, but . . ." The threatening smile spread across his mouth. "Should you disobey me again, I will lesson you in the proper respect for your lord's wishes. I will take you to my bed and keep you there until you repent your spiteful ways."

"I am stubborn, my lord," she vowed, her dancing eyes reflecting the love ashine in his. "Very stubborn."

"So I hope, my lady," he breathed.

Her smiling mouth lured Tristan to sip the taste of her. A sip which led to a deeper draft that yet left him wanting more. He feared his thirst would never be quenched and put it to the question. Nay, never would he tire of this sweetness.

His questing tongue touched a roughness on her lip and tasted the salt tang of blood. He raised his head, frowning, as he tilted her face to the weak light sputtering from the torch. A light that revealed the bruises on her jaw and neck, a chilling reminder of why they were there. His head pounded with the insistent rhythm of rising wrath.

"He hurt you," he growled.

Amicia, unwilling to allow any intrusion on her joyful mood, raised her hands to cover his. "It is naught, my lord," she soothed. "It will mend."

"Why? Why did he do it?"

She stared up at him, surprised by the question. "Surely Aimery told you what happened—"

"God's Wounds!" He raised her hands, staring down at the broken and bloodied nails, then flipped them palms up and flinched at the sight of the blisters and oozing scrapes. "What happened to your hands? What have you—"

"My lord, Aimery must have told you—"

"He told me naught. He fled this place like a base-born coward before I entered the gate."

"Fled?" Amicia's breath dwindled to a trickle of air squeezing through the painful constriction of her throat. "Tristan! He is away to Carrickmuir! Megotta is in danger!"

"Megotta?" he asked. "My mother has what she wants from me. Megotta is of no further use to her, and so is safe."

"Nay, my lord! Nay, she is not! Aimery came to me with your letter and I . . . I threw it in yonder fire! I burned it!"

Tristan stared down at her. Fear darkened her gaze and pain quivered across her mouth, but resolve molded the delicate line of her jaw. Burned it. The senseless, pointless words echoed and re-echoed. Burned it. The letter, whose every word had caused him agony such as he had never experienced. Burned it.

"Why?" he asked softly, unable to believe it was done. "It was the only way I could save you. The only way I could protect Megotta."

"Tristan! Does it matter why I did it?" Amicia cried. "Megotta is in danger!"

"As you were!" His numb surprise rapidly eroded beneath the sandy grit of fear for her, the harsh rasp of his own anger. His hands clenched around her arms and pulled her close, and he bent his head and scowled down at her. "You could have been killed! He could have slain you in this chamber, and none hard by to give you aid. Why? Why did you do it?"

Her hands touched his cheeks, cradling them in tenderness. "Must you ask me why, my own dear lord? You, who were willing to sacrifice all you believe in for me," she whispered, her eyes searching his. "I could not let you do it. It would have tainted our love. You would have grown to hate yourself and me, and I would not allow that to happen. I could not allow you to be made less in your own eyes."

Tristan stared down at her earnest face with the same look of awe and wonder he might have turned up to a heavenly angel perched on the turret of Castle Eden. He saw in her a strength, a courage, and a loyalty that surprised him. Never had he seen such in a woman. Never had he believed such was possible for a woman. Always he had thought them weak creatures, incapable of the finer, deeper emotions that a man gave to a man.

Yet, here she stood, telling him she had risked her own life for him. He remembered telling her once that he would find it all the sweeter when she yielded her all to him. But never had he dreamed what that all would be. A love that enriched him; a loyalty that shamed him.

Bereft of words to express the love that sent his heart soaring free, Tristan dropped his mouth to hers and sealed the vow he had taken months before. The vow to take Amicia of Bellay to wife, to honor her as she deserved.

His lips trailed from hers, caressing the bruise on her jaw, sliding down to cherish the vulnerable column of her throat. His fingers took the place of his mouth, the tips wafting across the livid marks of Aimery's angry hands.

"I do not deserve such love and and loyalty, Amicia," he whispered.

"You deserve it all and more, my lord."

"I would that I could stay with you and take you as wife once more, but I must be away to Carrickmuir to wrest Megotta from them. I will give order that you be taken to Kenilworth and placed in Earl Simon's keeping—"

"Nay, my lord! I will not go so far away. Let me return to Castle Eden—"

"Nay! Should I fail . . ." He raked his hand through his hair, frowning a curious mixture of love and frustration. "Amicia, I have no time for this—"

"Then I will go to Holmby Priory and await you there."

"And when I come, my lady"—he bent a baleful eye upon her—"we will discuss who will rule in Castle Eden."

Her gaze dropped and her chin dipped submissively. "There is no question of that, my lord. You will rule as ever."

"Will I?" he asked softly. "I wonder."

# Chapter 23

The unmistakable scent of cowslips filtered into Tristan's mind. *The meadow is aquiver with cowslips and the wood bright with gorse and the robins are anesting,* he heard Amicia say as if she stood beside him and whispered in his ear, tempting him as she had that day in the willow brake. Every breath he drew sucked in the perfumes of youthful spring, the signs of life all around him. He knew a moment of intense yearning for that promise of life, for he feared death awaited him beyond the curtain wall of Carrickmuir.

The crescent moon, peeking through a bank of silver-edged clouds, lent an unearthly glow to the wall planted in a rubbled-stone scarp on the crest of the near hill. Staring out from the dusky shadow of a sheltering oak, Tristan studied it and brooded about the changes in himself. Once he courted death as a lover who would release him from the pain of life. Now he saw it as a bitter foe who would take him from Amicia, from her promise of pleasure and peace and love.

It would not be easy to bring Megotta out under the best of circumstances, but with his mother waiting for him it would be impossible. Yet he had to try; and if he died, it would be best for all. All but him. Megotta's secret would be kept; Amicia would be safe in the Earl's keeping.

"You cannot enter that viper's nest alone, my lord!" Rolf protested.

"I must bring Megotta away by stealth," Tristan said, his mouth drawn into a line as grim as his resolve. "Better one man than two for that."

"If you had called out your vassals, we could have taken Carrickmuir down stone by stone and had them all out."

"And Megotta killed for it?" Tristan questioned. "Nay, she must be got away safely at any cost, but later . . . later, Rolf, if I live, I will have my hour of reckoning."

Tristan hefted a coil of rope, slipped his arm through the center opening, and settled it on his shoulder. Bracing the grapnel against his side, he slanted a narrow look at his master-at-arms. "If I do not return by the nooning when the sun is high, you are to ride as fast as you may to Holmby Priory and guide my lady to Kenilworth. Give her my order that she is to tell Earl Simon all she knows and to leave punishment of these to him. Tell her, also, that I . . ." The firm sure tone of his voice faltered and his gaze slid away.

Tell Amicia what? That she had taught him more of life and love and loyalty than he had ever known. That she, a mere woman, had taught him the meaning of honor and how to be as true to himself and those he loved as she was.

"Tell her that . . . I love her."

"L-love her, my lord?" Rolf faltered.

"Ay." Tristan canted an ill-favored look at his man. "Is it so surprising?"

"Nay, my lord," Rolf hastened to say. Presuming on his long service with Tristan, he grinned broadly. "I have only been wondering when you were going to see it yourself. She is worthy of you as no lady I have met ere now has been. Did you know she dug the stones from her window to escape and give you warning? Odo said she near killed him when she pushed the stone out."

Her hands. Her fragile hands all bloodied and torn, just to give him warning. Was he worthy of her? What had he done to earn such love and loyalty? Would he have the chance to take pleasure in it his life long? If only there had been time to say more to her, to tell her of the fleeting joy she had given him. But there had not been.

Megotta was within, and only he could bring her out.

Tristan shrugged off his regrets, and began to move away. "Await me here, Rolf."

"My lord, surely you cannot expect me to leave you here!"

"If I do not return, I will be dead and will have no need of you. I put my lady in your keeping. Do for her what you would for me. Honor her, for she above all women has earned it."

He strode out into the moon-silvered night, his feet sinking deep into rotting leaf-mold. The odor of the fecund earth rose on vaporous curls of ground-hugging mist. Moving cautiously, a stalking hunter, he slipped from the deep shadow of an oak to a blackthorn hedge in fragrant blossom. He trampled nodding beds of bluebells and primroses swaying on slender stems, then knelt behind a crumbling cairn to survey the terrain ahead.

Fog, up from the boggy bank of the River Clee, crawled along the shallow vale at the foot of the hill. The ghostly curtain of white slowly climbed the steep rise to the curtain wall. A rise covered with tall grasses and spreading whortleberries. Perfect concealment for a man bent on mischief—and a poor testimony for the castellan who should have kept the rise so clean not a hare could move across it unseen.

His stern gaze returned to the crenellated curtain wall polished by moonlight. Unbroken by towers, apparently unmanned, it spanned the crest of the hill with the keep rising from the ward beyond like a thick black fist threatening the dark sapphire sky. He moved slowly, dodging from shelter to shelter, into the shallow dip at the foot, up the steep slope. His eyes watched the battlement and saw no guard upon it.

Crouched low, he ran the last few steps with the rubbled stone scarp crunching beneath his feet. At the foot of the curtain wall, he paused and heard footsteps on the parapet overhead. He flung himself against the wall, his shoulders melting against the stone.

"Why do you stand like a moonling watching the south?"

Lady Sybilla's voice traveled clearly, reaching Tristan with its slow drawl of disapproval. He hung there, splayed against the wall with his heart hammering and hate rising like an odor in his nostrils. Ay, when Megotta and Amicia were safe, he would return for his day of reckoning. The reckoning he had dwelt upon during these days of hard riding, of sleepless hours snatched to rest the horses, of parched oats chewed to save every precious moment. The reckoning that would give his mother a reason to rue the day he was born.

"Do you remember how Ruella stood in this very spot." Aimery's forlorn murmur traveled down the curtain wall. "Watching, always watching the south, in hopes Tristan would come."

Below, Tristan jerked taut, his eyes arching up, but seeing naught but the solidity of stone and mortar and, above, the sickle moon slipping behind a cloud. Ruella? When had she come to Carrickmuir, and why? His teeth clenched tight. A cuckolded fool's question that was! To be with her lover, his brother, away from the censure of his folk.

"You are a fool, Aimery! She is dead and gone. You have worries enough without mourning her. Better you should fear what Tristan will do to you when he comes, as he surely will."

"I loved her," Aimery moaned. "I do swear I loved her. Why? Why did she fight me? Why did she make me beat her, when all I wished to do was love her."

Despite the cool embrace of the night, sweat broke across Tristan's brow. Beat her? Why need he beat her, if . . .

"You should think of what Tristan will do, should he ever learn you raped her."

Raped! God! His mother's voice faded while Tristan's blind stare held a vision of Ruella's face. Freckles sprinkling her small nose as they sprinkled Megotta's. Ebony hair, so black it held the blue sheen of a raven's wing. Gentle and comely and eager to please. So very eager to please. So hurt when she could not. How could he have believed she would be unfaithful? Yet believe it, he had. So strongly that he left her to die alone, suffering in body and spirit.

Bile surged into the back of his throat and he swallowed. Swallowed his rage and disgust and guilt, but he could not rid himself of the wrenching vision of Ruella cowering before Aimery's blows. She had not deserved the pain she suffered, neither Aimery's beating, nor his own studied indifference. An indifference he used to protect her from his mother, though that was no comfort now.

The rage billowed up. The mindless, merciless beast's rage he thought he had quelled. His chest heaved as if he had run a long distance. His fingers curled into claws, so strong was his wish to feel Aimery's neck in their grip.

"You will forget her soon enough, now that Bellay has promised you will wed Amicia when Tristan is dead."

Her low cynical laugh raised the hair on the back of Tristan's neck.

"Think on it, Aimery. When you are wed to her and her father is dead as he will be—we will see to that!—you will be the Lord of Eden *and* Bellay. We will rule lands and hold knights' fees that will give even Simon of Leicester pause should he wish to do us harm. And you, my dearest son, will hold a place high in the King's council."

Her deep voice was soft, cajoling, almost flirtatious. It was a mood Tristan had often seen her use upon Aimery. One that his brother was powerless to resist. Always he melted like butter and followed her will in the least matter. Never did he think—think as he should have now, that Simon of Leicester could bring the might of the kingdom swarming about their heads or that the King looked to the greatest men of the land for council. Nay, he thought only, if he thought at all, of the love he wished to be his.

"Am I your dearest son?" Aimery asked in a lilting child's plea for approval.

Tristan's rage seeped away, pity taking its place. Was Aimery's hunger for her love so great she could use it to drive him to any end? He was not evil, only weak. Tristan clenched his hand into a fist. His scorn, his anger blundered astray. She, their mother—though she had never been a mother to either of them—should be heir to his vengeance.

"Certain it is that you are," she cooed like a wooing maid. "Soon, soon, you will be the Lord of Eden and Bellay, and I will see you dressed in finery fit for a king. I will sit at your right hand and together we—"

"Nay, it cannot be. What of Megotta? Earl Simon thinks her Tristan's daughter. He will take her as ward and hold Eden—"

"Ay"—her voice dropped so low Tristan strained to hear—"there is Megotta."

Each measured, thoughtful word slammed into Tristan's belly like a fist. Megotta stood between his mother and what she wanted. Only he stood between Megotta and his mother. Should all go awry and he die, he dared not hope that Aimery might, this once, withstand his mother's will.

Tristan rested his head against the stone. The fog, rolling up from his feet in a smothering blanket of white, cooled his flushed face. He knew what he must do, but it sickened him to the depths of his soul. He wished his rage had not fled and his decision had not been made in the cold light of reason. Whatever his mother was, she was also the woman who had given him life. Whatever Aimery had become, he was also the brother he had loved and protected as a child. It would have been easier to strike in the heat of anger, than to later live with the knowledge that it had been done in cold deliberation. Yet as long as they lived Megotta's life was threatened, and she, above all, was guiltless and innocent.

Drawn by a vision of Megotta sitting on his lap with her small finger tugging down her lower lip to reveal the space where a tooth had been, Tristan crept along the wall. Testing each step before it was taken, he reached the corner and eased around it. He paused to listen for a man-at-arms above, but heard naught.

The fog grew thicker by the moment, surging higher and higher up the stone wall until it swallowed the battlement overhead. Tristan counted his steps, estimating the center where he would be less likely to stumble onto a man-at-arms.

He stepped out with the coil of rope looped over one hand and the grapnel in the other. Wrapped in strips of linen and bound with leather to deaden the sound, the four claws whirled around and around the lengthening end of the rope, flew upward, and vanished in the thick cloud of white. He heard a muffled thump, tugged, and felt it hold fast. Waiting a moment, he listened for a warning cry, the clatter of arms, the slap of feet on the parapet, but heard only the forlorn trill of a bird heralding morning's approach.

Naught was left to do but test his weight on the rope and scale the wall. Mist beading on his lashes, he stared up into the obscuring curtain of white with a deep foreboding. He should have seen men-at-arms patrolling. He should have heard them coughing and shifting restlessly as men bored by a long watch will do. That he had neither seen them nor heard them, could mean only one thing. They waited in silence—for him.

He had but one hope, that the fog would conceal him.

Catching the rope, he pulled himself up. Up and up to the battlement, and he slid into the gap sheltered by the square teeth rising on either side. He reached out, gripping the inside and pulling himself through—and felt the pressure of a blade pushing the linked mail of his hood into the vulnerable flesh between his jaw and neck.

Thrills of alarm racing across his scalp and down the deep runnel of his spine, Tristan heard, "A good greeting to you, my lord. Lady Sybilla awaits your pleasure. If you will but step out—Carefully, my lord! Carefully!"

The thrills of alarm resolving themselves into coursing waves of goosebumps, Tristan eased onto the parapet and allowed himself to be prodded along by the man-at-arms. He would offer no resistance, not while there was the slightest hope, and if he knew his mother, there would be. She would not resist her chance at a last triumphant moment of tormenting him, and that might be his salvation.

A breath of a breeze swirled through the fog, revealing the row of men-at-arms scampering up from crouches along the parapet. A torch was lighted, another and another, until the night was bright with them. Both led and followed by men shabbily garbed, thin shanked, and muttering, Tristan rounded the corner and approached his mother and Aimery. The breeze strengthened, shredding the fog into transparent ribbons that swirled eerily about them.

Lady Sybilla, her mantle thrown back over her shoulders and her plum-colored wimple faultlessly folded about her face, smiled at his approach. "So you have come," she murmured, her fine brows arching in satisfaction.

"As you knew I would," Tristan replied, his gaze wandering to his brother.

Dusty and mud-splattered, as though he had not taken time to bathe or change since riding into the keep only hours ahead of his pursuers, Aimery leaned against the battlement, stubbornly studying his feet. He looked haggard and worn, his skin sagging at the jaws and a nervous twitch squinting his eye.

"Aimery," Tristan said softly. Neither greeting nor question, he simply sought to see if his brother had courage enough to meet his eyes. He did not. Aimery was only brave with helpless women and children. The thought set a spark to Tristan's dampened anger.

"St. George, come to slay the dragon!" Lady Sybilla scoffed. "Is your sword sharp, Tristan of Eden?"

His eyes narrowed, swiveling upon his mother. What game did she play now? Would she have him fight in melee against her men-at-arms? Or did she have a champion chosen to best him?

"Sharp enough!" he answered.

Her fingers snapped. The men-at-arms jerked to vigilant attention. "Move back and make room. Torch carriers to the front. We will have here a duel"—she paused, her eyes sliding toward Aimery and a sly smile pinching her mouth—"brother against brother."

Aimery sprang from his slouch against the wall, his eyes wide with shock and disbelief. "He . . . he will kill me! You know what I have done! He will kill me for it!"

Tristan, listening to the light voice climb on keening notes of fear, closed his eyes and swallowed bitter gall. He had been long in seeing the end his mother desired, but now he saw it only too clearly.

"And if he kills you," she said, her voice as hard as the stone wall at Aimery's back, "I will know that you do not deserve all I have planned for you. Think on it, Aimery." Her voice softened to the wheedling tone of a flirtatious maid. "Lord of Eden and Bellay. Amicia as your wife, and I, your mother, there at your side. Ay, wherever you go, whatever you do, I will be there to gaze upon you with a mother's pride, a mother's love. My son. My only son. The one upon whom I will spend all of my love."

While she spoke, Tristan listened and despaired. He had climbed the wall with cold calculation, planning to kill them both and end the threat to Megotta's life. Yet now he knew he could not do it. He could not kill the pitiful thing Aimery had become. He could not kill his mother, for she was bereft of all reason—a madwoman who should be locked in a tower where her ravings could hurt none. He should have done it, could have done it, long ago, when first he became Lord of Eden. But then he had not known what lengths her madness would drive her to. He could not now make Aimery's head forfeit for his own mistake.

Tristan strained against the hands holding him straightly. "Nay, Aimery! You will never have her love, for there is none in her to give! You must see what she wants! To have us both dead! Look at her, Aimery! Look at her eyes! She will eat you alive if you let her!"

"Draw your sword, my dearest son," Lady Sybilla urged. "Draw your sword and show me who is the better man."

Aimery, his thick body swaying in the grip of terror, swung his head from Tristan to his mother like a dog-baited bear. His face contorted with the conflict raging inside him, he settled an unsteady hand on the hilt of his sword.

"Nay, Aimery!" Tristan shouted. "Do not give her this satisfaction! Look at her, Aimery! Look at her! She slavers like a wolf at the kill!"

"Show me, Aimery! Prove yourself the better man!"

Aimery's lower lip jutted in a familiar stubborn and implacable pose, and Tristan's heart sank. He watched his brother straighten, his thick shoulders squaring, even as his eyes clung to his mother, pleading, yearning, frightened.

"Draw . . ." The word whistled high and shrill, and Aimery swallowed and frowned. "Draw your sword, Tristan!"

The hard hands holding him fell away, but he made no move to touch his sword. "Nay, Aimery! I will not fight you! Can you slaughter me where I stand?"

"Ay, brother! Always, always, you have stood between me and what I wanted!"

Aimery's sword hissed from its sheath. He lunged forward, the well-honed blade whirring in a sideways slash. Tristan leaped backward, but was brought up short by the pressing wall of men-at-arms. The glittering point grated across his hauberk, scoring his chest beneath, and shifted away, moving slowly by the men at his back.

"Aimery, think! Think what she will want when she has me dead! Where will her hate turn then?"

"Kill him! Kill him!"

His mother's scream seemed to add strength to the thrust of Aimery's sword. A thrust that slashed Tristan's upper arm and pinned his hauberk against the stone wall. For a moment his eyes met Aimery's, and he caught a heartening glimpse of his loved and loving brother of old. A faint flicker of astonishment deep in the spice-brown eyes, as if Aimery asked himself what he was doing and why.

Tristan wrenched free and dodged to the side. The sword whipped through the air, its blade set ablaze by the torchlight. He dove away, rolling and springing to his feet. "Aimery, remember when we were boys together." He played desperately on that moment of weakness. "Remember when I taught you to use your first wooden sword. Remember—"

"Nay! I will not!" Aimery lumbered toward him, his face tracked with tears. "You loved me well then! You hate me now!"

"Kill him! *Kill him!*"

"Nay!" Tristan shouted down his mother's shriek. "I did when first I learned what you had done, but I do not any longer. You are . . ."

Aimery slashed wildly. Tristan teetered on the edge of the parapet. The sharp point scored his cheek, leaving it stinging and bloody. While Aimery clumsily followed through on his swing, stumbling like a sotted knight, Tristan lunged across the parapet to put the wall at his back.

"Aimery, hear me! Hear what I say!" he shouted over the muttering of the men-at-arms, the sobbing of Aimery's breath, his mother's low litany of "Kill him! Kill him!"

"Nay," Aimery bellowed, and came at him once more. A sharp thrust. Tristan rolled away, while the blade scraped against the stone. A slash, and he danced to the side.

"You are brother to me, Aimery," he said, desperately seeking some sign that he was heard. "I will help you. Naught will I do of ill unto you, for the love we have shared our life long. Remember that, Aimery. Remember . . ."

"I cannot!" Aimery cried. "I cannot! You must see! You must see what I am! You must see what she has made me! Even I can . . ."

He brought the sword up and over, putting all of his strength into it. It came whistling down at Tristan's shoulder. He spun away. The point struck the parapet and a chip of wood flew toward the gaping circle of men-at-arms. Tristan fell against the stone wall, panting, wondering how much longer he could avoid the death that would surely be his.

"Kill him! Kill him now!" Lady Sybilla trod on Aimery's heels and flicked an angry hand across his back. "Do it now!"

"Can you, Aimery?" Tristan asked as he watched the tears flood his brother's cheeks and saw his chest swell on a deep indrawn sob. "Can you kill me, who has loved you, who has protected you and taught you? Can you kill me for her, who has never loved any?"

The point of the sword wavered and sank, carrying with it the last of Aimery's strength. "Nay," he sobbed. "I cannot! I cannot do it!"

"You are a weakling, Aimery!" came his mother's venomous voice. "That is why I despised you from your birth. Even in the cradle you whined and cowered. Do you really think I could love you? What a fool you are! Almost as great a fool as your father. He would not take that he so dearly wanted for his honor's sake, yet he ever mourned her till his death. He was a fool not to reach out and take, no matter the cost."

Aimery drew his sleeve across his nose and blinked the tears from his eyes. "Have you told me naught but lies?" He quavered, as if he could not believe the proof of his ears. "The plans we made, were those false? As false as your heart?"

"What do you think?" She stood tall, the first light of

morning reaching over the hills to flush her face in dawn's rosy glow. A glow of freshness and innocence that did not soften the sinister sneer curling her lip. "Do you think I wanted to spend the rest of my life with you? *You?*" she jeered.

Aimery shuddered, his sword falling from his hand and thunking against the timbered parapet. "You would have had me killed, as you have tried to have Tristan killed," he said, his voice softly wondering. His eyes, blind with pain, turned to Tristan. "You told me and I would not listen. You said there is no love in her to give. Amicia told me, too. She said I should fear where my mother's hate would turn, just as you did now. Have I been the only one who could not see what she wanted? Have I . . ." He fell silent, his eyes widening with sick comprehension. "Tristan, what have I become?"

"Aimery—" he began, but could not continue. His throat was locked in a vise of pain. Nor could he look at the anguish twisting his brother's face any longer. He could not watch Aimery's shattered hopes destroying him inch by inch.

His gaze shifted to the circle of men-at-arms. A circle growing larger and larger as they slunk back, their faces twisted with the knowledge of the evil they witnessed. Mayhap, he hoped, they would give him aid in getting Megotta away, whatever happened here.

So thinking, Tristan heard Aimery ask their mother, "What were you planning to do with Megotta when we were dead?"

The question, soft, strangely neutral, sent Tristan's gaze spinning to his mother to see what her answer would be.

She stared at Aimery, supreme confidence molding her face. "Does it matter?"

"Nay, my lady." His whisper was a sunken sound of defeat, but the eyes that touched Tristan and lingered on his face were no longer the eyes of a faltering child wandering alone and lost in a wilderness of despair. Instead, they were filled with love and resolve. A resolve that shared odd quarters with his subdued expression. "I cannot make amends for the evil I have done you and . . . others, but mayhap I can do one thing. Our mother"— the term dripped with bitterness—"has sent word to Eustace of Bellay that our father's letter resides with the Prioress of Holmby. He has been ordered to send it to Earl Simon."

Prioress of Holmby! Tristan blanched. Amicia was there and her father on the way!

"Little good it will do him to know it!" Lady Sybilla mocked. "I will have you both now! Guar—"

Aimery's drooping body uncoiled. His arm snaked out, looping around his mother and yanking her close to his side. She screamed, a sound drenched in outrage. One thundering step and he leaped into a square gap in the battlement. The men-at-arms raised a shout. Lady Sybilla's scream now came fraught with fear. Tristan froze, his eyes locking with Aimery's for one fateful second. In those eyes shone the unscarred love of brother for brother: the unquestioning love of youth and, too late, the enlightened love of manhood.

"There is no other way," Aimery whispered, and plunged over the side, taking his mother with him.

"Nay! Nay!" Tristan shouted, lunging for the gap and reaching out, though he knew it was too late. Lady Sybilla's terrified scream—so quickly choked off by a thud—rang in his ears as he stared down at the broken bodies sprawled across the rocky scarp.

Aimery and his mother, her arms holding him in death as she never had in life.

# Chapter 24

Silence lay heavy in the cloister where Amicia of Bellay sat on the stone bench beneath the apple tree. Its gnarly limbs twisting overhead were bedecked by a cloud of blush-tinted blossoms that sweetly scented the night air. From the door of the church there came the silvery notes of the nuns' voices rising in the Evensong. Silvery notes in perfect harmony, save for the vigorous monotone of plump Sister Edwenna.

A wistful smile wended its way across Amicia's mouth. Naught had changed. Sister Edwenna was as harried and harassed as ever, and Sister Catherine, as stern. The clump of butter-yellow celandine bloomed against the wall as it had every spring she could remember. The silence was the same, broken only by the soft scuffing of leather shoes or the hushed murmur of reverent voices. Ay, naught had changed. One day was as the next from month to month and year to year.

Only she was different. The hushed silence, once welcomed, was now an intrusive presence. She longed instead for the grunting of swine and the yelping of hounds, the chatter of women drawing water from the well, the pounding of the carter's hammer and the whoosh of the smith's bellows. She longed for the raucous life astir in the ward of Castle Eden.

The serenity of the cloister was hers no longer, though she struggled to feel it as once she had. She had become too much a part of the secular world to find peace in quiet contemplation. Here, life was a stream flowing smooth and untested. Out there—Amicia's gaze lifted to the knifelike cleft glowing blue against the black shadows of the mountains—the stream of life crashed against rocks, fought across shoals, and flung headlong down steep falls. Out there, pain was leavened by a joy that was the sweeter for it.

A joy she had known so briefly it seemed more dream than reality. Had Tristan really said the words she had longed to hear? *I love you, sweet witch. I know not how it happened or when. I only know I cannot bear to think of a life without you.* Ay, he had said them, huskily soft and wondering, as she heard them now.

He loved her. Bellay's daughter, his wife, she had found a place in his heart as he had made a place in hers. Had it come too late? Would they never know more than that fleeting moment when their hearts touched in life's most hallowed communion?

"Tristan, Tristan." Her plaintive mourning sigh whispered like the blossoms shivering in the breeze overhead. "God guard and guide you, my own dear lord."

What was happening? she wondered, struggling to breathe against the pain binding her chest. Nearly two weeks it had been since he had torn himself from her arms and set out after Megotta. By now, he would have won her out of Carrickmuir . . . or his mother and Aimery would have . . .

Nay, she would not believe that! If anything had happened to him, she would know it! She must believe that Megotta was safe and that Tristan was now riding over hill and dale, coming for her. She must believe that he would take her to Castle Eden and that her span of life would be spent there in his loving embrace. She must believe it!

Chafed by fear as she was, Amicia could sit no longer. She climbed to her feet and made her way to the prioress's hall. It was better to keep her hands busy and her mind occupied, else the visions of Tristan tortured and tormented by Lady Sybilla would drive her mad. Yet, in the solar above was a sight to sadden her immeasurably. Mother Margaret wasted and wan upon her pallet, clinging to the last thread of life in the hope that she might just once look upon the son her beloved Robert had sired.

The chamber was fully lit by the candles flickering atop tall iron holders and set in dishes all about. A waste, Sister Catherine would have claimed it, had they not been for Mother Margaret's comfort. She craved the light, both day and night, and none would say her nay in this, her last wish. Amicia moved quietly to the novice, whose nodding sleep threatened to send her tumbling from her stool.

"Wake, Sister. Go and take your ease. I will sit with her through the night."

The novice blinked owlishly and settled a shamed gaze on Amicia's face. "Forgive me, my lady. I should have—"

"Naught is there to forgive. You are weary. Go and take your ease in comfort."

"God be with you, my lady."

Her head bent, her lips moving in prayer, and her hands clasped at her waist, the novice left with the unhurried steps of all in the order, and Amicia's gaze followed her. She remembered the time, just months past, when she had so ardently desired to become one with these who moved in the serene knowledge of God's grace.

"Do you regret the path your life has taken, my child?" Mother Margaret's voice rustled like dead leaves.

Amicia moved to her, dropping to her knees beside the pallet. Her sorrowing gaze lingered on the face, once ethereally unlined, now shrunk upon the framework of the skull and striated by pain and suffering. "You should be resting, Mother," she chided gently.

"I will sleep through eternity, child. Do not grudge me the hours left," she whispered, and stopped to breathe heavily, as if those few words had robbed her of strength. Her hand, a skeletal claw, struggled up from her side. "Do you regret not becoming one of us?"

Amicia took her hand, feeling it so frail and cold and dry between hers. "Nay, Mother. I regret it not, for I have found I am not suited for the cloister."

"Ay, you have tasted life and love," the prioress breathed softly, her fingers weakly pressing Amicia's hand. "Tell me again, child. Tell me of his son."

It was a request she had made often as the days crawled

by, and one that never failed to bring tears to Amicia's
eyes. "He is tall, Mother, and strong. When first I saw
him, I thought I beheld a giant of old."

"Ay, his father was so. His arm was thick and his grip
strong. I once saw him joust through the morn and fight in
the melee till eventide, then dance the night away. He
smiled often, my Robert did. Does his son?"

Nay, he did not, but she could not tell Mother Margaret
that. Not when she had so carefully spun a minstrel's tale
of love and joy about all in Eden Castle, especially the
new-wed pair. Not when she had explained her presence at
Holmby as the indulgence of a loving husband for the
whim of a beloved wife. Though she had prayed fitfully in
penance for her deceit, she could see it as no great sin.
And when the tale stained Mother Margaret's cheeks with
the pink of pleasure and brought a shine to her dull,
care-worn gaze, Amicia knew it was a positive good.

"He has a comely smile, Mother," she said softly.
Remembering the smile spreading across his mouth and
illuminating his eyes, she fell silent. *Should you disobey
me again, I will lesson you in the proper respect for your
lord's wishes. I will take you to my bed and keep you there
until you repent your spiteful ways,* she heard him saying
as clearly as if she stood in the gentle embrace of his arms
once again. Pray God, he would return and she would
know that happiness once more.

"Your memories of him are happy, child. I am glad
hearted," Mother Margaret murmured as if she, too, sought
refuge in memories and found happiness there.

"Rest, Mother—"

"Nay, I wish to know more of him. Do not beseech me,
child. Tell me of him."

Amicia's smile was bittersweet. "His eyes are the soft
blue of a midsummer sky and they grow bright with
laughter. His cheeks crease around his mouth and his curly
hair falls across his brow, a bright reddish-gold."

"He sounds a handsome man, child. Tell me again of
his people, and how they love him."

Amicia spoke softly, telling of Enid and thumbless Giles,
of small Guy of Lancasterdale and the sweet-scented squire,
Roger. Softer and softer she spoke, until she crooned the

words as a lullaby in hopes the prioress would sleep and rest.

"Tell me again of Robert, child," Mother Margaret whispered.

Amicia lifted the nun's skeletal hand to her lips and pressed a kiss to the cold fingers. "He loved you well, Mother, and never forgot you. Tristan told me that he spoke of you in the most loving of ways and dwelt long on your comeliness and gentleness. And when he lay dying, he called your name at the end."

The prioress's violet gaze, tormented by a sudden fear, turned to Amicia. "He did not suffer—"

"Nay, he did not suffer," she assured her.

"He did not regret—"

"Nay, Mother." Amicia lied once more. "He lived a long and happy life, siring three sons as strong as he was."

"I am glad. So very glad. I would not have him suffer as . . ." She sighed, a dolorous sound steeped in a lifetime's pain. "I would not have him suffer or regret what he did. He could do naught else. Being the man he was, he could do naught else."

Her lashes, wispy fans of white that had once been long and thick and dark, drifted down to her cheeks and she sighed softly. Amicia waited a moment, watching her sunken chest for the even rise and fall of sleep, then laid Mother Margaret's bony hand atop her waist and stroked it gently. When the thin fingers crept to the length of split cane, seeking that comfort even in slumber, Amicia climbed heavily to her feet and moved to the stool.

From the woven reed basket at her side, she lifted her stitching, a snowy white altar cloth encrusted with gold thread in an intricate design that demanded her full attention. An attention she could not give it. Three stitches, all to be undone, and she abandoned the attempt. The cloth lying forgotten in her lap, she breathed deep of the scent of apple blossoms wafting on the night air.

*Tristan, Tristan,* she called silently. *Return to me, my own dear lord. Return to me, and let me love you as I would. Let me banish your pain and sorrow. Let me give you my heart and soul, sons of my body to honor you and daughters to love you. Tristan, do not let me end my life as Mother Margaret does hers, mourning a lost love and a life spent in suffering and regret.*

Her gaze, heavy with tears, moved slowly about the chamber, ascetically barren of comfort, of hope, of the vital breath of life. Such would be her fate should aught befall her love, for there would be no life without him, no hope, no comfort. Yet, she could not find in herself the seeds of the acceptance Mother Margaret had found. Mayhap her faith was too weak; mayhap her worldly ways were too strong. She would find no rest until those who had brought him down had suffered a like fate.

Amicia's gaze lingered on the prioress, stroking up the wasted body that barely rippled the woolen coverlet, touching the face that found no surcease from pain even in slumber. What great depth of love lodged in her heart that she could find room in it for the daughter of Eustace of Bellay, the man who had destroyed her life?

The sawing songs of crickets, adrift on the breeze, was overlaid by the distant ring of the gate bell—an impatient triplet of notes. Amicia started, her gaze leaping to the window. Tristan? Would he chance the dangerous defile in the dark of night? Nay, he would not. More likely it was a serf come from the village to seek Sister Catherine to attend a birthing or Père Brocard to ease a death.

She forced her gaze from the window, but could not rid herself of the knot of excitement aflutter beneath her breast. It was foolish, she knew. Even Tristan, bold and daring as he was, would not risk his men when morning would come soon enough. Her legs trembling with the need to leap up and away, Amicia made herself sit quietly through the minutes that spun long and long—until a disturbance in the hall below raised the fine hairs on her nape. Tristan? Invading the sanctuary of the priory? Nay, never would he do such, but if not he, then . . .

*An impatient triplet of notes!* Ever had her father rung the bell so! Had he learned she was here and come for her? Would he try to use her against Tristan as Aimery and Lady Sybilla had? Would his hate know no end and his evil, no limit?

Her pulse thundering like hoofbeats, Amicia climbed on

knees as wobbly as a new lamb's. A quick glance found Mother Margaret's slumber undisturbed, and she moved to the door.

"My lord! My lord!" Sister Edwenna keened in dismay. " 'Tis sacrilege, my lord! Alas! Alas! You may not . . . nay, my lord—"

"Get from my sight!" Eustace of Bellay shouted. "I will not be delayed by a twittering churchling! I must see her! Begone!"

Above, Amicia froze. *I must see her*. Who had told him she was here? Did this mean that Tristan . . . Nay! She would not believe ill had happened to him! Yet her father was come for her and none else knew where she was. A terrible grief lay its cold, cruel hands upon her, but she dared not yield to it. At any cost, Eustace of Bellay must be kept from the prioress's solar. He must never know that the woman dying above was Lady Margaret of Castle Rydding.

Never had a step been so hard to take as the one that carried her onto the landing at the top of the stairs. At the foot her father shook off Sister Edwenna's clutching hands, and the rattle-pated nun wailed and danced like a headless hen.

"There is no need to abuse her, my lord!" Amicia's voice rang out crystal clear. "Nor is there a need for you to violate the sanctuary of this place. If my husband is dead, I care not what you do to me. Take me, and leave all here in peace."

His head snapped up, the light of a wall torch falling across the hateful features gone slack with astonishment. "You! What do you do here?" he growled.

"My lady! My lady! I tried to tell him . . . I did . . . I did," Sister Edwenna mewed. "My lady, what shall I do?"

The fluttering nun's question lightly intruded on Amicia's stunned incomprehension. Her father had not come for her! He had not even known she was there. Then, why? Why would he come? Had he learned about Mother Margaret . . .

"So, you are here." He recovered his poise, an evil smile slanting crookedly across his slash of a mouth. "It is better than I planned. Lady Sybilla says Eden is mad for you, though he does not admit it to himself. When I am done with the prioress, you will—''

"Why do you wish to see her? She is ill, dying. Naught can she tell you!" Amicia moved down the steps hoping to lure him away.

"A letter was given into her keeping. I have come for it," he said flatly as he began climbing one step after the other.

Amicia went so cold her cheeks and fingers felt stiff. Trembling like the butter-yellow celandine in a stiff wind, she stared down at him. A letter? *The* letter? It could be no other. Whatever happened he must not have it!

She moved down another step and braced her cold hand against the smooth stone. "The prioress is ill unto death! You may not see her! I forbid you to pass, my lord."

He stopped, canting his head up. A derisive look, half amused, half angry, pinned her in place. "You forbid?" he asked mildly. "Who are you to forbid me aught? Do you have a meinie of men to leap from these shadows at your bidding?" he asked, his voice growing stronger, harder. "If you do not, I would suggest that you move aside, else I will move you and you will not like it."

The look he settled upon her was one Amicia knew well. A look of virulent loathing glittering from his time- and temper-ravaged face that, even now, weakened her knees and threatened to send them sinking beneath her. She struggled against the inner trembling and drew herself up.

"Would you imperil your soul, my lord, for naught but a letter?" she tried a different course. "You violate—''

"My soul gives me no worry." He rapidly climbed the stairs, his patience obviously ended. "I have no doubt I will go straight to the devil. What is one more sin added to the rest?"

Below, Sister Edwenna moaned and fluttered.

Amicia shrank back, but his hand whipped out and clamped around her arm. "Come, daughter, we will go above to see this dying prioress you protect so hardily."

"Nay, my lord, I will not—''

"Ay, but you will!"

He roughly yanked her along, despite her resistance. She tried to peel back his fingers, bands of steel digging into her flesh. It was useless. "Sister Edwenna!" she screamed. "Go for Odo! Bring my man here!"

"*Your* man? I vow you will be disappointed if you expect him to protect you from me. I own him, daughter, body and soul. He is my man, no other's."

Flinging a look back over her shoulder to watch Sister Edwenna clumsily fleeing the hall, Amicia could only hope her father was wrong. If it came to a choice, she was not sure what Odo would do. Ever did he cling to his hope that her father would see the error of his ways and amend them.

Dragged up the stairs like a hound on a tether, Amicia scraped her hip against the wall and stumped her ankle against the edge of a stone step. Pain lanced through her, a physical pain far less keen than the aching of her heart. How bitter it was that Mother Margaret, now in her weakest moment, must confront the fiend who destroyed her.

"I beg of you, my lord! Do not do this thing! I beg of you!" she sobbed and pleaded, knowing her efforts were useless. There was no pity in him. There was no swaying him. If only she could get the letter and burn it as she had the other, but here there was no hearth fire ablaze, only candles and those too slow for the deed.

He thrust her through the doorway. A hard, swift shove sent her reeling, falling, skidding across the floor in a gathering mound of dusty rushes. As she skidded, she gathered herself, lunging and scooting toward the pallet like a crawling babe to use her body as a shield.

"Mother," she whispered frantically, staring into the prioress's startled eyes, "he comes for the letter. I beg you! Hide it! Hide it, quick—"

His hand hammered into Amicia's shoulder, his fingers grappling, lifting, tossing her backward. She fell with a spine-jarring thump and rolled to her side, tangling in the lively thickness of her hair. One hand sweeping up to fling a heavy chestnut-brown swatch back, she saw her father set his legs apart and hook his thumbs in his belt— conquering man's age-old stance.

"With the leave of Lady Sybilla of Carrickmuir, I am

come for the letter she left here with you," he said, staring down at the prioress on her pallet. "I would have it as soon as may, for I must ride south. Come, woman!" he growled impatiently. "Do not dally! I have no time for this!"

"Eustace!" The sibilant whisper hissed in the chamber.

Amicia froze in the act of rising. Her gaze dropped from the stiffness crawling across her father's back to the horrified expression Mother Margaret wore. An expression so pained it sent chills scrambling across her flesh.

"Eustace!" came the hiss once again. "Do you not know me?"

He fell back a step, his hand trembling against the hilt of his sword. "Nay, my lady," he said, his voice deep and hoarse. "I—I know you not."

For all his denial, Amicia heard a thread of recognition, a thread of horror, a stunned awareness that pulled her up and sent her stumbling to the pallet. "Nay, Mother," she choked out. "Do not rise. You have not the strength for it."

"Ay, but I do. I have waited a lifetime, and I will find the strength now." Her violet gaze, lighted by the bright flame of resolve, clung to Bellay's sagging face as she struggled up with Amicia's aid. "Ay, Eustace, you know me of old. I am Margaret. Margaret of Castle Rydding, who you long ago claimed to love."

His face paled to a pasty white that etched the spider-webbing of veins across nose and cheeks in blood's bright color. His eyes widened, the blue darkening to hell's own black. "Nay!" His head shook. "Nay, it cannot be. You died on the moors. You died!"

"Nay, Eustace! Though many is the time I wished I had."

Weak as she was, her voice was stronger than his. As if, Amicia thought, she fed on the strength that fled him.

"It is I, Margaret, whose life you destroyed as you nearly did my body with your brutish lust. All done in the name of a love whose meaning you have never known. I tell you now"—she drew herself up, rejecting Amicia's supporting arm—"it is ended! You will never hurt another!"

"Nay! There is more I must do! He took you from me

. . .'' He paused, his desperate plea dying in the stillness of the room. His eyes narrowed viciously, his mouth twisting in a snarl. ''He took you from me,'' he began again, stony voiced and vengeful. ''I vowed to end his line, and I will, Margaret. I will!''

Though Amicia quaked at the power returning to him as his shock faded, Mother Margaret stood firm and steady. ''I was never yours, Eustace, for I loved him well and you not at all. Ever did you destroy what you could not have. I tell you now—it is ended!''

''It will never be done until I have dragged his memory through the muck of dishonor,'' he roared. ''Until I have slain his sons and taken his lands for my own. I will have the letter he wrote, Margaret.''

''I will not yield it to you!''

''But you will, Margaret. Have you forgotten what lengths I will go to achieve my desire?''

Uncoiling like a snake, he struck without warning. Amicia, expecting some such from him, leaped to put herself between him and Mother Margaret, only to discover she was his quarry all along. Before she could regain her balance, she had been dragged hard against his chest and the cold blade of his dagger was poised at her throat.

''Yield the letter to me, or she dies.''

''Nay, Moth—''

The blade sliced through Amicia's skin, bringing the warm welling of blood.

''She is your daughter, Eustace!'' Mother Margaret cried. ''You would not!''

Amicia watched her move forward an unsteady step, her fleshless hands reaching out in supplication. She tried to believe there had been conviction in her voice, but she could not. She, no less than Mother Margaret, knew what her father was capable of doing.

''But I would,'' he said implacably. ''She stole her mother from me, sorry as she was. Do you know why I took her to wife, Margaret? Because she was the image of you, and I could think it was you that I held and you that I bedded. And, while I had her, the dreams did not come, Margaret.'' He spoke with an eerie break in his voice. ''Those dreams of you fighting me and screaming at me and telling me of your love for him and your hate for me. Those dreams where I woke to find you gone and knew that you were ever lost. She"—his voice grew hard and hating—"this daughter of mine, took that from me. Why should she live?"

"Eustace, do not hurt her!" Mother Margaret's face betrayed the first sign of fear. "I will give you the letter if you give me your word—"

"Nay, Mother! I would rather be dead—"

The thick arm beneath Amicia's breasts tightened painfully while the dagger sliced deeper. "Have a care, daughter; or I will oblige you."

She dared not speak again, but her eyes pleaded with the prioress not to give him the letter, not to destroy the honored memory of Tristan's father, not to destroy Tristan's pride. And while she watched, she saw the febrile spurt of strength draining away, leaving the nun shaken and wan in defeat.

"Ay, Eustace. You will have it, only give me your word you will release her."

"You have it."

She watched in horror while Mother Margaret fumbled the knotted cord from the length of split cane at her waist. Nay! Nay! Amicia's heart cried, while her mind scurried in frantic plans—until the scuff of a shoe at the door stopped even her heart.

Odo? Would he cleave to her side or give his loyalty to her father? *Oh, God!* she prayed. *Let him see my father for what he is! Let him help me now! Let him put end to the torment my father has caused!*

Mother Margaret gingerly extended the worn-smooth cane, reaching out for Amicia with the other hand. The dagger inched away from her throat and his arm fell away from her, and Amicia moved forward a step while he reached and grasped the means of his vengeance upon Robert of Eden and his son. And as he grasped it, he grabbed her once more, pulling her back against his chest so abruptly she had no time to cry out or wrench away.

His laugh clawed at her ear, a vicious sound utterly lacking in humor. "My word, as you should have known, Margaret, is worthless."

Amicia writhed wildly in his cruel embrace. Lifting her foot to kick backward, she made painful contact with his shin.

"God rot you! Hold fast, or I will kill you here!" he growled, and set the knife to her throat once more, bringing her to quivering quietude. "By God!" he exulted. "I have him now! I will ruin his memory and slay his son. Then, daughter, I will see to you."

"Nay, Eustace, I beg of you! Leave her here!" Mother Margaret stumbled forward. "Oh, God! God, answer me now! Send down your mighty wrath and end his wicked life. Suffer his evil no more!"

"You pray to Him who gives no answer!" he said with a cruel laugh as he backed to the door, dragging Amicia with him. "Where was He when you cried for Him at Castle Rydding, Margaret? Where was He then?"

Mother Margaret stumbled and fell to her knees. "Oh, God! I pray you hear me! I pray you . . ." Her eyes rolled up and she crumpled onto the rushes. "I pray . . ." She gasped and said no more.

Amicia strained against the arm binding her tight. "Mother! Mother Margaret!" she screamed.

"She cannot hear you," her father muttered. "She is gone now, as he is. I will have Tristan next, and then you. You, daughter, will suffer for what you have stolen from me. You will know pain and sorrow. I will keep you alive. Ay, alive to know . . ."

He stiffened abruptly. A single gasp whistled at Amicia's ear, and his arm convulsed around her, then slackened. She trembled a moment in indecision before lurching away and wheeling to face him. His eyes, round with astonishment, stared at her.

"What . . . What . . ." His breath eased out in a long slow sigh, and he pitched forward, thudding heavily against the floor. Seeping through the broken gash in his hauberk was the bright red of blood.

Behind him, Odo stood with his dagger dripping and his scarred face twisted by new and deeper scars of the soul. His hand opened, fingers spreading. The dagger rolled from his palm and fell to the rushes. His deep, racking sob echoed about the solar and he stumbled forward. Kneeling, he took Eustace of Bellay's head gently on his lap and leaned to press a kiss to the furrowed brow.

"Father, forgive me," he wept. "I could not let you do it. I could not let you hurt her. She told me you were steeped in evil, but I would not see it, for I loved you well. So often I turned my face from your cruelty, but this time I could not. I could not!"

Amicia, stunned by a new comprehension, moved toward Odo haltingly. Father, he had said. Was it true? Was he . . .

"My lady"—his single eye, glistening with a tear, lifted to her in pleading—"I could not let him hurt you. You are his blood, and the only good he ever brought forth. Yet, he would have crushed you as he has so many others."

"Odo," she whispered, reaching out to touch his cheek, "are you . . . my brother?"

"Ay," he said softly, "though you would not claim me, my lady. My mother was but a serf the lord lay with in the fields when the mood took him. I was naught to him. I am naught to you."

"Nay, do not say it! You are much to me. A friend long ere now. I am glad, so very glad, to claim you as kin."

"My lady!" His glistening eye assumed the merest hint of its old chiding. "I vow they kept you as innocent as a babe in this priory of yours. Do you not know that none of noble blood claim kinship with such as me!"

"I do and I will," she said softly, and turned away to kneel at Mother Margaret's side. "I will claim you as brother before any in this land from the highest to the lowest."

# Chapter 25

The morning sun was probing the mist-shrouded tors with golden daggers of light when Tristan caught his first sight of Holmby Vale through the narrow defile wedged between precipitous granite slopes. He did not pause to look upon the pastoral serenity below. Instead, he spurred his flagging destrier on.

In the days since he had parted from Rolf and Megotta, leaving them to go on to Castle Eden, he had stopped only to rest Vainqueur. During those stops he had rolled himself in his mantle and lain upon the hard earth, but neither rest nor sleep did he find. Then, as now, he was driven by a single thought: Amicia waited at Holmby Priory, unsuspecting. Then, as now, he flagellated himself for his heedlessness. He should not have yielded to her! She would be safe at Kenilworth, if he had not! A stubborn wench she was, he thought, torn between pride and frustration. But no more. From hence she would bend to his will . . . was she alive to do so.

He cursed the slow pace, but dared not rush his destrier down the steep slopes and hooked turns of the trail. A pace that gave him more time to think than he wanted. With thought came the memory of Aimery and his mother sprawled across the rocky scarp. With thought came a grief he never expected to feel.

Lady Sybilla was his mother, but a mother she had never been to him. So why this wrenching at his vitals, this terrible pain over her loss? Was he so bound to her in hate that he could not bear to lose her? Or was this something else Amicia had given to him? This ability to grieve for the emptiness of his mother's life. If she had known happiness, contentment, and love, she might have been a different woman. One that had no room for hate.

The hate that was the fruit born of his father's decision so long ago. That choice of honor had slain the woman Robert of Eden loved and turned the woman he married into a despicable creature ruled by her thwarted passions. Tristan shied from further thought of what his father had done, what he himself had so nearly done. He knew he was not yet ready to think it through, to decide whether that decision had been right or wrong. He had lived too long with the certitude that the choice had been inevitable.

Nor could he allow himself to think of Aimery, for that grief was truly unbearable. He bitterly blamed himself for what Aimery had become. He should have seen what was happening to his brother. He should have helped him.

So many thoughts he dared not think, and Ruella was another. Never would he forgive himself for what had happened to her. He could only try to make amends through her daughter, Megotta. He would see that she lacked for nothing, that her life was all he could make of it. So much he would do for love of her and in memory of her mother.

And Amicia would be there to help him, should he go astray, he dreamed. She would sweep the musty corners of his soul as free of pain as she had swept the musty corners of his hall free of dust. She would teach him to laugh as she laughed, to smile freely over naught. She would love him, and teach him to love. He would love her, and teach her that all men were not as her father.

As if the thought had summoned the man as trouble does the devil, Tristan saw the file of men-at-arms led by Bellay's whipping banner. In stunned disbelief, he watched them snake across the lush green turf of the vale below, heading for the path at the foot of the mountain, away from Holmby Priory. Too late! He was too late!

He had neared the band of trees rimming the lowest slope like a band of verdant green embroidery round the hem of a woman's cotte. Now he plunged down the widening path into those trees, cursing himself for his failure to bring his own men-at-arms with him. He had been forced to choose between speed and men, and had chosen the first in the hope he could get Amicia away before her father came. Now both he and she might pay the forfeit for his error.

He secreted Vainqueur far enough away that he would not answer the whicker of the horses, then crept back to climb a venerable oak and lie flat along the thick limb sprawling across the path. If he could do naught else, he would leap upon Bellay and end his sorry life.

He waited there listening to the drone of the bees sipping nectar from the hawthorn blossoms and the birds twittering gaily overhead. It was better to listen to those cheery sounds, than to dwell on the heavy thud of his heart and the thick sludging pulse of his blood. What if Amicia had angered her father and he had . . .

The chink of harness closed Tristan's mind to all but a well-trained knight's concentration on the task at hand. The first man came into sight. The dipping banner passed so near he could have touched it. Waiting, he watched for Bellay. Yet, man after man plodded beneath him, men-at-arms all; and, slung across a great black destrier, a body wrapped in coarse linen. Bellay was not with them, nor Amicia.

Where was she?

The last man vanished from sight and Tristan searched the trail behind. No other came . . .

Nay, one did. He could hear the faint clopping of hooves. Bellay? By the Mass, let it be! His every muscle grew taut, his mind alert, and there, round the bend, came Odo, slumped despondently in his saddle. Tristan, his heart trembling in his chest, listened for the hoofbeats of another horse—but heard naught. There was no one but Odo, whom he had sent with Amicia to keep her from harm. Now the man was riding with Bellay's men and Amicia was nowhere in sight!

Rage pummeled him to action. He lifted himself up and poised, waiting for Odo to draw nearer. When the man was directly below, he leaped from the limb with a snarl. Odo's head jerked up, his mouth flopping open and his

eyes rounding in the split second before Tristan fell full
upon him.

Together, they tumbled awkwardly from the rearing
mount. Tristan's shoulder hit a root, and white-hot pain
coursed through him, but he did not release his death grip
on Odo's throat.

"I left you to protect her! You gave your word that you
would give your first loyalty to her, yet I find you here
with her father's men. Where is she? God rot your soul in
hell! What has he done to her?"

"My lord," Odo choked out, "she is unhurt. She awaits
you . . ." The pressure of Tristan's fingers eased, and
Odo sucked in a sobbing breath. "I vow I will do naught
to cross you, my lord. You have near slain me for naught.
Your lady is as you left her. She awaits you in the priory."

"Why are you here with Bellay's men? Where is he?"
Tristan asked suspiciously, not daring yet to give vent to
the elation he felt. He would see her soon. Soon!

A look of pain leaped into Odo's eyes before he glanced
away. "Dead, my lord. He rides ahead, and I go to see
him buried—"

"Dead!" Tristan rolled away, only now reaching up to
massage his aching shoulder. "I can scarce believe it true.
Bellay, dead."

"Nor can I, my lord, and I . . . I did the deed."

The grief in his voice pulled Tristan's eyes to him.
"You were given a choice?" he asked softly, knowing
naught else would drive Odo to this end. Only if Amicia's
life was threatened would he kill the man who was . . .
what to him?

"Ay, my lord." Odo stood, dusting himself off. "The
child, my lord. You have her safe?"

"Ay."

"The lady awaits you, my lord. Go to her."

Tristan stood. Eager though he was to be on his way, he
paused to settle a comforting hand on Odo's shoulder.
"When he is buried, come to us at Castle Eden. You will
have a place of honor at my hearth."

"Nay, my lord." Odo's haunted gaze touched him and
and fled. "I must return here to do penance."

"What penance can there be for saving a life?" Tristan frowned.

"In that saving, my lord, I took the life of my own father. I must do penance for that."

Tristan's hand tightened its grip on Odo's shoulder, the painful offering of comfort from one hard man to another. Bellay's son. He was not surprised, for he had long suspected it.

"Does she know?" he asked.

"Ay, my lord, she knows now."

"She loves you well. Naught would keep her from claiming you as kin."

"So she told me, my lord," Odo said with a faint smile. "But you and I are not innocent of the ways of this land. It would not do for her to claim kinship with such as me. Besides, it is time that I see to my soul, and leave you to see to her happiness."

"You have my word that I will do all in my power to make her the most blissful of women."

"You have naught to do but love her, my lord. Naught else does she need."

Naught else does she need, but much else would he give her, Tristan thought as he flung himself from Vainqueur's back and leaped at the gate bell. Its urgent ring clamored in the stillness, a joyful intrusion on the serenity of the cloister.

He waited with ill-concealed impatience. Aware, suddenly, that he stank of horse and sweat, he shoved back his mail hood and arming coif to rake agitated fingers through his flattened hair. He wished he had taken time to bathe in the beck. He wished he could have come to her clean and clothed as befitted her. He swatted a clump of dried mud from his surcoat and pounded the dust from it. He shifted from foot to foot, suffering the agonizing uncertainty of an unfledged boy wooing his first maid.

She was in no way changeable, he assured himself, yet perversely feared that she was. Had it all been a dream? Would he come to her now, heart in hand, to find she loved him not? Would . . .

The peephole in the gate opened and a misty blue eye peered through. "How may I serve you, my lord?"

"I am Tristan, Lord of Eden, come for my wife." He silently cursed the tremor in his voice.

The eye blinked and scanned him rapidly, then twinkled. "Demoiselle . . . nay, she is that no longer, is she? Lady Amicia . . . there I have it right, have I not? Lady Amicia is your wife?"

Tristan, stepping back and hunching his shoulders with the need to batter the gate down, frowned in irritation. "Ay, Lady Amicia is my wife. I was told she awaited me. Bring her forth in all haste!"

"I may not, my lord!" The eye blinked rapidly, and the nun's head shifted to reveal a rosy plump cheek. "I was given strict order to bring you to the prioress's solar when you arrived."

"The prioress's solar?" Tristan questioned in disbelief. The private quarters of a nun, prioress or no, were never visited by any man. "Why am I to be taken there?"

"I know not, my lord, and I fear it is unseemly. But I must follow Mother Margaret's order, must I not?"

The light abstracted voice set Tristan to gritting his teeth. Of all the times to be wasting precious minutes in dealing with a lack-witted nun! he thought in frustration, then set his jaw and reined in his temper. "Then," he began as gently as was possible, though his nerves were jangling worse than the bell, "open the gate, Sister . . ."

"Edwenna," she said dutifully. "Sister Edwenna."

"Then open the gate, Sister Edwenna, that I might enter. And, tell me why my wife may not come out!" His voice climbed, despite his best intent.

"There is no need to shout, my lord!" the nun dithered. "Lady Amicia is with Mother Margaret. I fear she will not be with us long. The Lord is gathering her to his fold—"

"Amicia!" Tristan choked out, a terrible fear twisting his heart. "Amicia is—"

"Nay, my lord! Mother Margaret!"

"God's Wounds!" Tristan's slammed his hands against the gate. "Open it, or I will break it down!"

The crossbar scraped and the gate swung open. "There is no need to curse, my lord!" The plump nun jiggled and fluttered and wheeled about with a quivery, "Follow me, if you will, my lord."

His rapid strides treading at Sister Edwenna's scurrying heels, he followed into the prioress's hall, dimly lit by the evenly spaced columns of sunlight reaching through the narrow windows, and up the stairs. All the while his heart was beating a wild rhythm and his breath was fitful and shallow.

There must be some reason he was being taken to the prioress. Mother Margaret, the nun had called her, he thought with a frown. Why would a dying nun want to see him? Unless she loved Amicia well and wished to see her husband for herself. Mayhap, he thought, his tension seeping away, she but wished to bless their joining. Surely—he relaxed further—it was naught but that.

At the top of the stairs, Sister Edwenna turned and dipped a clumsy curtsy. "Through this door, my lord. They await you."

He felt an odd reluctance to cross the portal. A reluctance strangely at odds with a rising eagerness to see Amicia. He chided himself for his faint-hearted forebodings and stepped into the solar. His eyes moved unerringly to his wife, kneeling beside a pallet that seemed to be naught but a pile of rumpled coverlets.

He paused to drink in the sight of her: gently flaring hips perched upon her heels; her hair spilling down her back, gloriously reddened by the firelight, springy and shining and sinuously coiling with her every slight move. He neither moved nor spoke, but she turned slowly, her face tilting up. Her eyes, darkened by grief, lightened on sight of him and filled with the gentle passion of love. The sight of her snatched Tristan's breath from him, and left him curiously lightheaded, lighthearted.

"My lady," he said, his voice diving to guttural depths, "I was brought here on order of the . . . the prioress."

It was not what he wanted to say at all. He wanted to declare his love, his passion, his need, but those would profane this hallowed chamber.

"Megotta?" she questioned.

"Is safe," he responded.

"I am glad, my lord. Come"—she stretched out her hand—"she has waited for you."

He moved slowly, drawn by the love in Amicia's eyes. His hand entwined with hers, and he reveled in that nearness so dearly won, so nearly lost. She tugged lightly, and he knelt beside the pallet, staring down into the prioress's luminous violet eyes. Eyes that gazed up at him with a startling sweetness and love.

"His son," the woman whispered in a cracked and fading voice. "Robert's son, and so like him I can almost believe he has returned to me."

Tristan darted a questioning look at Amicia, and she leaned close to him. "My lord, this is Mother Margaret, the Prioress of Holmby. She is . . . was Margaret of Castle Rydding."

Margaret! The woman his father had condemned so long ago. The woman he had thought dead of his deed. The woman that could have been—should have been his own mother. He stared down at her, seeing the lines of suffering etched into her skin. There was little of the comeliness his father had spoken of. Naught but a suggestion in the bone structure and the fine line of her nose. But of her gentleness and love, all was there in her eyes. Those luminous eyes that spoke so eloquently of love and compassion and forgiveness. How, he wondered, had his father done it? How had he denied the love of this woman?

"I beg of you, lean down that I may touch you," she whispered.

He bent forward and her fleshless hands cupped his cheeks, the trembling fingertips stroking him lightly, lovingly. A mother's touch it was. A touch he had never had, and one he had never missed—until now. Now, when he realized what it was.

"You have your father's jaw. So strong, so stubborn a jaw he had. And his nose. So proud and straight. So much of him I see in you. So much." Tears welled in her eyes and spilled across her temples. "I would that you had been my son to bear in love and raise in joy."

"I would that you had been my mother," Tristan said hoarsely. He took her hands—those pitiful, skeletal hands—

and brought them to his lips. "He loved you well till the
end of his days. Never did he forget you."

"I am glad," she sighed. "It is selfish of me, but I am
so very glad."

"My lady, I must know . . ." He swallowed hard,
telling himself he should not ask, and knowing that he
must. "Did you blame him for—"

"Nay." She smiled sadly. "Nay, I could not blame
him. I could not . . ."

Her face contorted with pain, a pain Tristan felt as
though it were his own. Why should that be? he wondered.
She was a stranger to him but moments ago, yet he
grieved for her. A pure grief untainted by the conflicting
emotions he felt for his mother.

The pain passed and she sank back weakly. "Amicia,
you remember what I told you?"

"Ay, Mother, I remember it well." She reached out and
placed her hand atop theirs. "Naught will I forget of all
you have taught me. Naught will I forget of the love you
have given me. You have been a true mother to me. The
only mother I have known."

"And you my true daughter. Be happy, my children.
Cleave one unto the other in love and joy. Be—"

She stopped suddenly, her head tilting as if she listened
to a voice. Her eyes shifted from them, gazing up at the
foot of her pallet. A smile touched her lips, growing
stronger, wider, happier until joy lent a youthful radiance
to her face.

"He has come for me," she whispered, straining to
rise, reaching out with an eager hand. "Robert has come.
Beloved . . . beloved . . ."

She sighed softly and sank back, and sighed no more.

For long and long no whisper of sound intruded on the
sanctity of the solar. Even thought was suspended in the
holy air of that place. Tristan, who had shed no tears for
either grief or cheer since a youngling, now felt them
streaming unchecked. He reached out blindly, and felt
Amicia's small hand creep forlornly into his. Still he could
not speak.

Beside him, Amicia wept in silence, until the burden of
grief sought outlet in a sob. "I should not weep in sor-

row,'' she quavered softly, ''for she went in joy. Mayhap grief is selfish. I would have her near to love and guide me as she ever has.''

''Nay, Amicia,'' he whispered sadly. ''Let her go in peace.''

''Do you . . . do you think he really came for her? Could love be so strong it could reach out from the grave?'' she asked.

He cradled her hand in both of his and brought it to his lips. ''Once, I would have said it could not, but now'' —his loving gaze searched hers—''now I know it can. Where love is as deep and abiding as theirs was''—he paused and reached out to snare a tear from her cheek with the gentle pad of his thumb—''as ours is, then death is no hindrance.''

*As ours is.* The words sang in Amicia's mind like a melodic refrain during the hard days of travel that followed Mother Margaret's interment with the letter her beloved Robert had written so long ago. With time and distance Amicia's grief eased, and she could be glad that Margaret of Castle Rydding had found surcease from suffering. Each day she awakened lighter of heart, until a morning came when she awoke in Tristan's sheltering arms with true anticipation.

They were but a day's journey from Castle Eden and the wood was thick overhead and the earth clothed with swaying windflowers and heady drifts of columbine. A jay scolded a scampering squirrel and a hare thrust his twitching nose through the thick fronds of a fern, and Amicia gazed all about with a smile playing about her mouth. Though she and Tristan had exchanged tales of their parting, it seemed that only now did the realization come that they were free of hate and haters, free of deceptions and dangers, free of all . . . but each other.

A delightful thought. Her gaze abandoned the beauty of the morning for the beauty of the man beside her—and found him staring up at her with the hint of a smile softening his mouth.

''I must give you fair warning, my lady,'' he said, his

voice rough with vestiges of sleep. "I cannot abide a cheerful wench so early on the morn."

She gifted him with an unrepentent smile. "Then I shall take care to walk softly and growl often, my lord."

"So saucy, my lady?" he grinned. "Mayhap I should lesson you ere you get all out of hand."

"I am stubborn, my lord."

"Ay, so I have been told," he said with a wicked grin. "Mayhap it is time I began."

She gathered her feet under her to flee beyond the trees to the babbling beck, but he pounced like a sleek cat and bore her, giggling, down to the ground.

"My lord, you are heavy as a wine tun!"

"And you, my lady, are wiggly as worm, but you shall not escape . . ." Her gaze locked with his, and he breathed softly, all hint of humor gone. "You shall never escape me, Amicia. Never."

His mouth dropped to hers, molding its contours to his own in a kiss that spun long and sweet. And, at its end, she was as breathless as he.

"Tristan," she sighed, "how sad it is that Mother Margaret and your father never knew the happiness we have."

"Ay," he said solemnly, his finger trailing a fiery path to the hollow of her throat, "I feel as though we should try to live our lives for them. As though we should have twice the happiness so that they might look upon us and smile."

"It is a heavy burden, this happiness we need have." Her shining gaze caressed him. "Do you think we might do it?"

"Ay," his lips followed the path of his finger. "Ay, sweet witch. We will know such happiness as to make the angels in heaven weep."

*Authors of*
*exceptional promise*

*Historical novels*
*of superior quality!*

**ON THE WINDS OF LOVE**  Lori Leigh
75072-4/$3.95 US/$4.95 Can

**STORM OF PASSION**  Virginia Brown
89933-7/$3.95 US/$4.95 Can

**FIREGLOW**  Linda Ladd
89640-0/$3.95 US/$4.95 Can

**WILD LAND, WILD LOVE**  Mallory Burgess
75167-4/$3.95 US/$5.50 Can

**PRIDE'S PASSION**  Linda P. Sandifer
75171-2/$3.95 US/$5.50 Can

**RECKLESS YEARNING**  Victoria Pade
89880-2/$3.95 US/$5.50 Can

**AVON** Paperbacks